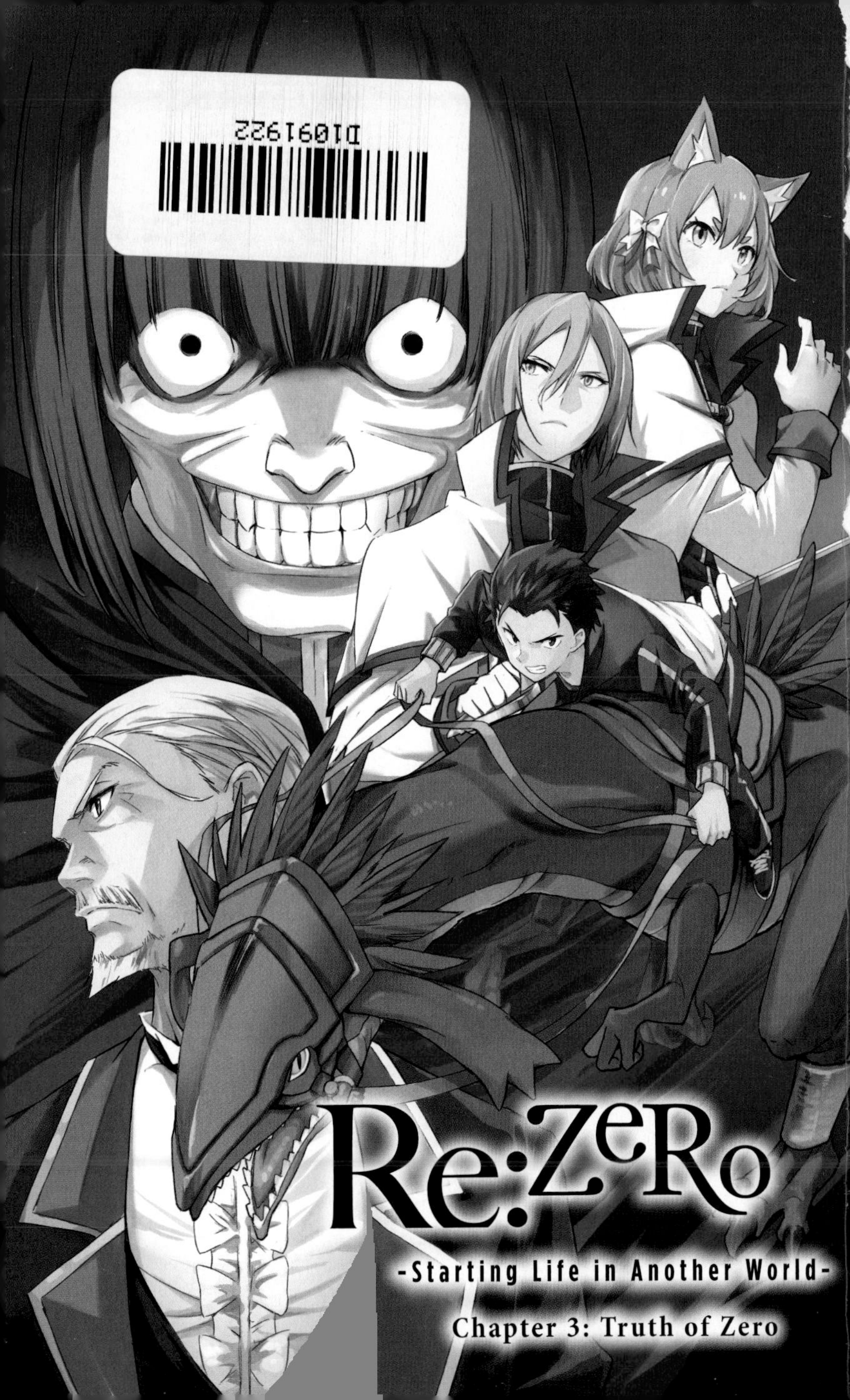
Re:ZeRo
-Starting Life in Another World-
Chapter 3: Truth of Zero

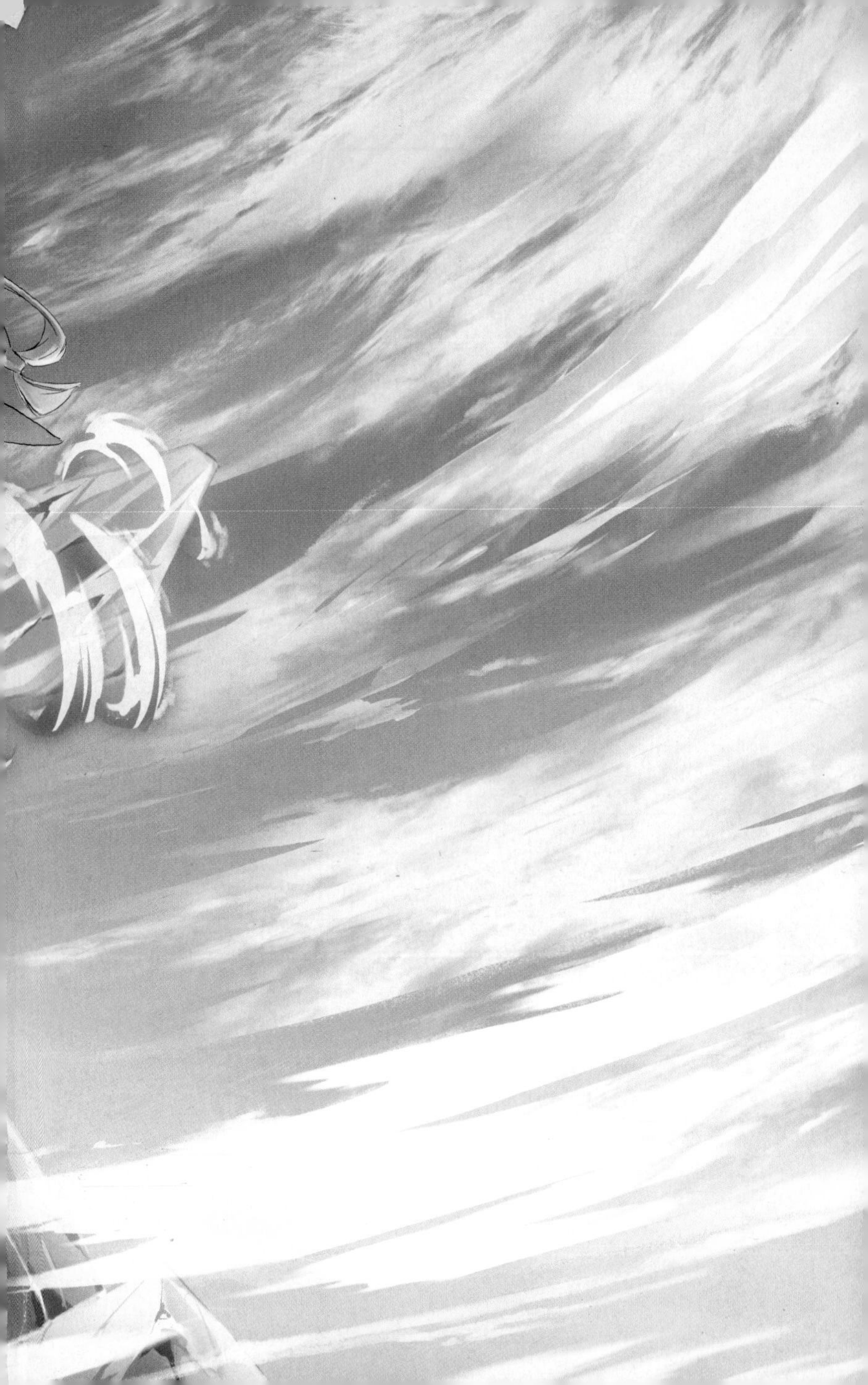

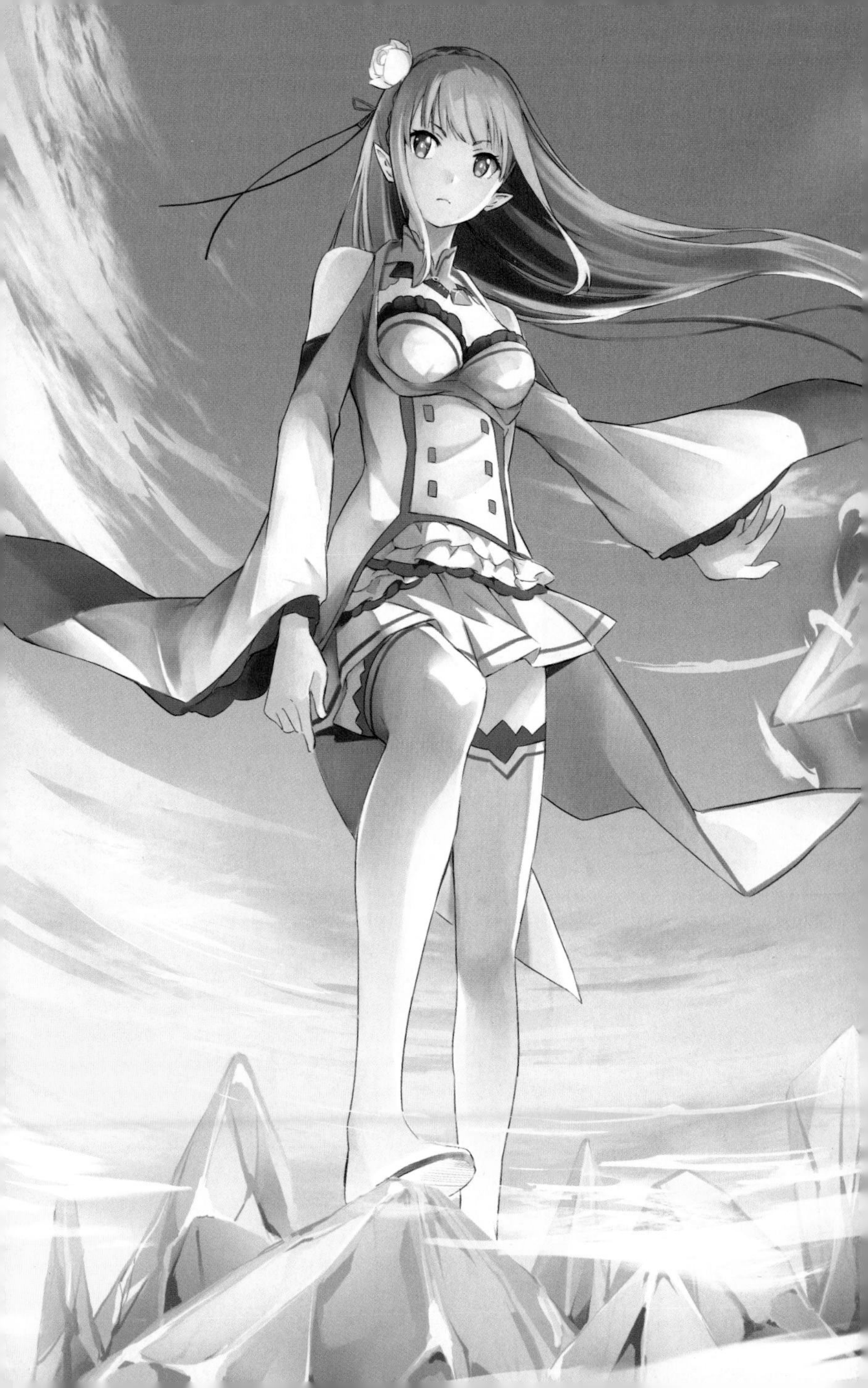

Re:ZERO -Starting Life in Another World-

Chapter 3: Truth of Zero

The only ability Subaru Natsuki gets when he's summoned to
another world is time travel via his own death. But to save her,
he'll die as many times as it takes.

Contents

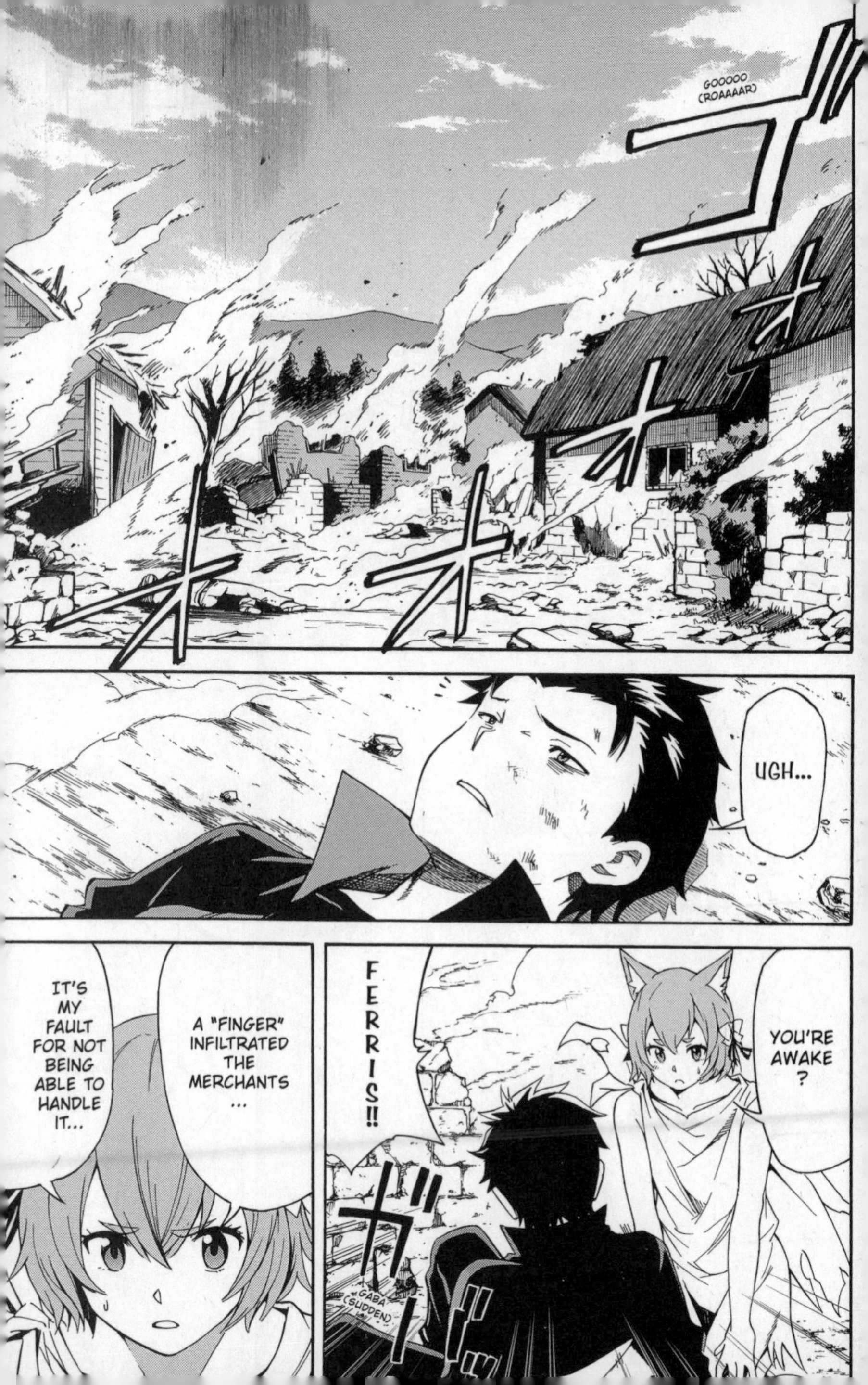
GOOOOO (ROAAAAR)
UGH...
YOU'RE AWAKE?
FERRIS!!
GABA (SUDDEN)
A "FINGER" INFILTRATED THE MERCHANTS...
IT'S MY FAULT FOR NOT BEING ABLE TO HANDLE IT...

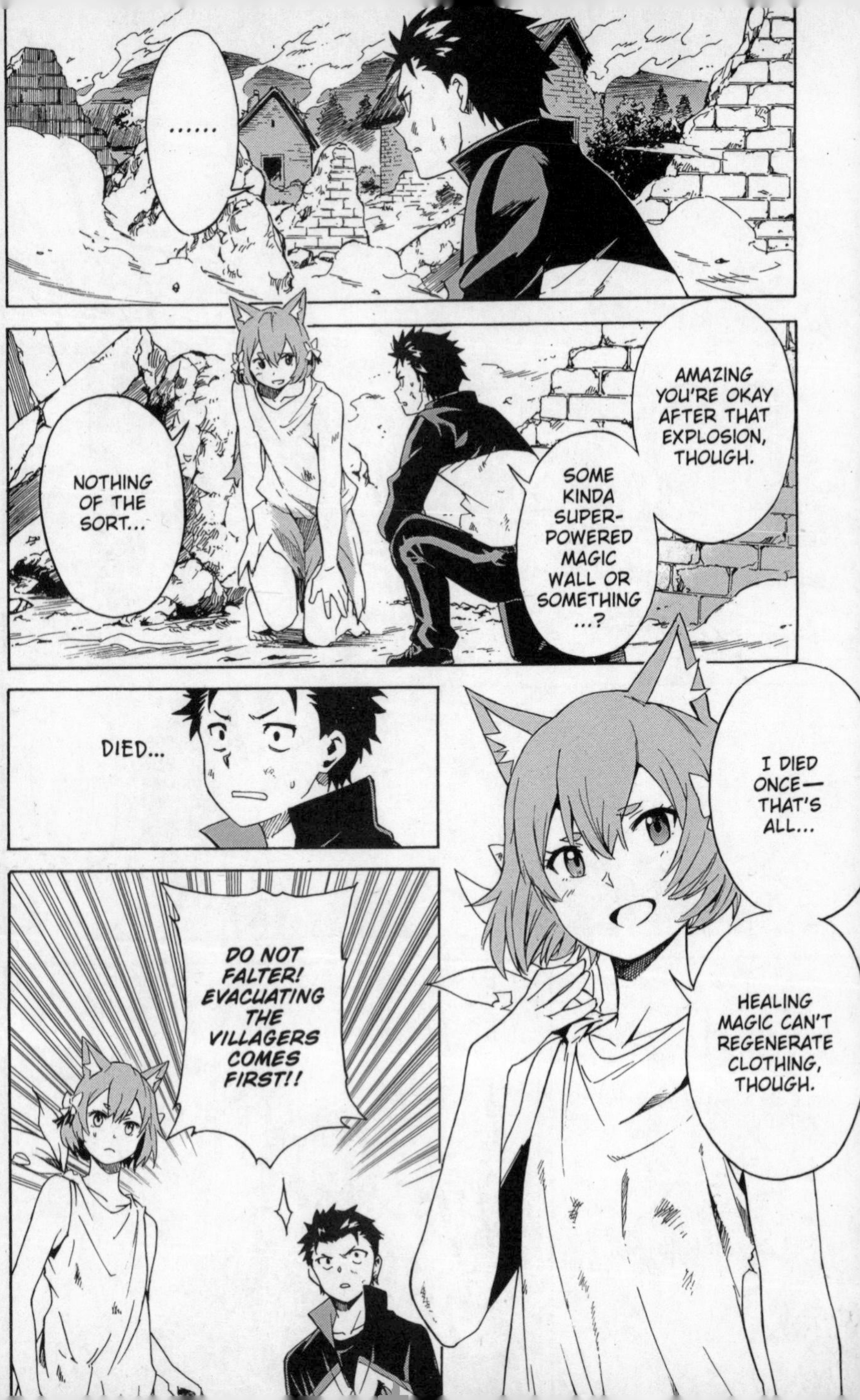
......
AMAZING YOU'RE OKAY AFTER THAT EXPLOSION, THOUGH.
SOME KINDA SUPER-POWERED MAGIC WALL OR SOMETHING ...?
NOTHING OF THE SORT...
I DIED ONCE—THAT'S ALL...
HEALING MAGIC CAN'T REGENERATE CLOTHING, THOUGH.
DIED...
DO NOT FALTER! EVACUATING THE VILLAGERS COMES FIRST!!

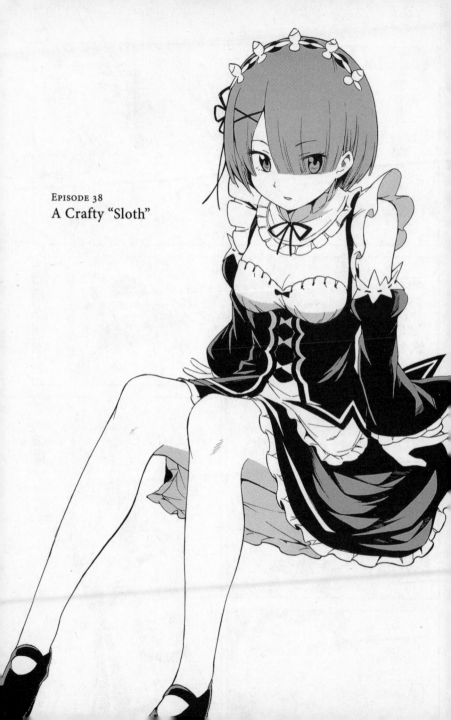

EPISODE 38
A Crafty "Sloth"

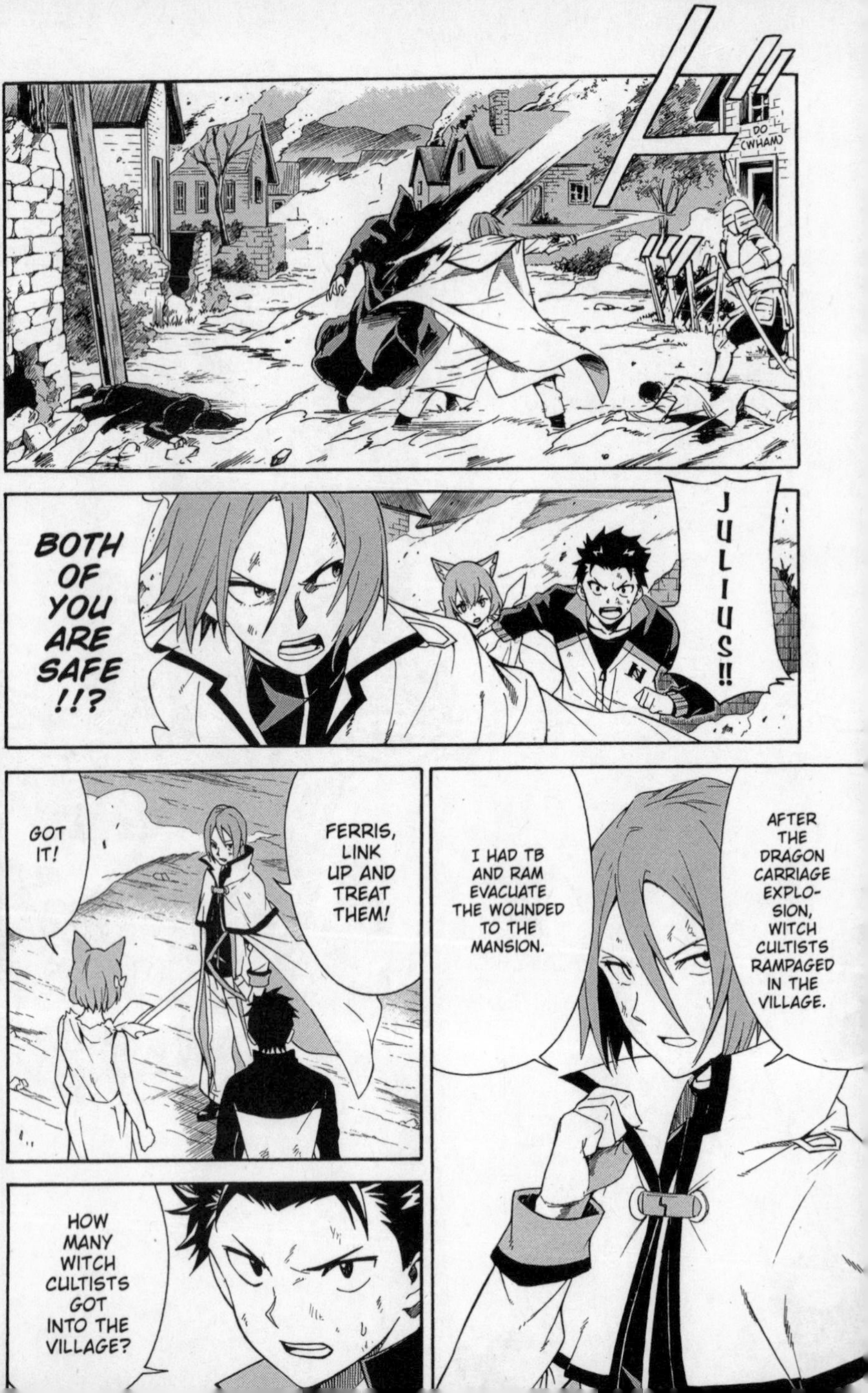
DO
(WHAM)
JULIUS!!
BOTH OF YOU ARE SAFE!!?
AFTER THE DRAGON CARRIAGE EXPLO-SION, WITCH CULTISTS RAMPAGED IN THE VILLAGE.
I HAD TB AND RAM EVACUATE THE WOUNDED TO THE MANSION.
FERRIS, LINK UP AND TREAT THEM!
GOT IT!
HOW MANY WITCH CULTISTS GOT INTO THE VILLAGE?

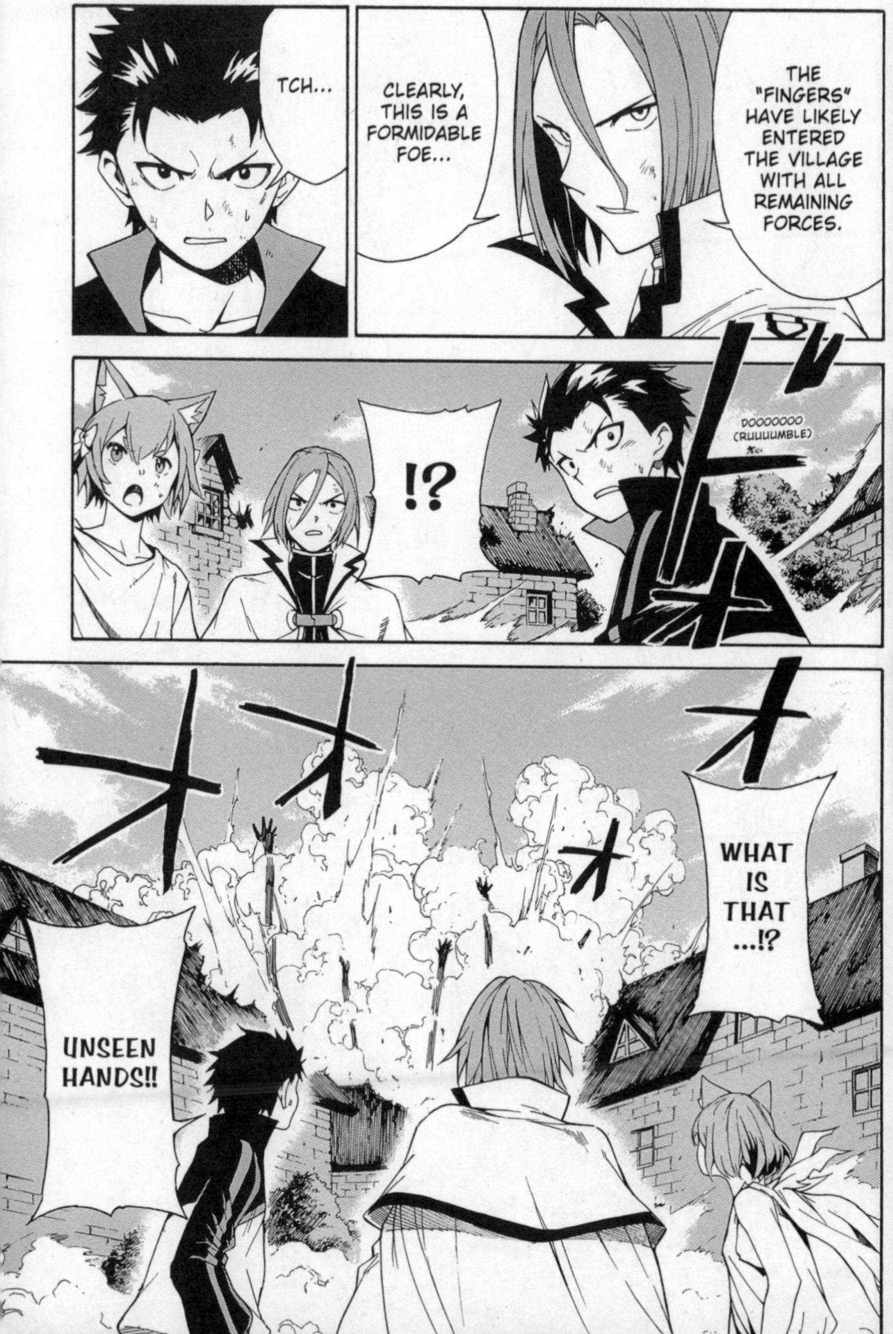
THE "FINGERS" HAVE LIKELY ENTERED THE VILLAGE WITH ALL REMAINING FORCES.
CLEARLY, THIS IS A FORMIDABLE FOE...
TCH...
DOOOOOOO (RUUUUMBLE)
!?
WHAT IS THAT ...!?
UNSEEN HANDS!!

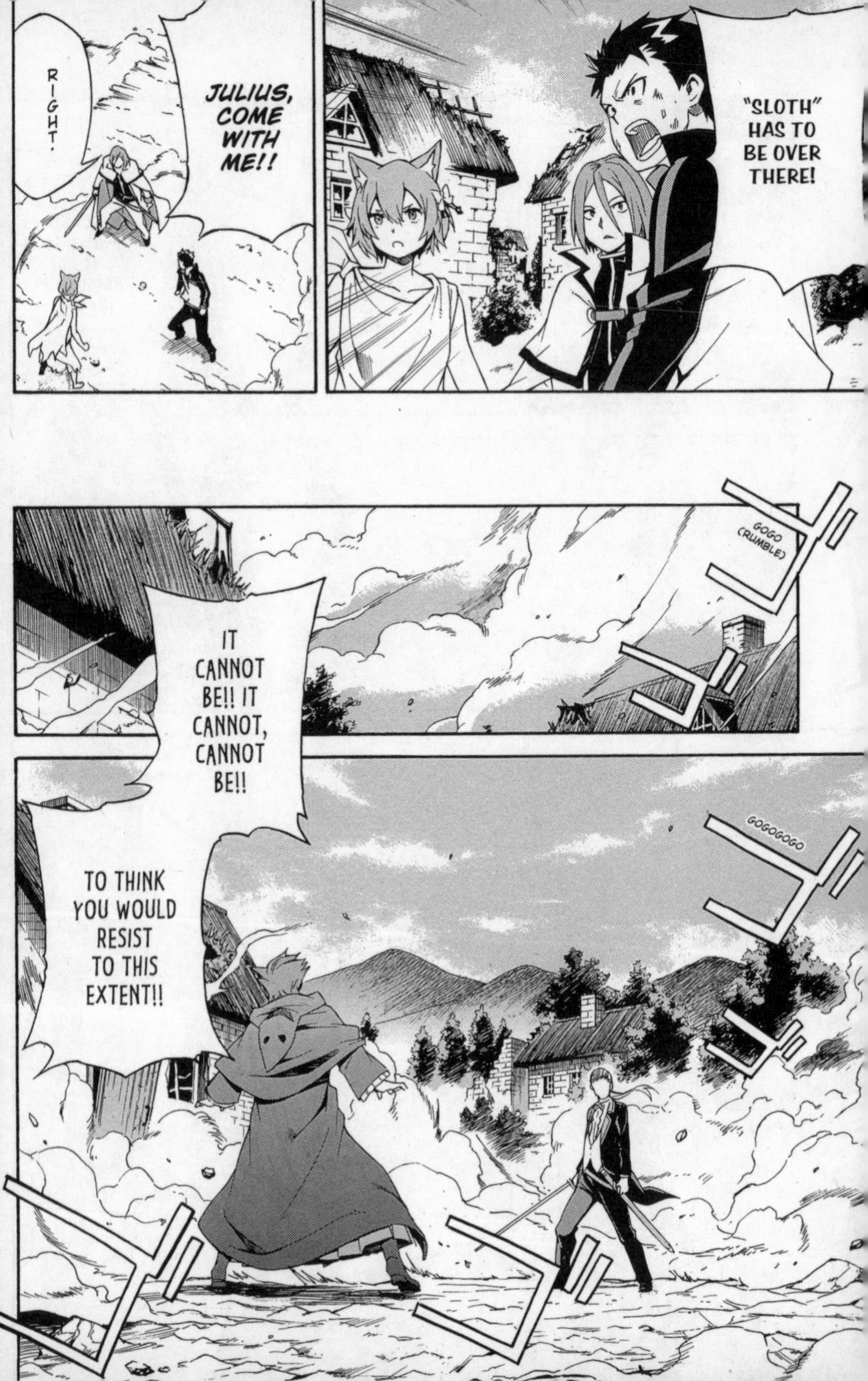
"SLOTH" HAS TO BE OVER THERE!
JULIUS, COME WITH ME!!
RIGHT!
GOGO (RUMBLE)
IT CANNOT BE!! IT CANNOT, CANNOT BE!!
GOGOGOGO
TO THINK YOU WOULD RESIST TO THIS EXTENT!!

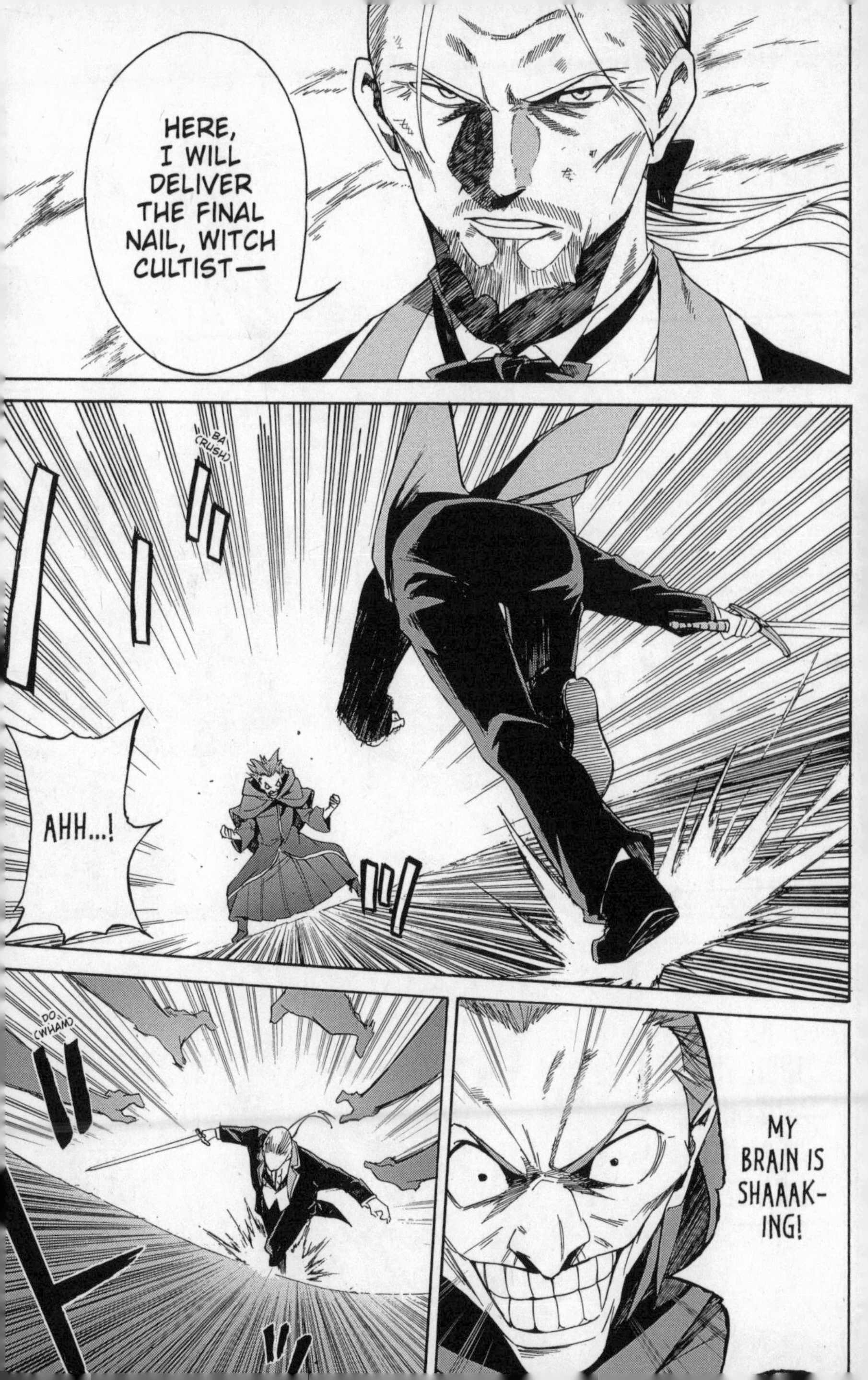
HERE, I WILL DELIVER THE FINAL NAIL, WITCH CULTIST—
BA (RUSH)
AHH...!
MY BRAIN IS SHAAAK-ING!
DO (WHAM)

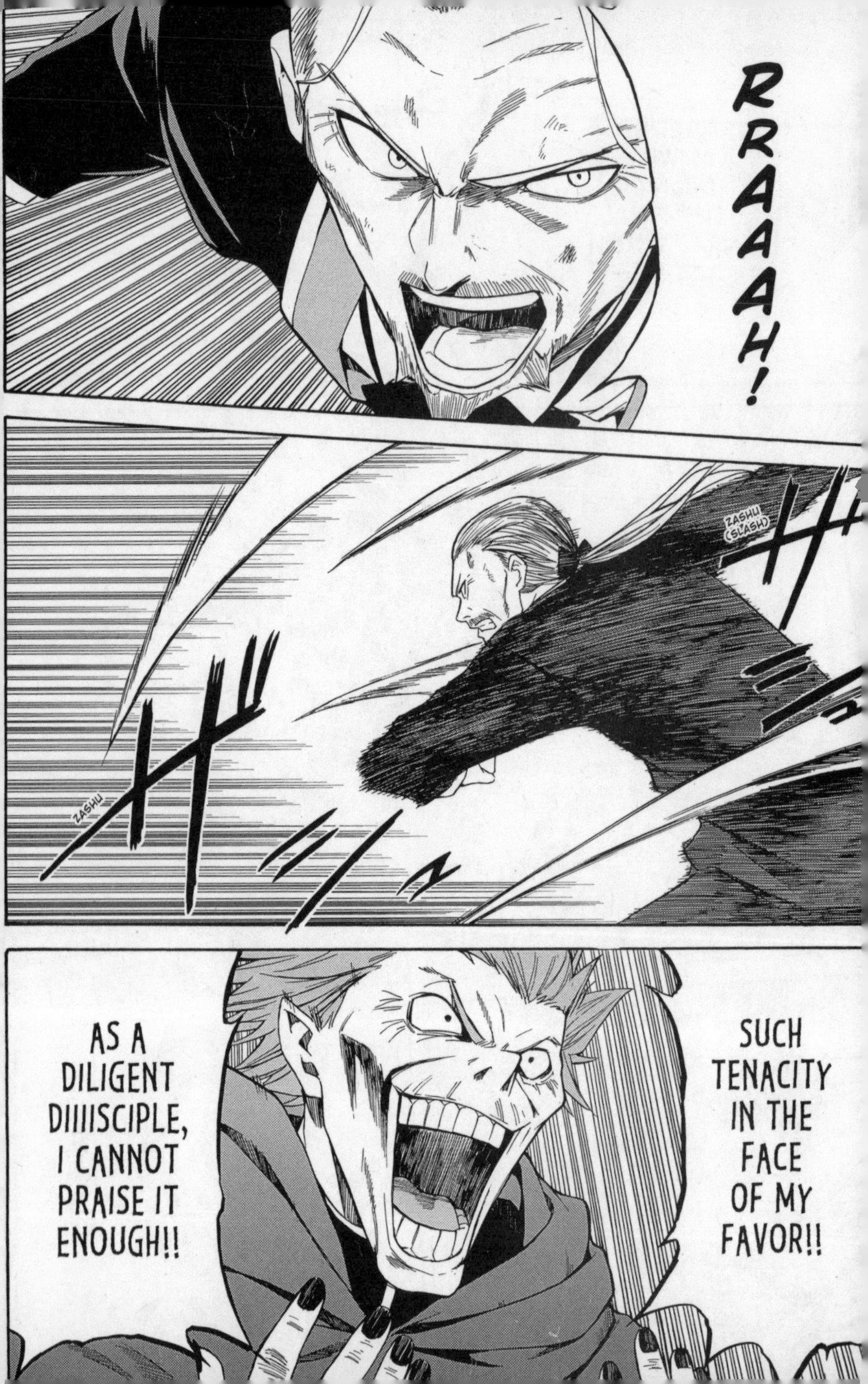
RRAAAAH!
ZASHU (SLASH)
ZASHU
SUCH TENACITY IN THE FACE OF MY FAVOR!!
AS A DILIGENT DIIIISCIPLE, I CANNOT PRAISE IT ENOUGH!!

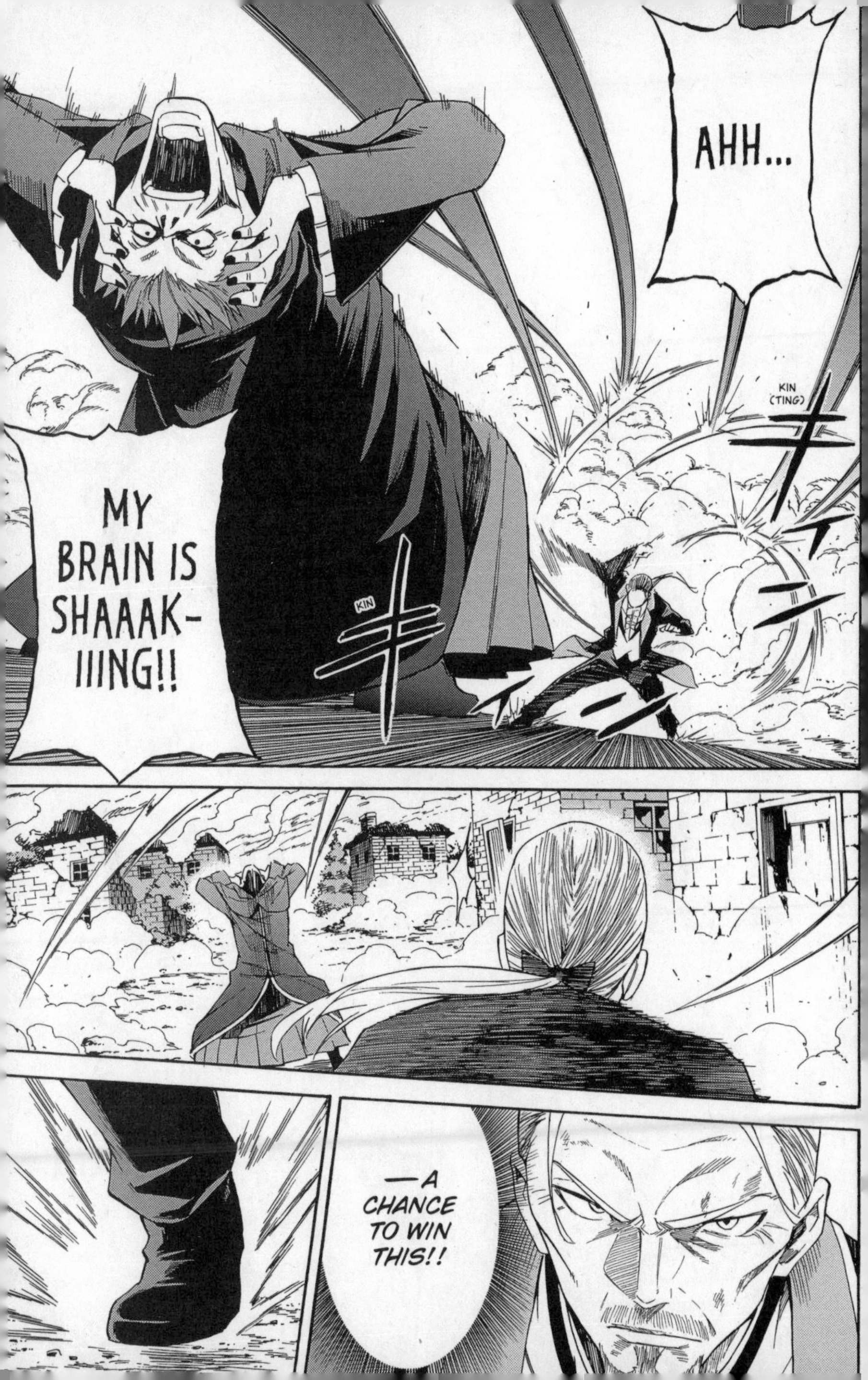
AHH...
KIN (TING)
KIN
MY BRAIN IS SHAAAK-IIING!!
—A CHANCE TO WIN THIS!!

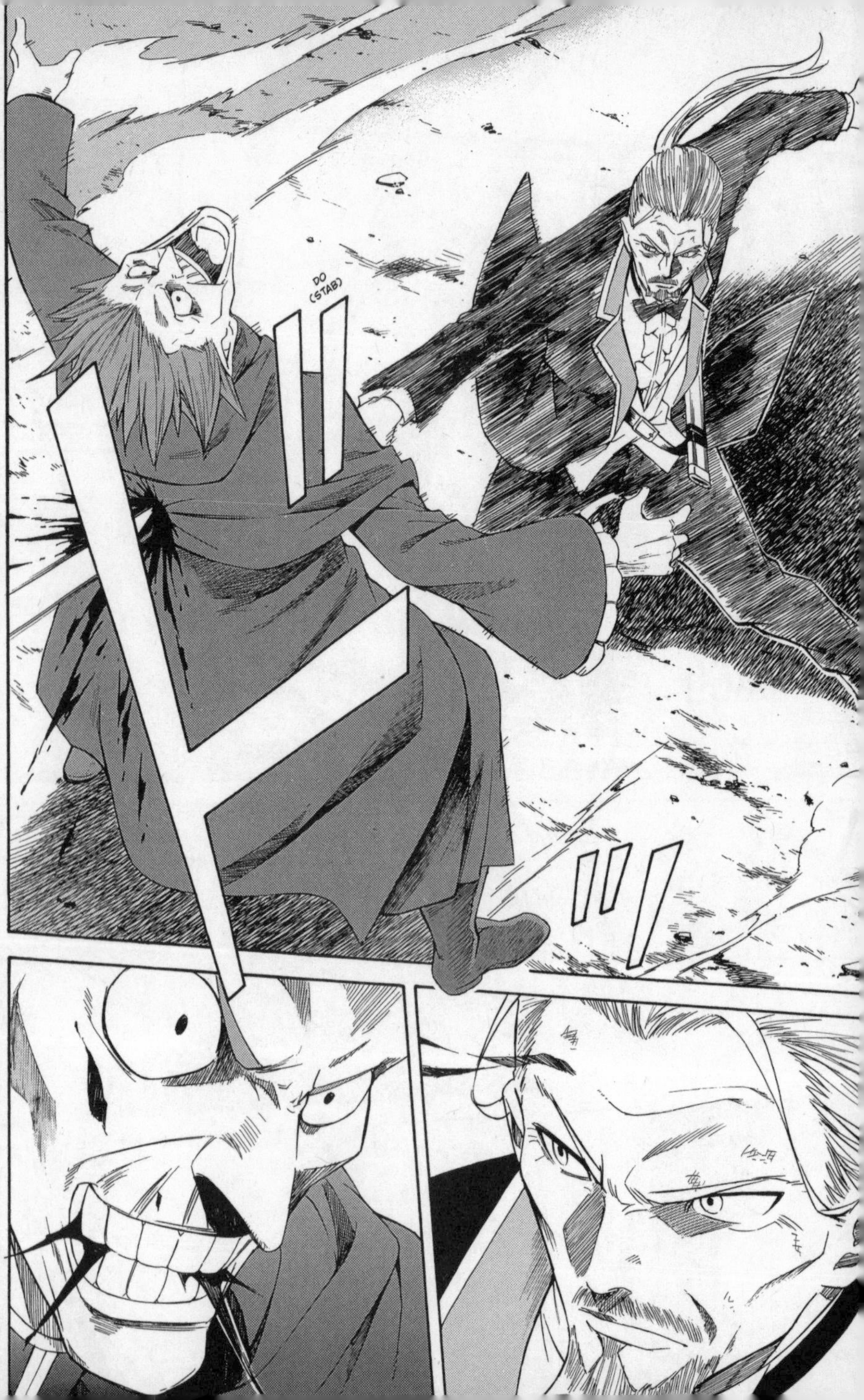
DO
(STAB)

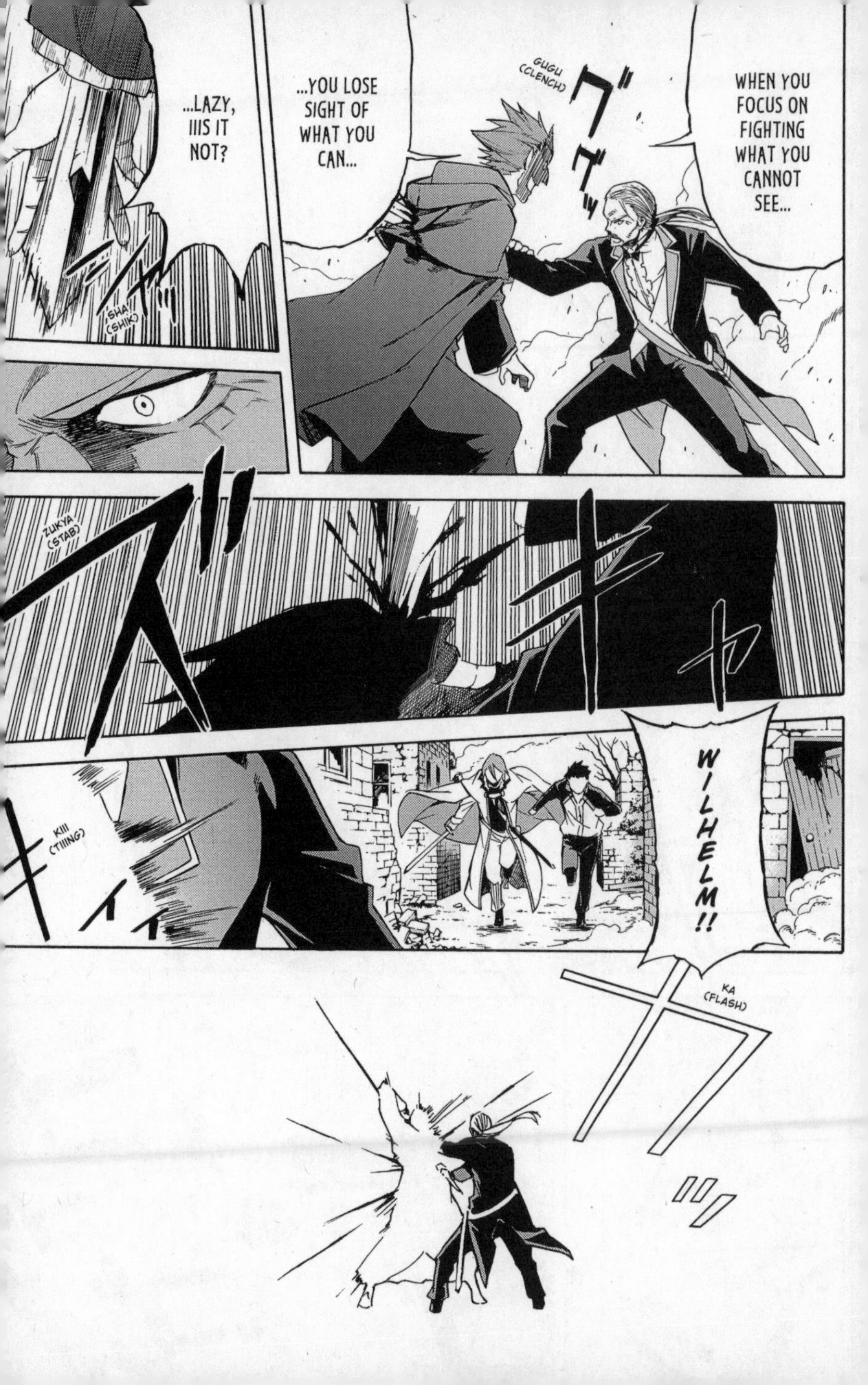
WHEN YOU FOCUS ON FIGHTING WHAT YOU CANNOT SEE...
GUGU (CLENCH)
...YOU LOSE SIGHT OF WHAT YOU CAN...
...LAZY, IIIS IT NOT?
SHA (SHIK)
ZUKYA (STAB)
WILHELM!!
KIII (TIIING)
KA (FLASH)

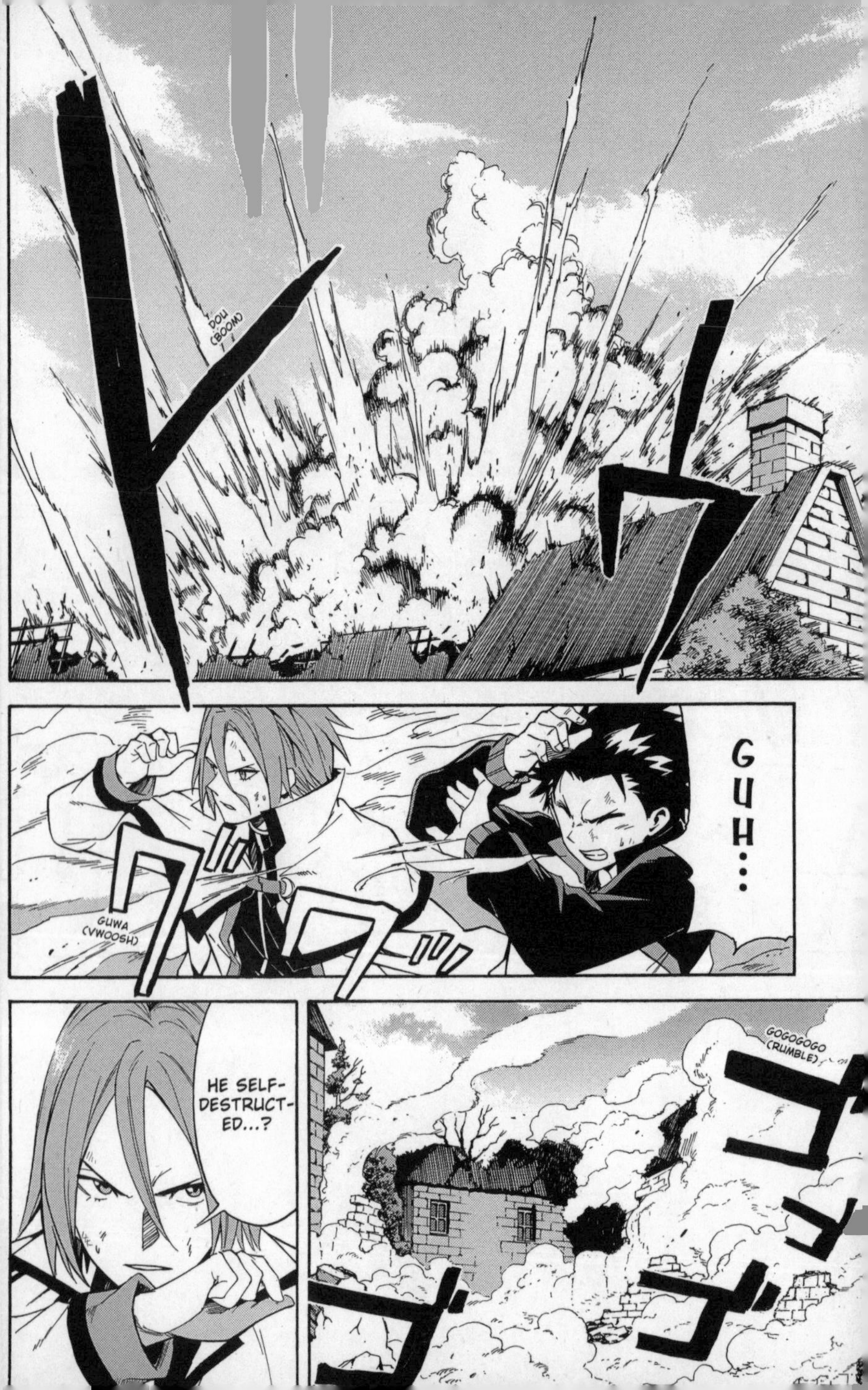
DOU (BOOM)
GUH...
GUWA (VWOOSH)
GOGOGOGO (RUMBLE)
HE SELF-DESTRUCTED...?

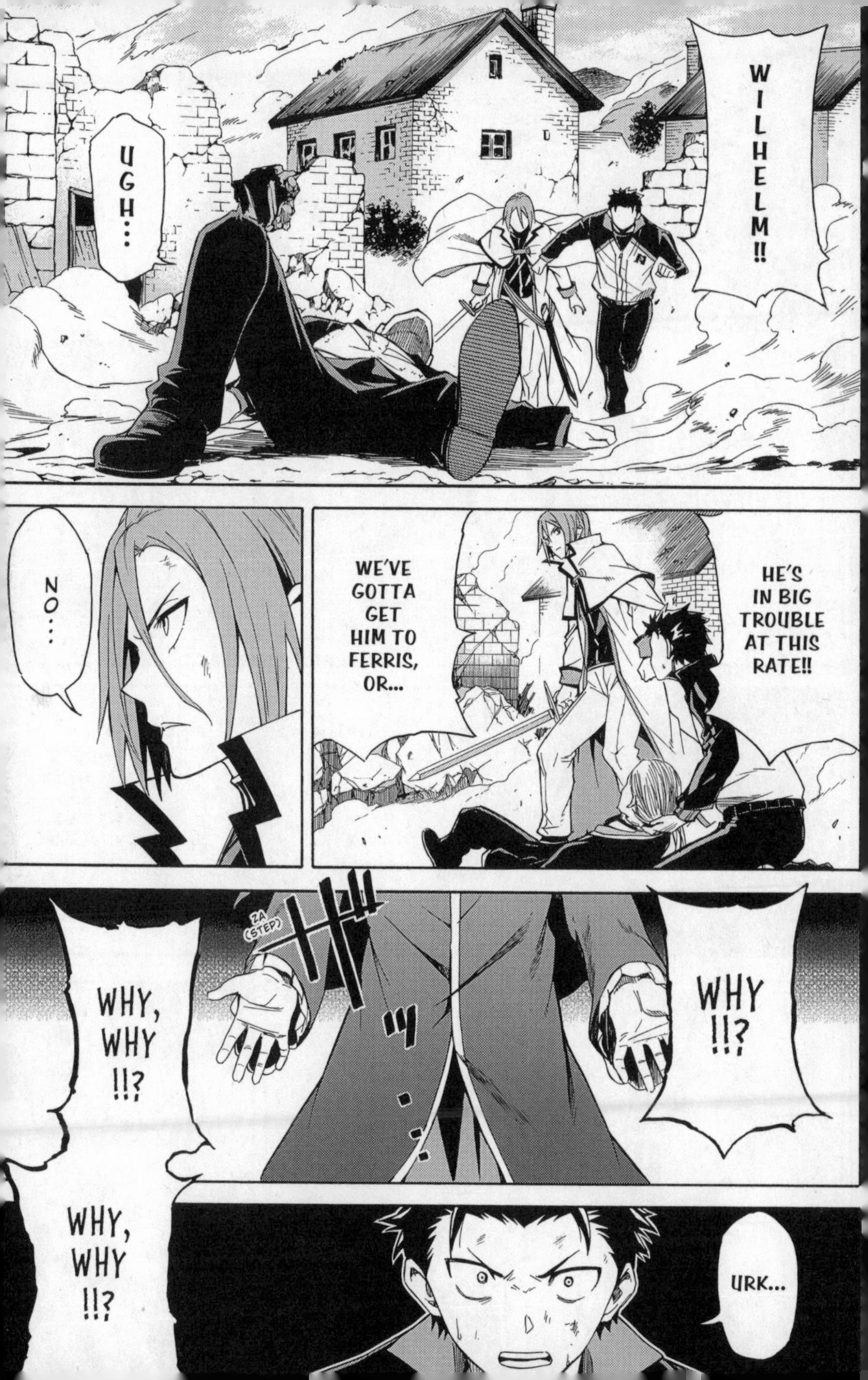
WILHELM!!
UGH...
HE'S IN BIG TROUBLE AT THIS RATE!!
WE'VE GOTTA GET HIM TO FERRIS, OR...
NO...
WHY!!?
ZA (STEP)
WHY, WHY!!?
URK...
WHY, WHY!!?

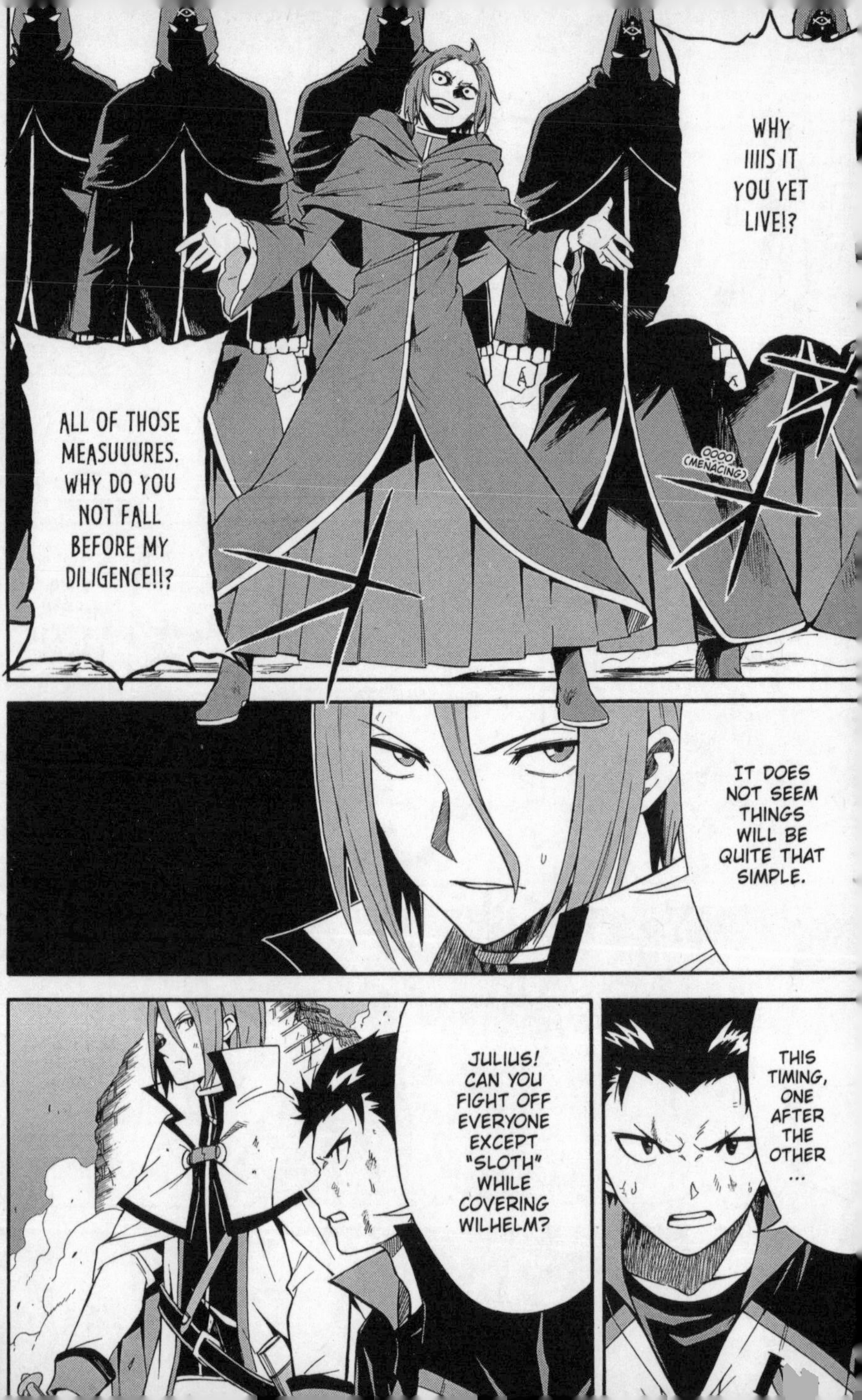
WHY IIIIS IT YOU YET LIVE!?
ALL OF THOSE MEASUUURES. WHY DO YOU NOT FALL BEFORE MY DILIGENCE!!?
OOOO (MENACING)
IT DOES NOT SEEM THINGS WILL BE QUITE THAT SIMPLE.
THIS TIMING, ONE AFTER THE OTHER ...
JULIUS! CAN YOU FIGHT OFF EVERYONE EXCEPT "SLOTH" WHILE COVERING WILHELM?

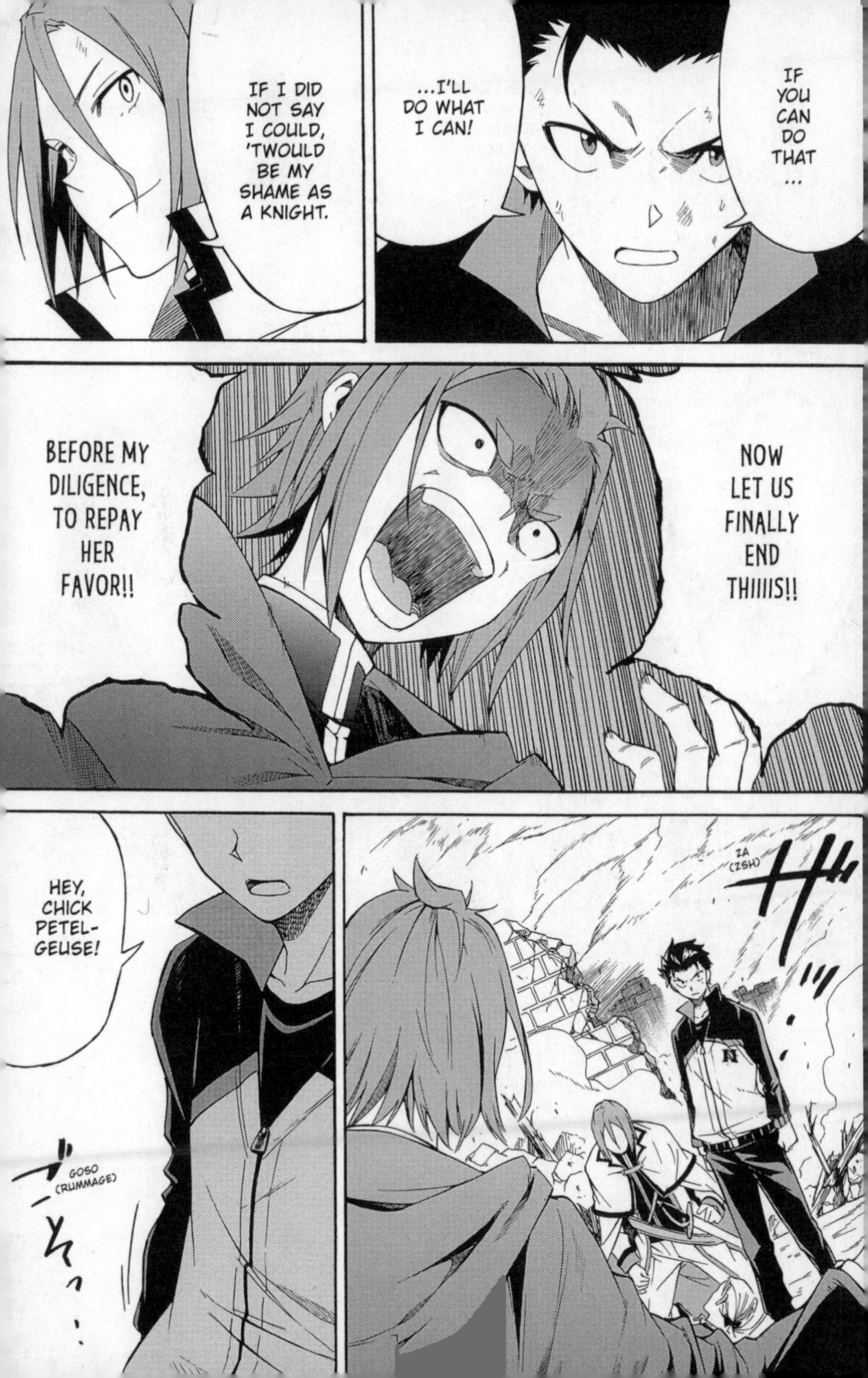
IF YOU CAN DO THAT...
...I'LL DO WHAT I CAN!
IF I DID NOT SAY I COULD, 'TWOULD BE MY SHAME AS A KNIGHT.
NOW LET US FINALLY END THIIIIS!!
BEFORE MY DILIGENCE, TO REPAY HER FAVOR!!
ZA (ZSH)
HEY, CHICK PETEL-GEUSE!
GOSO (RUMMAGE)

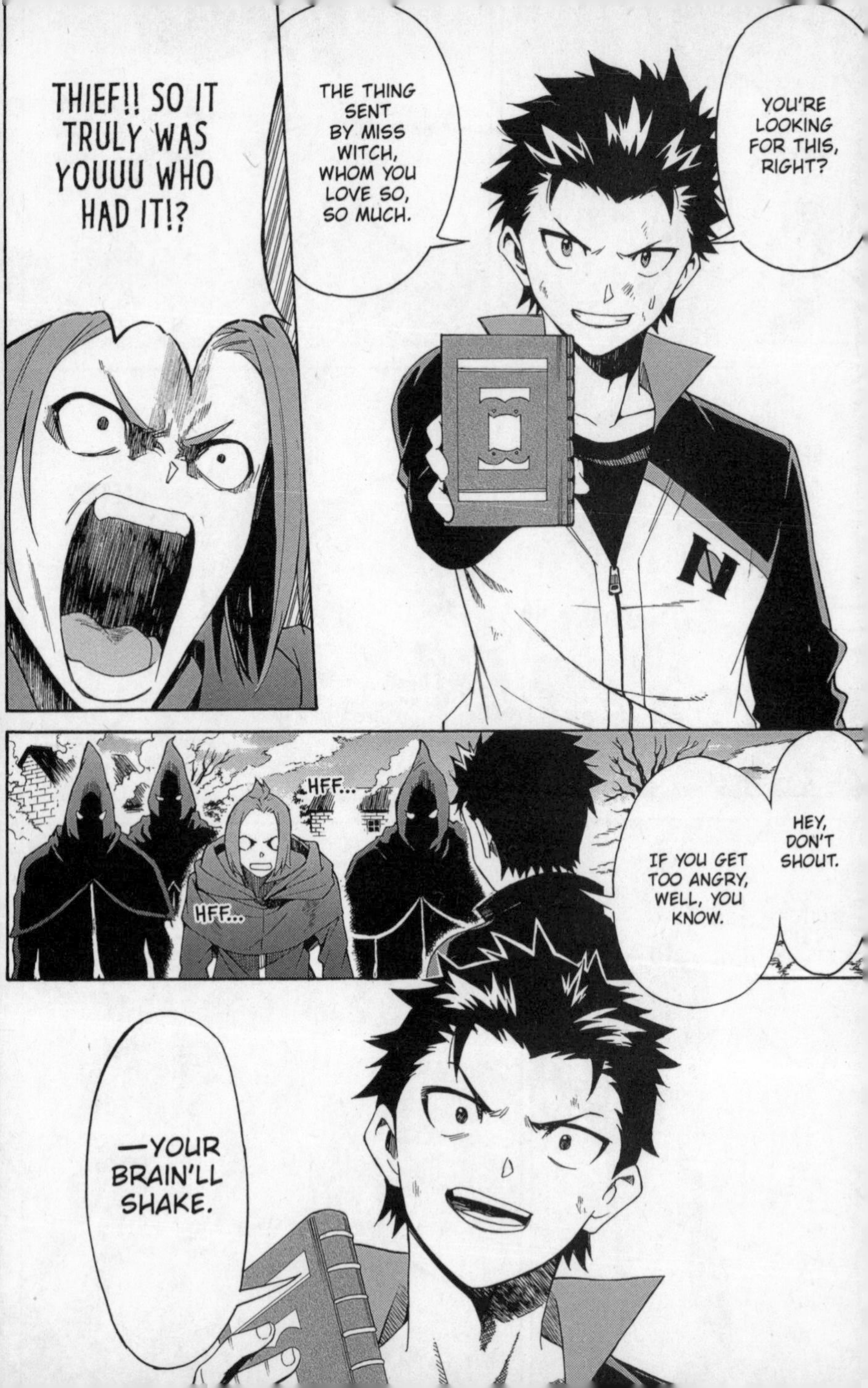
YOU'RE LOOKING FOR THIS, RIGHT?
THE THING SENT BY MISS WITCH, WHOM YOU LOVE SO, SO MUCH.
THIEF!! SO IT TRULY WAS YOUUU WHO HAD IT!?
HEY, DON'T SHOUT.
IF YOU GET TOO ANGRY, WELL, YOU KNOW.
HFF...
HFF...
—YOUR BRAIN'LL SHAKE.

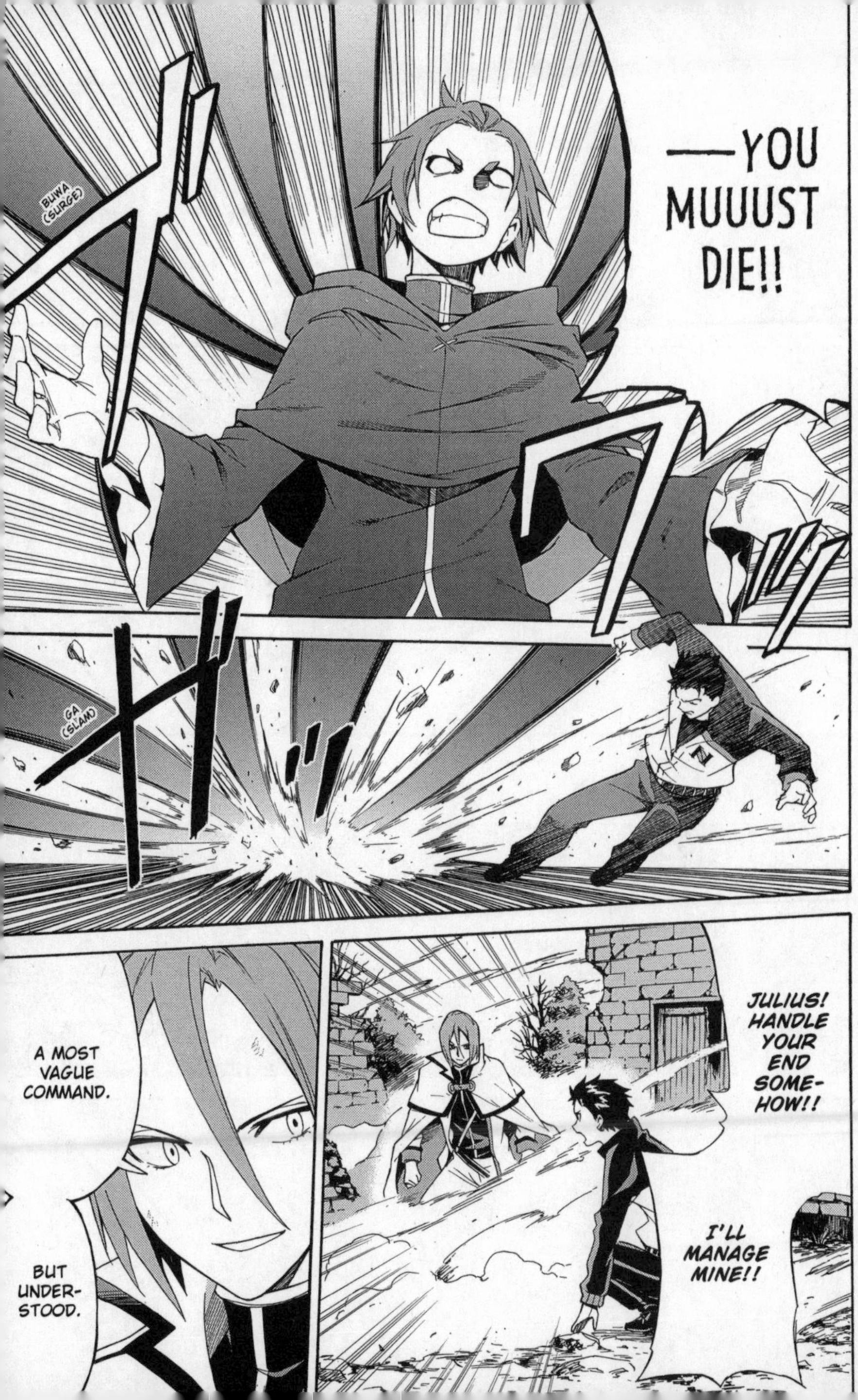
——YOU MUUUST DIE!!
BUWA (SURGE)
GA (SLAM)
JULIUS! HANDLE YOUR END SOME-HOW!!
I'LL MANAGE MINE!!
A MOST VAGUE COMMAND.
BUT UNDER-STOOD.

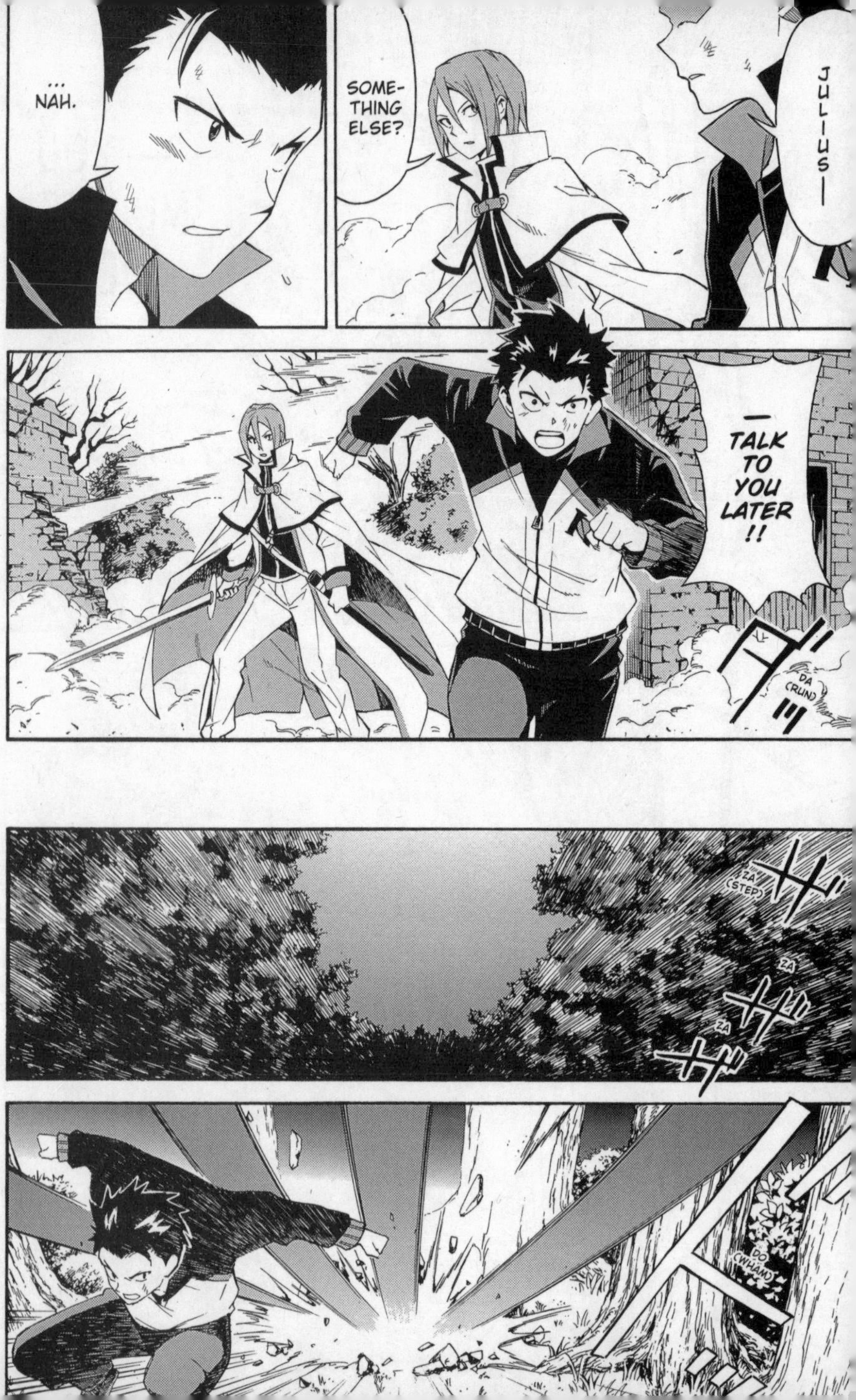
JULIUS—
SOMETHING ELSE?
...NAH.
—TALK TO YOU LATER!!
DA (RUN)
ZA (STEP)
ZA
ZA
DO (WHAM)

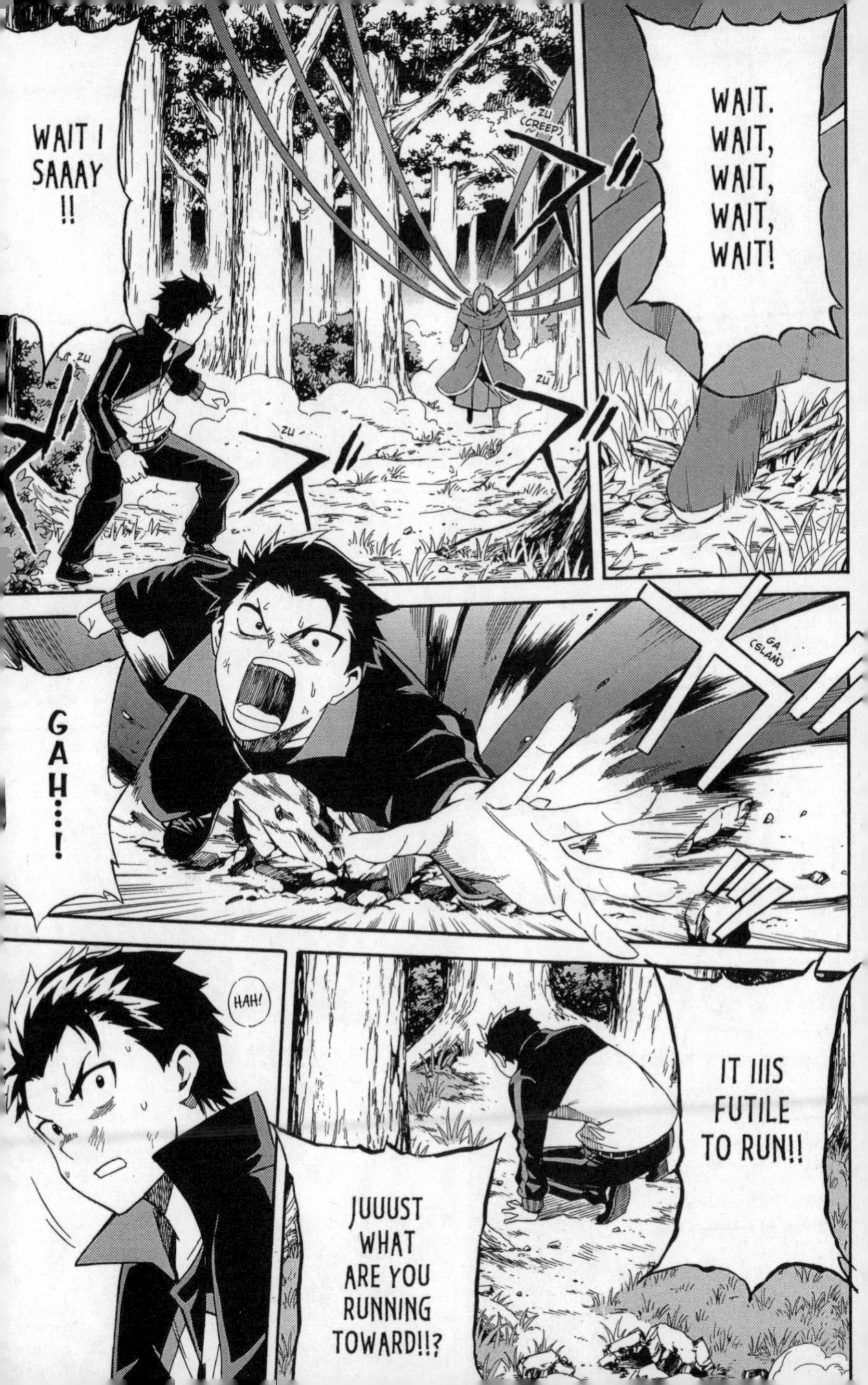
WAIT. WAIT, WAIT, WAIT, WAIT!
ZU (CREEP)
WAIT I SAAAY!!
ZU
ZU
ZU
GA (SLAM)
GAH…!
IT IIIS FUTILE TO RUN!!
JUUUST WHAT ARE YOU RUNNING TOWARD!!?
HAH!

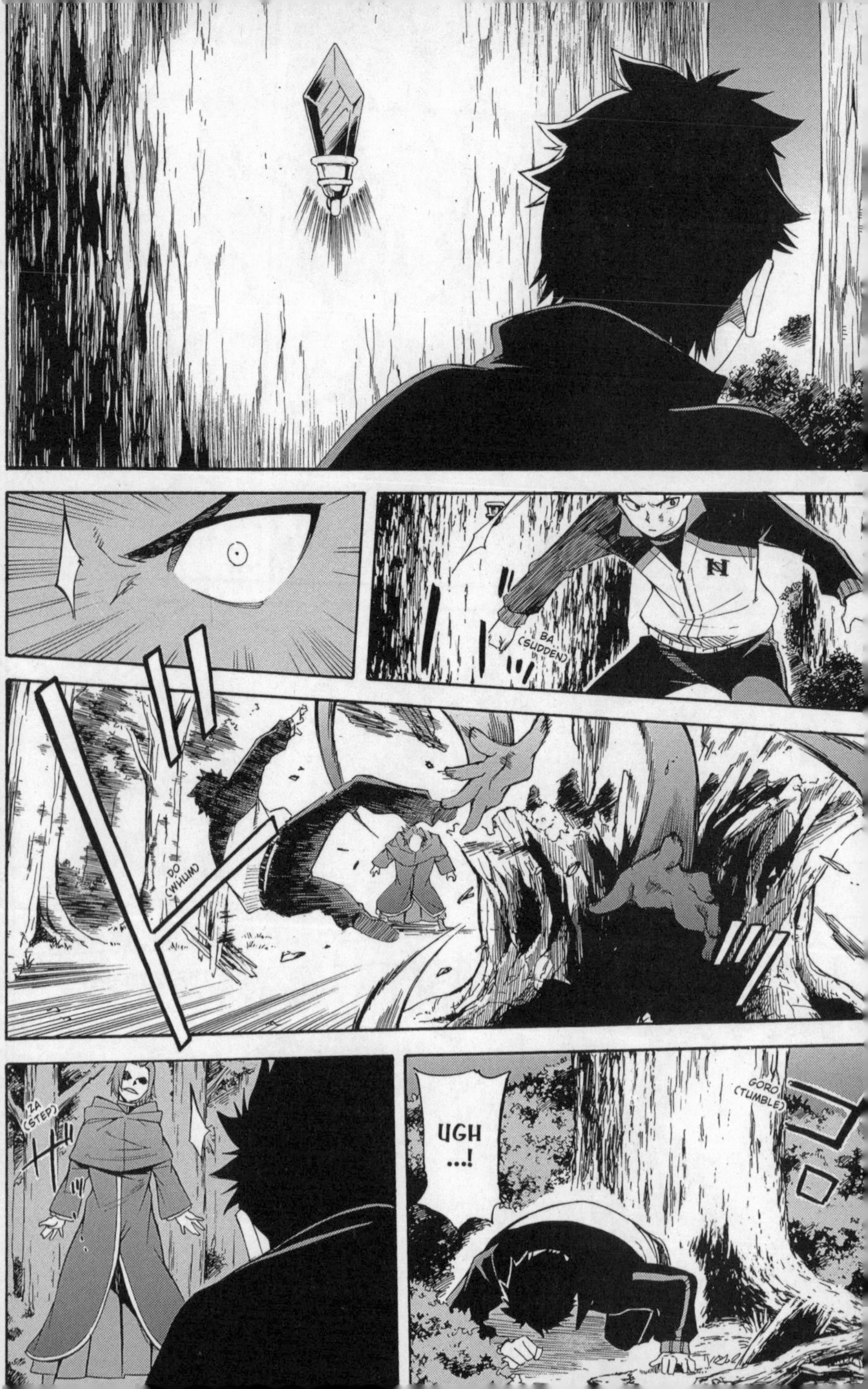
BA (SUDDEN)
DO (WHUMP)
GORO (TUMBLE)
UGH ...!
ZA (STEP)

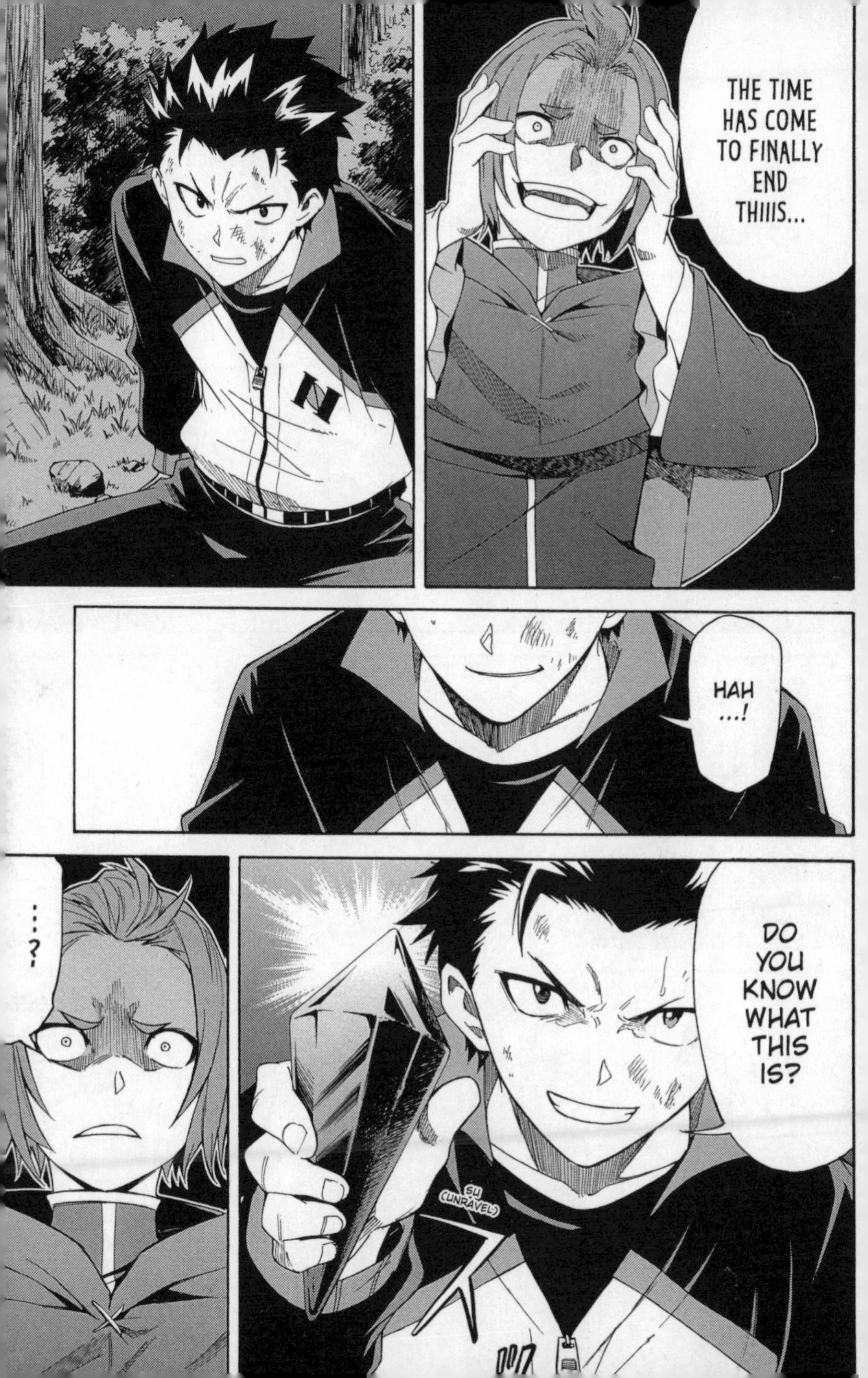
THE TIME HAS COME TO FINALLY END THIIIS...
HAH ...!
DO YOU KNOW WHAT THIS IS?
SU (UNRAVEL)
...?

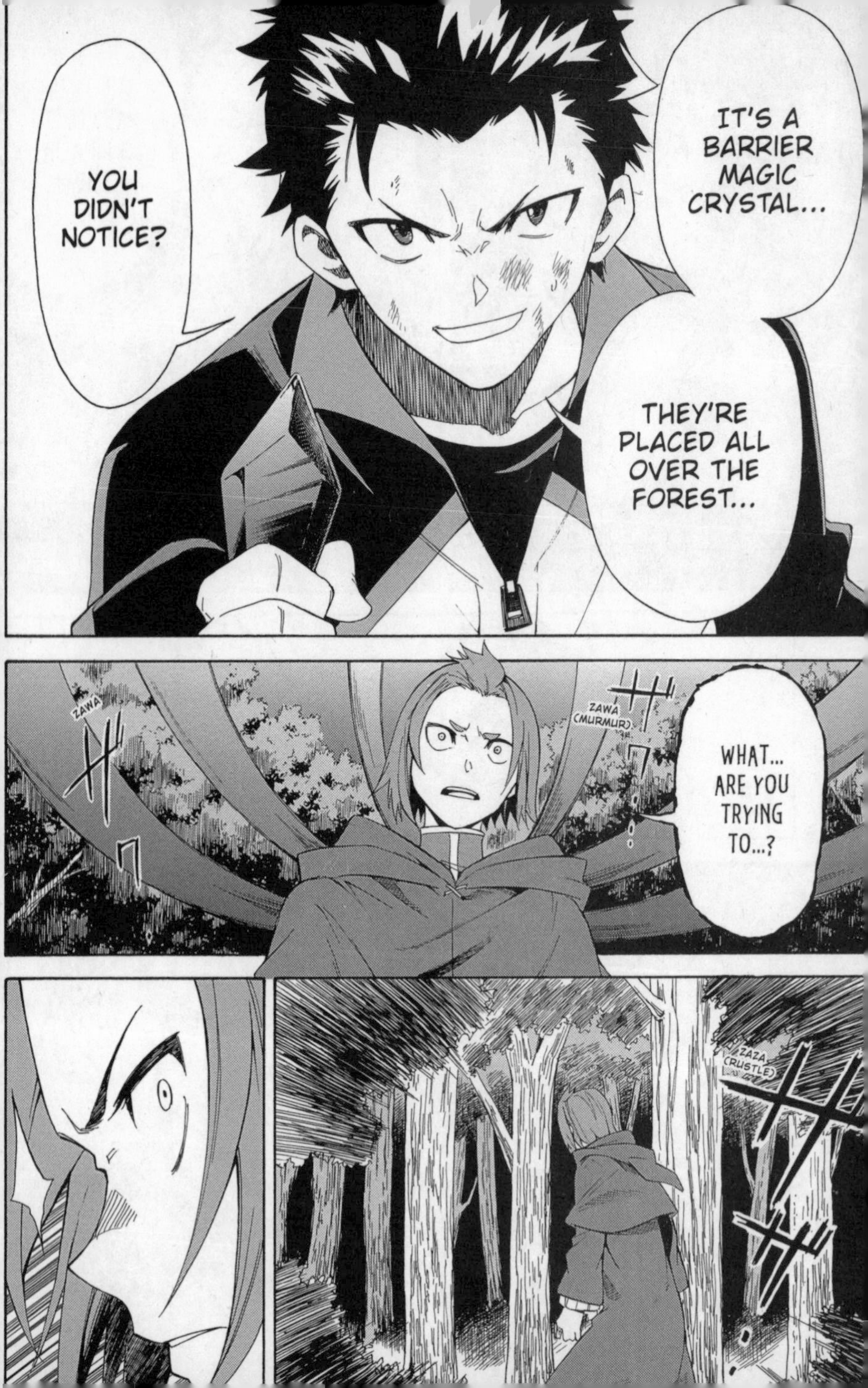
IT'S A BARRIER MAGIC CRYSTAL...
YOU DIDN'T NOTICE?
THEY'RE PLACED ALL OVER THE FOREST...
WHAT... ARE YOU TRYING TO...?
ZAWA (MURMUR)
ZAWA
ZAZA (RUSTLE)

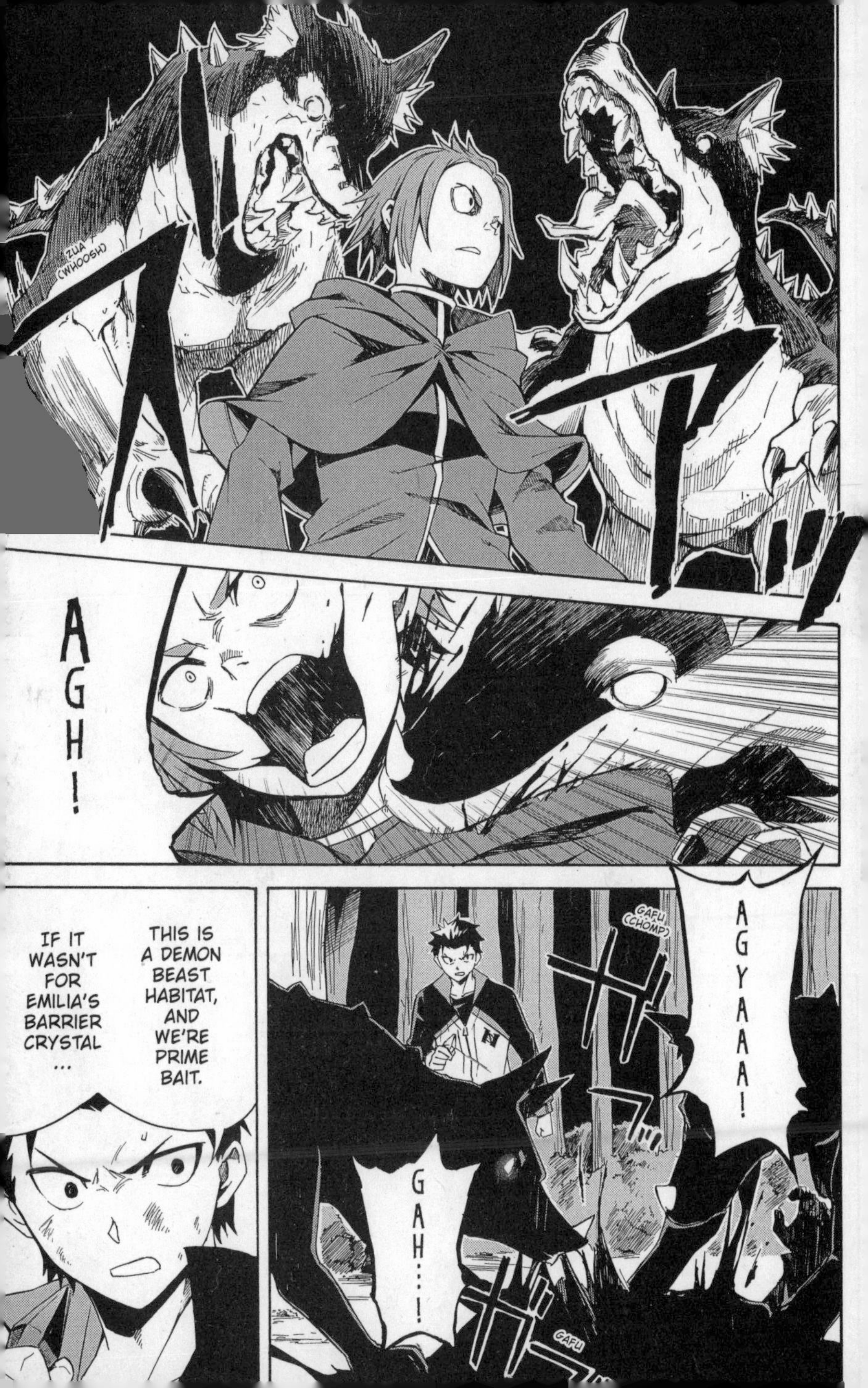
ZUA
(WHOOSH)
AGH!
AGYAAAA!
GAFU
(CHOMP)
GAFU
GAH...!
THIS IS A DEMON BEAST HABITAT, AND WE'RE PRIME BAIT.
IF IT WASN'T FOR EMILIA'S BARRIER CRYSTAL...

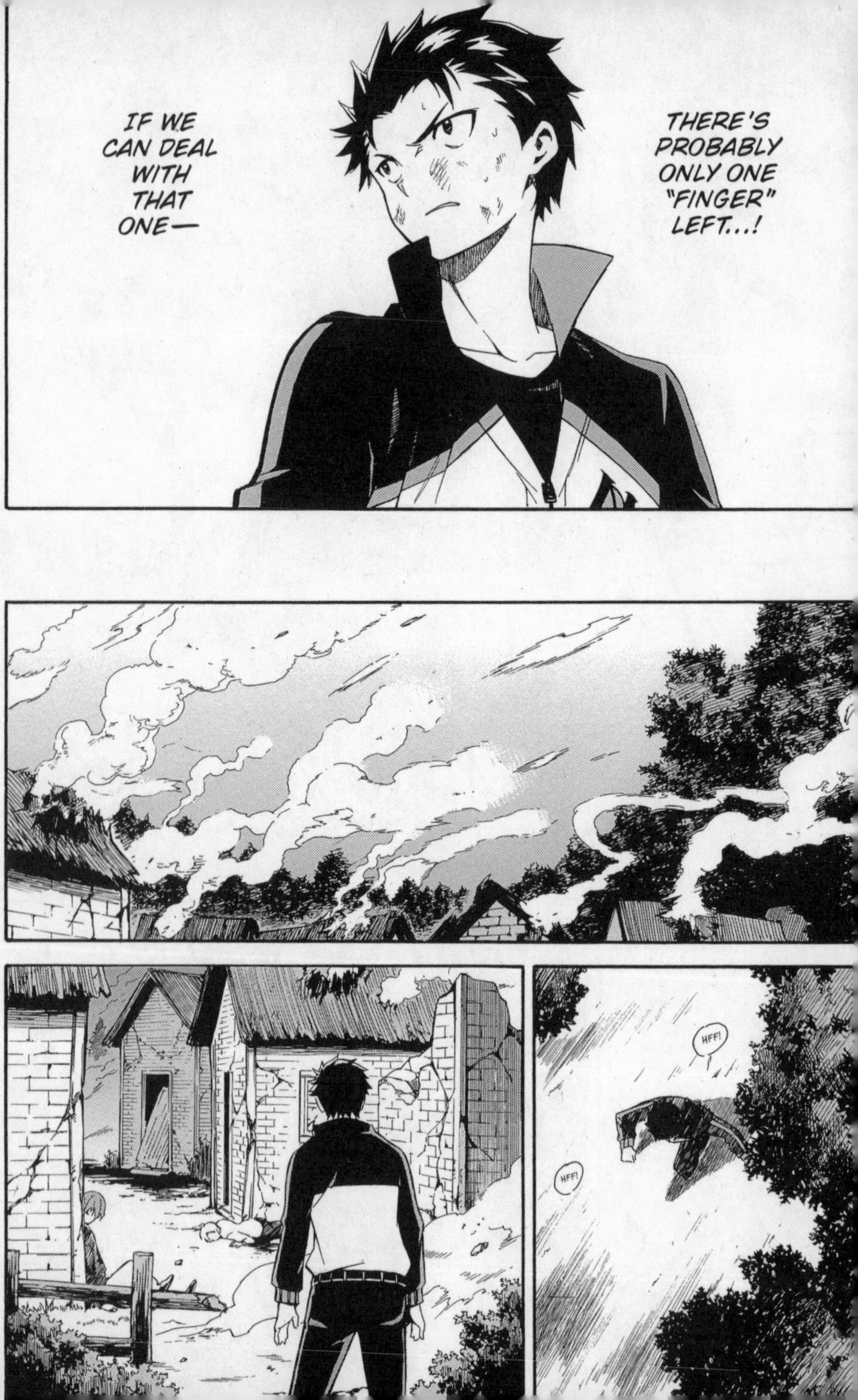
THERE'S PROBABLY ONLY ONE "FINGER" LEFT...!
IF WE CAN DEAL WITH THAT ONE—
HFF!
HFF!

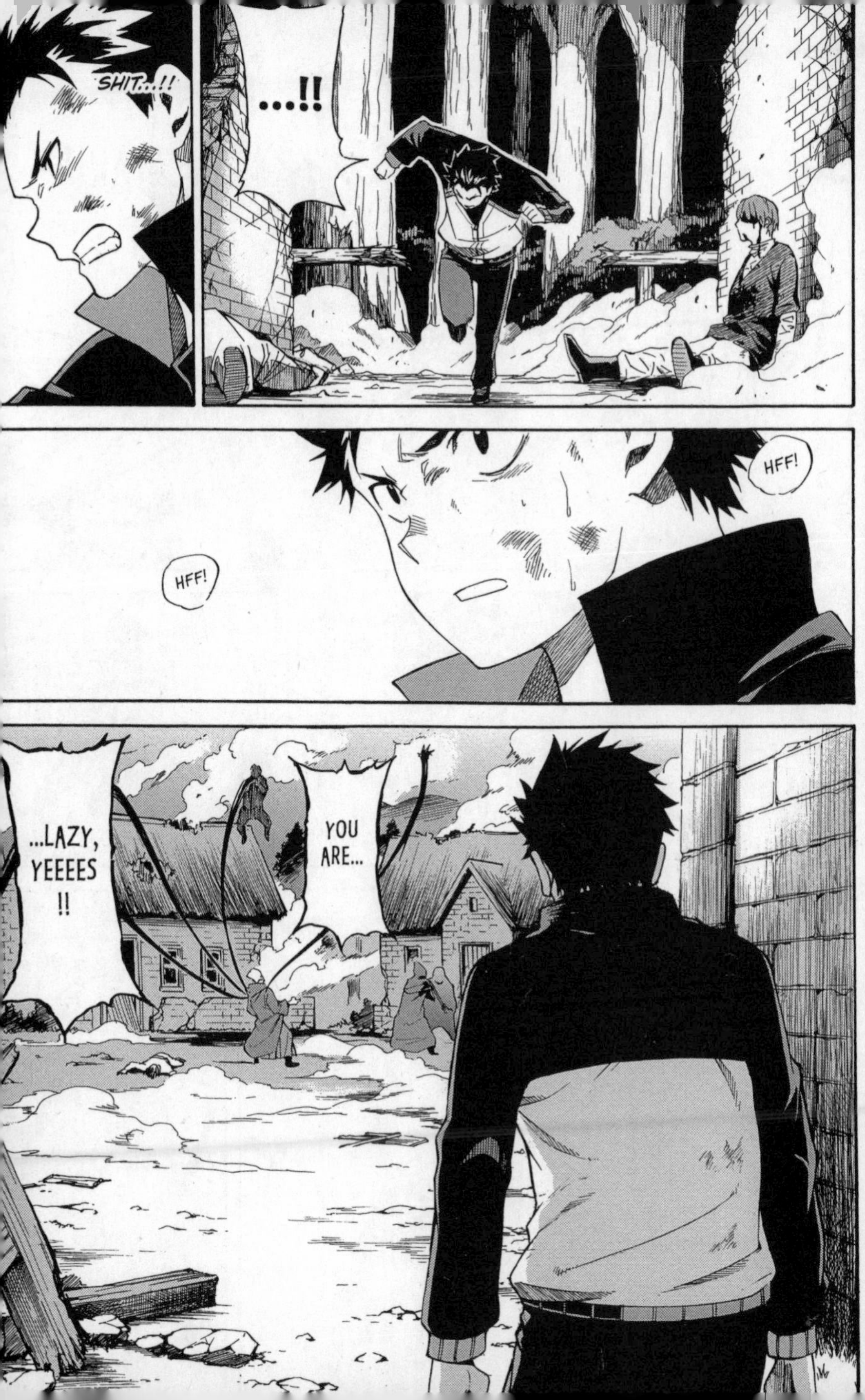
...!!
SHIT...!!
HFF!
HFF!
YOU ARE...
...LAZY, YEEEES !!

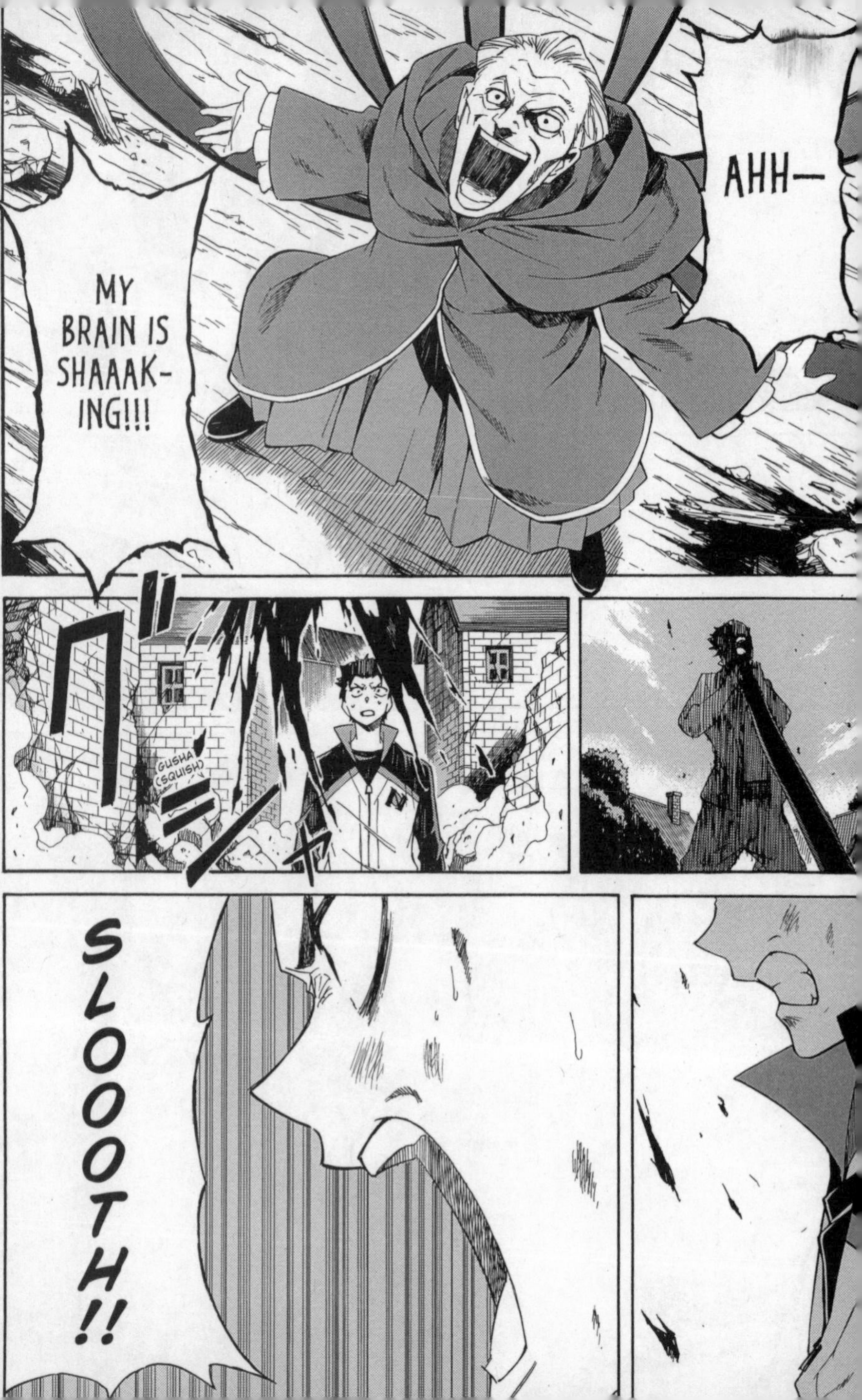
AHH—
MY BRAIN IS SHAAAK-ING!!!
GUSHA (SQUISH)
SLOOOOTH!!

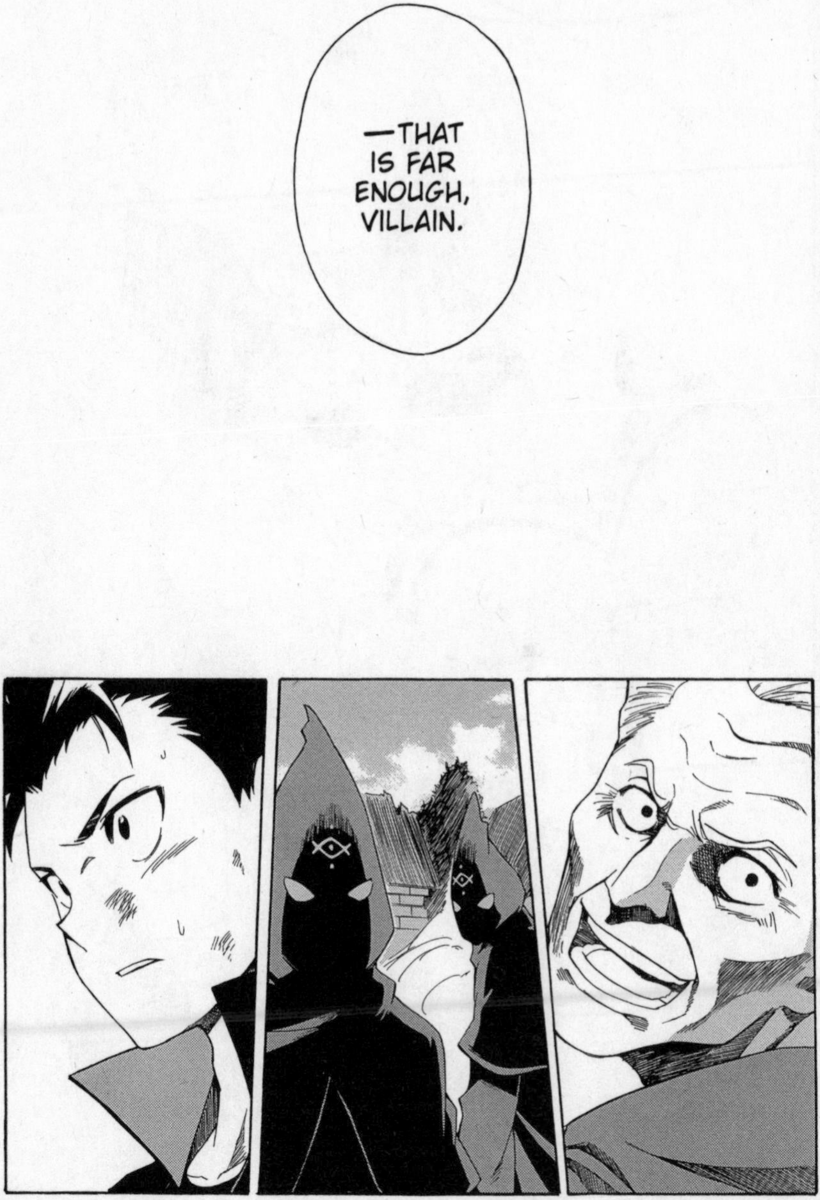
—THAT IS FAR ENOUGH, VILLAIN.

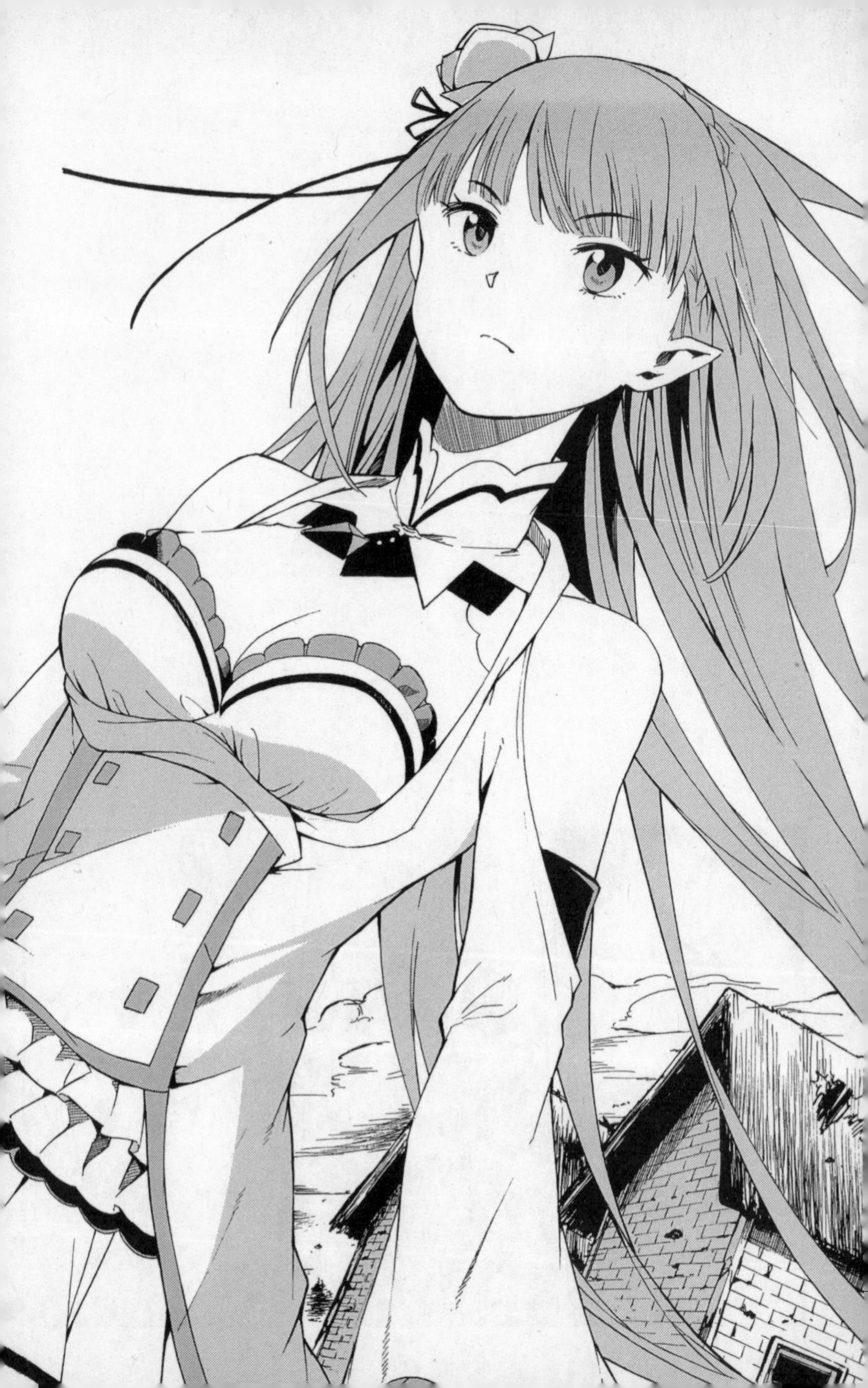

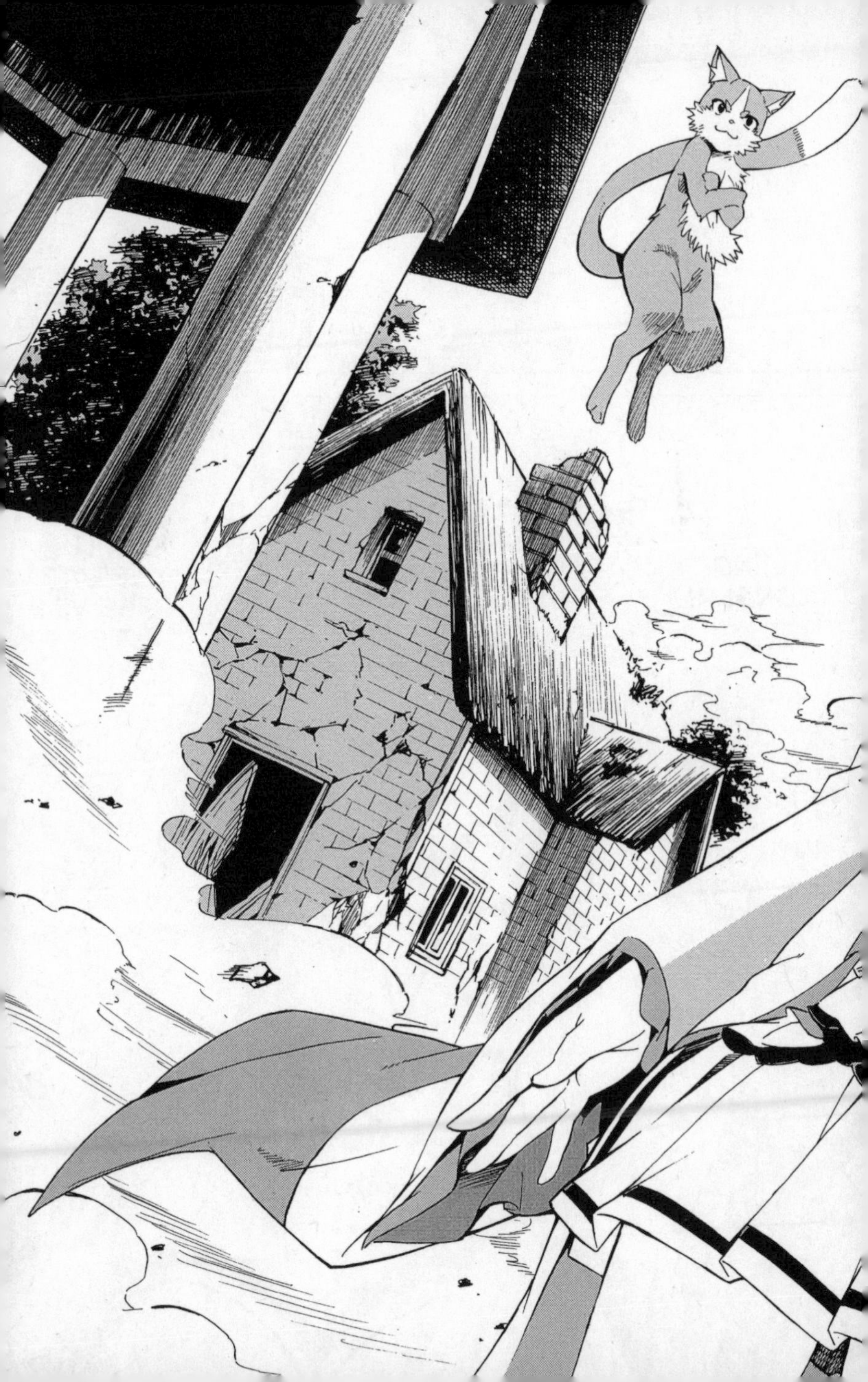

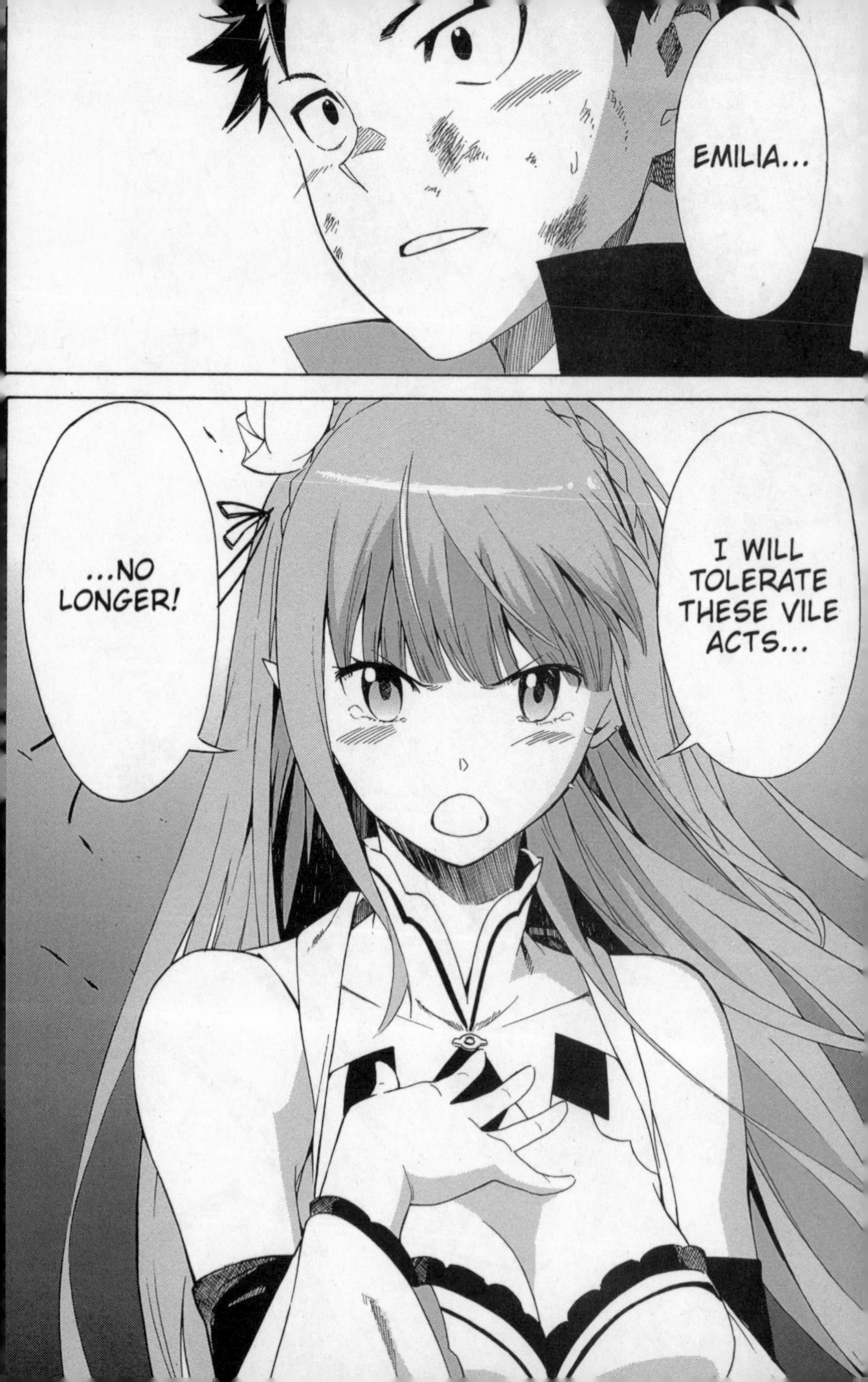
EMILIA...
I WILL TOLERATE THESE VILE ACTS...
...NO LONGER!

Re:ZERO -Starting Life in Another World-

The only ability Subaru Natsuki gets when he's summoned to another world is time travel via his own death. But to save her, he'll die as many times as it takes.

The only ability Subaru Natsuki gets when he's
summoned to another world is time travel via his own
death. But to save her, he'll die as many times as it takes.

Truth of Zero

Re:ZERO -Starting
Life in Another World-

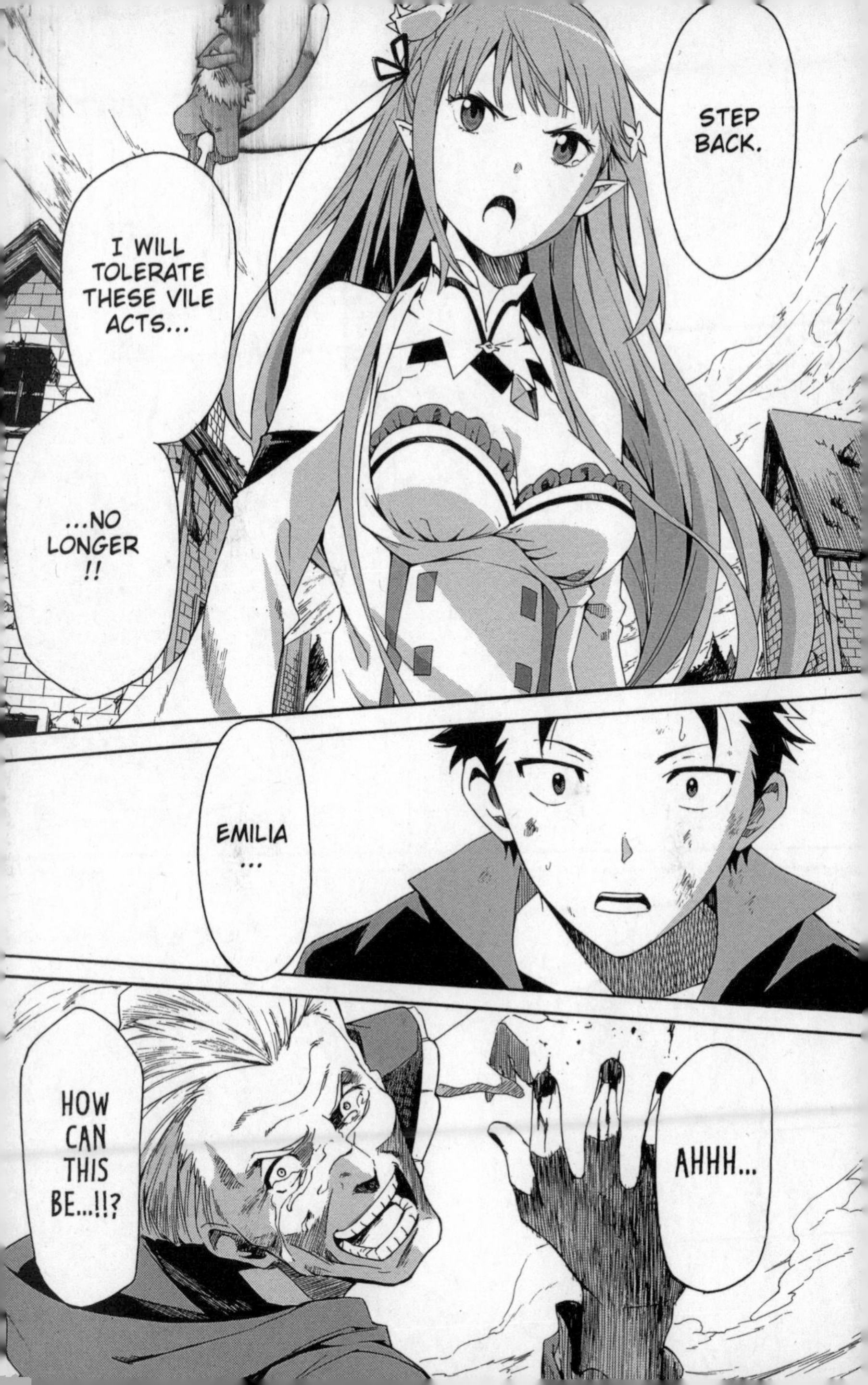
STEP BACK.
I WILL TOLERATE THESE VILE ACTS...
...NO LONGER!!
EMILIA...
AHHH...
HOW CAN THIS BE...!!?

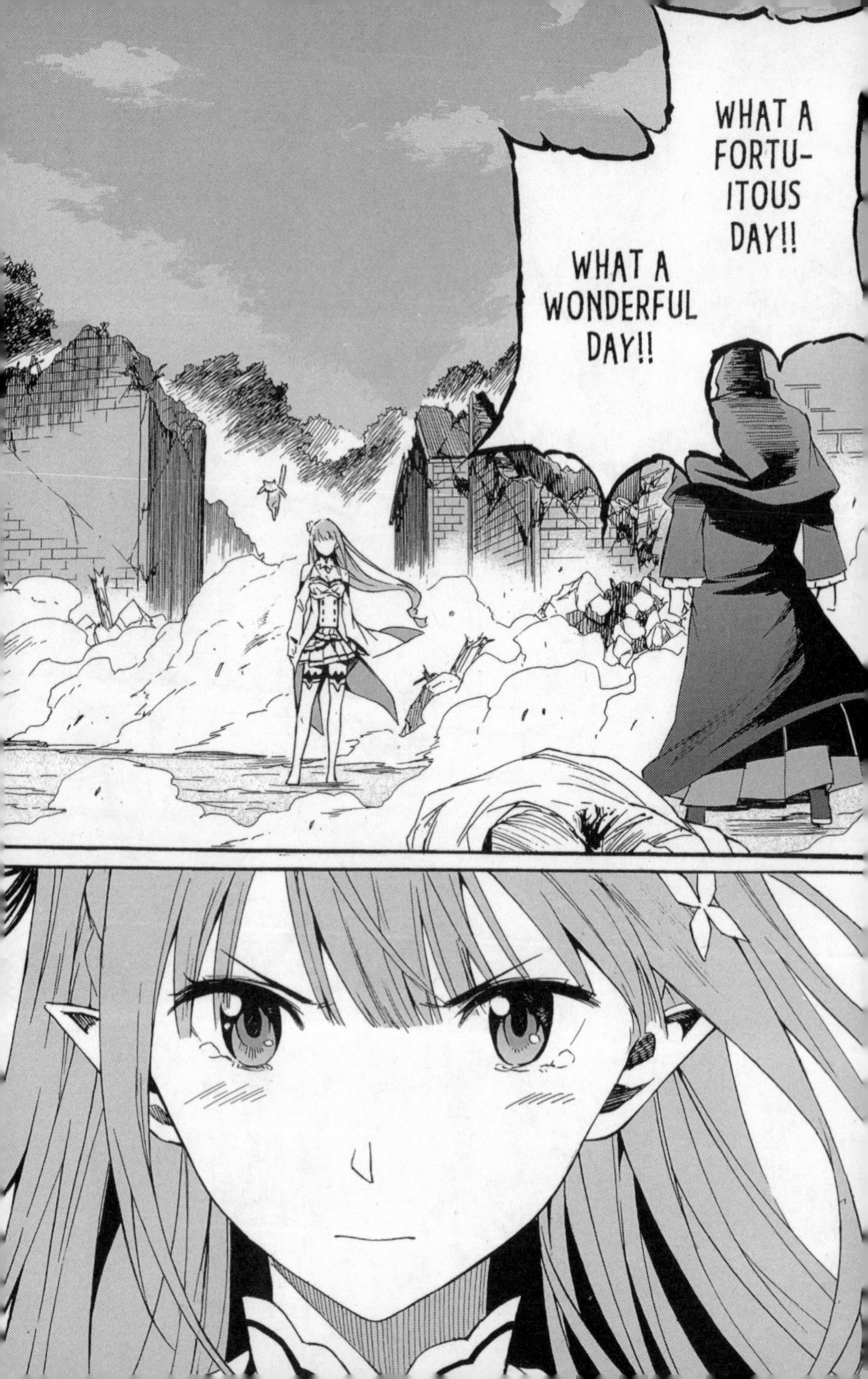
WHAT A FORTU-ITOUS DAY!!
WHAT A WONDERFUL DAY!!

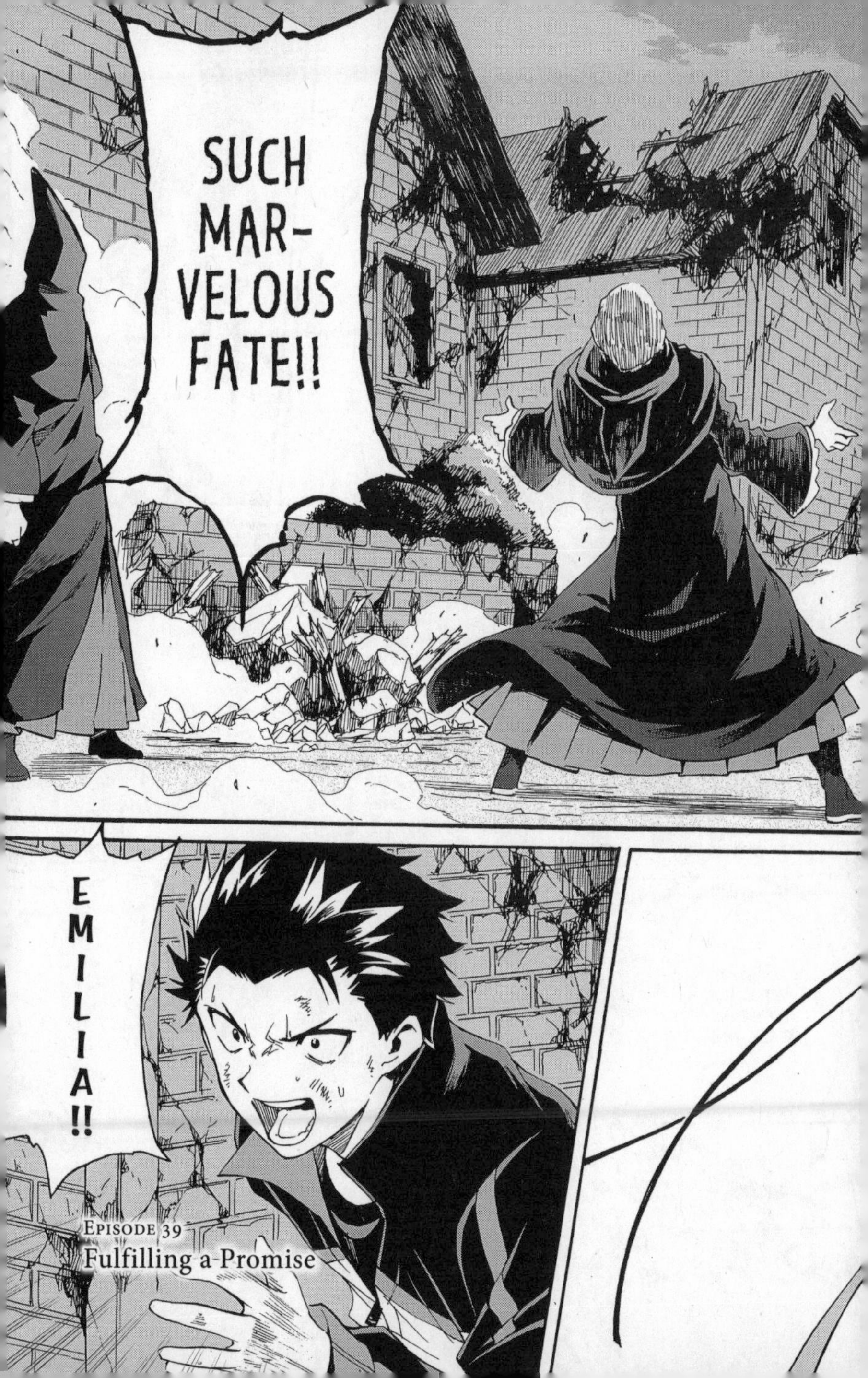
SUCH MAR-VELOUS FATE!!
EMILIA!!
Episode 39
Fulfilling a Promise

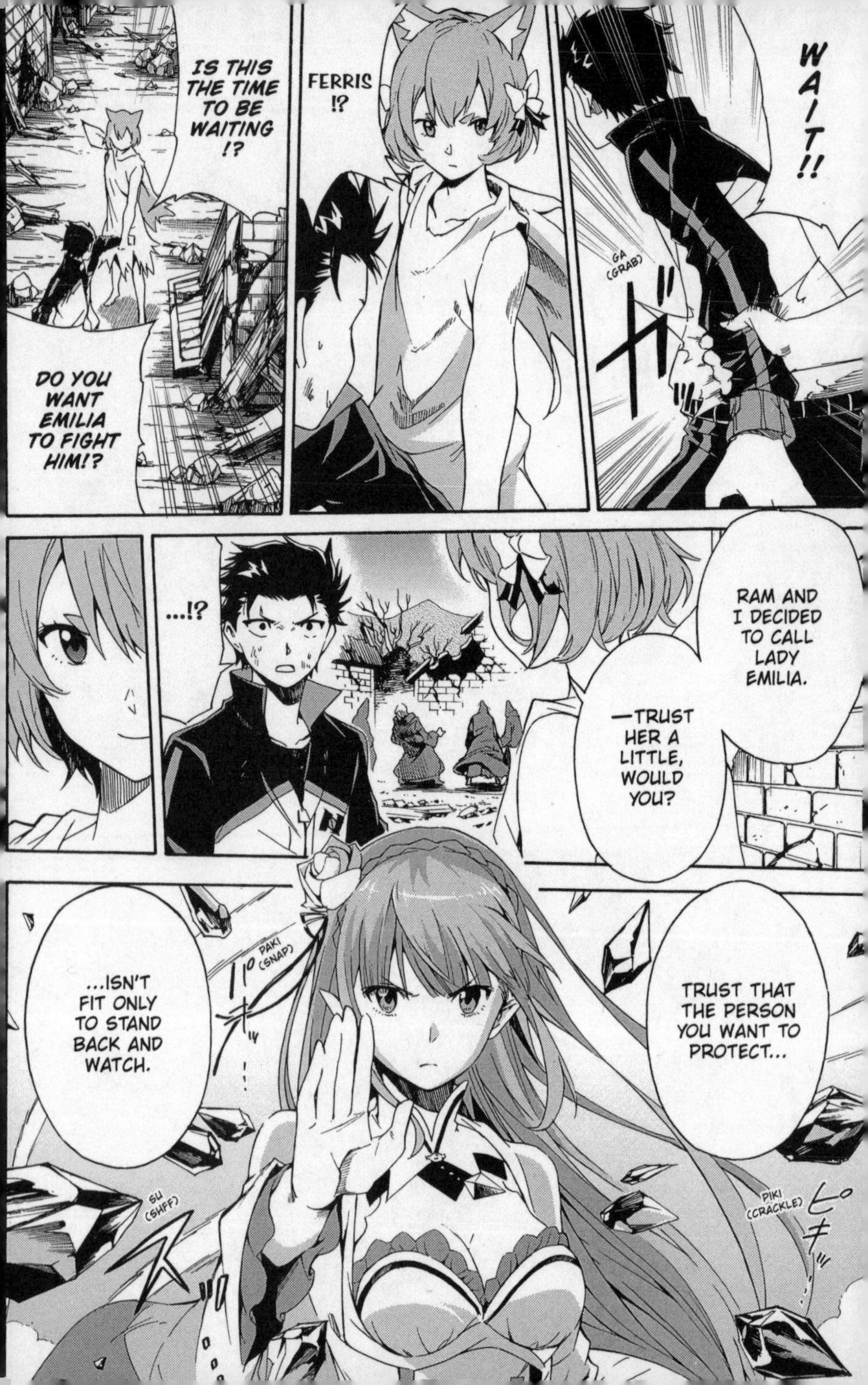
WAIT!!
GA (GRAB)
FERRIS !?
IS THIS THE TIME TO BE WAITING !?
DO YOU WANT EMILIA TO FIGHT HIM!?
RAM AND I DECIDED TO CALL LADY EMILIA.
—TRUST HER A LITTLE, WOULD YOU?
...!?
TRUST THAT THE PERSON YOU WANT TO PROTECT...
PIKI (CRACKLE)
PAKI (SNAP)
...ISN'T FIT ONLY TO STAND BACK AND WATCH.
SU (SHFF)

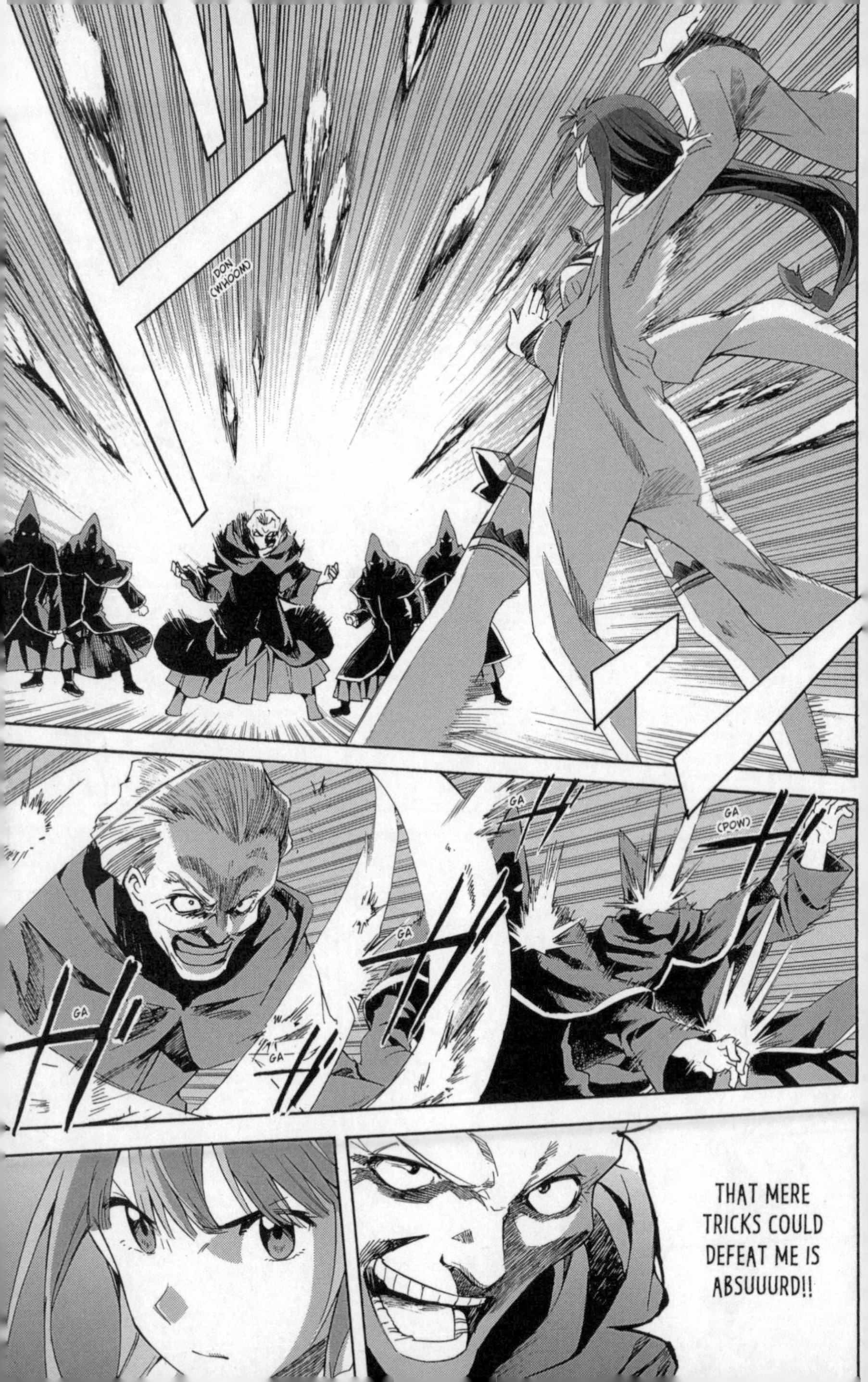
DON (WHOOM)
GA (POW)
GA
GA
GA
GA
THAT MERE TRICKS COULD DEFEAT ME IS ABSUUURD!!

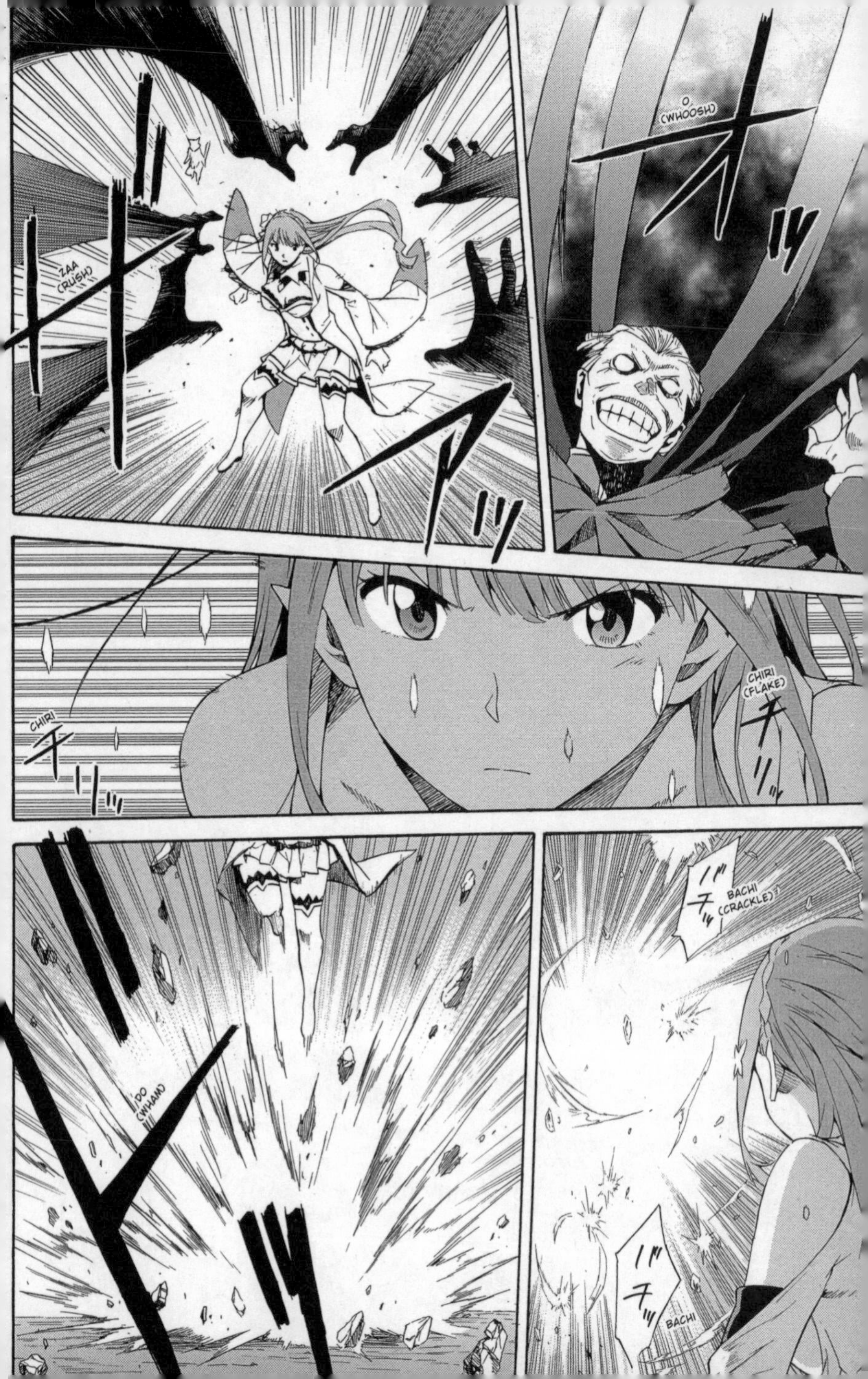
O
(WHOOSH)
ZAA
(RUSH)
CHIRI
(FLAKE)
CHIRI
BACHI
(CRACKLE)
BACHI
DO
(WHAM)

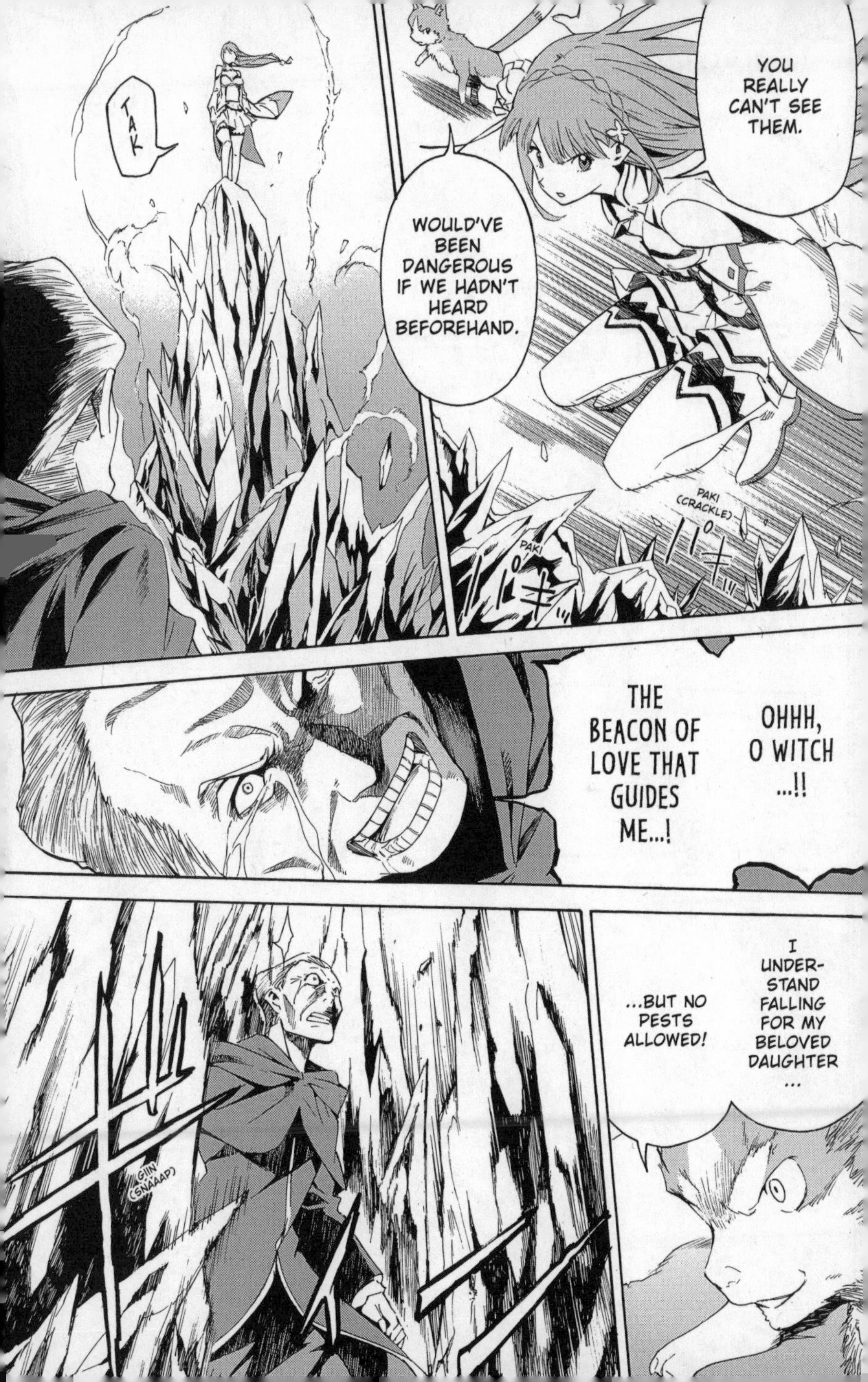
YOU REALLY CAN'T SEE THEM.
WOULD'VE BEEN DANGEROUS IF WE HADN'T HEARD BEFOREHAND.
PAKI (CRACKLE)
PAKI
TAK
OHHH, O WITCH ...!!
THE BEACON OF LOVE THAT GUIDES ME...!
I UNDER-STAND FALLING FOR MY BELOVED DAUGHTER ...
...BUT NO PESTS ALLOWED!
GIIN (SNAAAP)

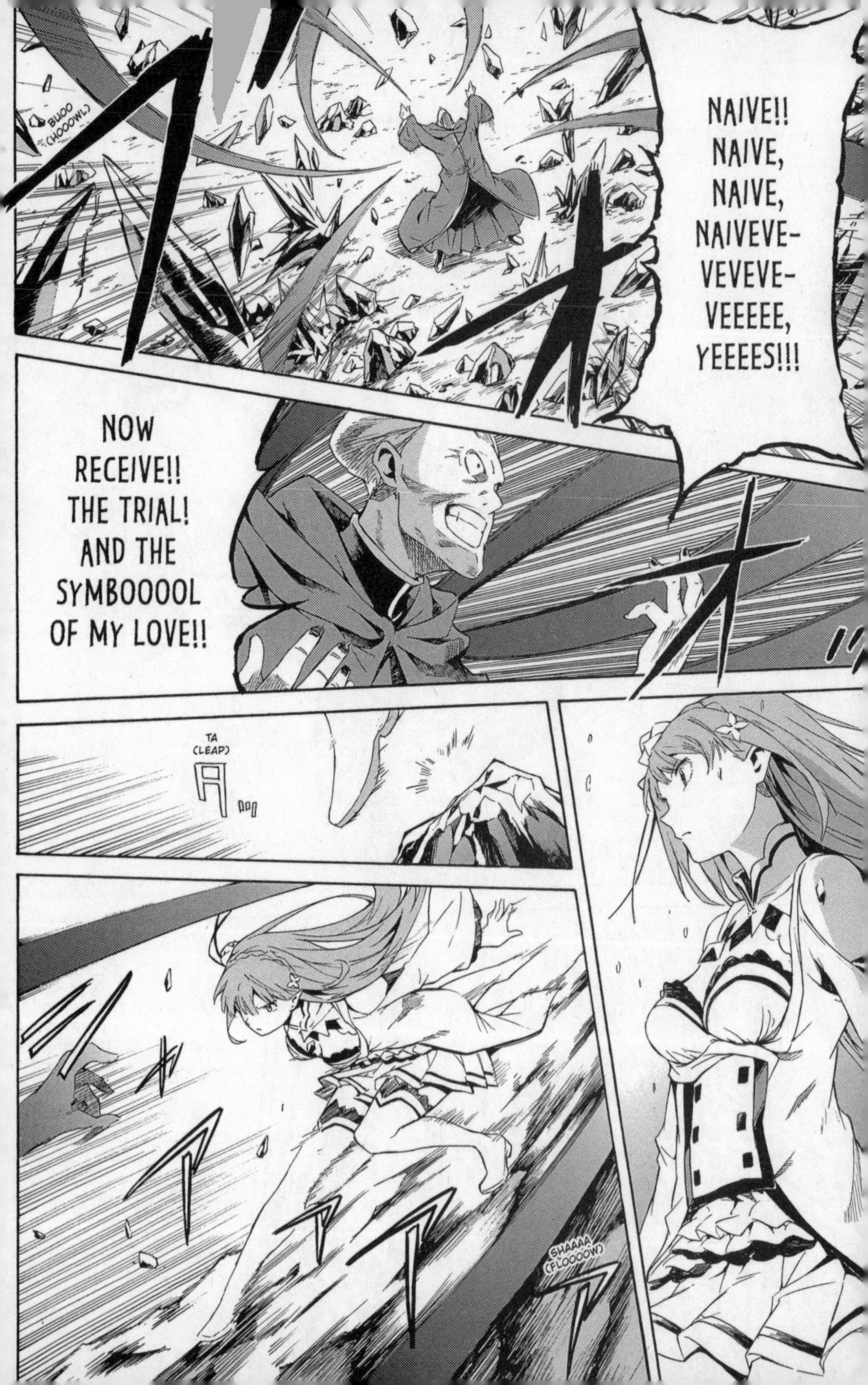
NAIVE!! NAIVE, NAIVE, NAIVEVE-VEVEVE-VEEEEE, YEEEES!!!
BUOO (CHOOOWL)
NOW RECEIVE!! THE TRIAL! AND THE SYMBOOOOL OF MY LOVE!!
SHAAAA (FLOOOOW)
TA (LEAP)

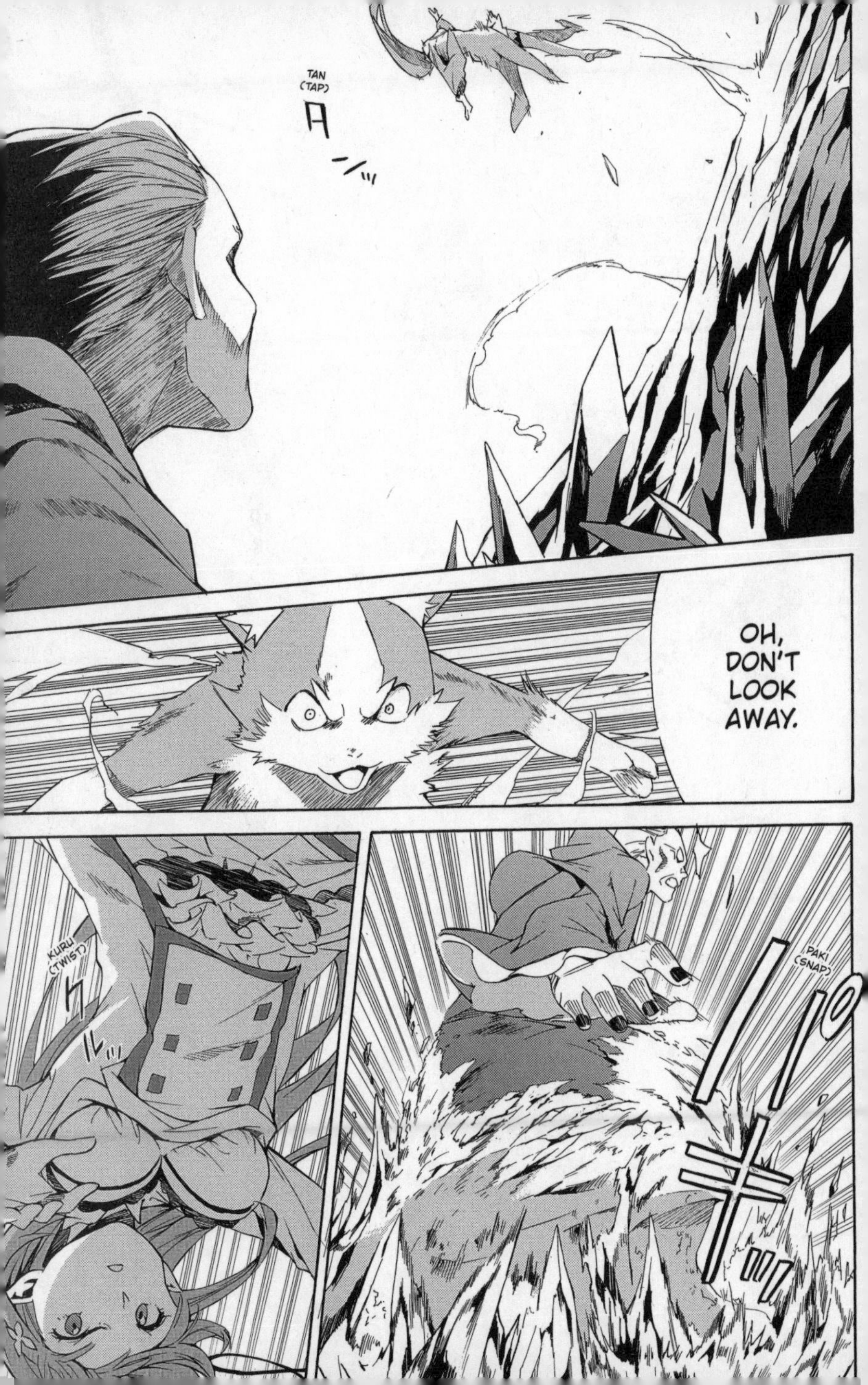
TAN (TAP)
OH, DON'T LOOK AWAY.
KURU (TWIST)
PAKI (SNAP)

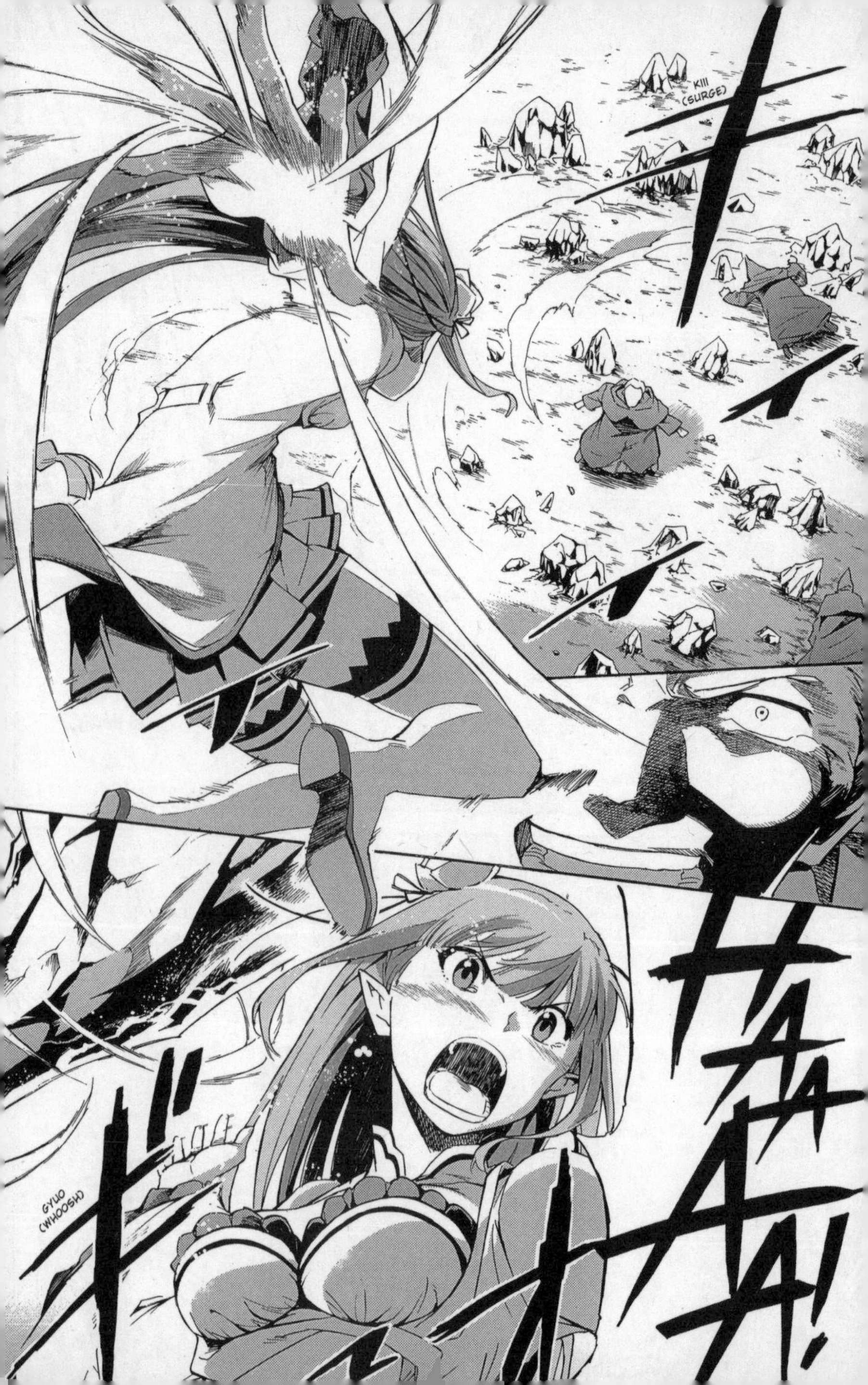
KIII
(SURGE)
HAAAA!
GYUO
(WHOOSH)

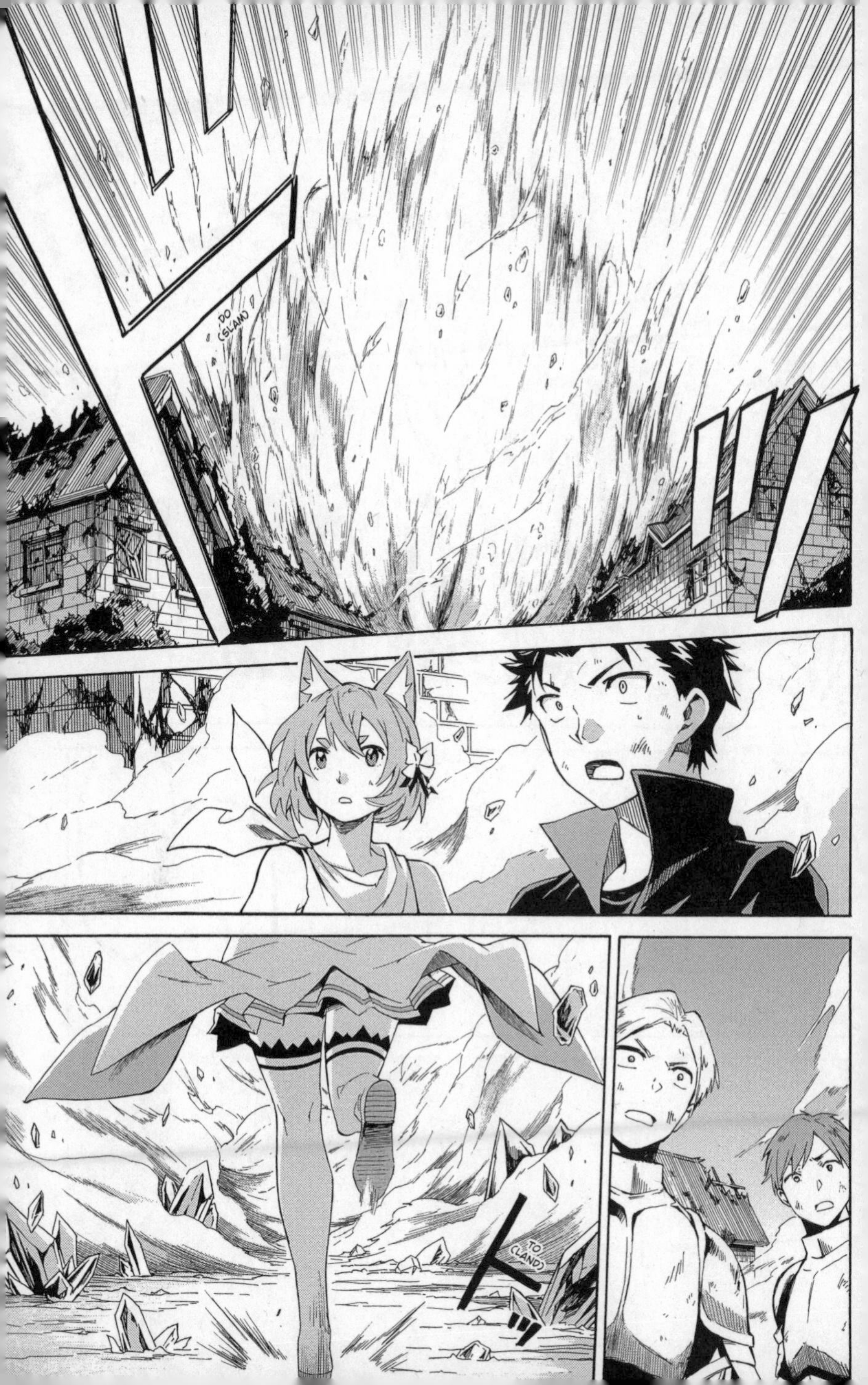
DO (SLAM)
TO (LAND)

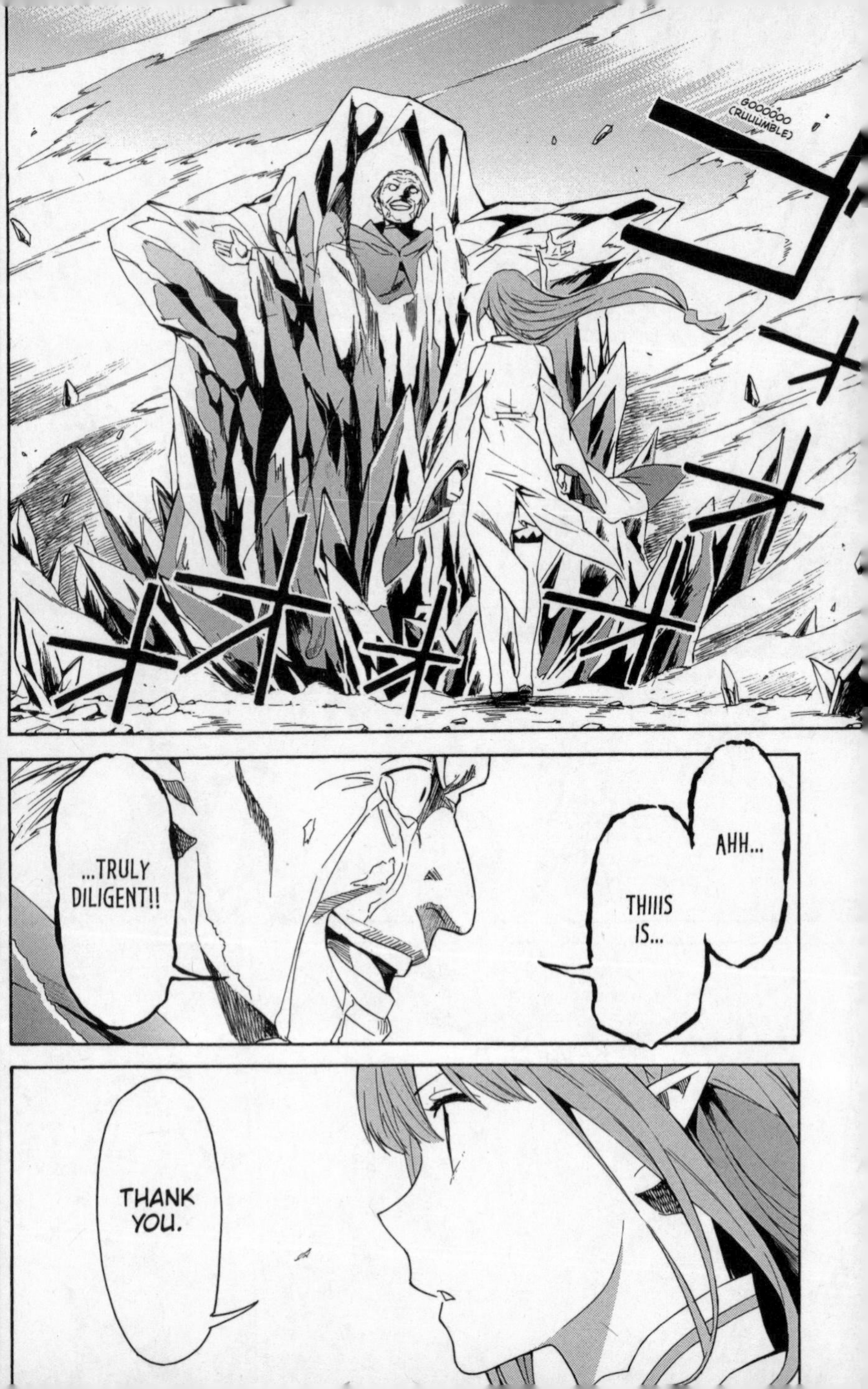
GOOOOOO
(RUUUMBLE)
AHH...
THIIIS IS...
...TRULY DILIGENT!!
THANK YOU.

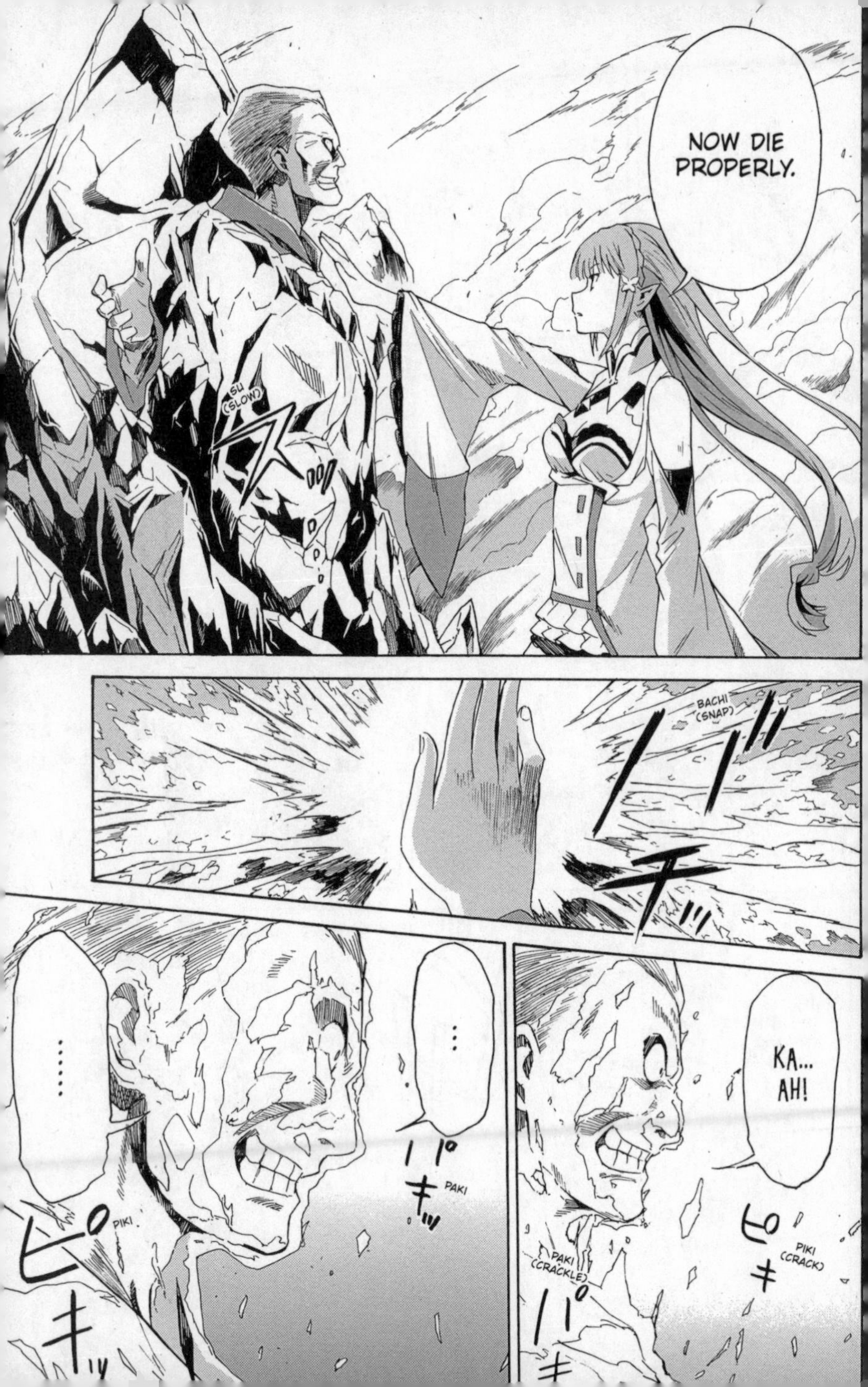
NOW DIE PROPERLY.
SU (SLOW)
BACHI (SNAP)
KA... AH!
PIKI (CRACK)
PAKI (CRACKLE)
...
......
PAKI
PIKI

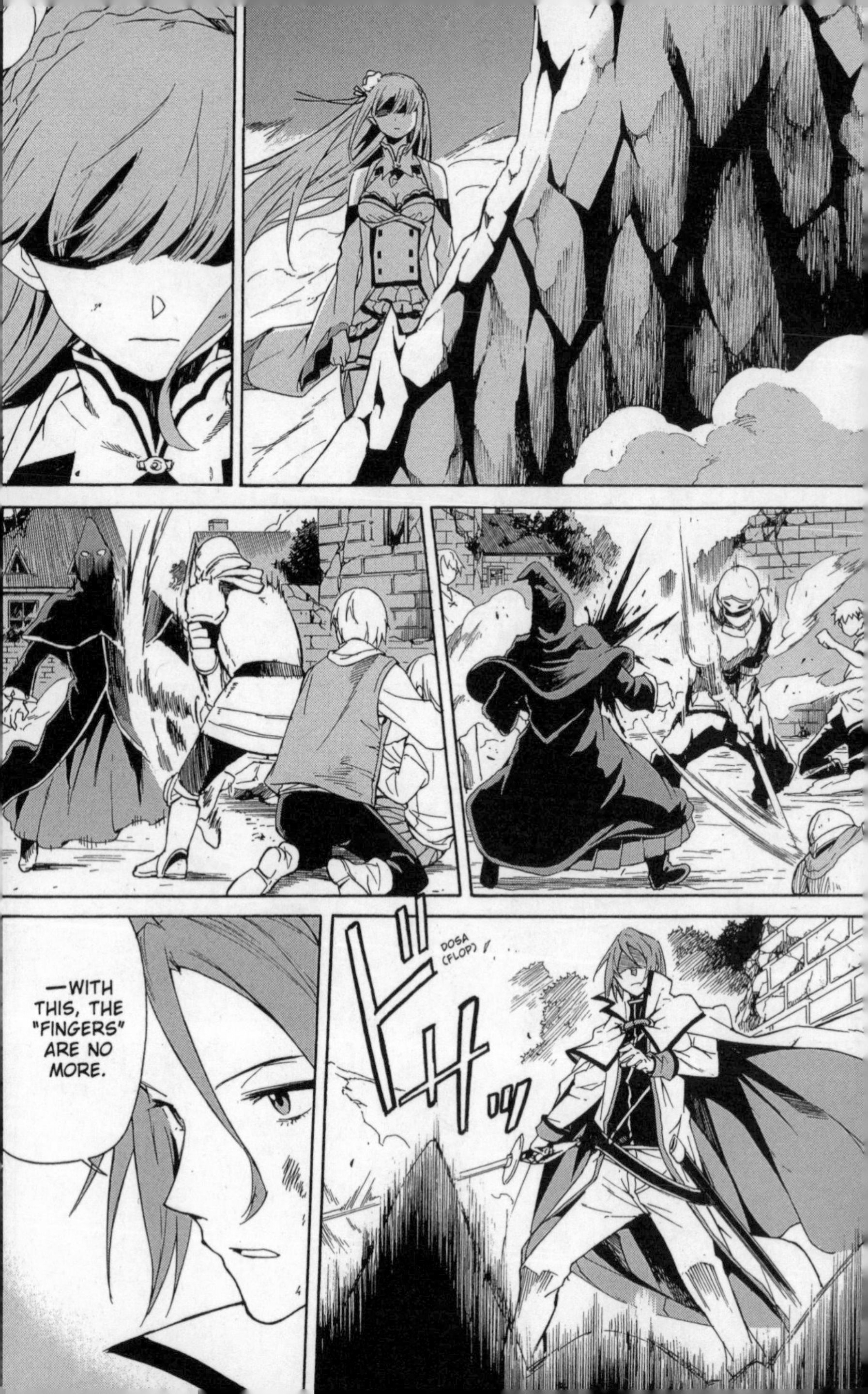
ドサッ
DOSA (FLOP)
—WITH THIS, THE "FINGERS" ARE NO MORE.

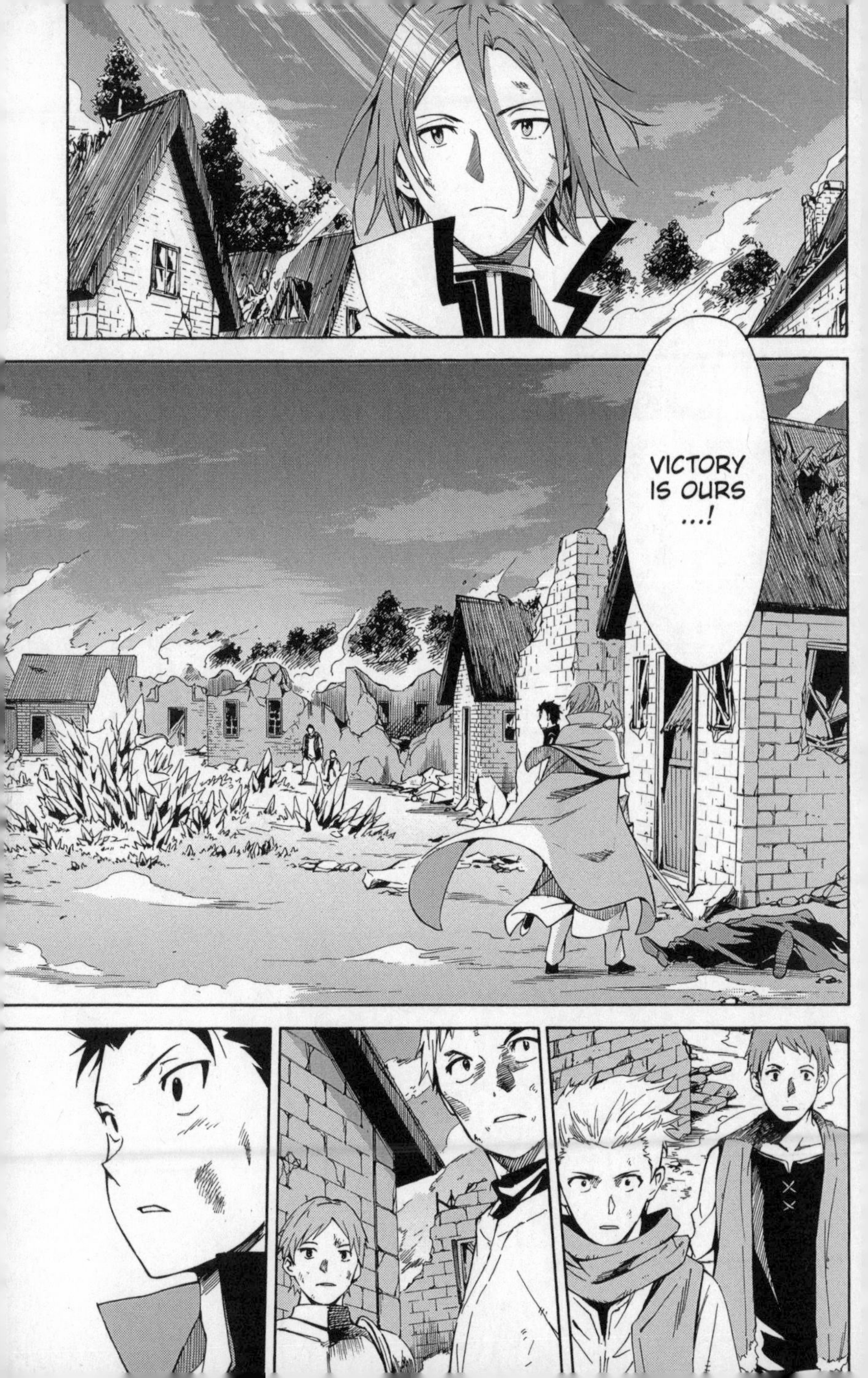
VICTORY IS OURS ...!

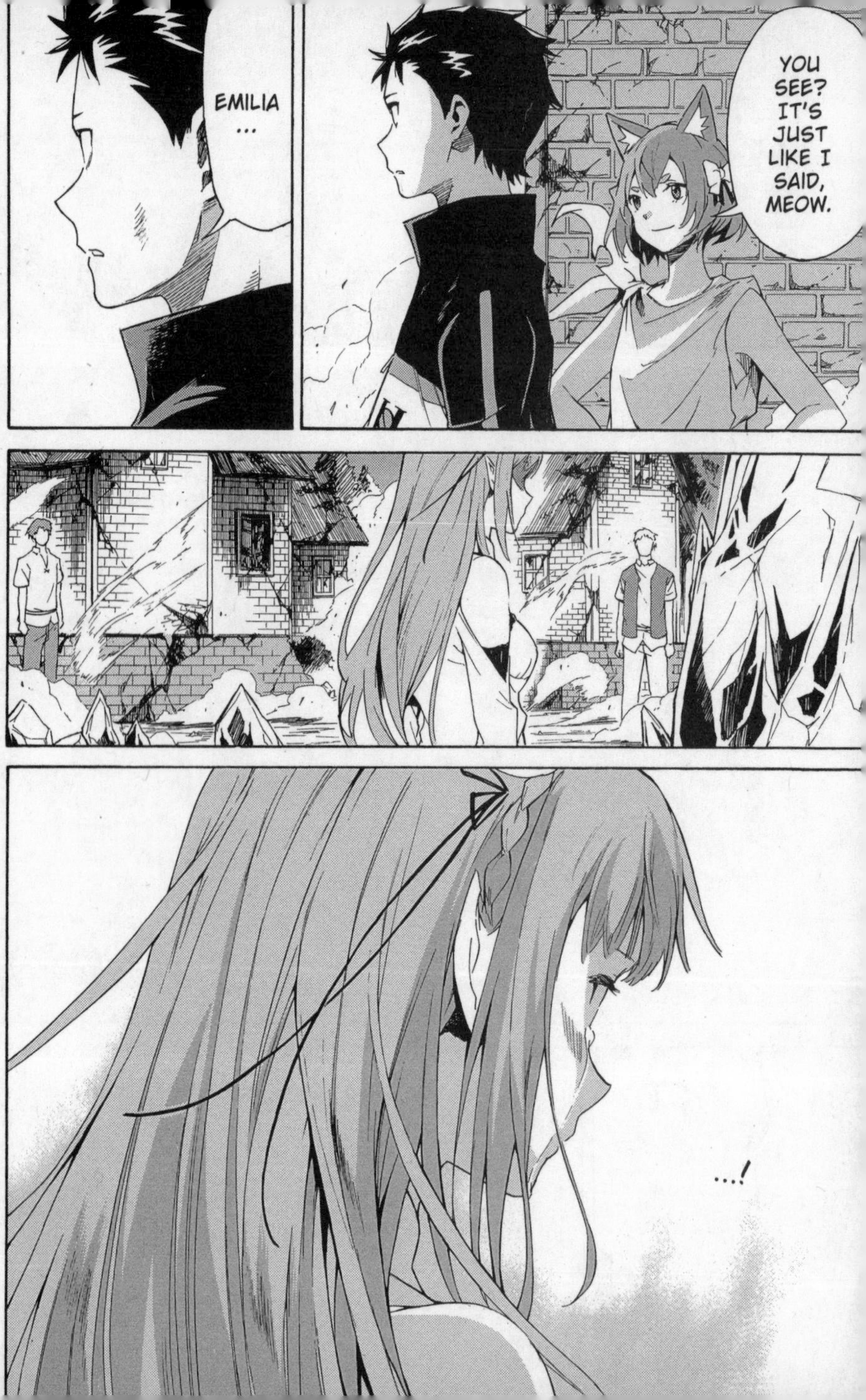
YOU SEE? IT'S JUST LIKE I SAID, MEOW.
EMILIA ...
...!

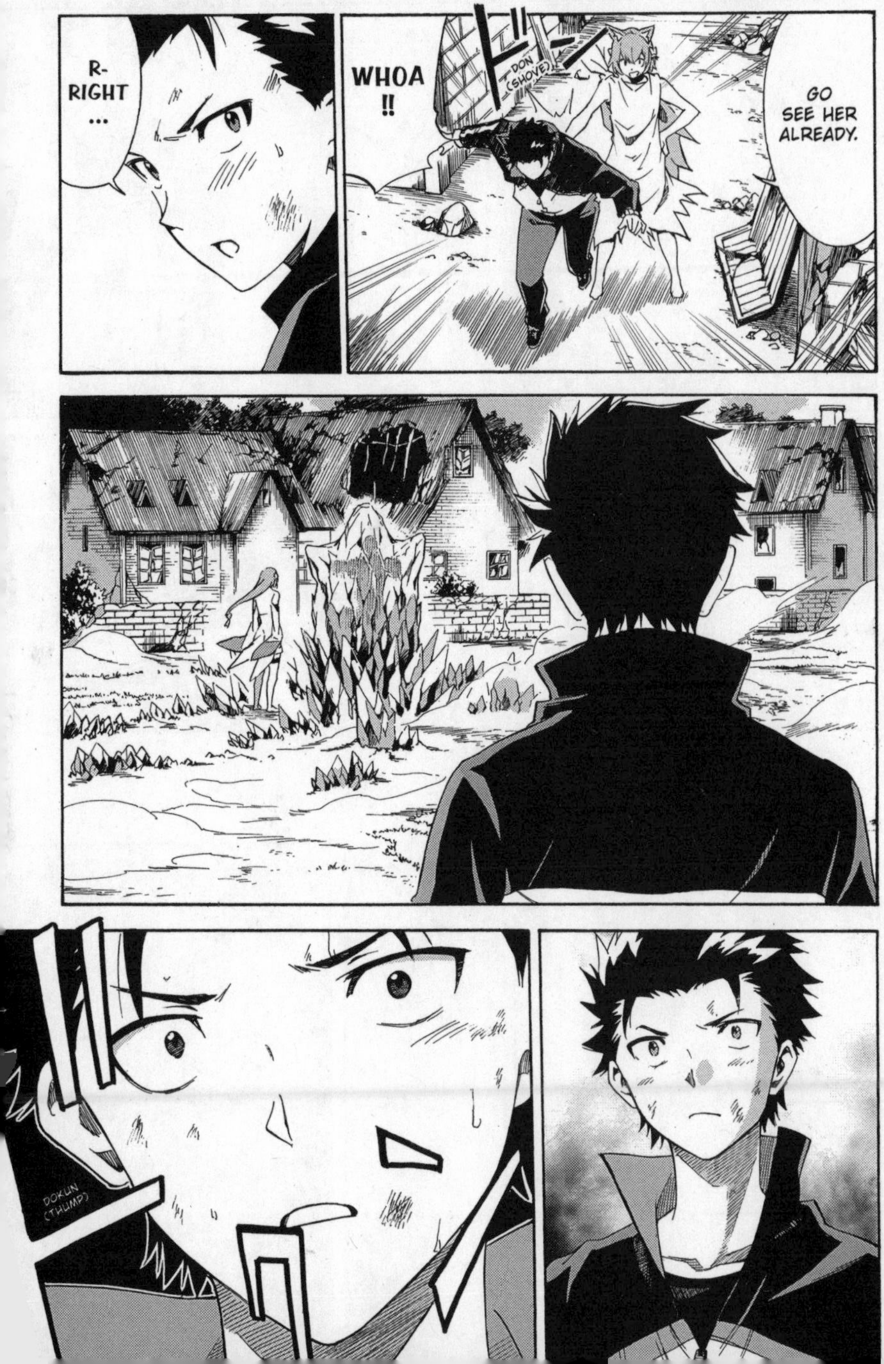
GO SEE HER ALREADY.
DON (SHOVE)
WHOA !!
R-RIGHT ...
DOKUN (THUMP)

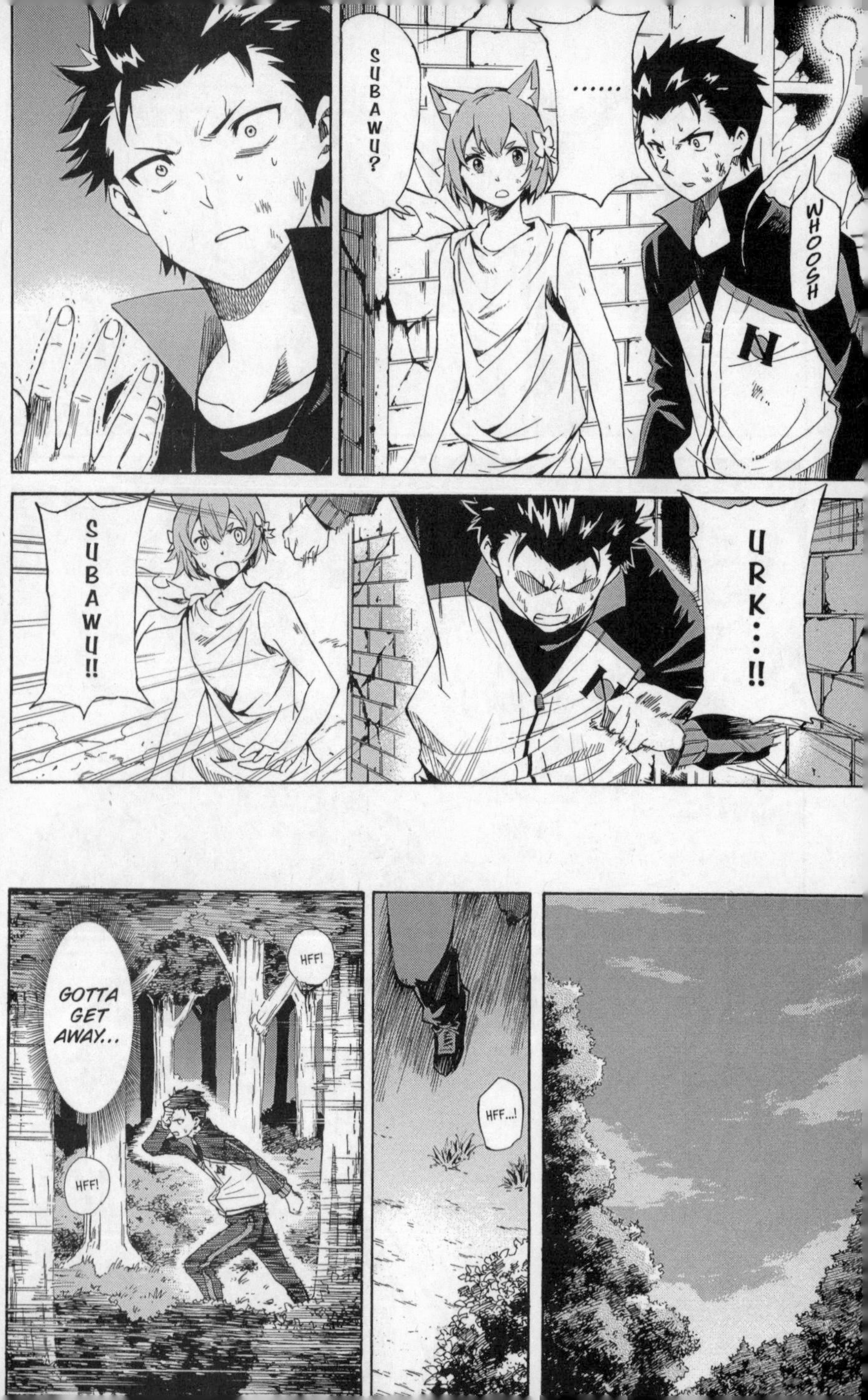
SUBAWU?
......
WHOOSH
URK...!!
SUBAWU!!
HFF...!
HFF!
GOTTA GET AWAY...
HFF!

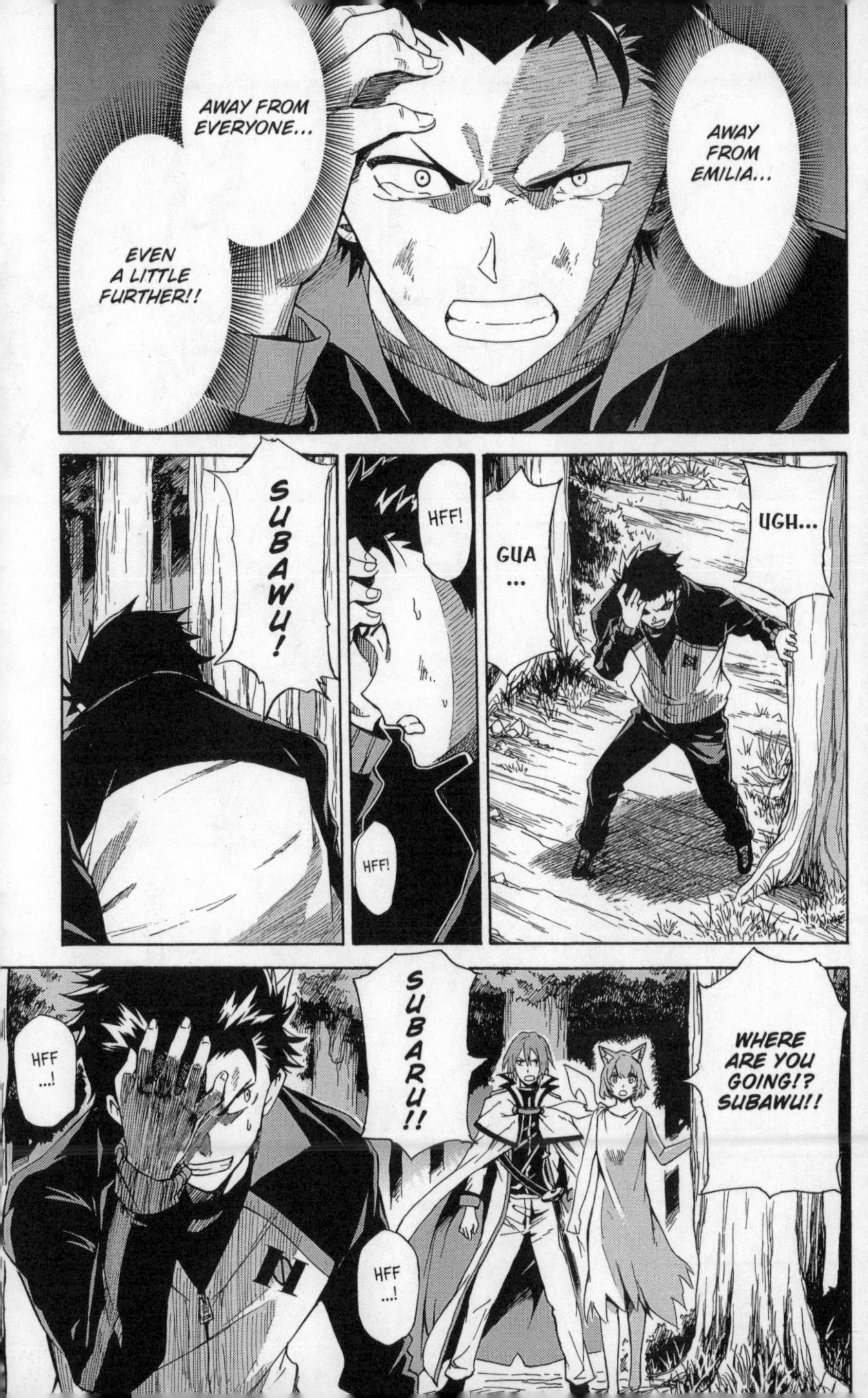
AWAY FROM EMILIA...
AWAY FROM EVERYONE...
EVEN A LITTLE FURTHER!!
UGH...
GUA ...
HFF!
HFF!
SUBAWU!
WHERE ARE YOU GOING!? SUBAWU!!
SUBARU!!
HFF ...!
HFF ...!

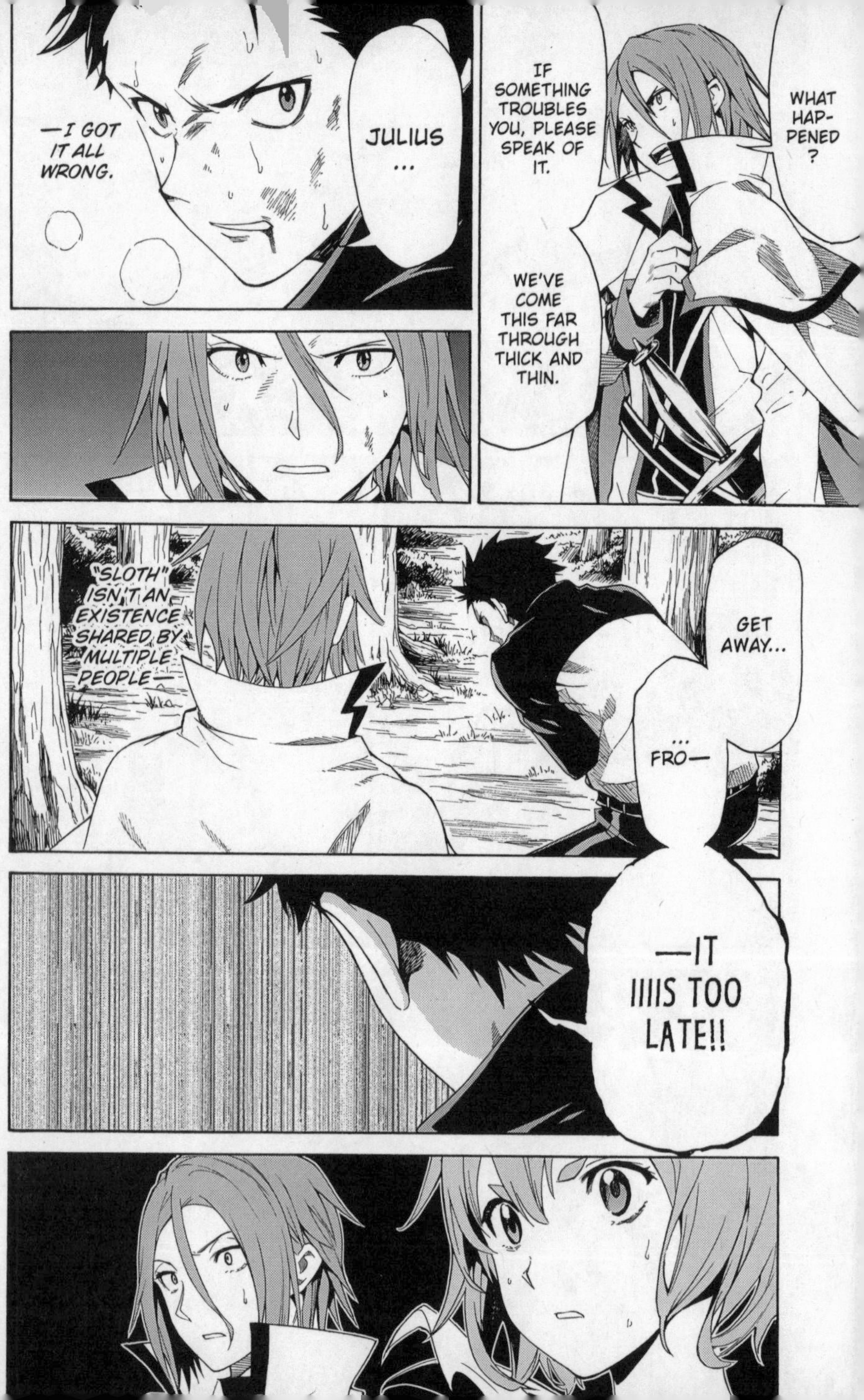
WHAT HAPPENED?
IF SOMETHING TROUBLES YOU, PLEASE SPEAK OF IT.
WE'VE COME THIS FAR THROUGH THICK AND THIN.
JULIUS...
—I GOT IT ALL WRONG.
GET AWAY...
...FRO—
"SLOTH" ISN'T AN EXISTENCE SHARED BY MULTIPLE PEOPLE—
—IT IIIIS TOO LATE!!

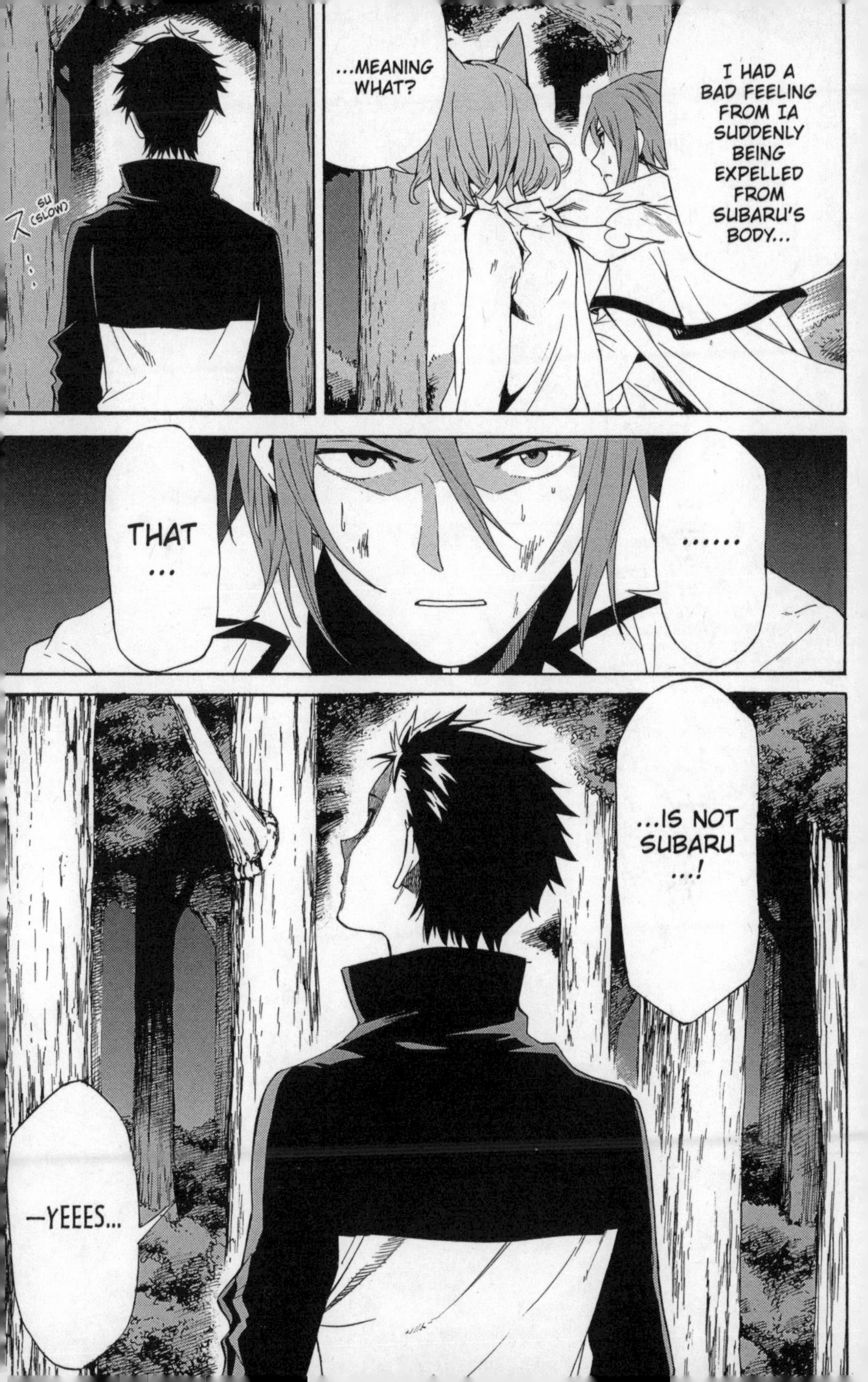
I HAD A BAD FEELING FROM IA SUDDENLY BEING EXPELLED FROM SUBARU'S BODY...
...MEANING WHAT?
ス
SU (SLOW)
......
THAT ...
...IS NOT SUBARU ...!
—YEEES...

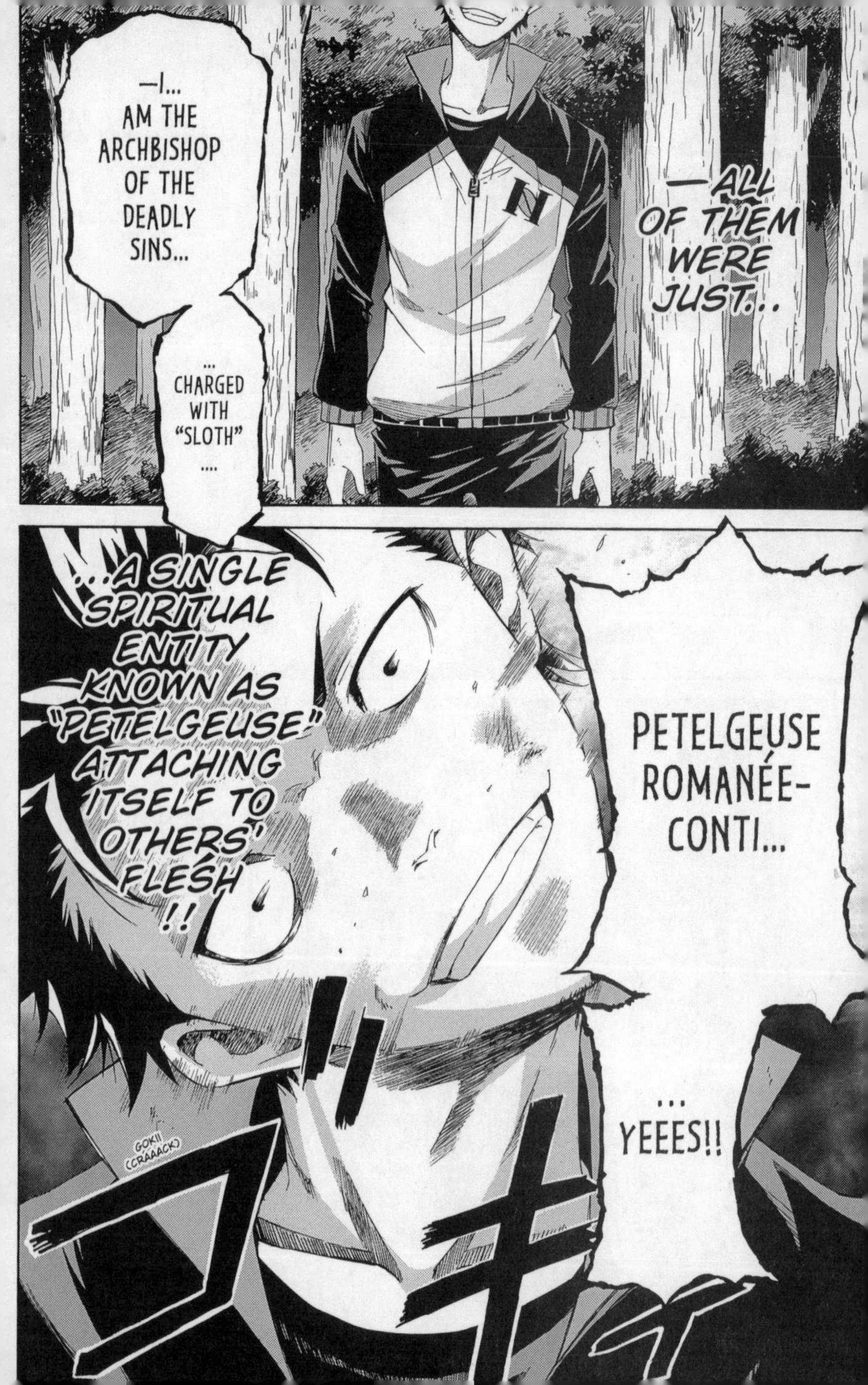
—ALL OF THEM WERE JUST...
—I... AM THE ARCHBISHOP OF THE DEADLY SINS...
...CHARGED WITH "SLOTH"....
PETELGEUSE ROMANÉE-CONTI...
...A SINGLE SPIRITUAL ENTITY KNOWN AS "PETELGEUSE" ATTACHING ITSELF TO OTHERS' FLESH!!
...YEEES!!
GOKII (CRÁAACK)

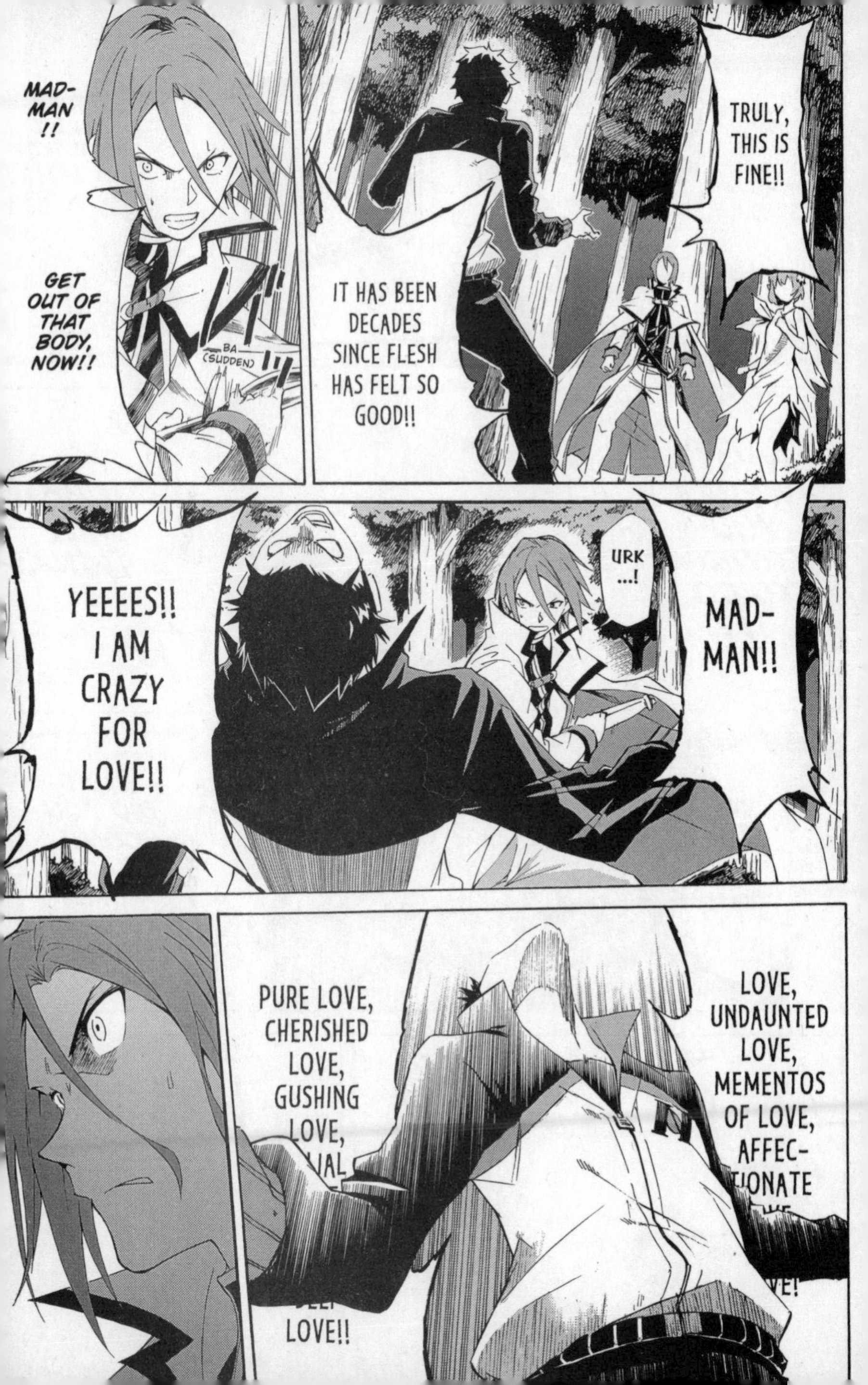
TRULY, THIS IS FINE!!
IT HAS BEEN DECADES SINCE FLESH HAS FELT SO GOOD!!
MAD-MAN!!
BA (SUDDEN)
GET OUT OF THAT BODY, NOW!!
MAD-MAN!!
URK ...!
YEEEES!! I AM CRAZY FOR LOVE!!
LOVE, UNDAUNTED LOVE, MEMENTOS OF LOVE, AFFEC-TIONATE
PURE LOVE, CHERISHED LOVE, GUSHING LOVE,
LOVE!!

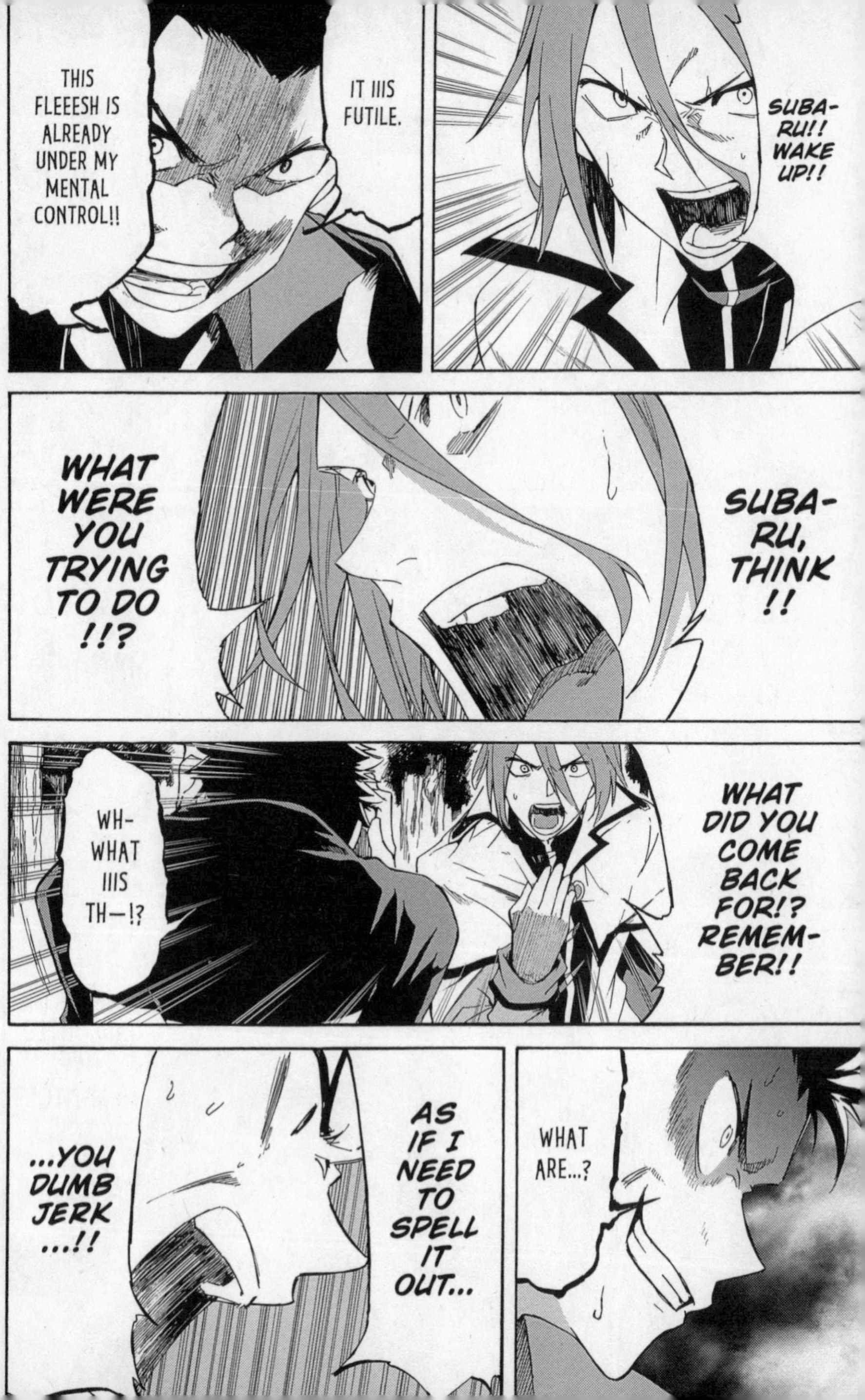
SUBA-RU!! WAKE UP!!
IT IIIS FUTILE.
THIS FLEEESH IS ALREADY UNDER MY MENTAL CONTROL!!
SUBA-RU, THINK!!
WHAT WERE YOU TRYING TO DO!!?
WHAT DID YOU COME BACK FOR!? REMEM-BER!!
WH-WHAT IIIS TH—!?
WHAT ARE...?
AS IF I NEED TO SPELL IT OUT...
...YOU DUMB JERK...!!

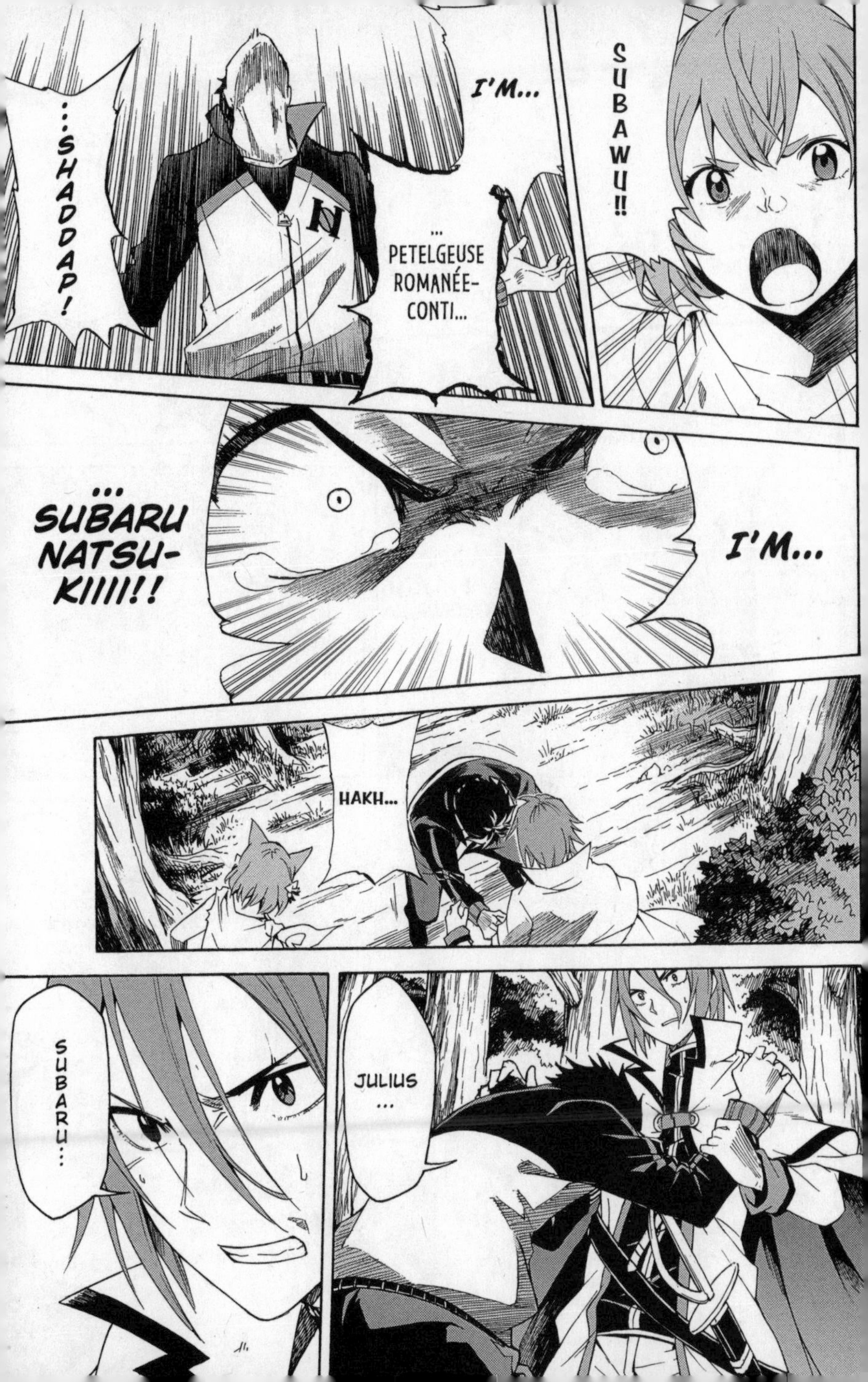
SUBAWU!!
I'M...
...PETELGEUSE ROMANÉE-CONTI...
...SHADDAP!
I'M...
...SUBARU NATSUKIIII!!
HAKH...
JULIUS...
SUBARU...

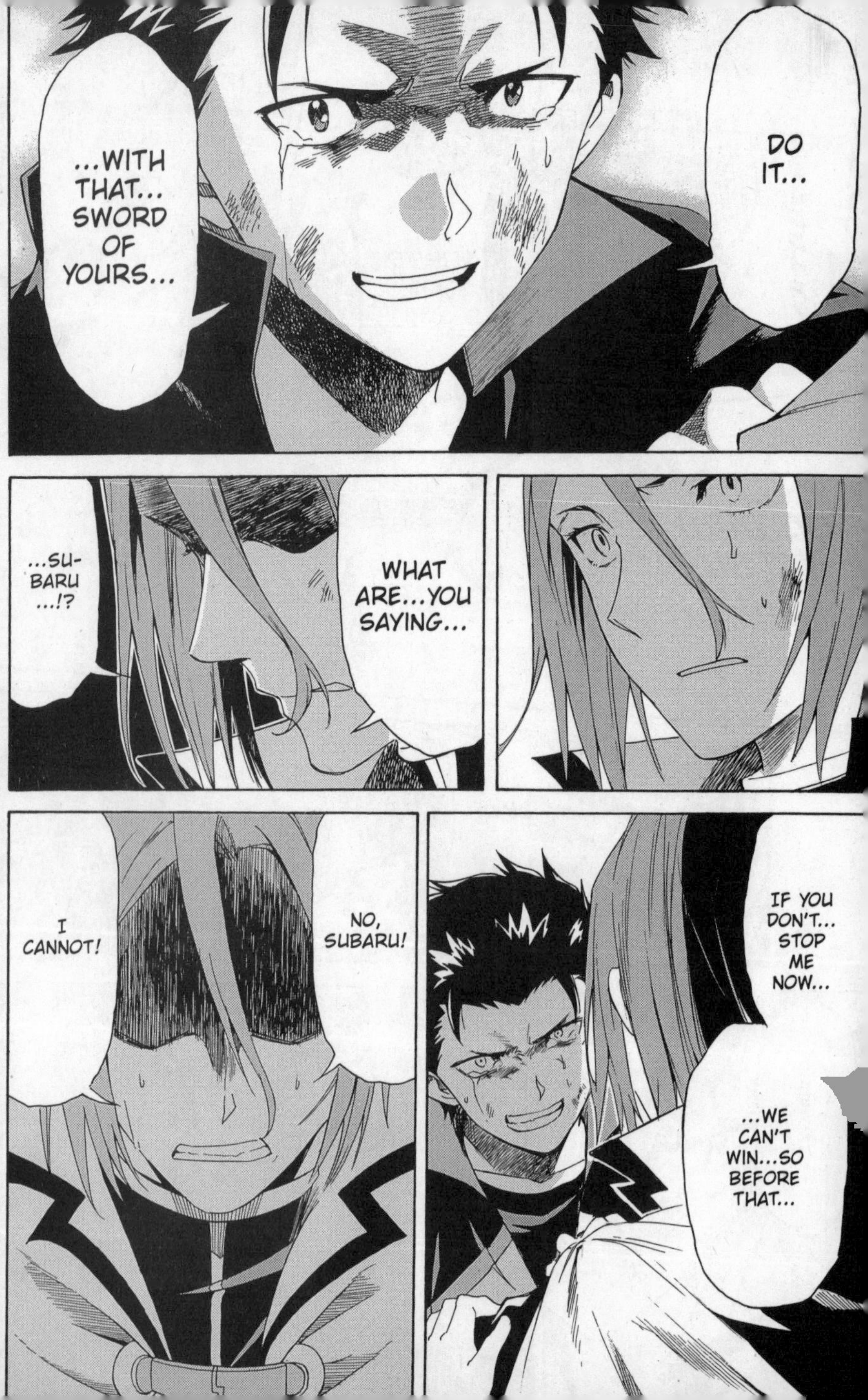
DO IT...
...WITH THAT... SWORD OF YOURS...
WHAT ARE...YOU SAYING...
...SU-BARU ...!?
IF YOU DON'T... STOP ME NOW...
...WE CAN'T WIN...SO BEFORE THAT...
NO, SUBARU!
I CANNOT!

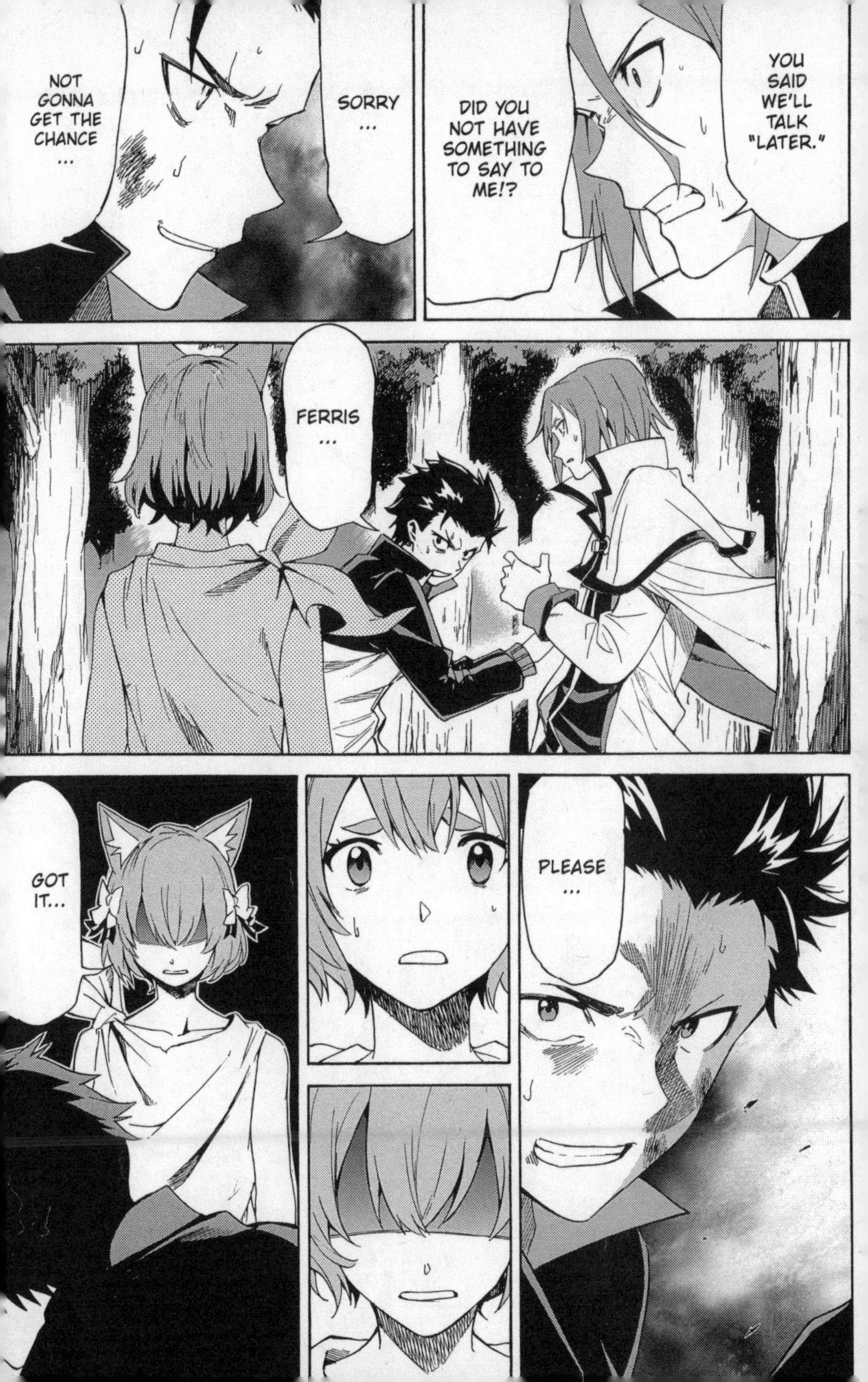
YOU SAID WE'LL TALK "LATER."
DID YOU NOT HAVE SOMETHING TO SAY TO ME!?
SORRY ...
NOT GONNA GET THE CHANCE ...
FERRIS ...
PLEASE ...
GOT IT...

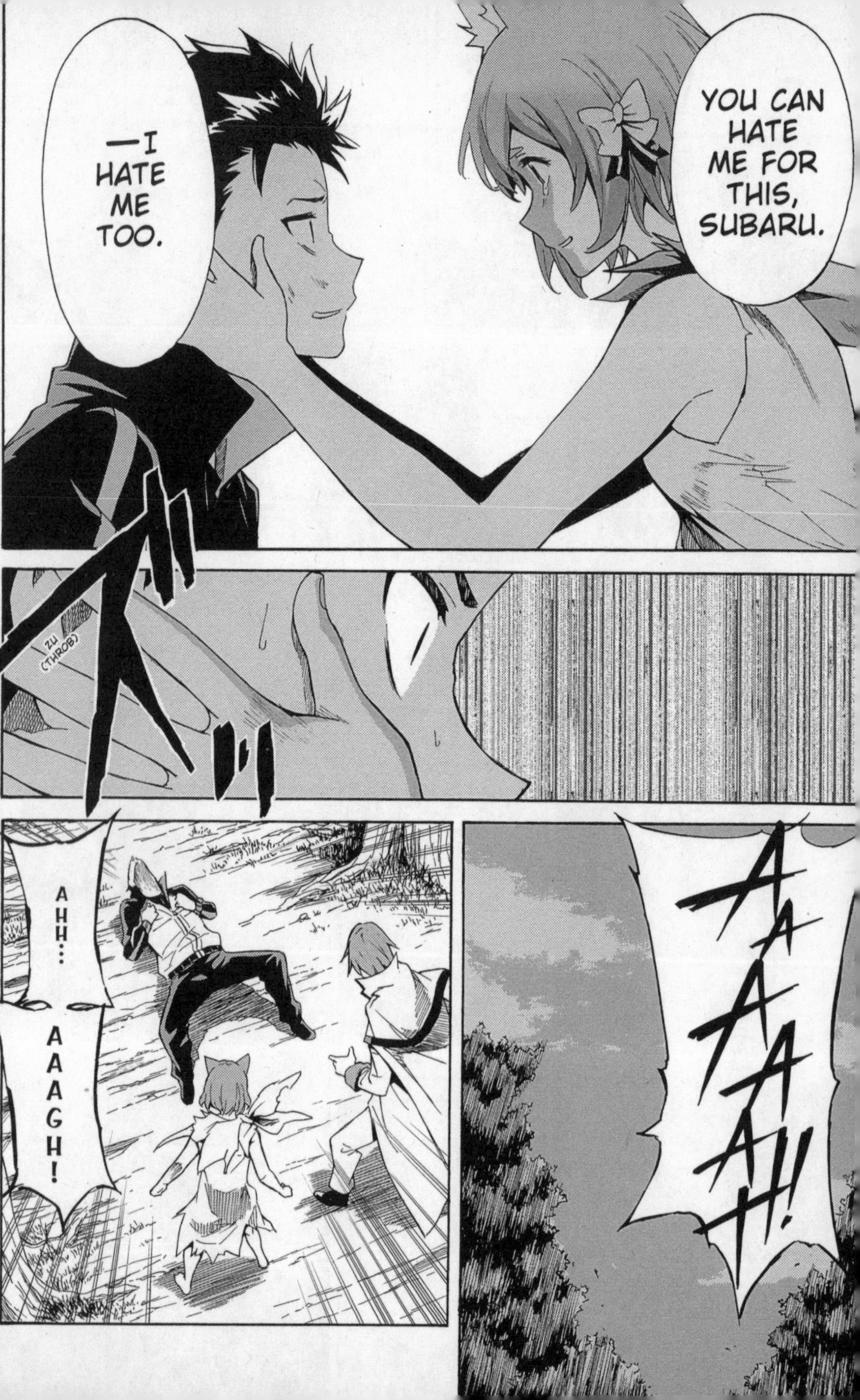
YOU CAN HATE ME FOR THIS, SUBARU.
—I HATE ME TOO.
ZU (THROB)
AAAAAH!
AHH...
AAAAGH!

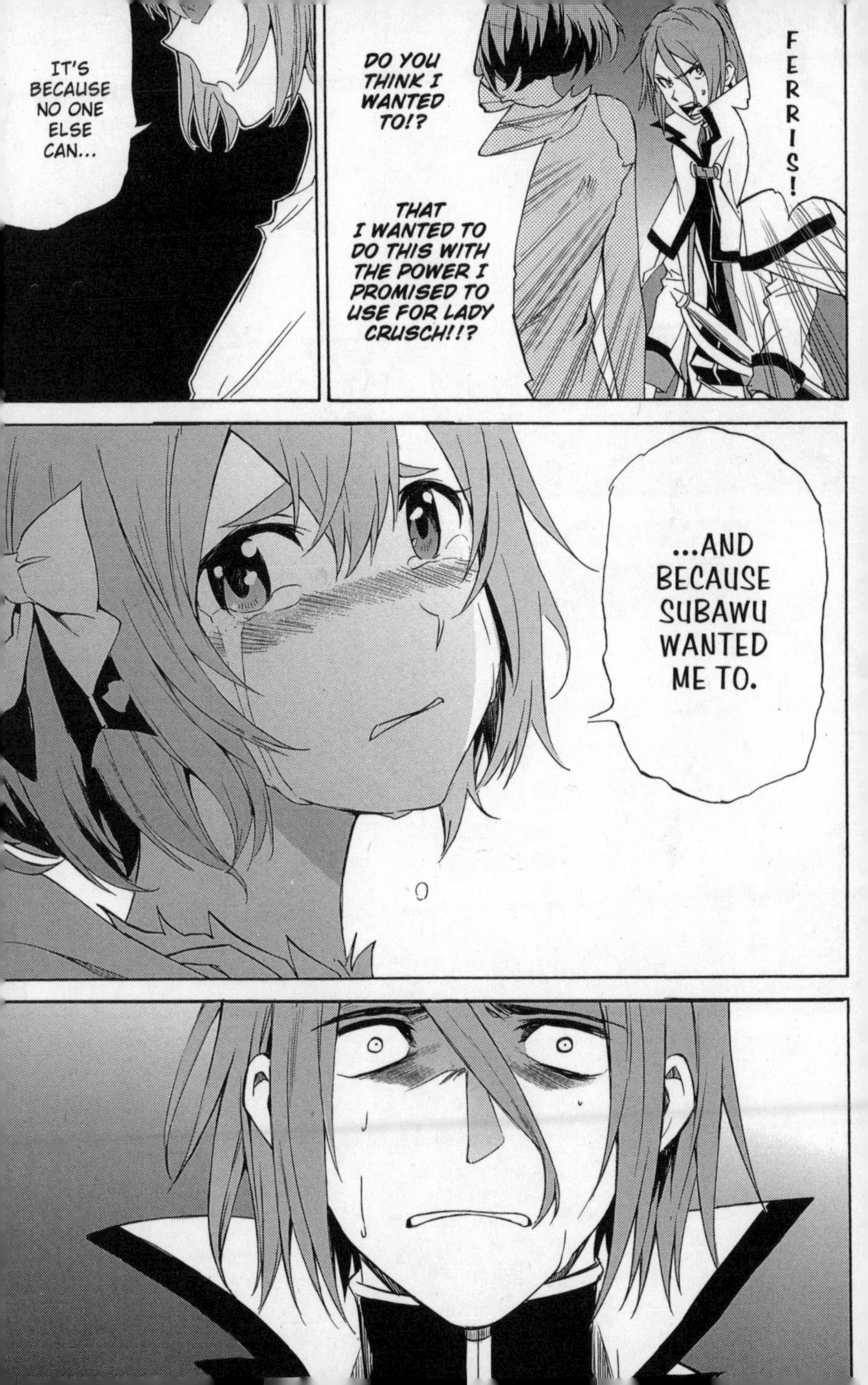
FERRIS!
DO YOU THINK I WANTED TO!?
THAT I WANTED TO DO THIS WITH THE POWER I PROMISED TO USE FOR LADY CRUSCH!!?
IT'S BECAUSE NO ONE ELSE CAN...
...AND BECAUSE SUBAWU WANTED ME TO.

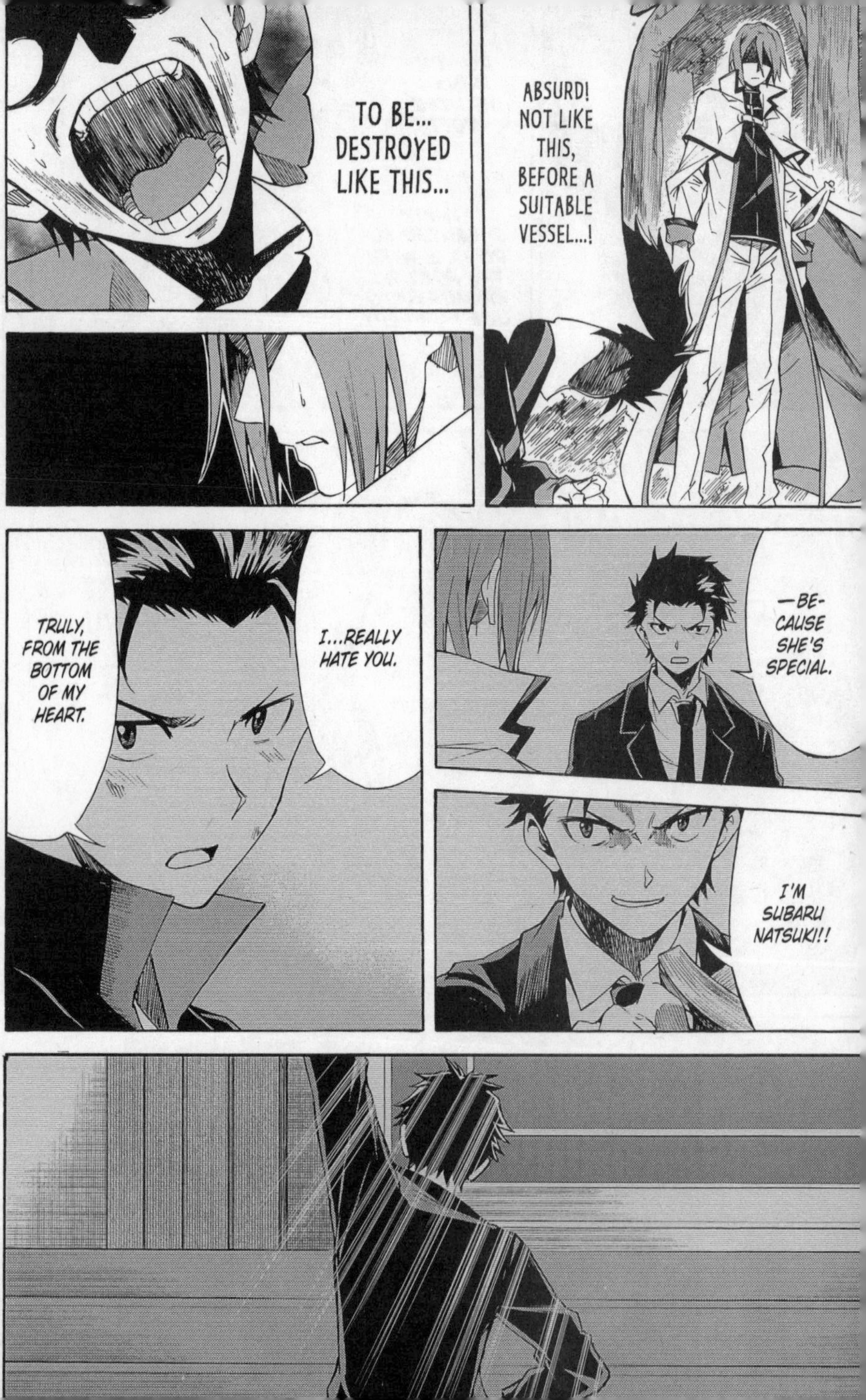
ABSURD! NOT LIKE THIS, BEFORE A SUITABLE VESSEL...!
TO BE... DESTROYED LIKE THIS...
—BE-CAUSE SHE'S SPECIAL.
I'M SUBARU NATSUKI!!
I...REALLY HATE YOU.
TRULY, FROM THE BOTTOM OF MY HEART.

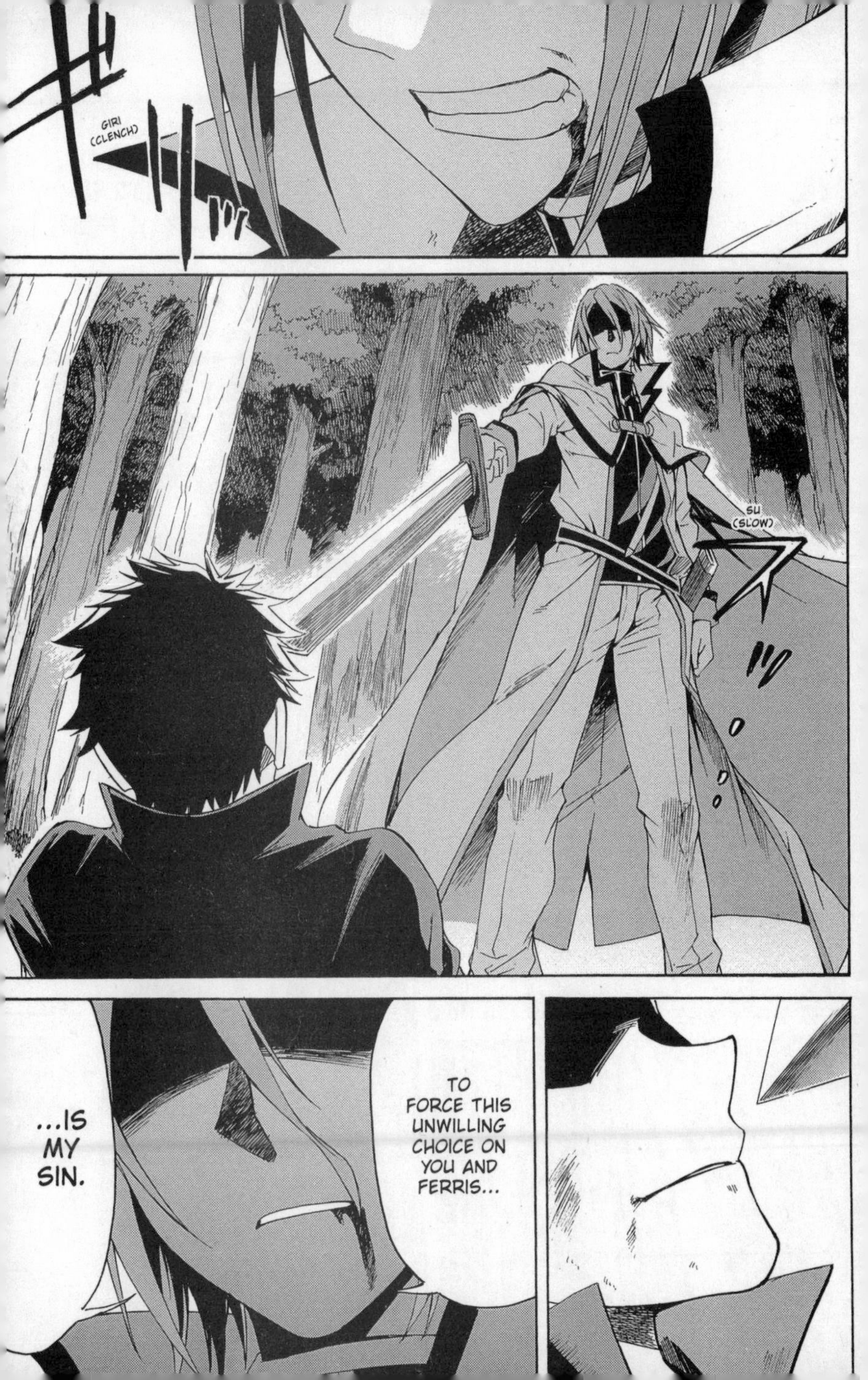
GIRI
(CLENCH)
SU
(SLOW)
TO FORCE THIS UNWILLING CHOICE ON YOU AND FERRIS...
...IS MY SIN.

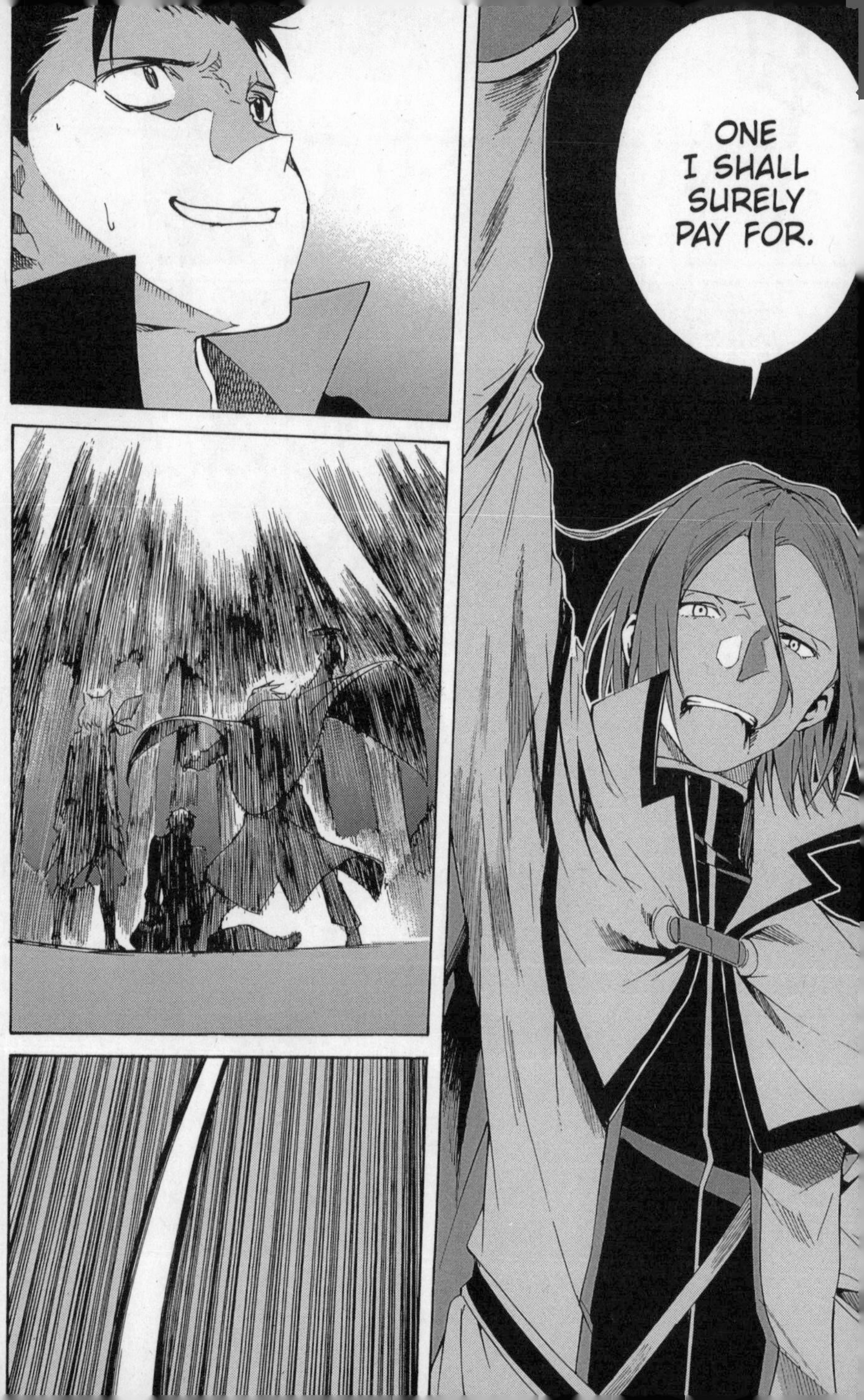
ONE I SHALL SURELY PAY FOR.

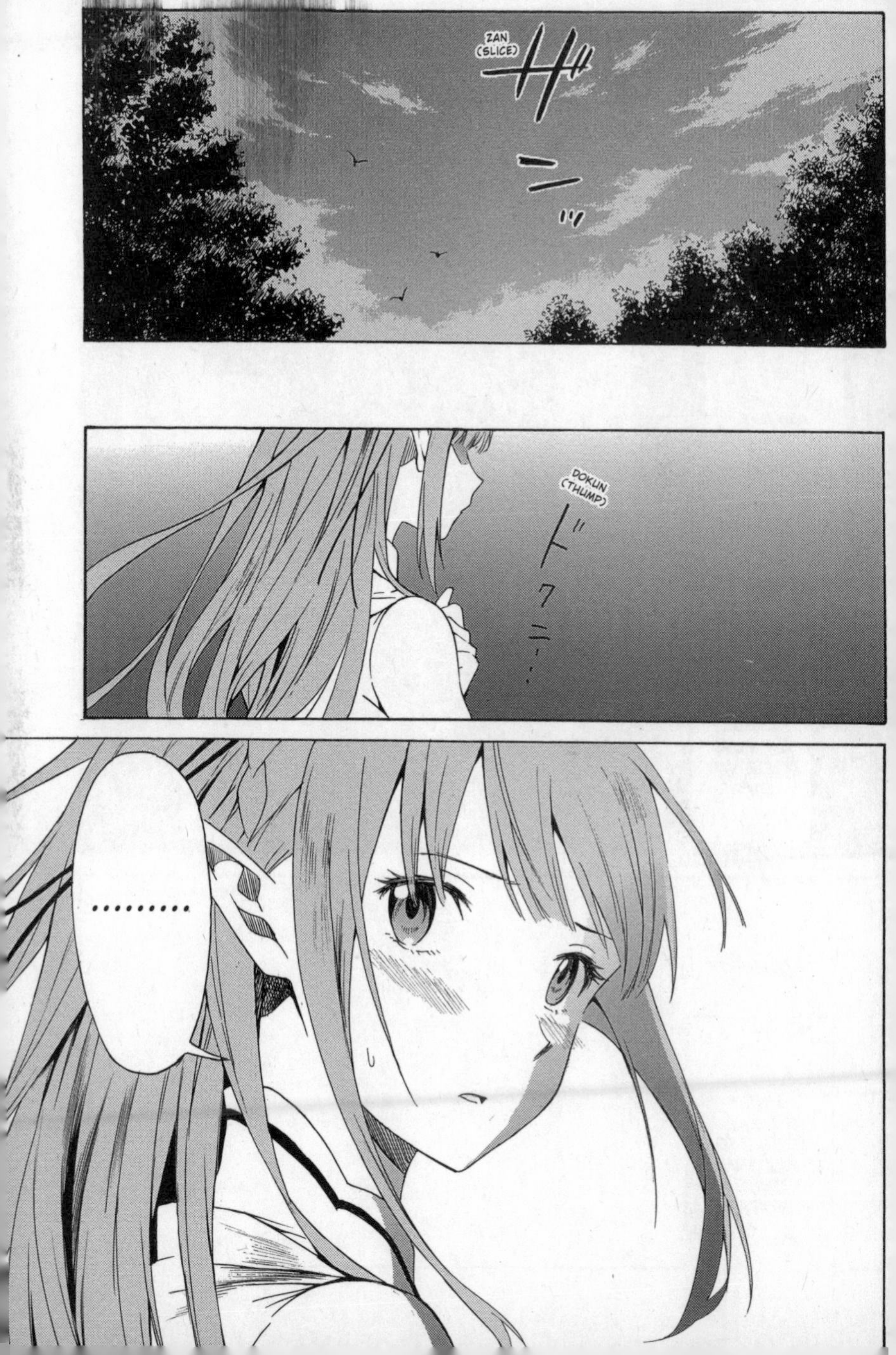
ZAN (SLICE)
ザン
DOKUN (THUMP)
ドクン…
………

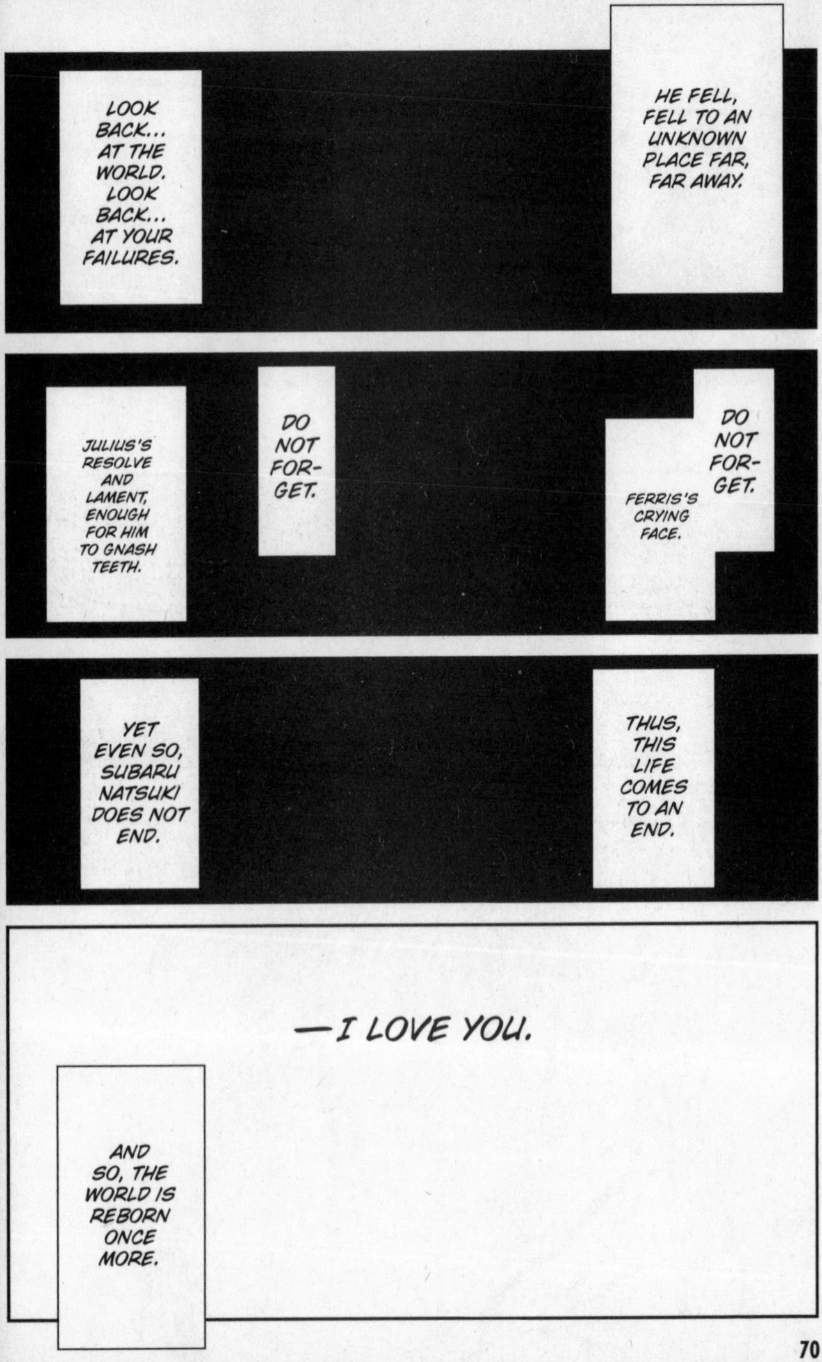
HE FELL, FELL TO AN UNKNOWN PLACE FAR, FAR AWAY.
LOOK BACK... AT THE WORLD. LOOK BACK... AT YOUR FAILURES.
DO NOT FOR-GET.
FERRIS'S CRYING FACE.
DO NOT FOR-GET.
JULIUS'S RESOLVE AND LAMENT, ENOUGH FOR HIM TO GNASH TEETH.
THUS, THIS LIFE COMES TO AN END.
YET EVEN SO, SUBARU NATSUKI DOES NOT END.
—I LOVE YOU.
AND SO, THE WORLD IS REBORN ONCE MORE.

Truth of Zero
The only ability Subaru Natsuki gets when he's summoned to another world is
time travel via his own death. But to save her, he'll die as many times as it takes.

Re:ZERO
-Starting Life in
Another World-

Re:ZERO
-Starting Life in Another World-

Truth of Zero

The only ability Subaru Natsuki gets when he's summoned to another world is time
travel via his own death. But to save her, he'll die as many times as it takes.

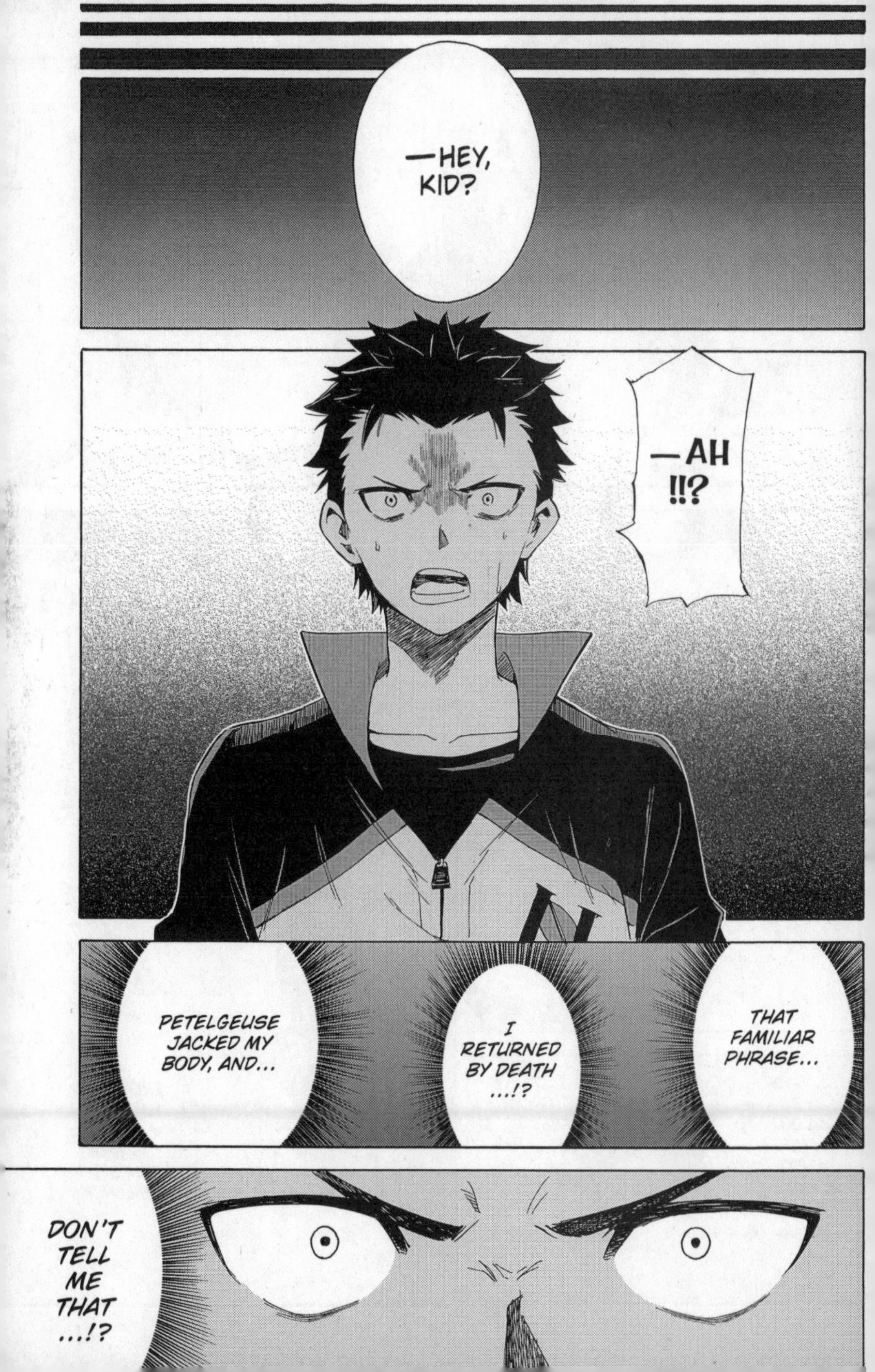
—HEY, KID?
—AH !!?
THAT FAMILIAR PHRASE...
I RETURNED BY DEATH ...!?
PETELGEUSE JACKED MY BODY, AND...
DON'T TELL ME THAT ...!?

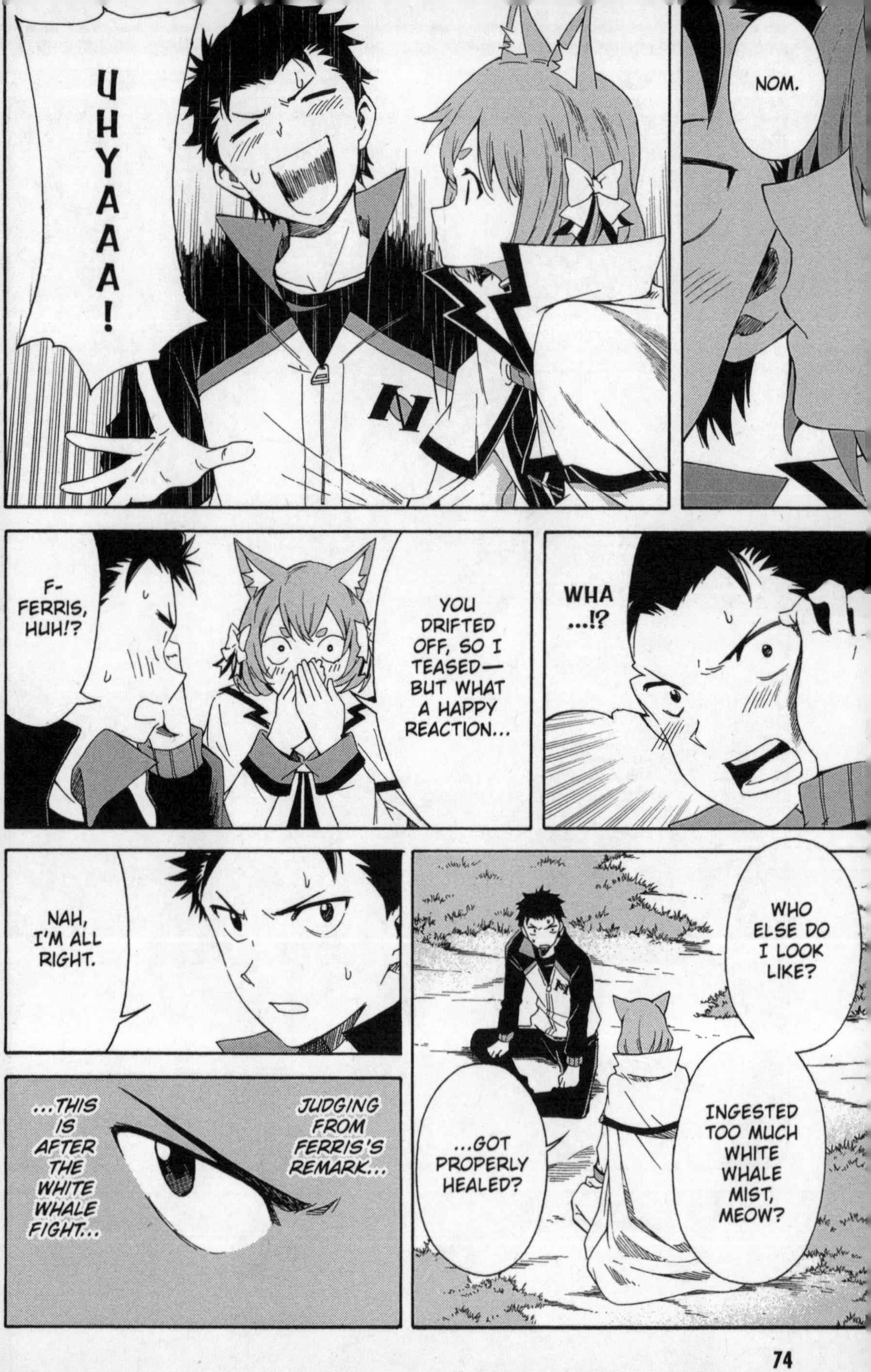
NOM.
UHYAAAA!
WHA ...!?
YOU DRIFTED OFF, SO I TEASED— BUT WHAT A HAPPY REACTION...
F- FERRIS, HUH!?
WHO ELSE DO I LOOK LIKE?
INGESTED TOO MUCH WHITE WHALE MIST, MEOW?
...GOT PROPERLY HEALED?
NAH, I'M ALL RIGHT.
JUDGING FROM FERRIS'S REMARK...
...THIS IS AFTER THE WHITE WHALE FIGHT...

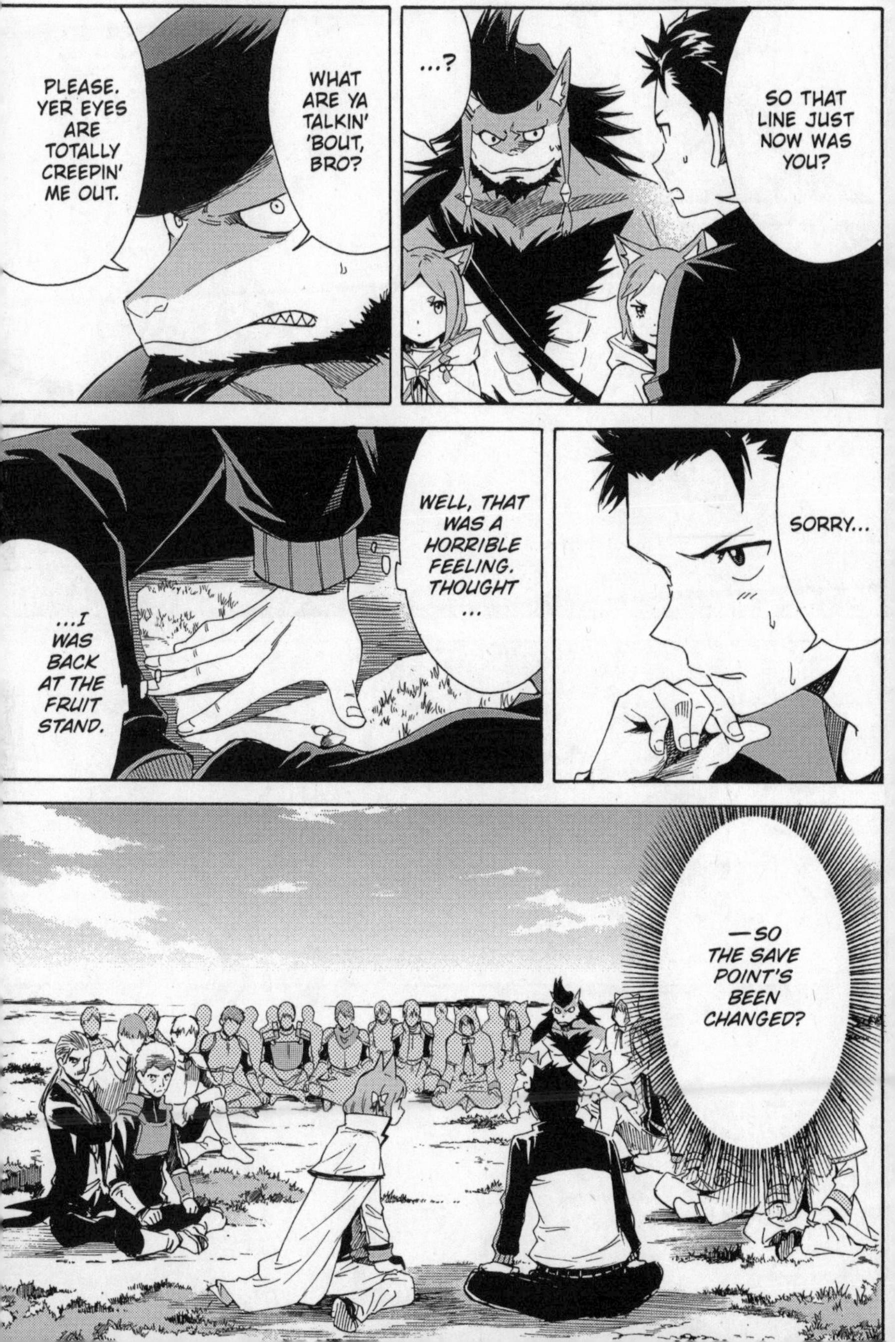
SO THAT LINE JUST NOW WAS YOU?
...?
WHAT ARE YA TALKIN' 'BOUT, BRO?
PLEASE. YER EYES ARE TOTALLY CREEPIN' ME OUT.
SORRY...
WELL, THAT WAS A HORRIBLE FEELING. THOUGHT ...
...I WAS BACK AT THE FRUIT STAND.
—SO THE SAVE POINT'S BEEN CHANGED?

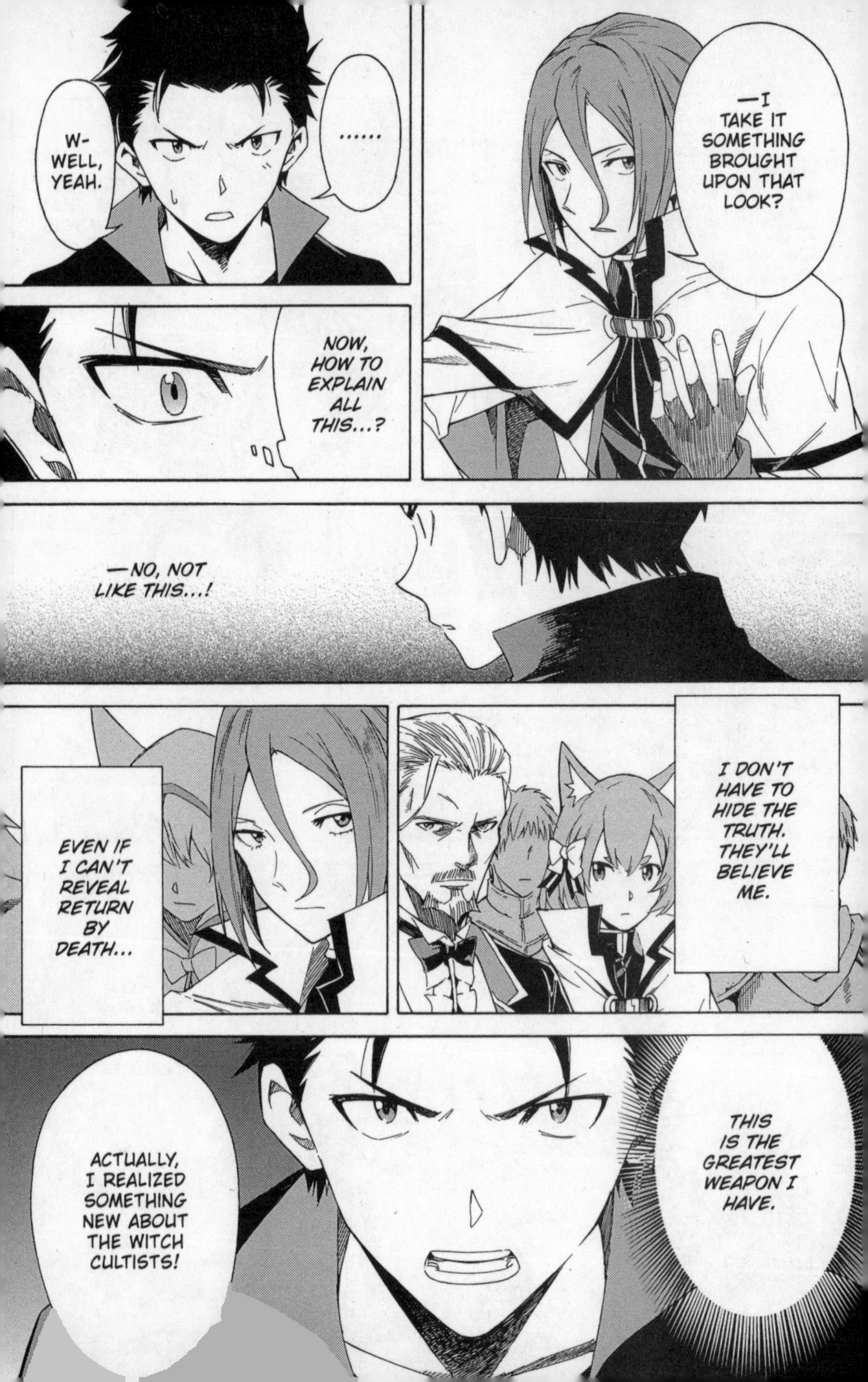
—I TAKE IT SOMETHING BROUGHT UPON THAT LOOK?
......
W-WELL, YEAH.
NOW, HOW TO EXPLAIN ALL THIS...?
—NO, NOT LIKE THIS...!
I DON'T HAVE TO HIDE THE TRUTH. THEY'LL BELIEVE ME.
EVEN IF I CAN'T REVEAL RETURN BY DEATH...
THIS IS THE GREATEST WEAPON I HAVE.
ACTUALLY, I REALIZED SOMETHING NEW ABOUT THE WITCH CULTISTS!

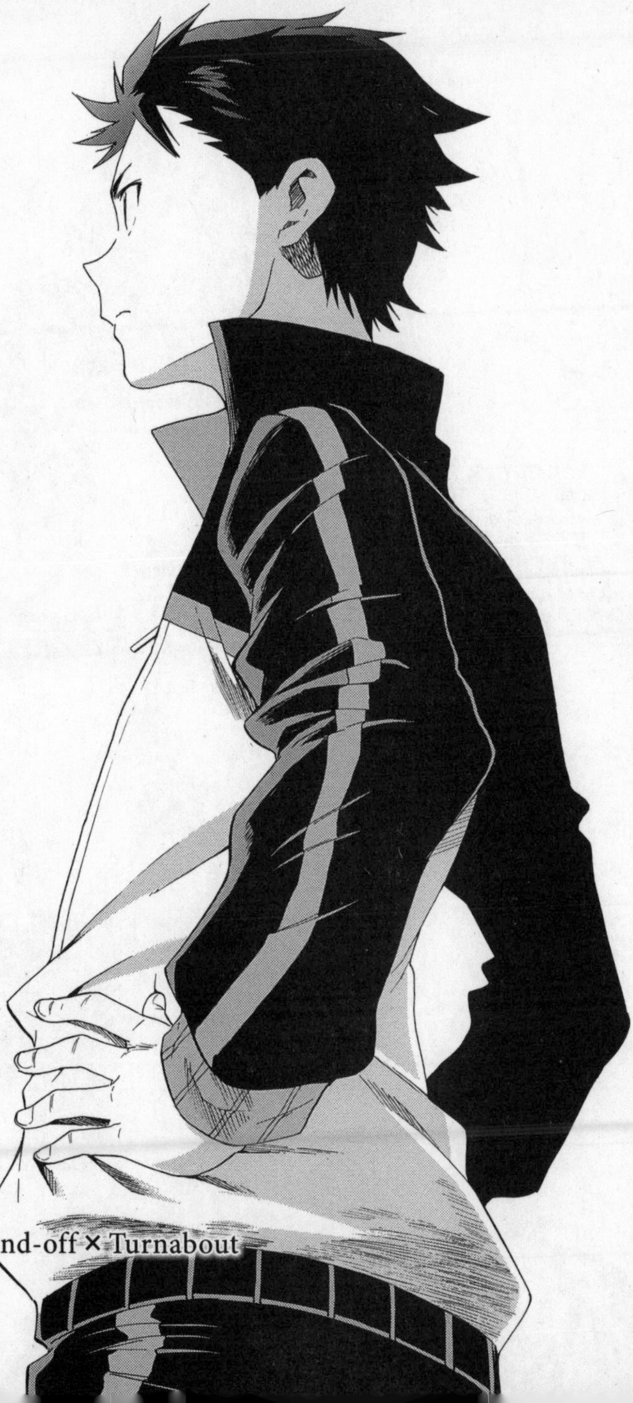

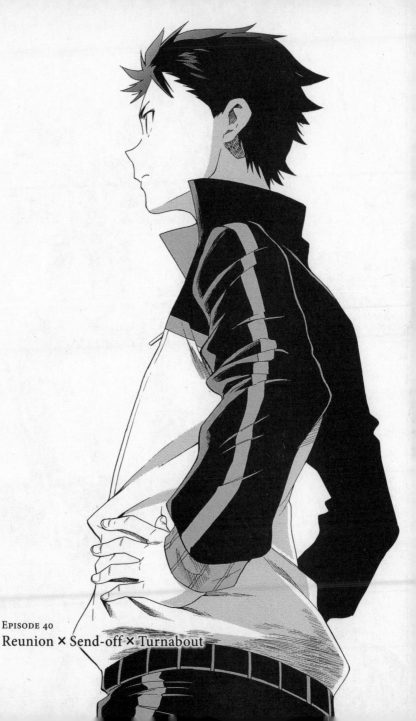

Episode 40
Reunion × Send-off × Turnabout

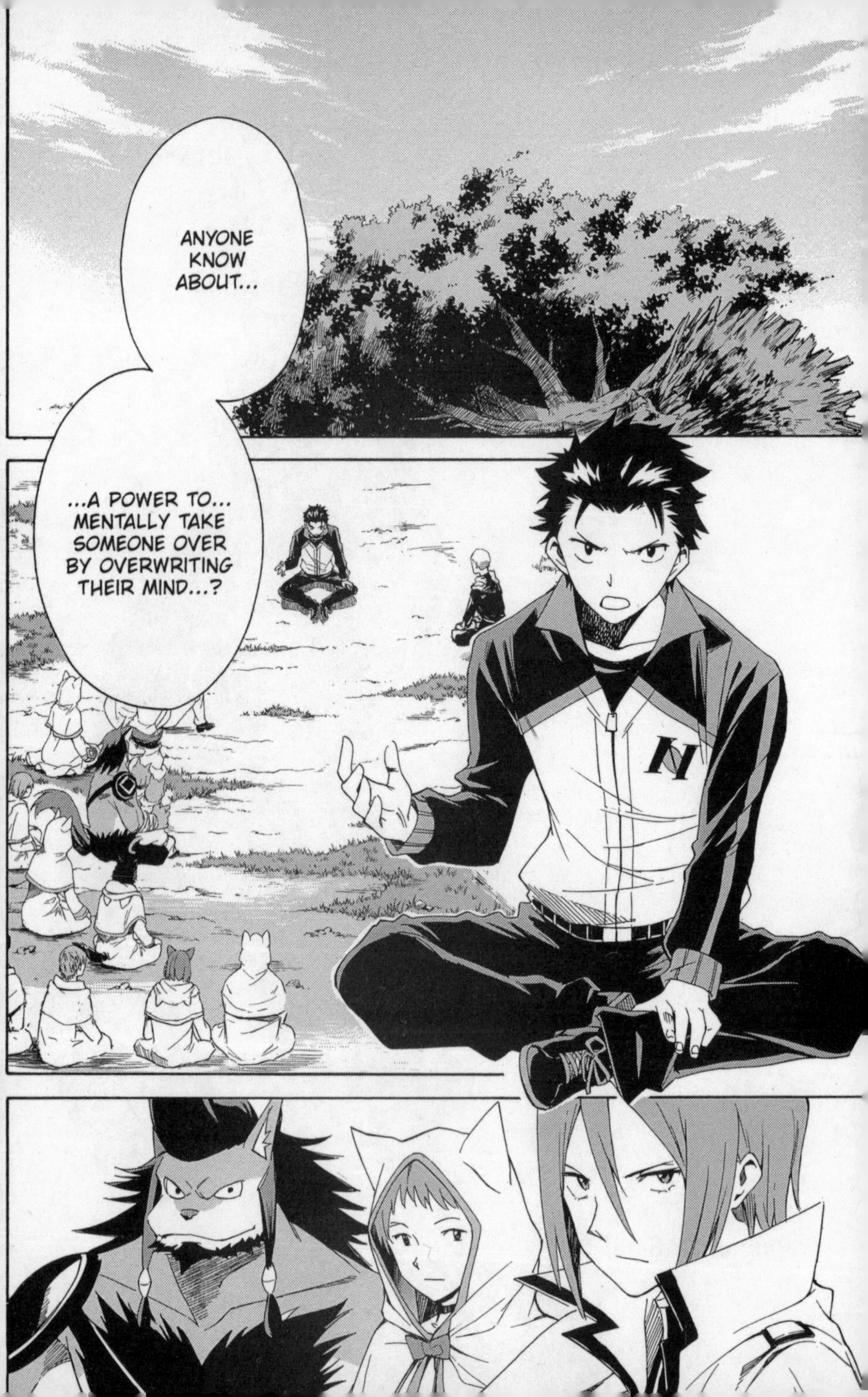
ANYONE KNOW ABOUT...
...A POWER TO... MENTALLY TAKE SOMEONE OVER BY OVERWRITING THEIR MIND...?

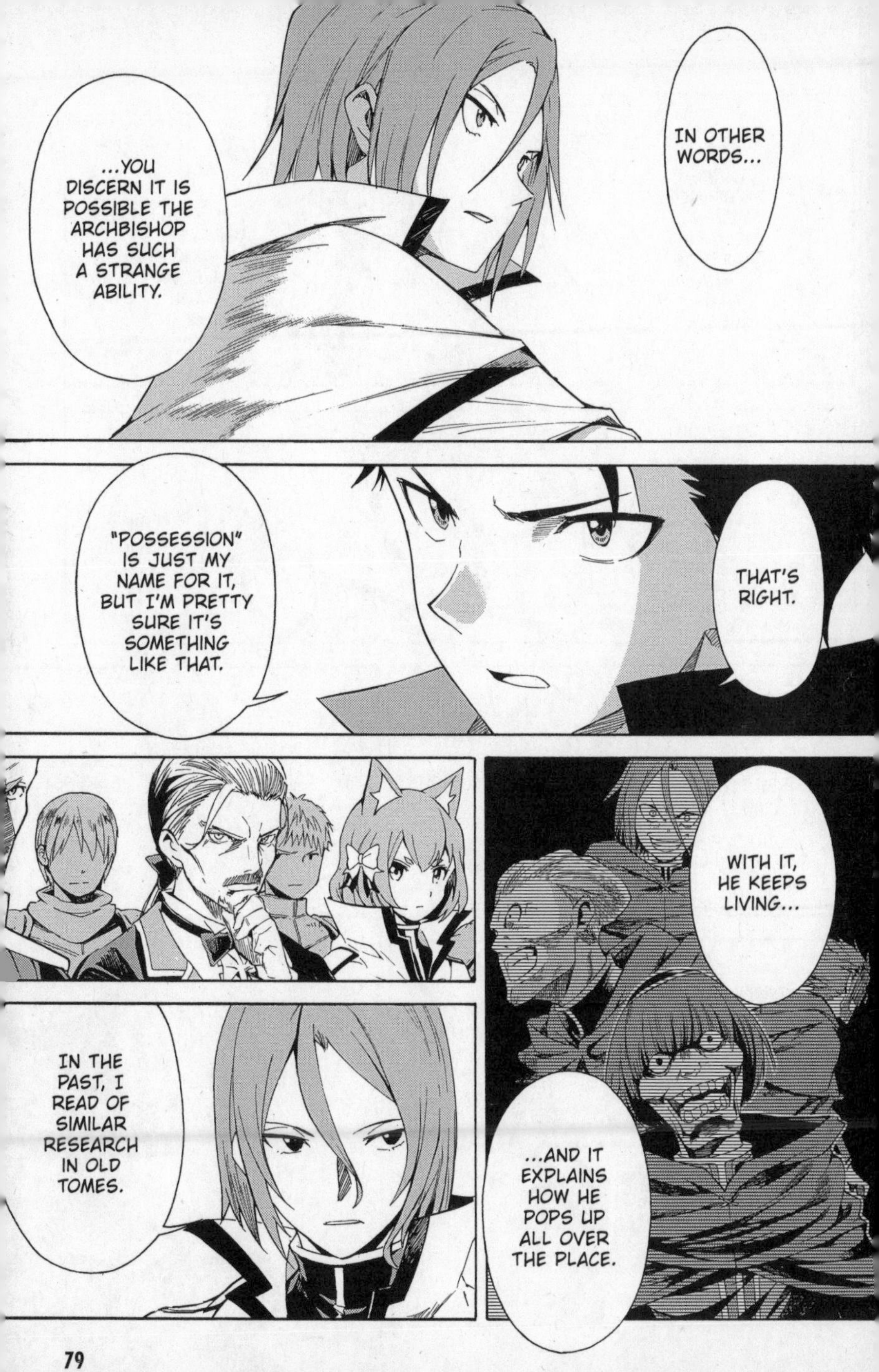
IN OTHER WORDS...
...YOU DISCERN IT IS POSSIBLE THE ARCHBISHOP HAS SUCH A STRANGE ABILITY.
THAT'S RIGHT.
"POSSESSION" IS JUST MY NAME FOR IT, BUT I'M PRETTY SURE IT'S SOMETHING LIKE THAT.
WITH IT, HE KEEPS LIVING...
...AND IT EXPLAINS HOW HE POPS UP ALL OVER THE PLACE.
IN THE PAST, I READ OF SIMILAR RESEARCH IN OLD TOMES.

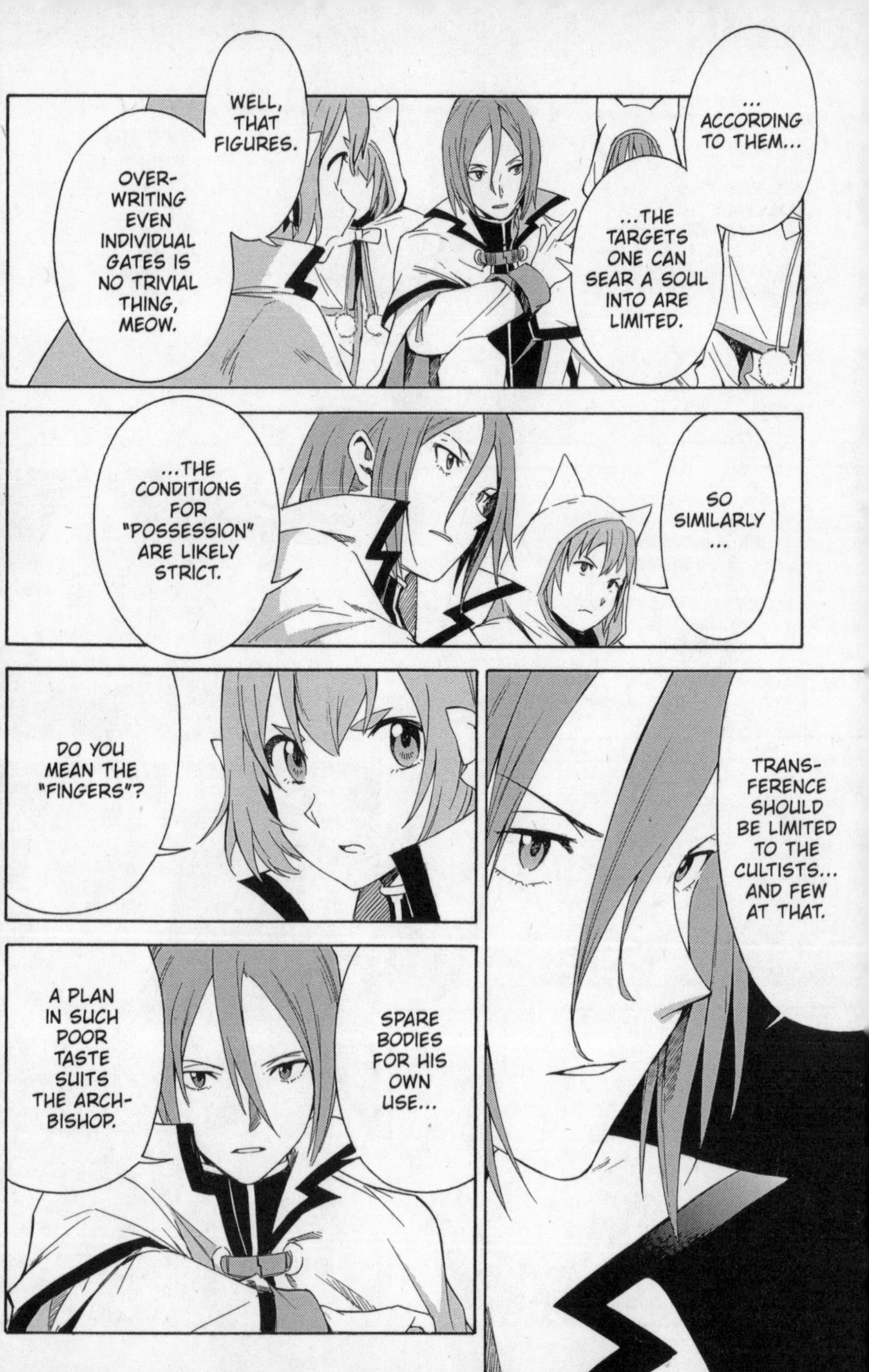
...ACCORDING TO THEM...
...THE TARGETS ONE CAN SEAR A SOUL INTO ARE LIMITED.
WELL, THAT FIGURES.
OVER-WRITING EVEN INDIVIDUAL GATES IS NO TRIVIAL THING, MEOW.
SO SIMILARLY ...
...THE CONDITIONS FOR "POSSESSION" ARE LIKELY STRICT.
TRANS-FERENCE SHOULD BE LIMITED TO THE CULTISTS... AND FEW AT THAT.
DO YOU MEAN THE "FINGERS"?
SPARE BODIES FOR HIS OWN USE...
A PLAN IN SUCH POOR TASTE SUITS THE ARCH-BISHOP.

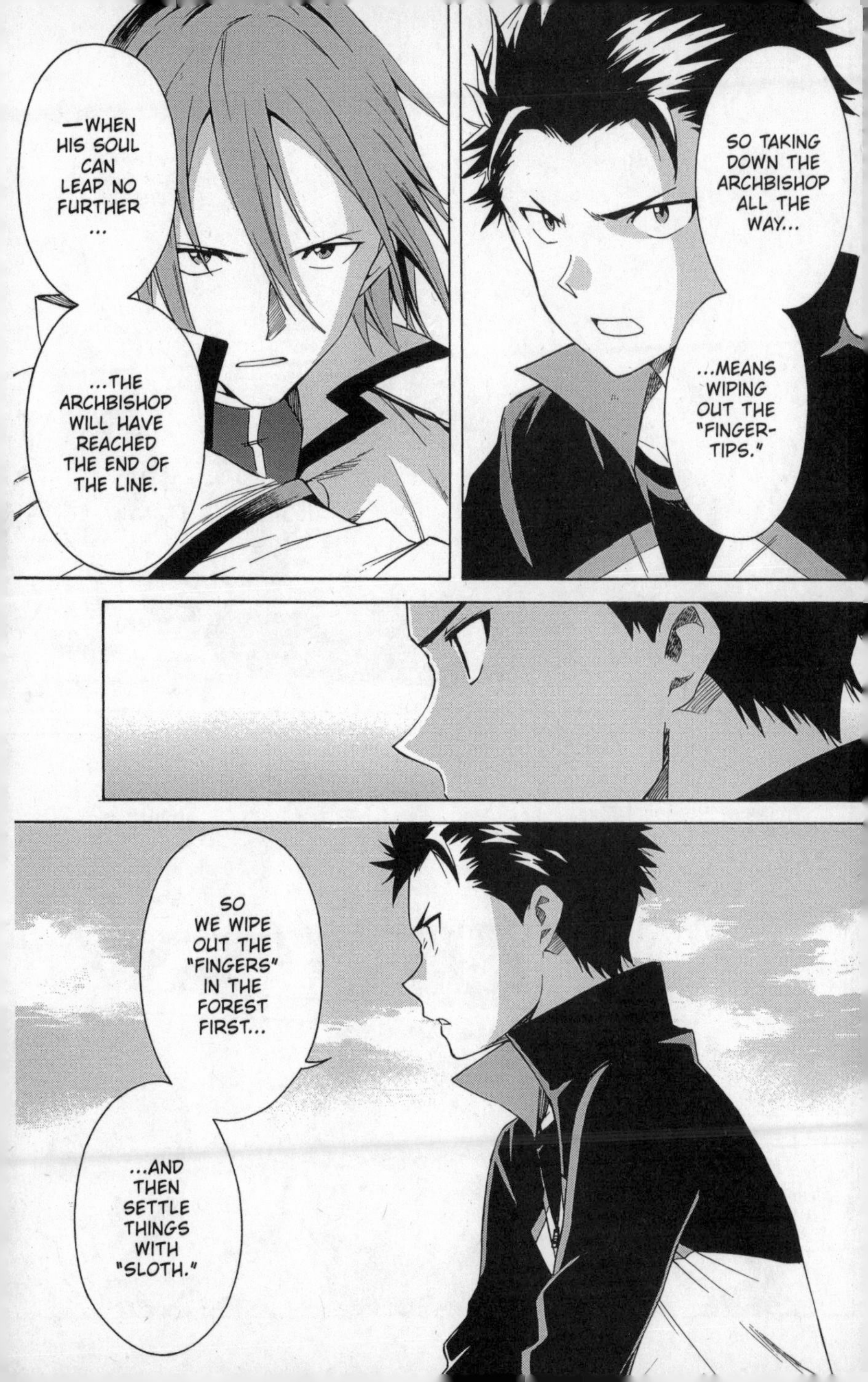
SO TAKING DOWN THE ARCHBISHOP ALL THE WAY...
...MEANS WIPING OUT THE "FINGER-TIPS."
—WHEN HIS SOUL CAN LEAP NO FURTHER ...
...THE ARCHBISHOP WILL HAVE REACHED THE END OF THE LINE.
SO WE WIPE OUT THE "FINGERS" IN THE FOREST FIRST...
...AND THEN SETTLE THINGS WITH "SLOTH."

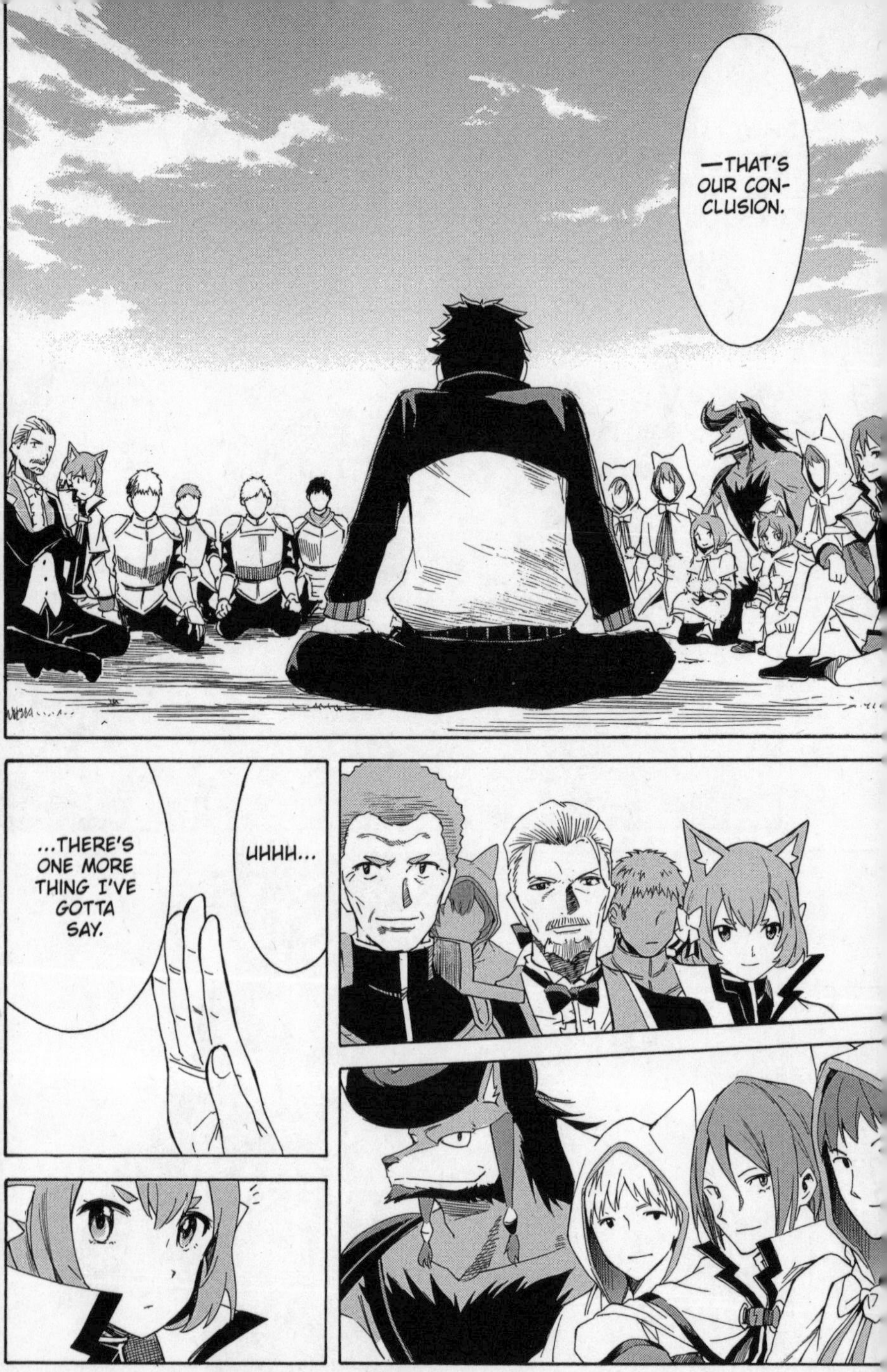
—THAT'S OUR CON-CLUSION.
UHHH...
...THERE'S ONE MORE THING I'VE GOTTA SAY.

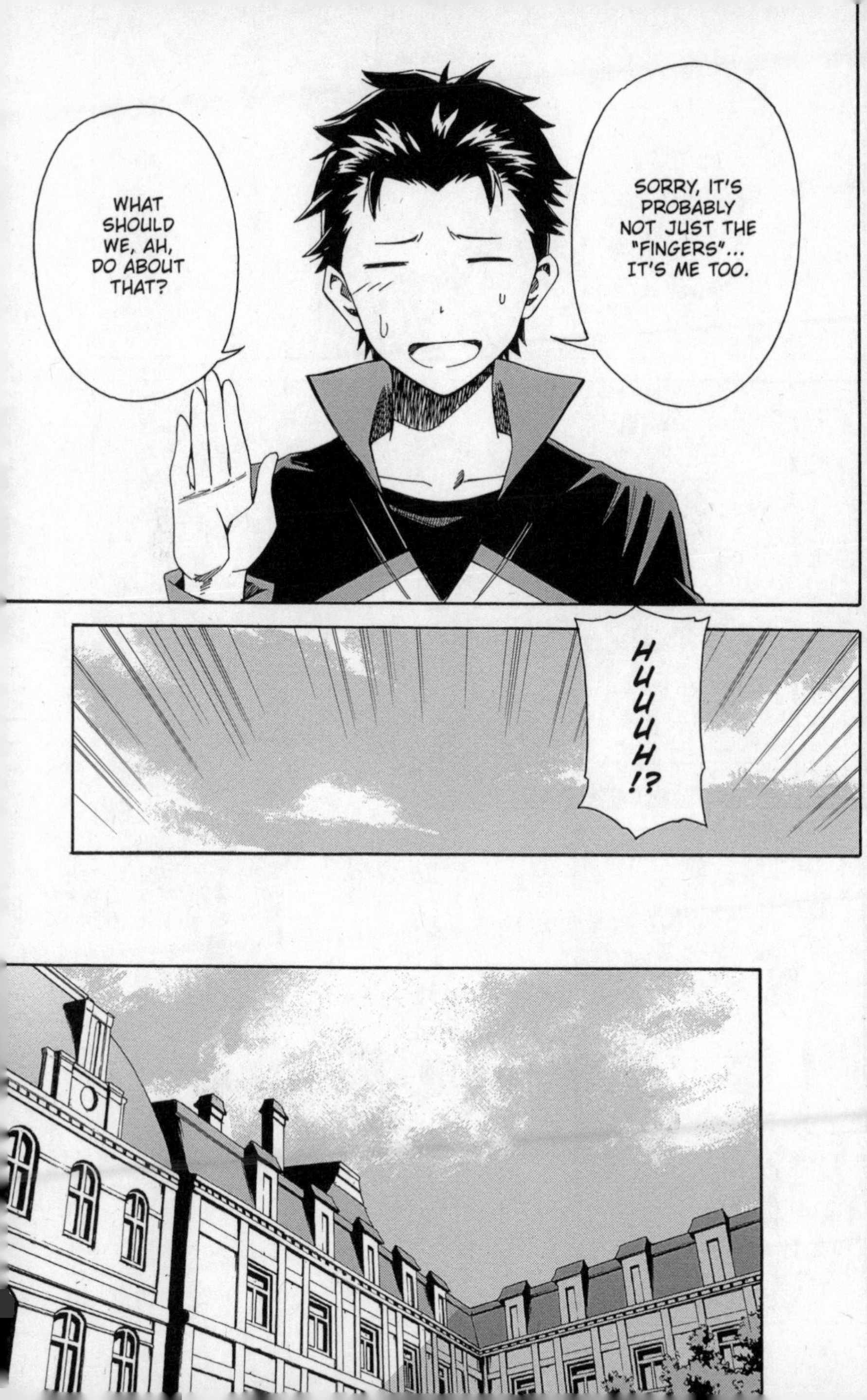
SORRY, IT'S PROBABLY NOT JUST THE "FINGERS"... IT'S ME TOO.
WHAT SHOULD WE, AH, DO ABOUT THAT?
HUUUH!?

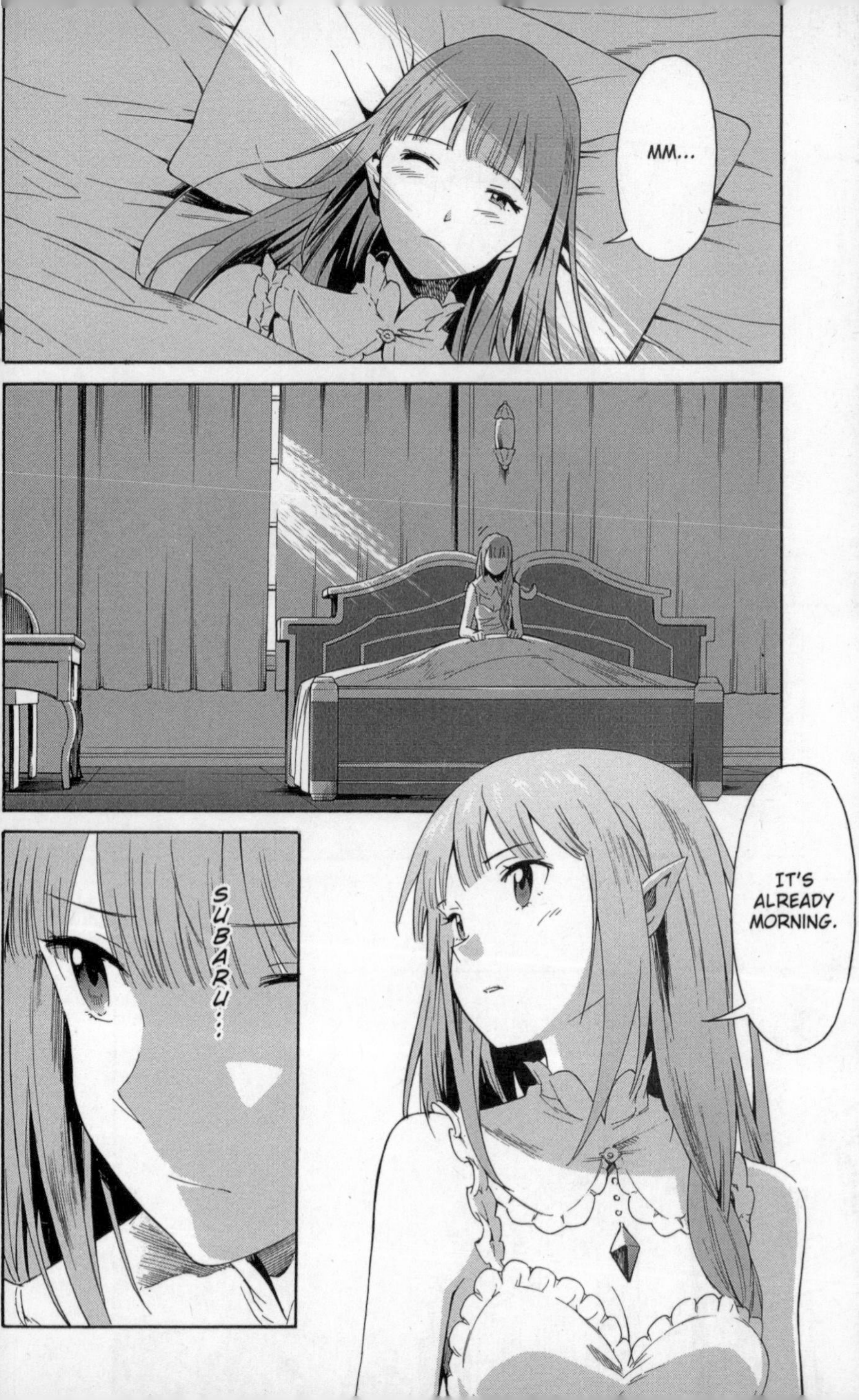
MM...
IT'S ALREADY MORNING.
SUBARU...

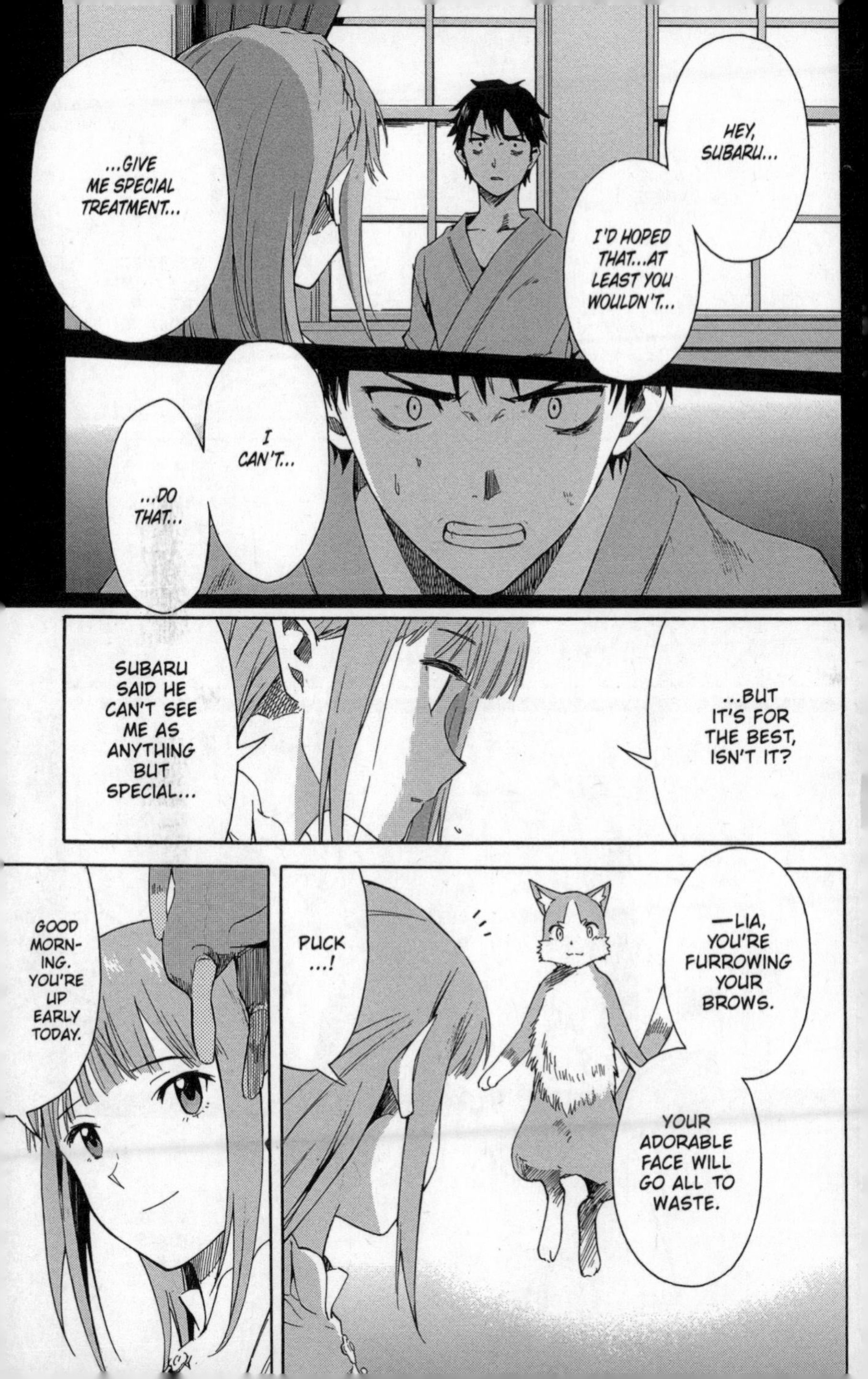
HEY, SUBARU...
I'D HOPED THAT...AT LEAST YOU WOULDN'T...
...GIVE ME SPECIAL TREATMENT...
I CAN'T...
...DO THAT...
SUBARU SAID HE CAN'T SEE ME AS ANYTHING BUT SPECIAL...
...BUT IT'S FOR THE BEST, ISN'T IT?
—LIA, YOU'RE FURROWING YOUR BROWS.
YOUR ADORABLE FACE WILL GO ALL TO WASTE.
PUCK ...!
GOOD MORNING. YOU'RE UP EARLY TODAY.

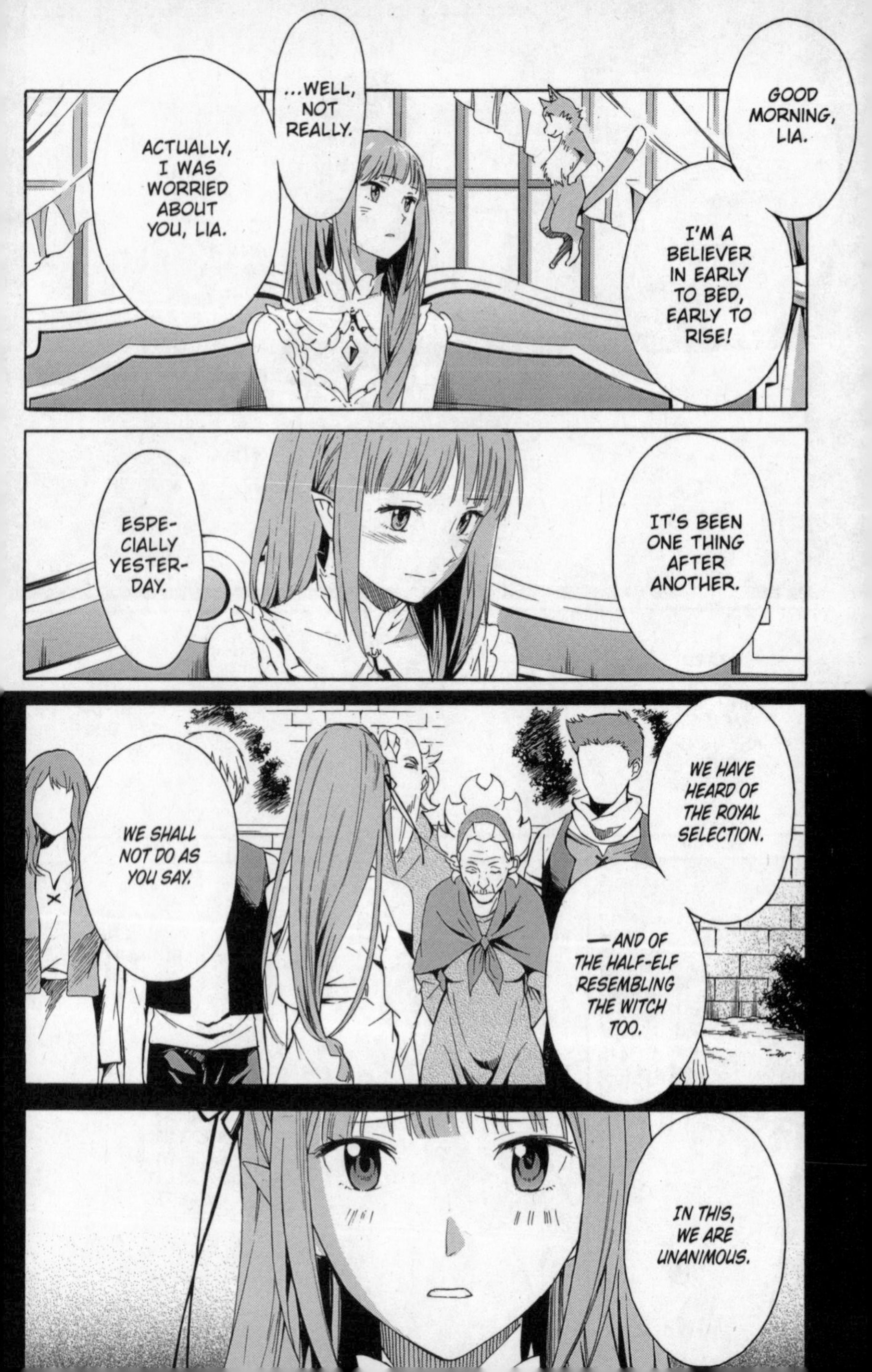
GOOD MORNING, LIA.
I'M A BELIEVER IN EARLY TO BED, EARLY TO RISE!
...WELL, NOT REALLY.
ACTUALLY, I WAS WORRIED ABOUT YOU, LIA.
IT'S BEEN ONE THING AFTER ANOTHER.
ESPE-CIALLY YESTER-DAY.
WE HAVE HEARD OF THE ROYAL SELECTION.
—AND OF THE HALF-ELF RESEMBLING THE WITCH TOO.
WE SHALL NOT DO AS YOU SAY.
IN THIS, WE ARE UNANIMOUS.

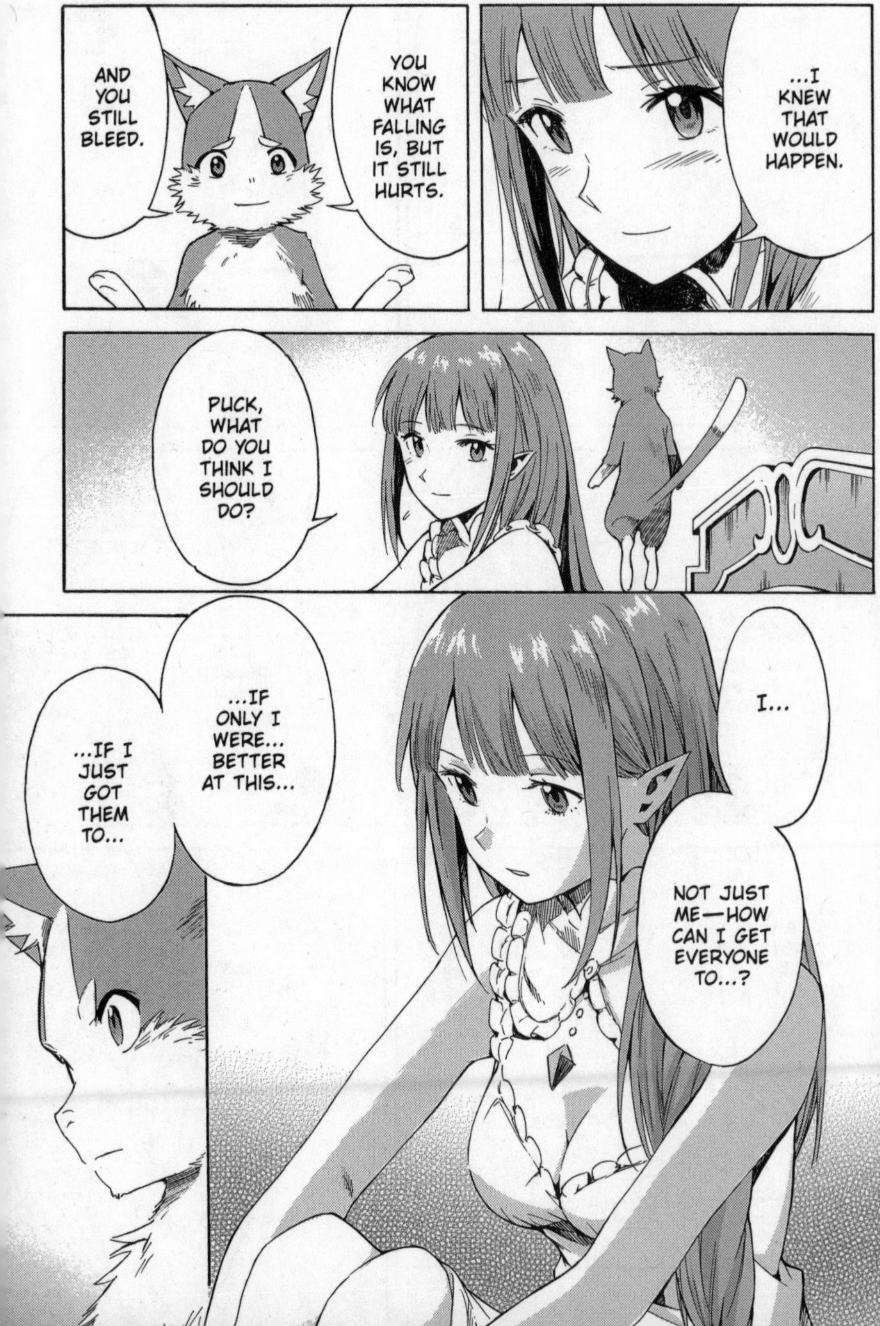
...I KNEW THAT WOULD HAPPEN.
YOU KNOW WHAT FALLING IS, BUT IT STILL HURTS.
AND YOU STILL BLEED.
PUCK, WHAT DO YOU THINK I SHOULD DO?
I...
NOT JUST ME—HOW CAN I GET EVERYONE TO...?
...IF ONLY I WERE... BETTER AT THIS...
...IF I JUST GOT THEM TO...

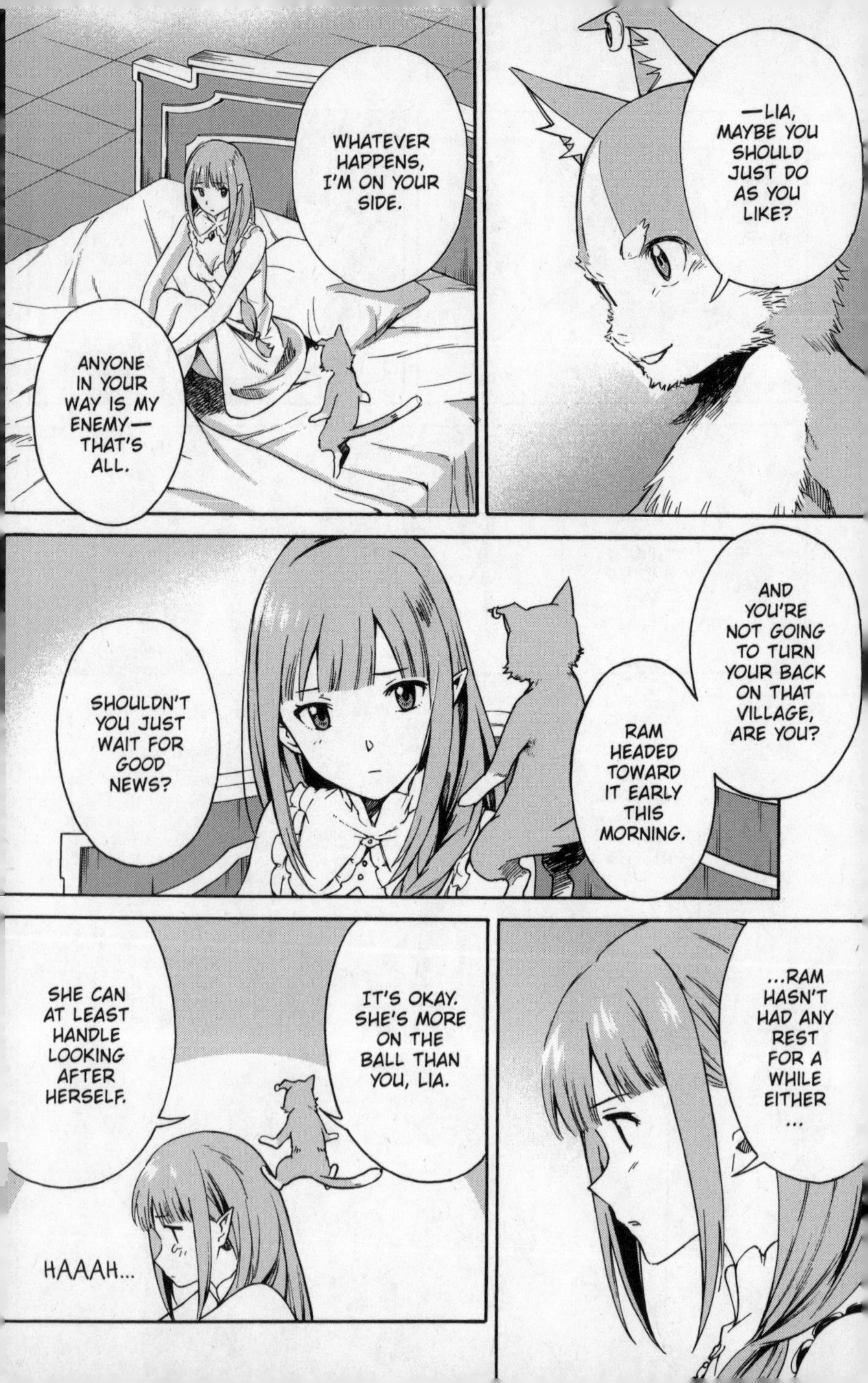
—LIA, MAYBE YOU SHOULD JUST DO AS YOU LIKE?
WHATEVER HAPPENS, I'M ON YOUR SIDE.
ANYONE IN YOUR WAY IS MY ENEMY—THAT'S ALL.
AND YOU'RE NOT GOING TO TURN YOUR BACK ON THAT VILLAGE, ARE YOU?
RAM HEADED TOWARD IT EARLY THIS MORNING.
SHOULDN'T YOU JUST WAIT FOR GOOD NEWS?
...RAM HASN'T HAD ANY REST FOR A WHILE EITHER...
IT'S OKAY. SHE'S MORE ON THE BALL THAN YOU, LIA.
SHE CAN AT LEAST HANDLE LOOKING AFTER HERSELF.
HAAAH...

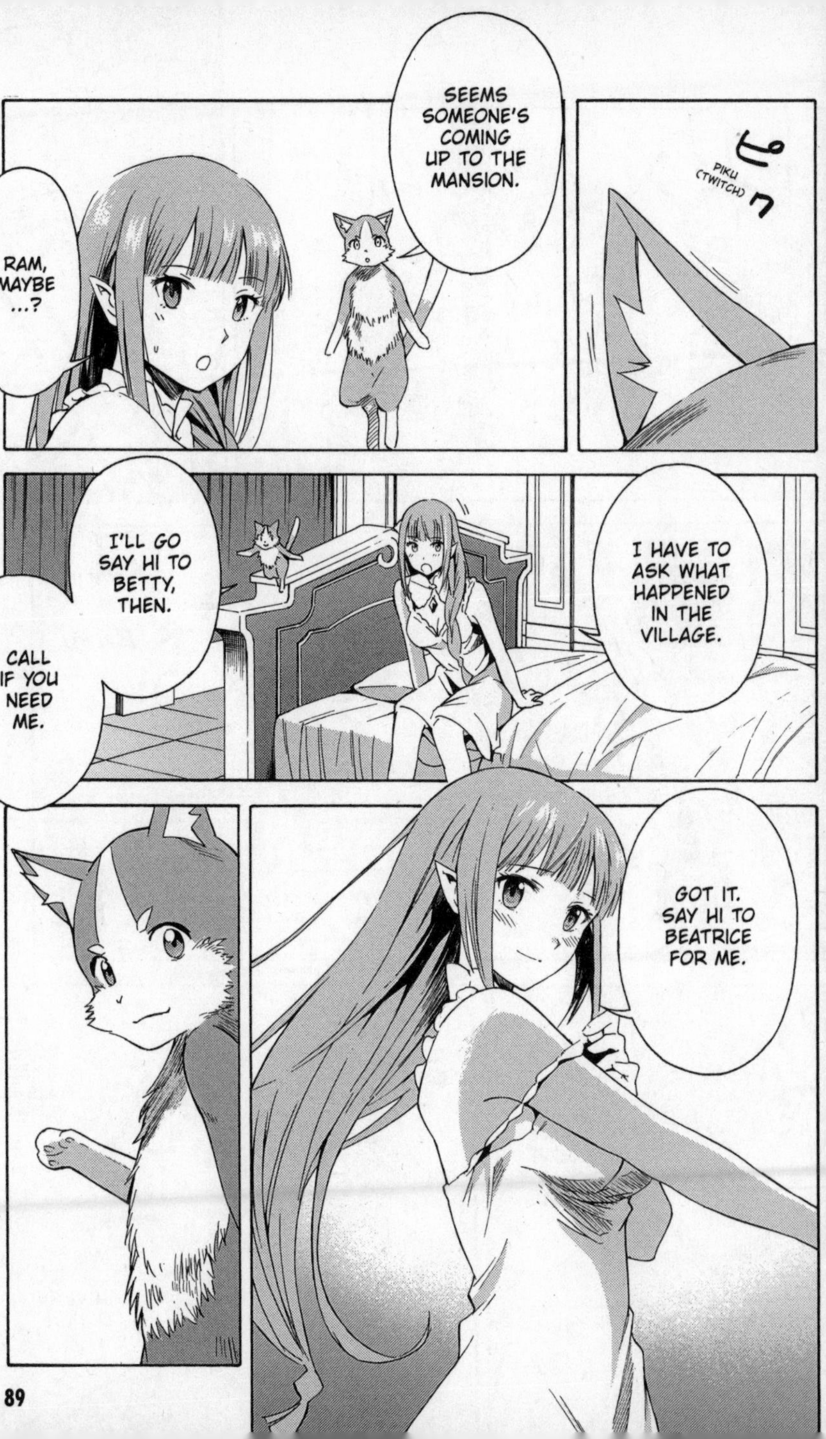
ピク
PIKU (TWITCH)
SEEMS SOMEONE'S COMING UP TO THE MANSION.
RAM, MAYBE ...?
I HAVE TO ASK WHAT HAPPENED IN THE VILLAGE.
I'LL GO SAY HI TO BETTY, THEN.
CALL IF YOU NEED ME.
GOT IT. SAY HI TO BEATRICE FOR ME.

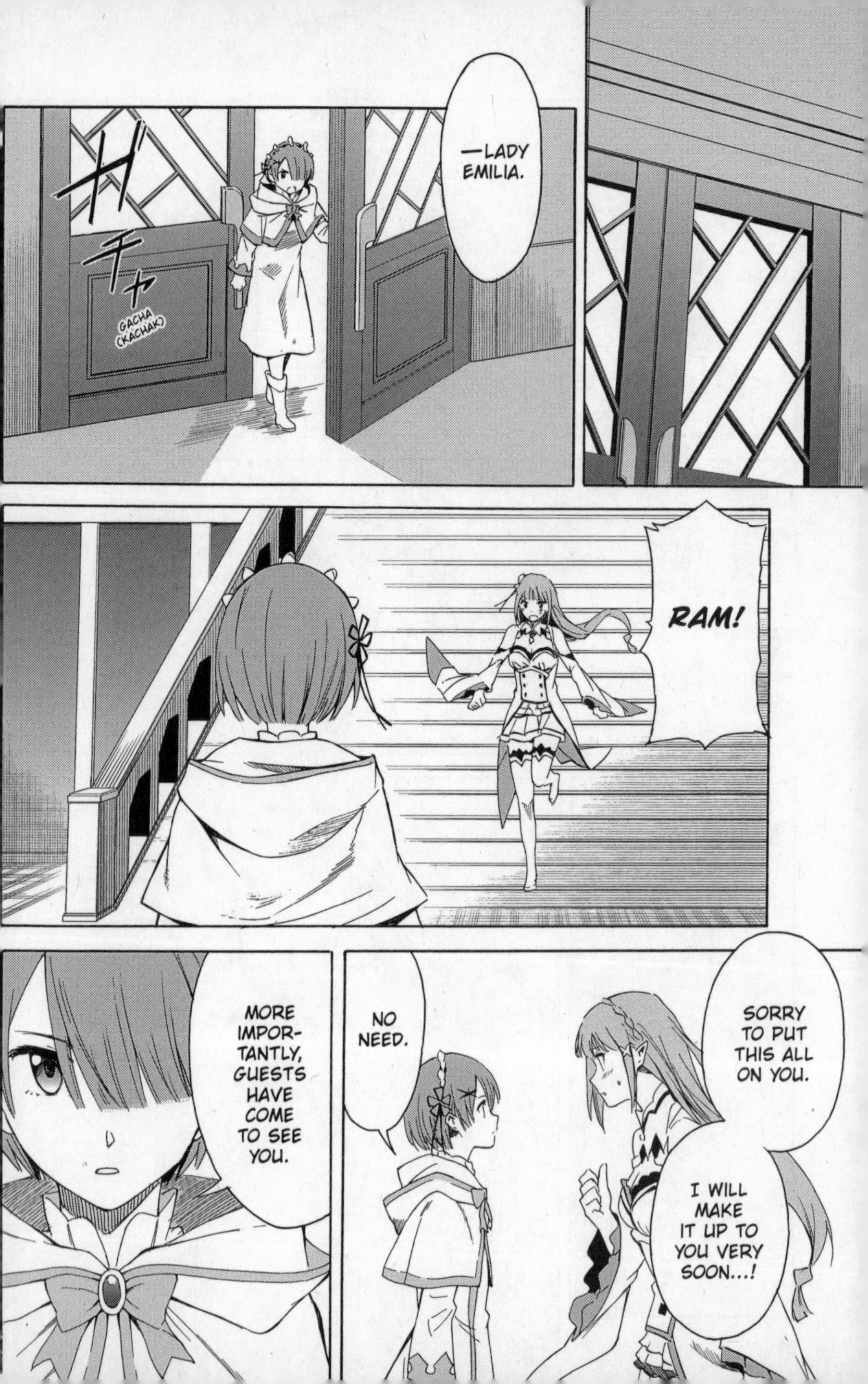
—LADY EMILIA.
ガチャ
GACHA (KACHAK)
RAM!
SORRY TO PUT THIS ALL ON YOU.
I WILL MAKE IT UP TO YOU VERY SOON...!
NO NEED.
MORE IMPOR-TANTLY, GUESTS HAVE COME TO SEE YOU.

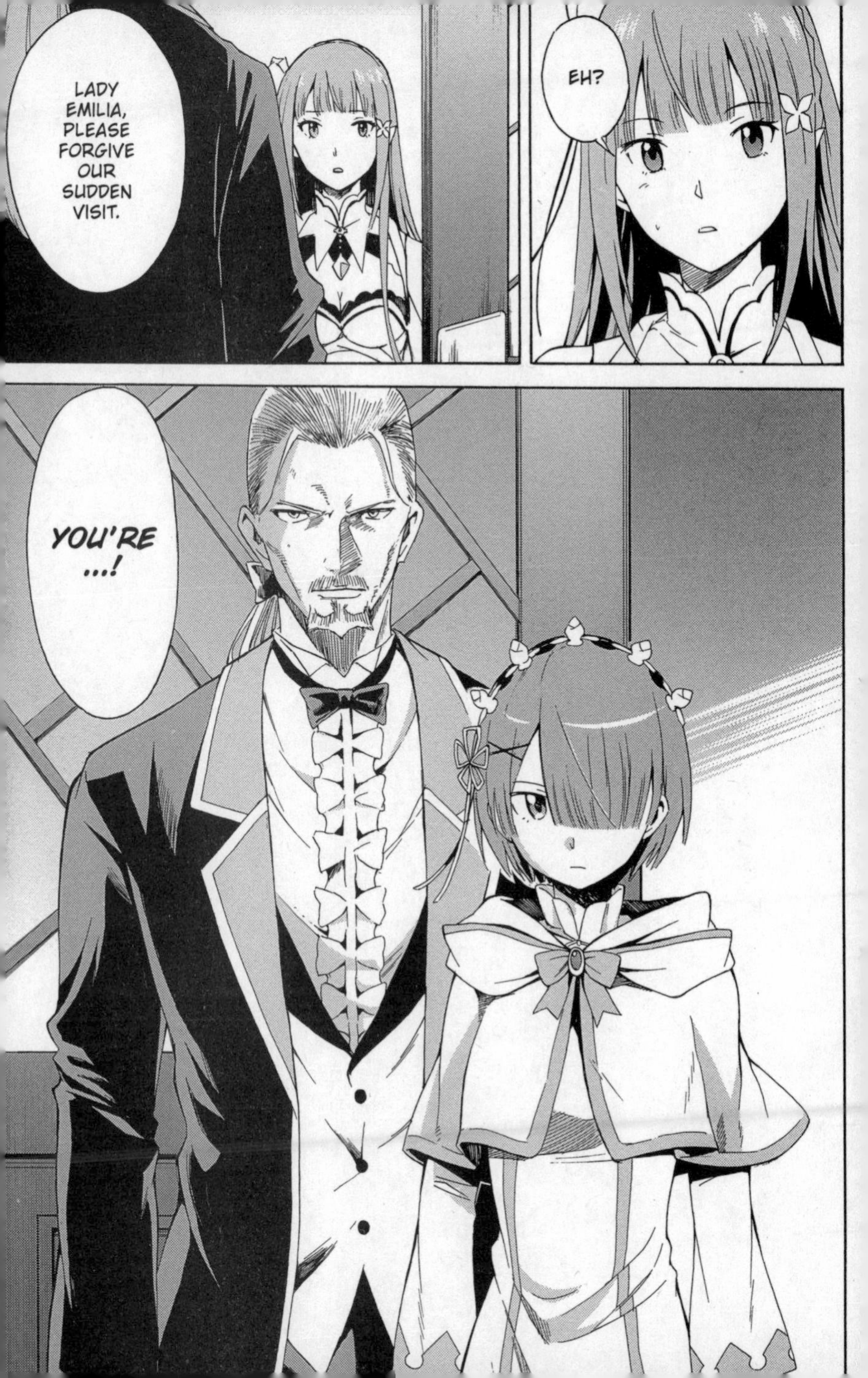
EH?
LADY EMILIA, PLEASE FORGIVE OUR SUDDEN VISIT.
YOU'RE ...!

Re:ZERO
-Starting Life in
Another World-

Truth of Zero
The only ability Subaru Natsuki gets when he's summoned
to another world is time travel via his own death.
But to save her, he'll die as many times as it takes.

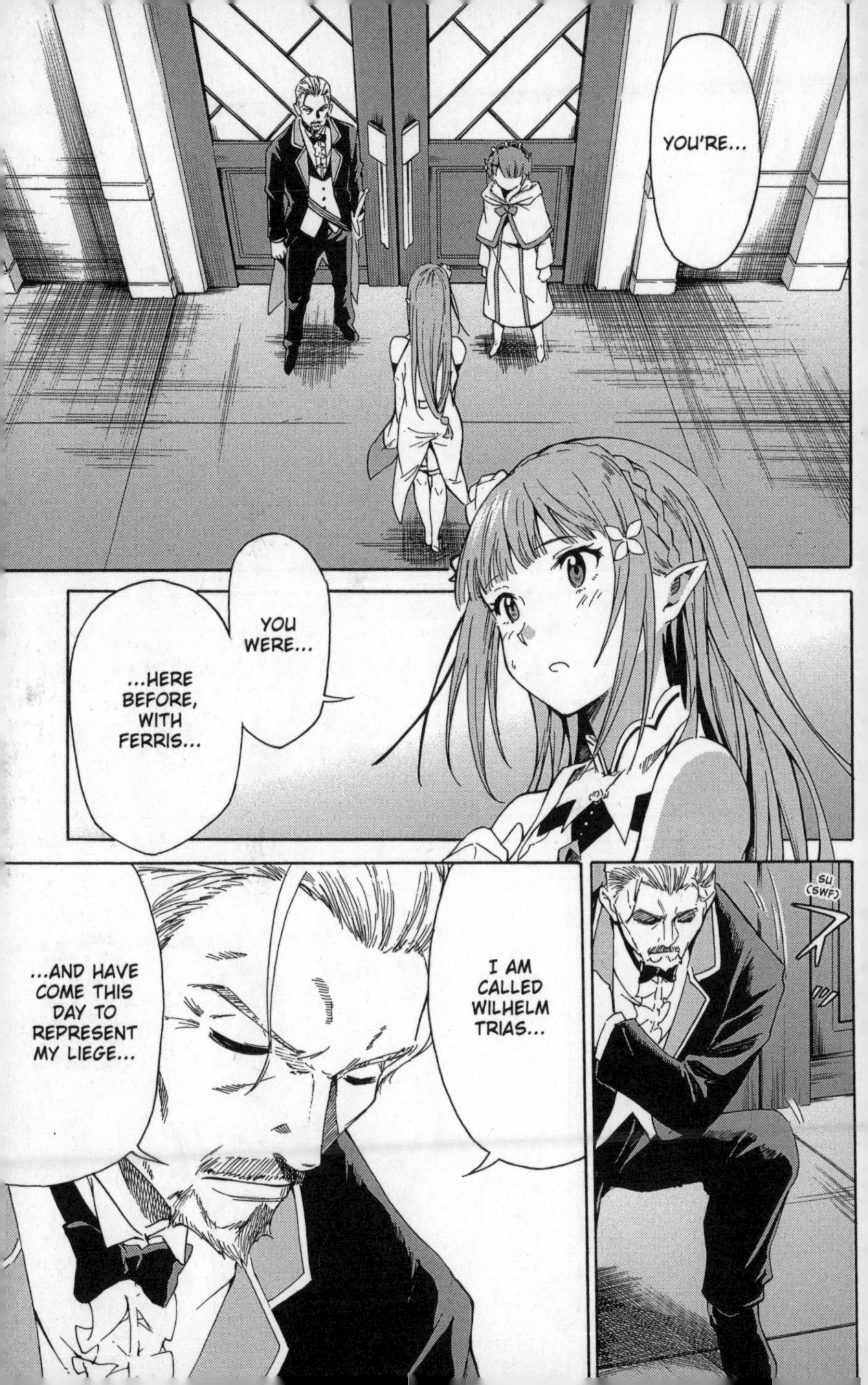
YOU'RE...
YOU WERE...
...HERE BEFORE, WITH FERRIS...
SU (SWF)
I AM CALLED WILHELM TRIAS...
...AND HAVE COME THIS DAY TO REPRESENT MY LIEGE...

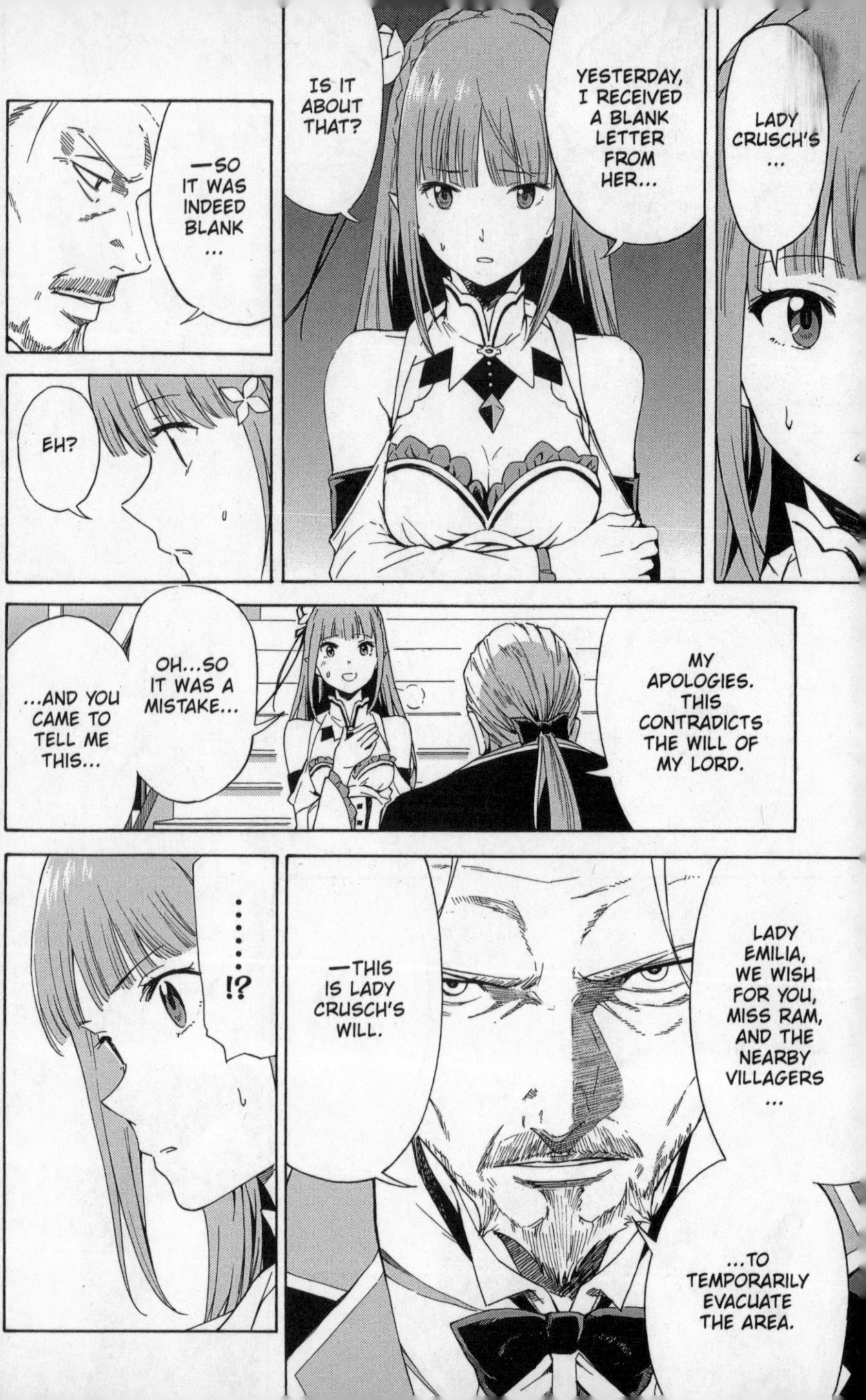
LADY CRUSCH'S ...
YESTERDAY, I RECEIVED A BLANK LETTER FROM HER...
IS IT ABOUT THAT?
—SO IT WAS INDEED BLANK ...
EH?
MY APOLOGIES. THIS CONTRADICTS THE WILL OF MY LORD.
OH...SO IT WAS A MISTAKE...
...AND YOU CAME TO TELL ME THIS...
LADY EMILIA, WE WISH FOR YOU, MISS RAM, AND THE NEARBY VILLAGERS ...
—THIS IS LADY CRUSCH'S WILL.
...TO TEMPORARILY EVACUATE THE AREA.
......!?

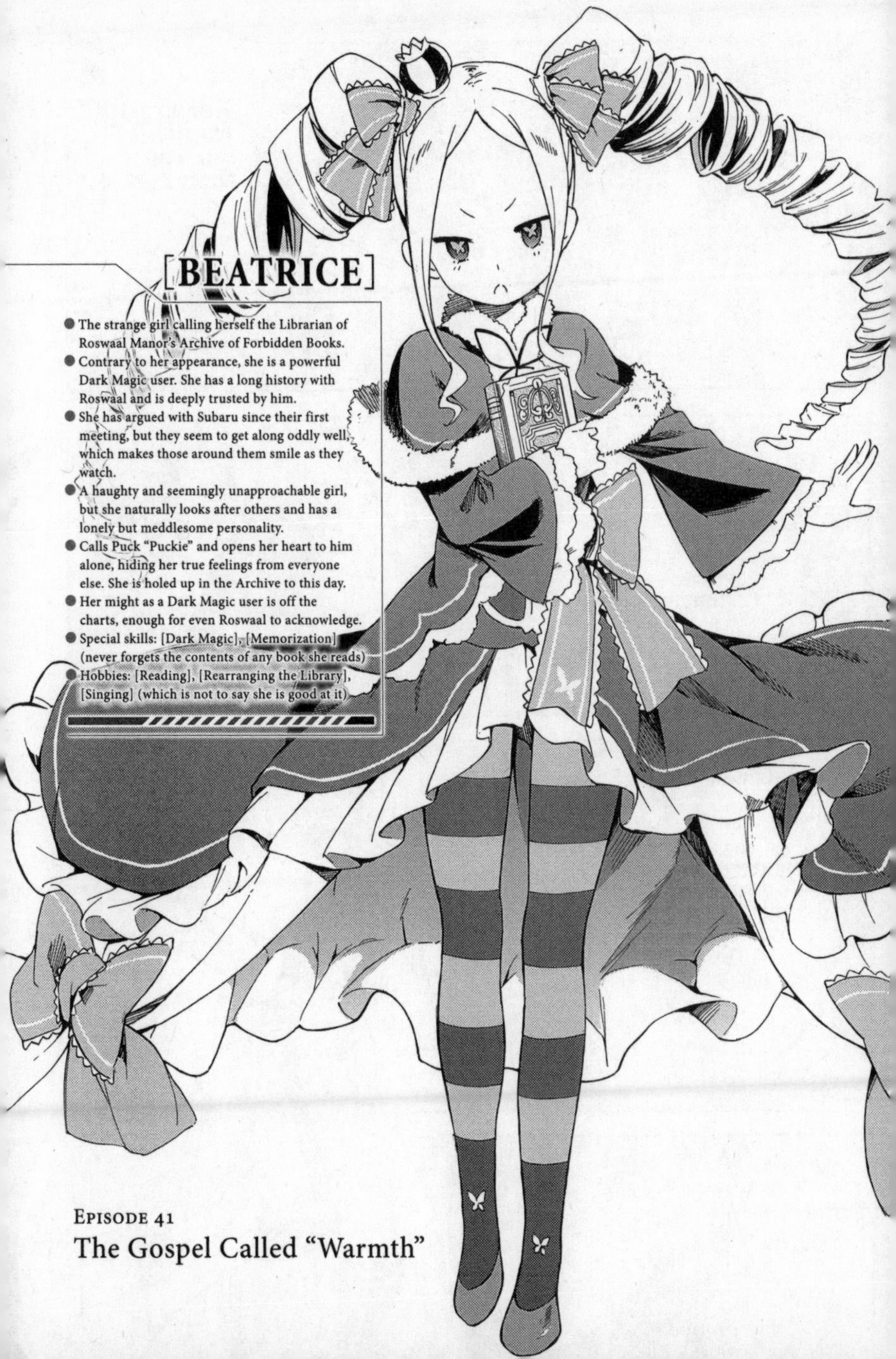

[BEATRICE]

- The strange girl calling herself the Librarian of Roswaal Manor's Archive of Forbidden Books.
- Contrary to her appearance, she is a powerful Dark Magic user. She has a long history with Roswaal and is deeply trusted by him.
- She has argued with Subaru since their first meeting, but they seem to get along oddly well, which makes those around them smile as they watch.
- A haughty and seemingly unapproachable girl, but she naturally looks after others and has a lonely but meddlesome personality.
- Calls Puck "Puckie" and opens her heart to him alone, hiding her true feelings from everyone else. She is holed up in the Archive to this day.
- Her might as a Dark Magic user is off the charts, enough for even Roswaal to acknowledge.
- Special skills: [Dark Magic], [Memorization] (never forgets the contents of any book she reads)
- Hobbies: [Reading], [Rearranging the Library], [Singing] (which is not to say she is good at it)

EPISODE 41

The Gospel Called "Warmth"

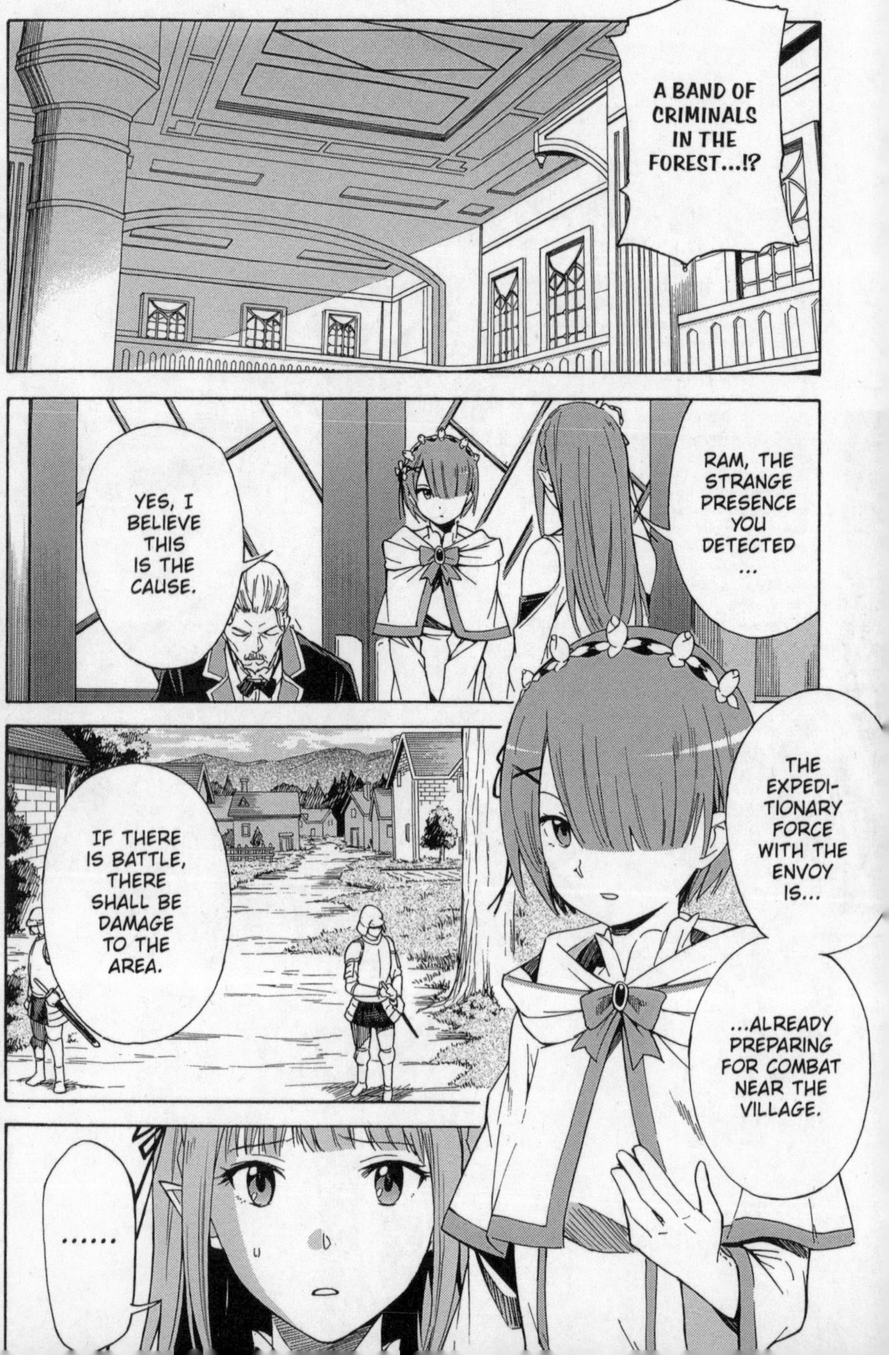
A BAND OF CRIMINALS IN THE FOREST...!?
RAM, THE STRANGE PRESENCE YOU DETECTED...
YES, I BELIEVE THIS IS THE CAUSE.
THE EXPEDITIONARY FORCE WITH THE ENVOY IS...
...ALREADY PREPARING FOR COMBAT NEAR THE VILLAGE.
IF THERE IS BATTLE, THERE SHALL BE DAMAGE TO THE AREA.
......

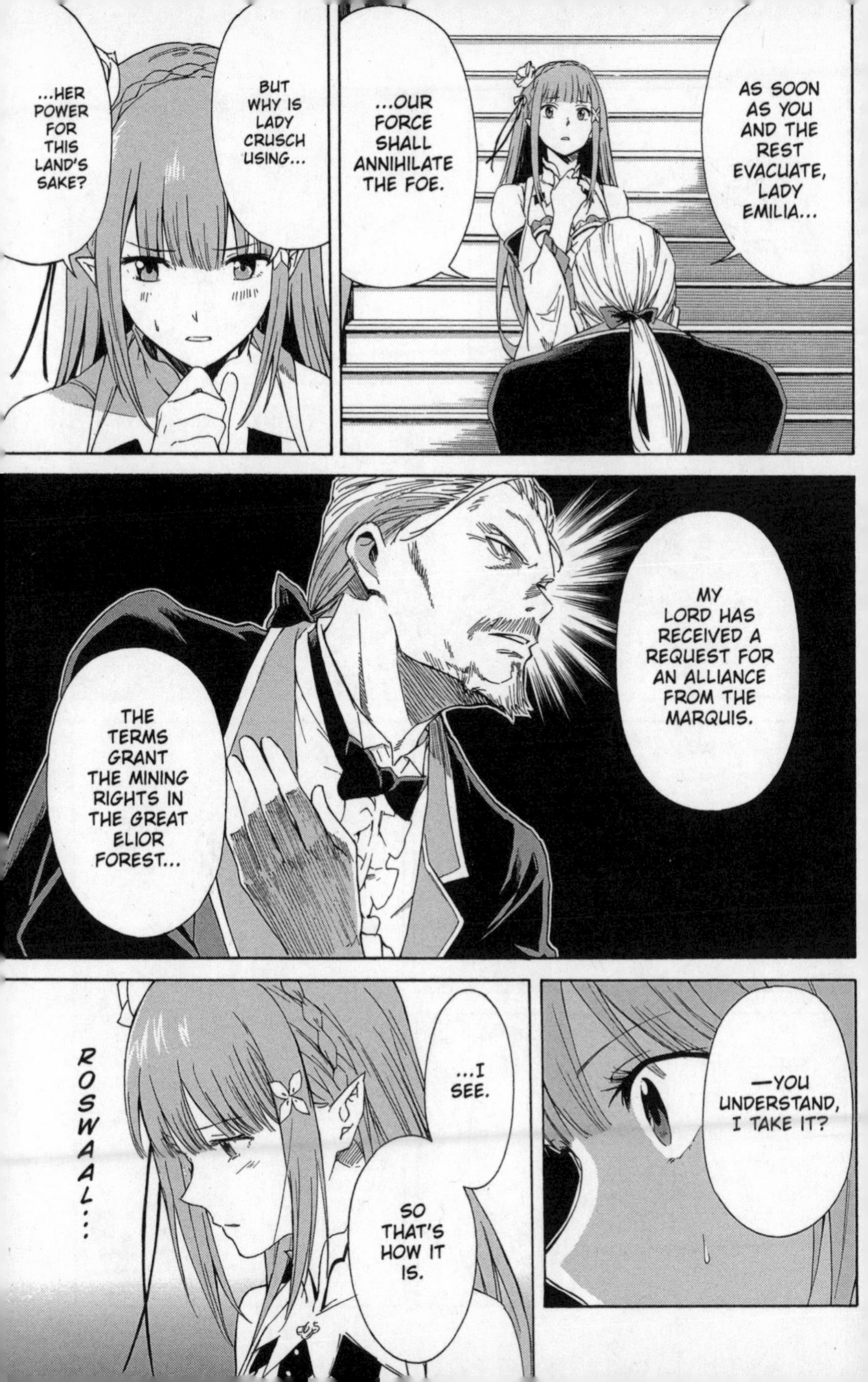
AS SOON AS YOU AND THE REST EVACUATE, LADY EMILIA...
...OUR FORCE SHALL ANNIHILATE THE FOE.
BUT WHY IS LADY CRUSCH USING...
...HER POWER FOR THIS LAND'S SAKE?
MY LORD HAS RECEIVED A REQUEST FOR AN ALLIANCE FROM THE MARQUIS.
THE TERMS GRANT THE MINING RIGHTS IN THE GREAT ELIOR FOREST...
—YOU UNDERSTAND, I TAKE IT?
...I SEE.
SO THAT'S HOW IT IS.
ROSWAAL...

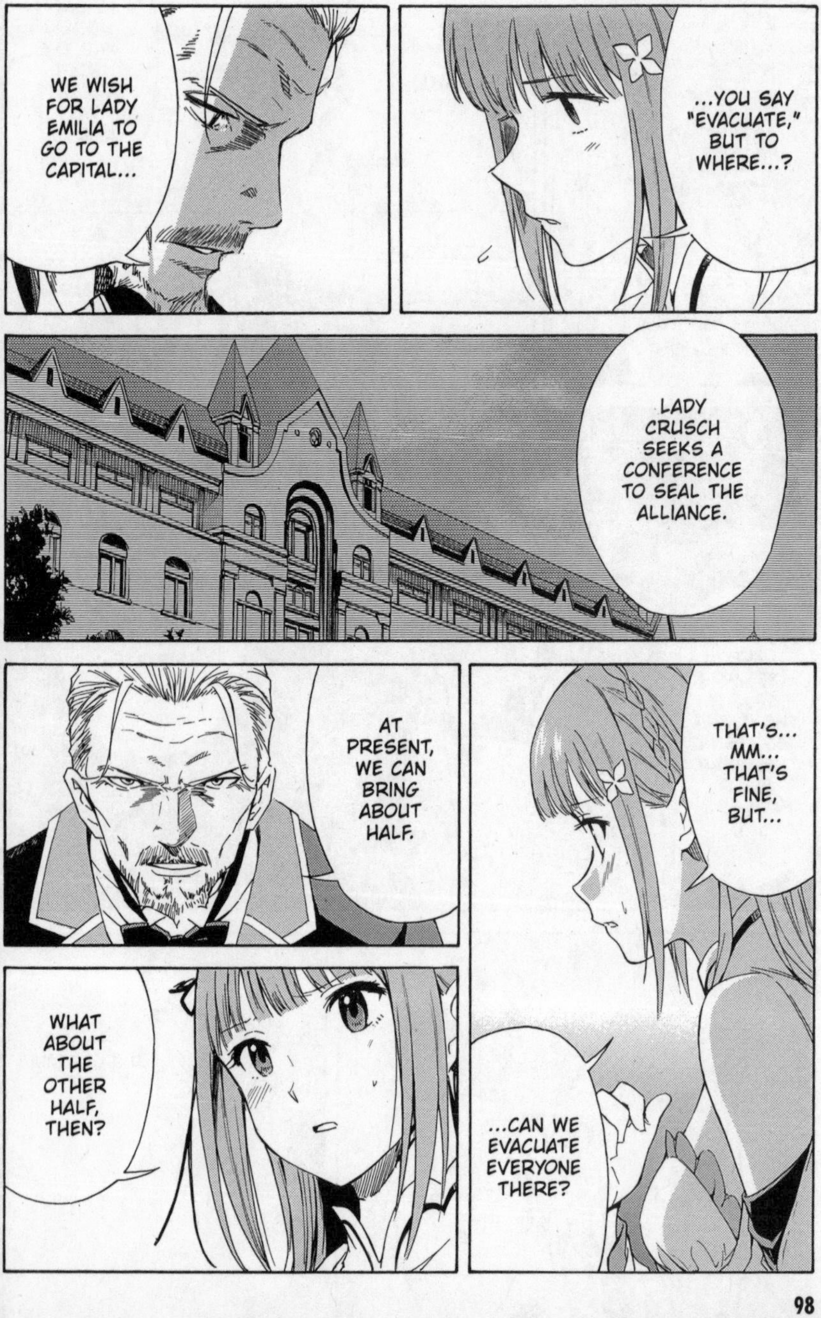
...YOU SAY "EVACUATE," BUT TO WHERE...?
WE WISH FOR LADY EMILIA TO GO TO THE CAPITAL...
LADY CRUSCH SEEKS A CONFERENCE TO SEAL THE ALLIANCE.
THAT'S... MM... THAT'S FINE, BUT...
...CAN WE EVACUATE EVERYONE THERE?
AT PRESENT, WE CAN BRING ABOUT HALF.
WHAT ABOUT THE OTHER HALF, THEN?

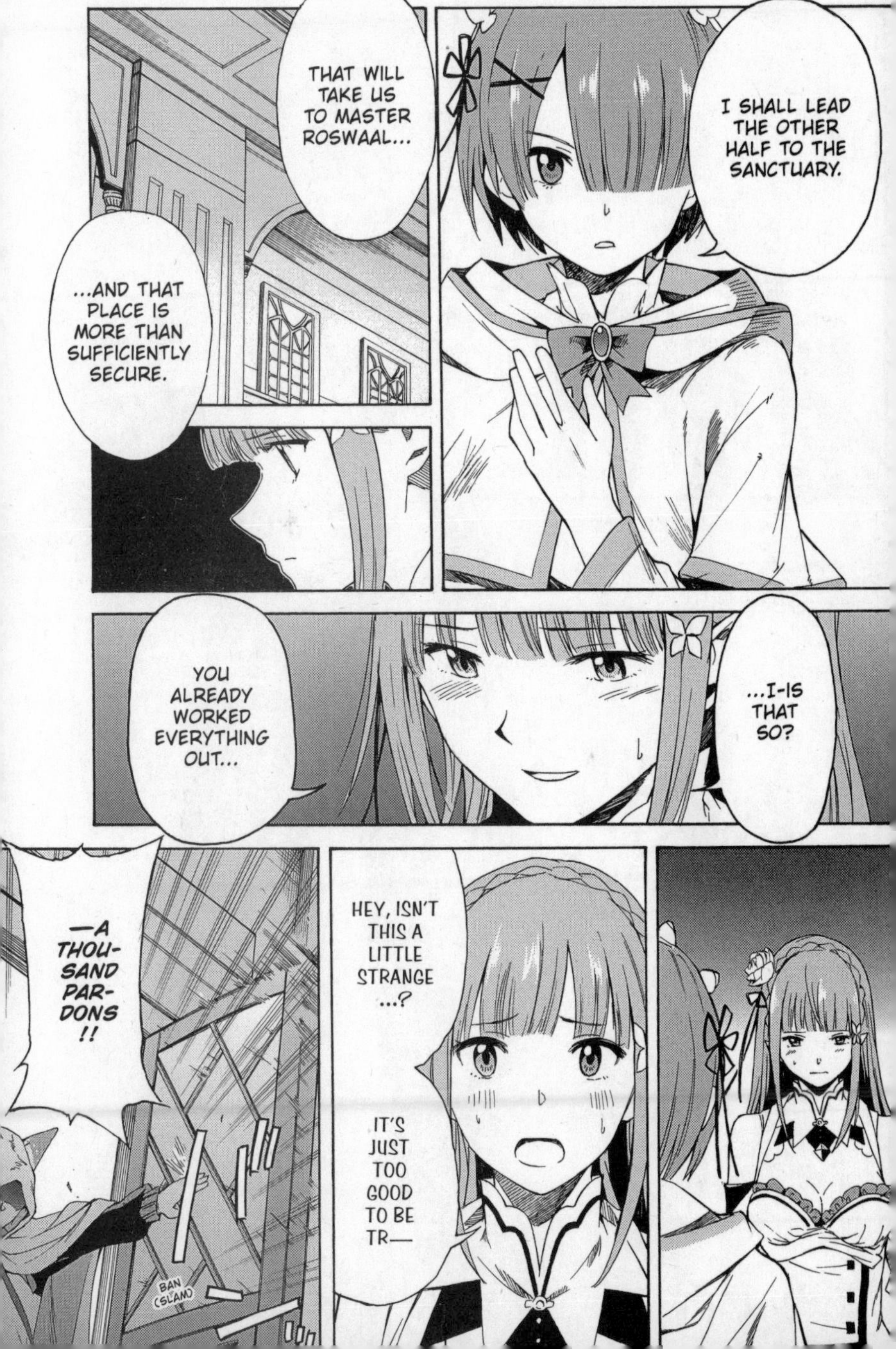
I SHALL LEAD THE OTHER HALF TO THE SANCTUARY.
THAT WILL TAKE US TO MASTER ROSWAAL...
...AND THAT PLACE IS MORE THAN SUFFICIENTLY SECURE.
...I-IS THAT SO?
YOU ALREADY WORKED EVERYTHING OUT...
HEY, ISN'T THIS A LITTLE STRANGE ...?
IT'S JUST TOO GOOD TO BE TR—
—A THOUSAND PARDONS !!
BAN (SLAM)

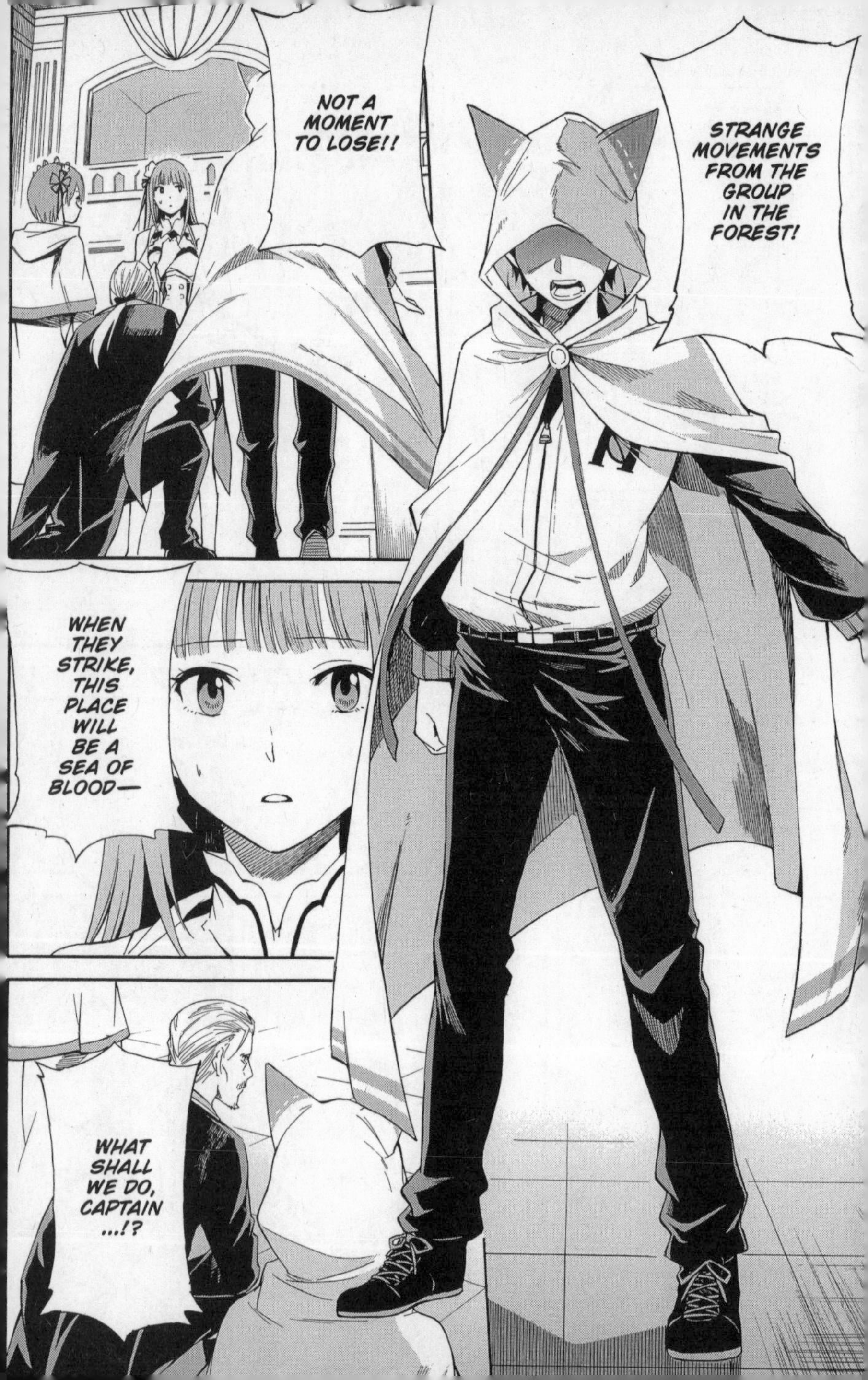
STRANGE MOVEMENTS FROM THE GROUP IN THE FOREST!
NOT A MOMENT TO LOSE!!
WHEN THEY STRIKE, THIS PLACE WILL BE A SEA OF BLOOD—
WHAT SHALL WE DO, CAPTAIN ...!?

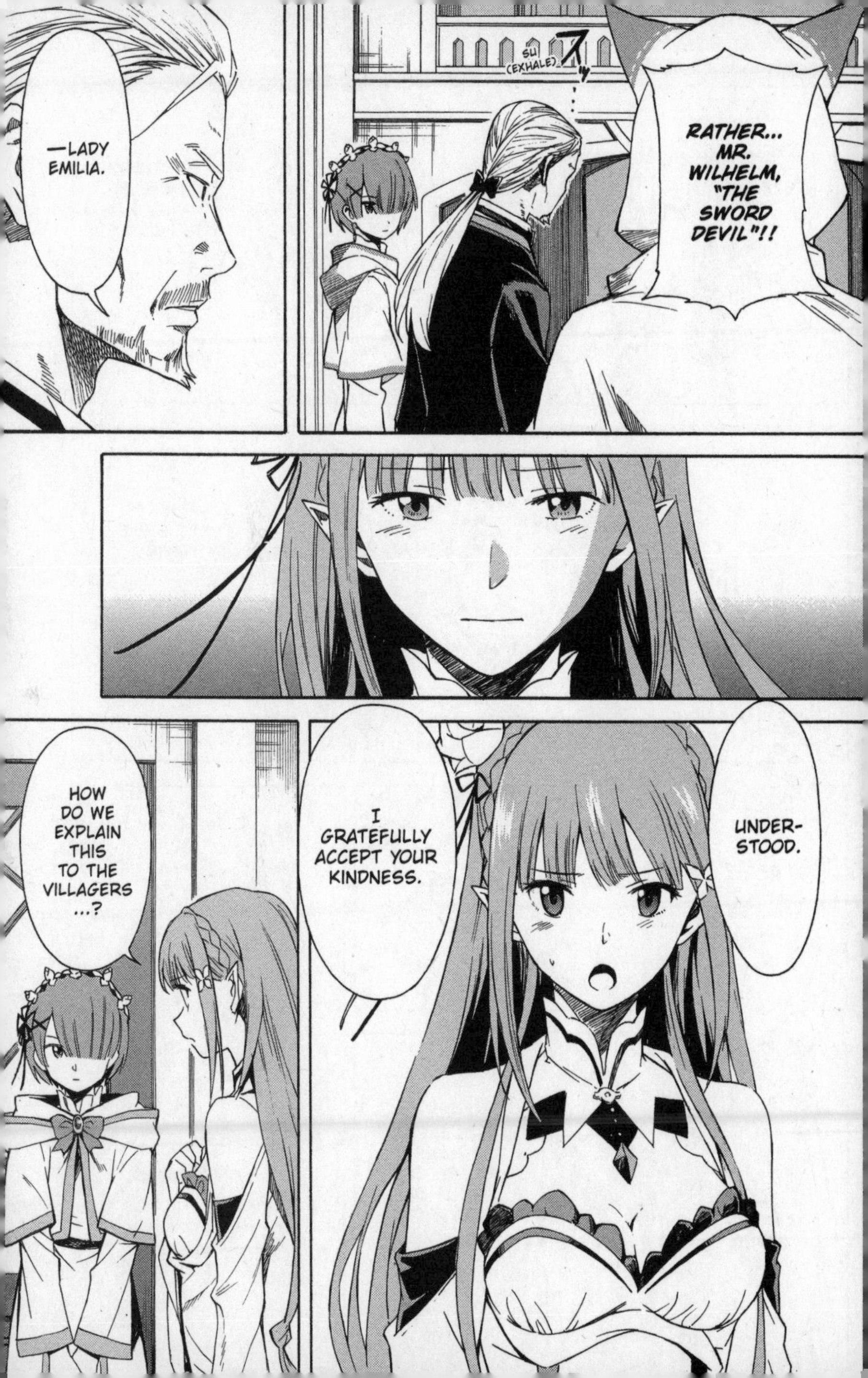
RATHER... MR. WILHELM, "THE SWORD DEVIL"!!
SU (EXHALE)
—LADY EMILIA.
UNDER-STOOD.
I GRATEFULLY ACCEPT YOUR KINDNESS.
HOW DO WE EXPLAIN THIS TO THE VILLAGERS ...?

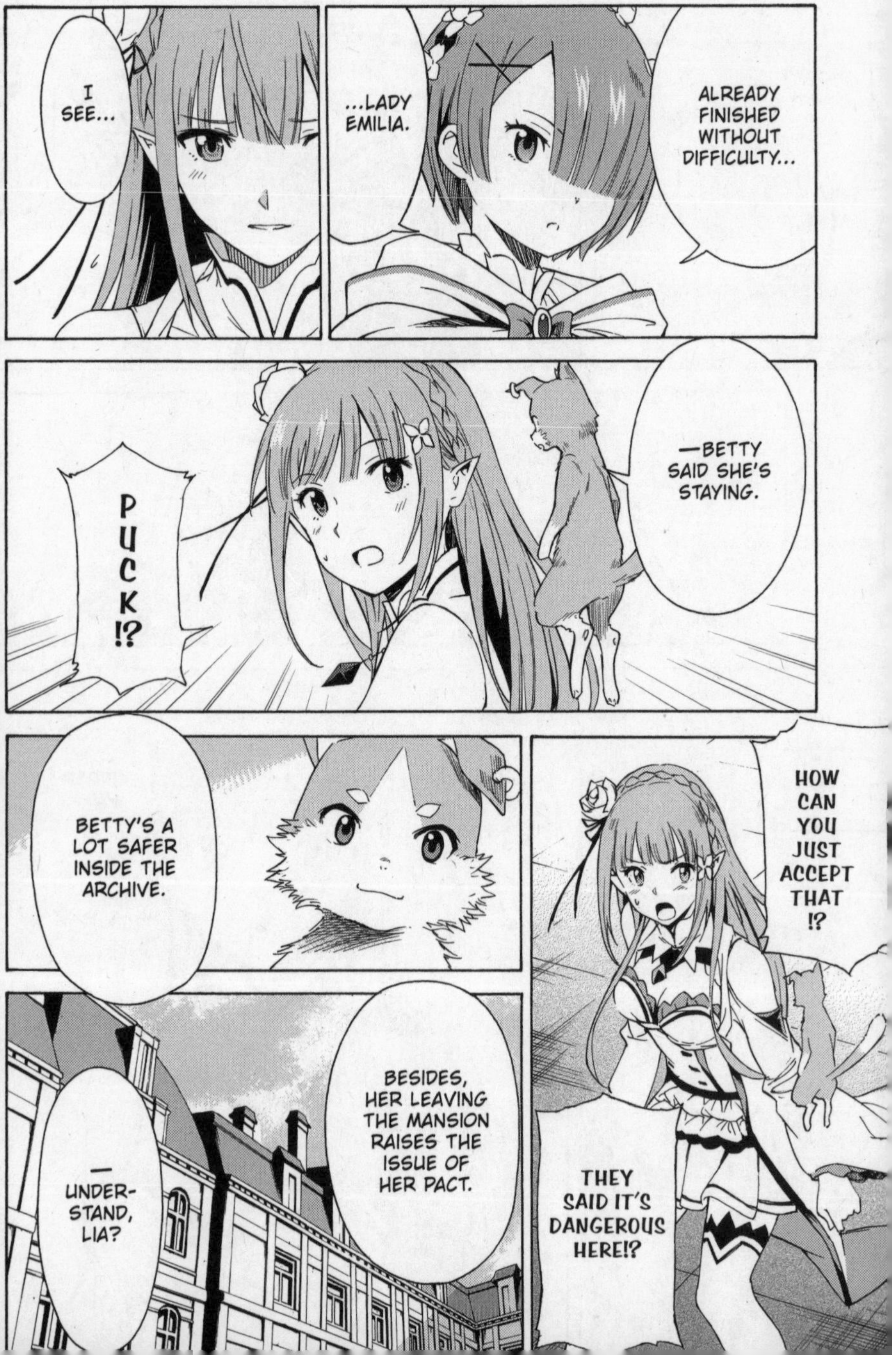
ALREADY FINISHED WITHOUT DIFFICULTY...
...LADY EMILIA.
I SEE...
—BETTY SAID SHE'S STAYING.
PUCK!?
HOW CAN YOU JUST ACCEPT THAT!?
THEY SAID IT'S DANGEROUS HERE!?
BETTY'S A LOT SAFER INSIDE THE ARCHIVE.
BESIDES, HER LEAVING THE MANSION RAISES THE ISSUE OF HER PACT.
—UNDER-STAND, LIA?

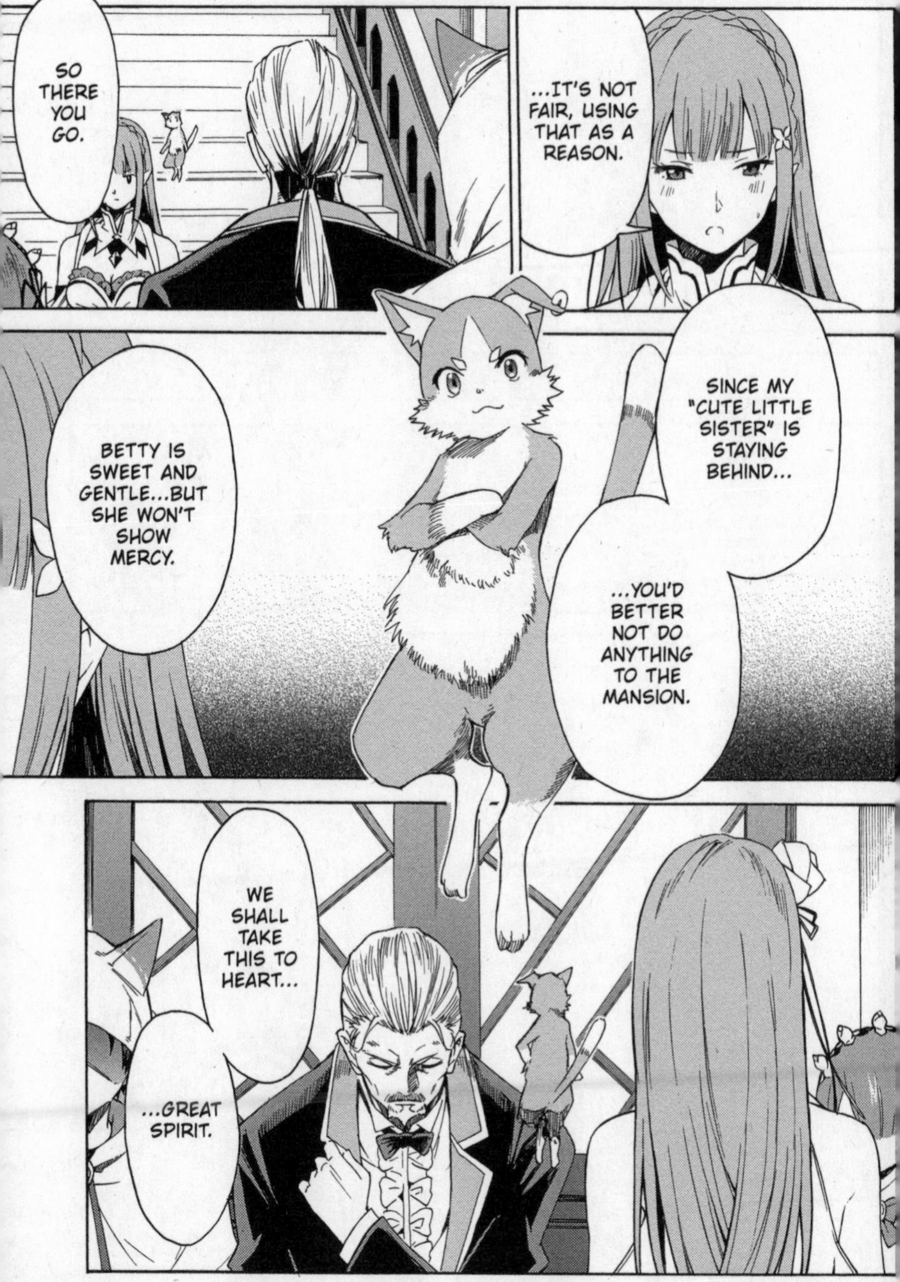
...IT'S NOT FAIR, USING THAT AS A REASON.
SO THERE YOU GO.
SINCE MY "CUTE LITTLE SISTER" IS STAYING BEHIND...
...YOU'D BETTER NOT DO ANYTHING TO THE MANSION.
BETTY IS SWEET AND GENTLE...BUT SHE WON'T SHOW MERCY.
WE SHALL TAKE THIS TO HEART...
...GREAT SPIRIT.

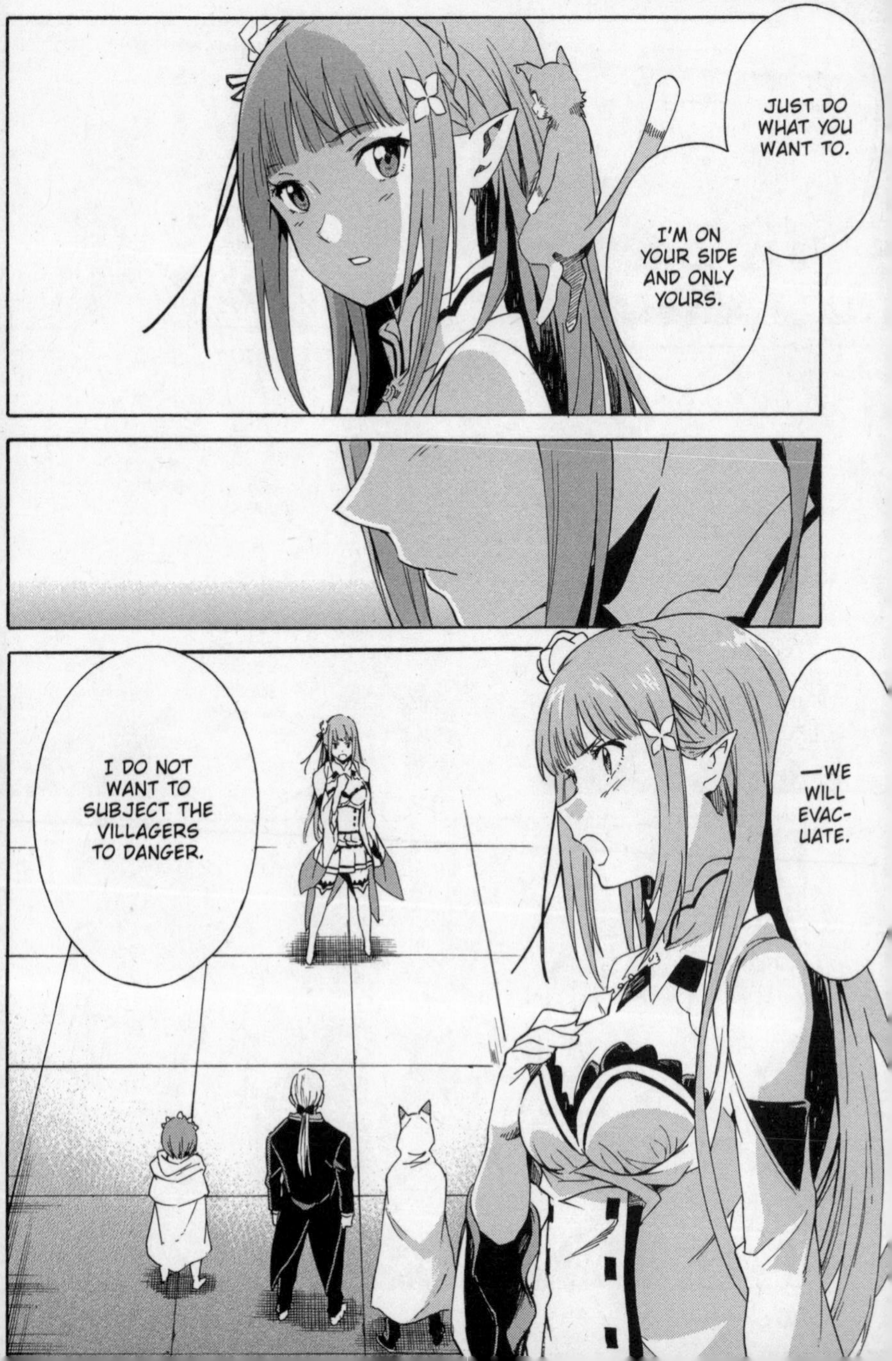
JUST DO WHAT YOU WANT TO.
I'M ON YOUR SIDE AND ONLY YOURS.
—WE WILL EVAC-UATE.
I DO NOT WANT TO SUBJECT THE VILLAGERS TO DANGER.

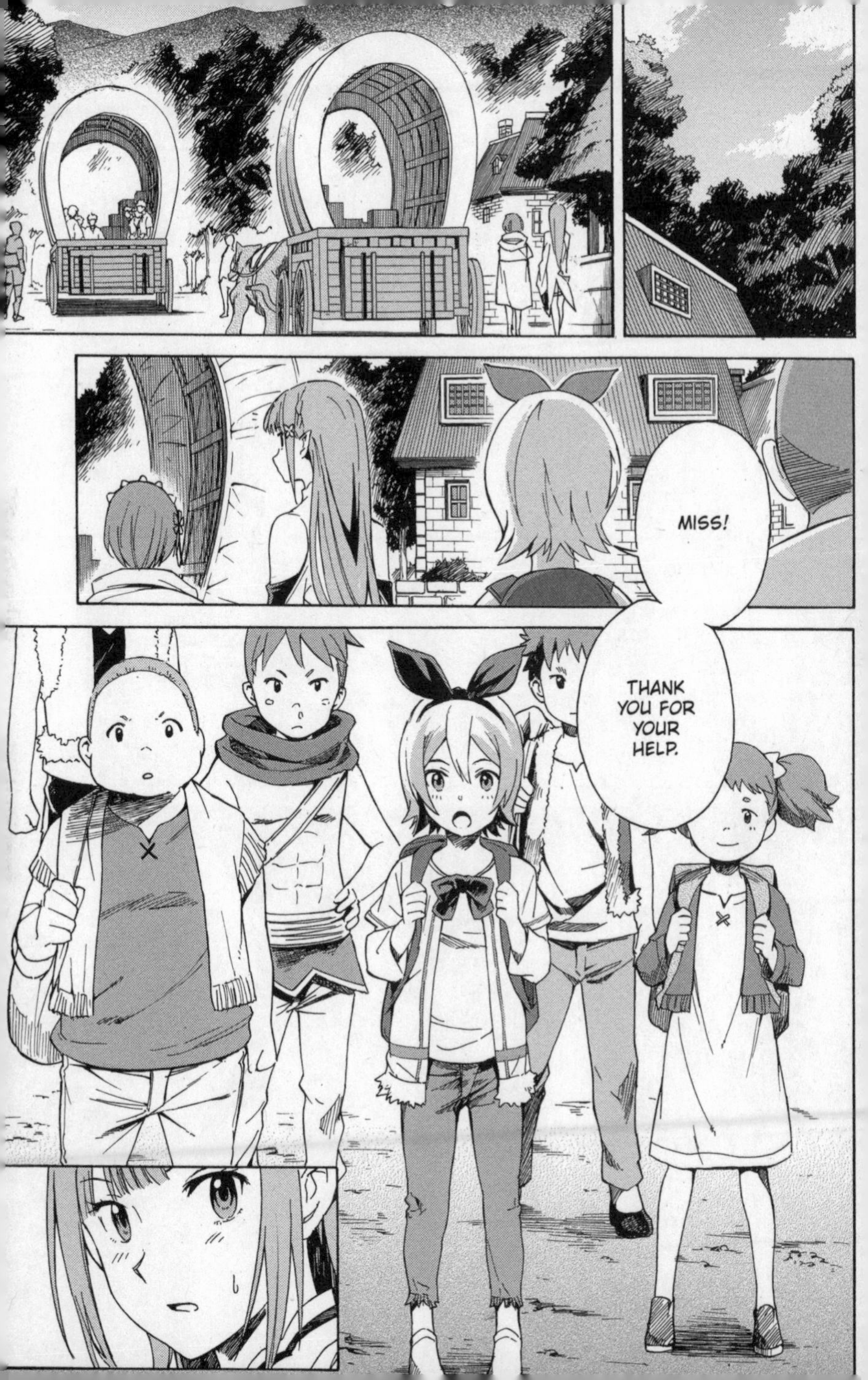
MISS!
THANK YOU FOR YOUR HELP.

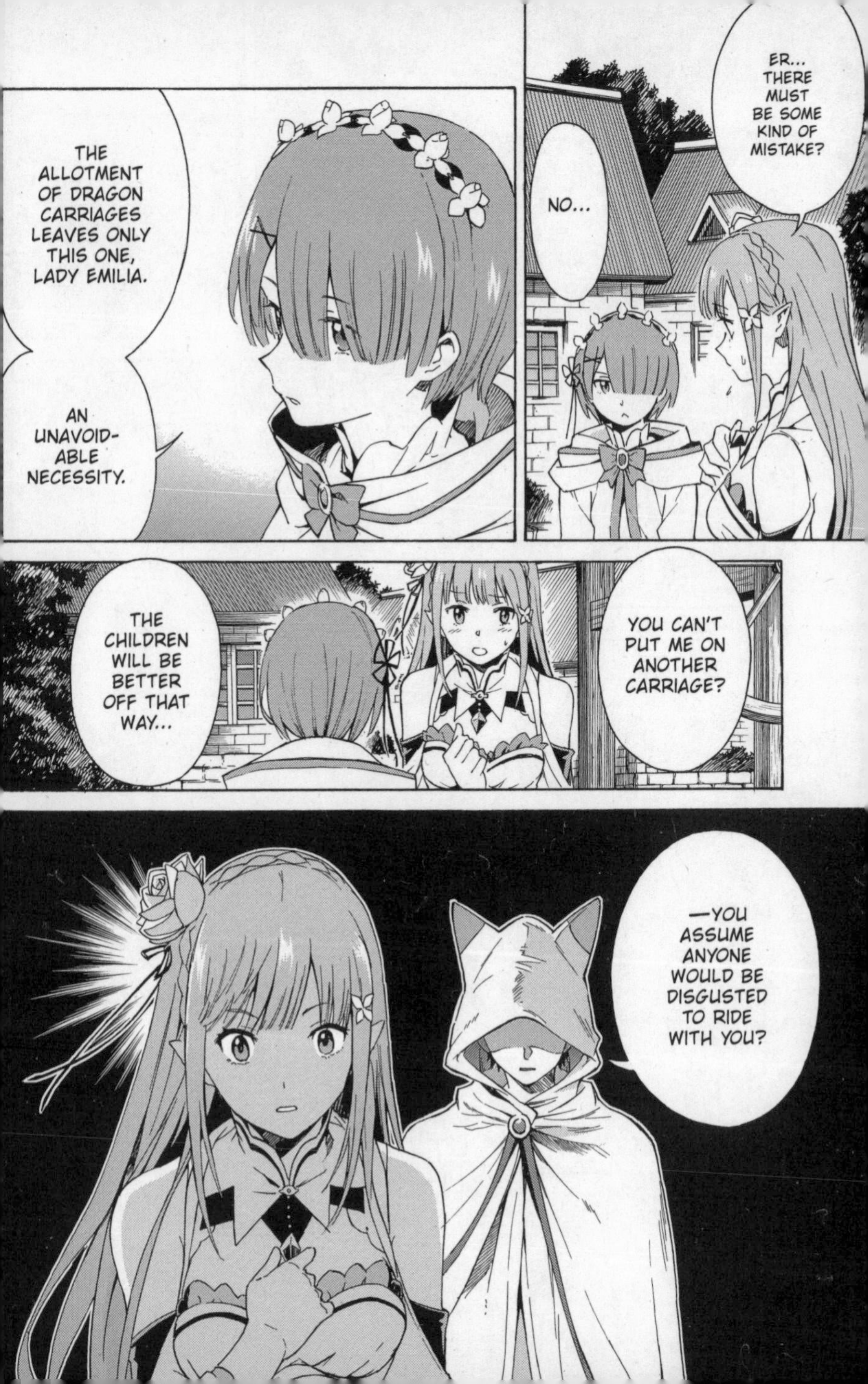
ER... THERE MUST BE SOME KIND OF MISTAKE?
NO...
THE ALLOTMENT OF DRAGON CARRIAGES LEAVES ONLY THIS ONE, LADY EMILIA.
AN UNAVOIDABLE NECESSITY.
YOU CAN'T PUT ME ON ANOTHER CARRIAGE?
THE CHILDREN WILL BE BETTER OFF THAT WAY...
—YOU ASSUME ANYONE WOULD BE DISGUSTED TO RIDE WITH YOU?

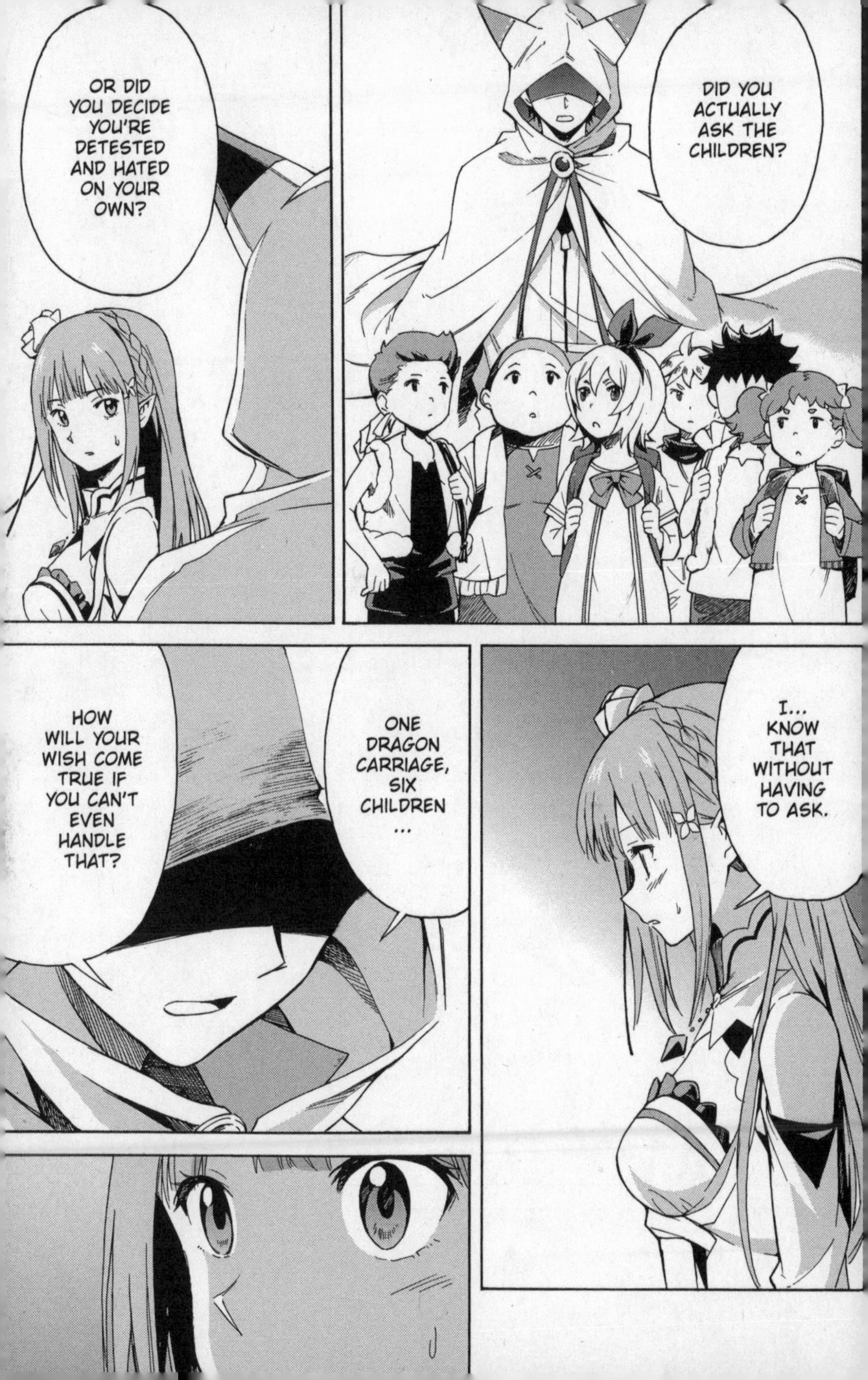
DID YOU ACTUALLY ASK THE CHILDREN?
OR DID YOU DECIDE YOU'RE DETESTED AND HATED ON YOUR OWN?
I... KNOW THAT WITHOUT HAVING TO ASK.
ONE DRAGON CARRIAGE, SIX CHILDREN ...
HOW WILL YOUR WISH COME TRUE IF YOU CAN'T EVEN HANDLE THAT?

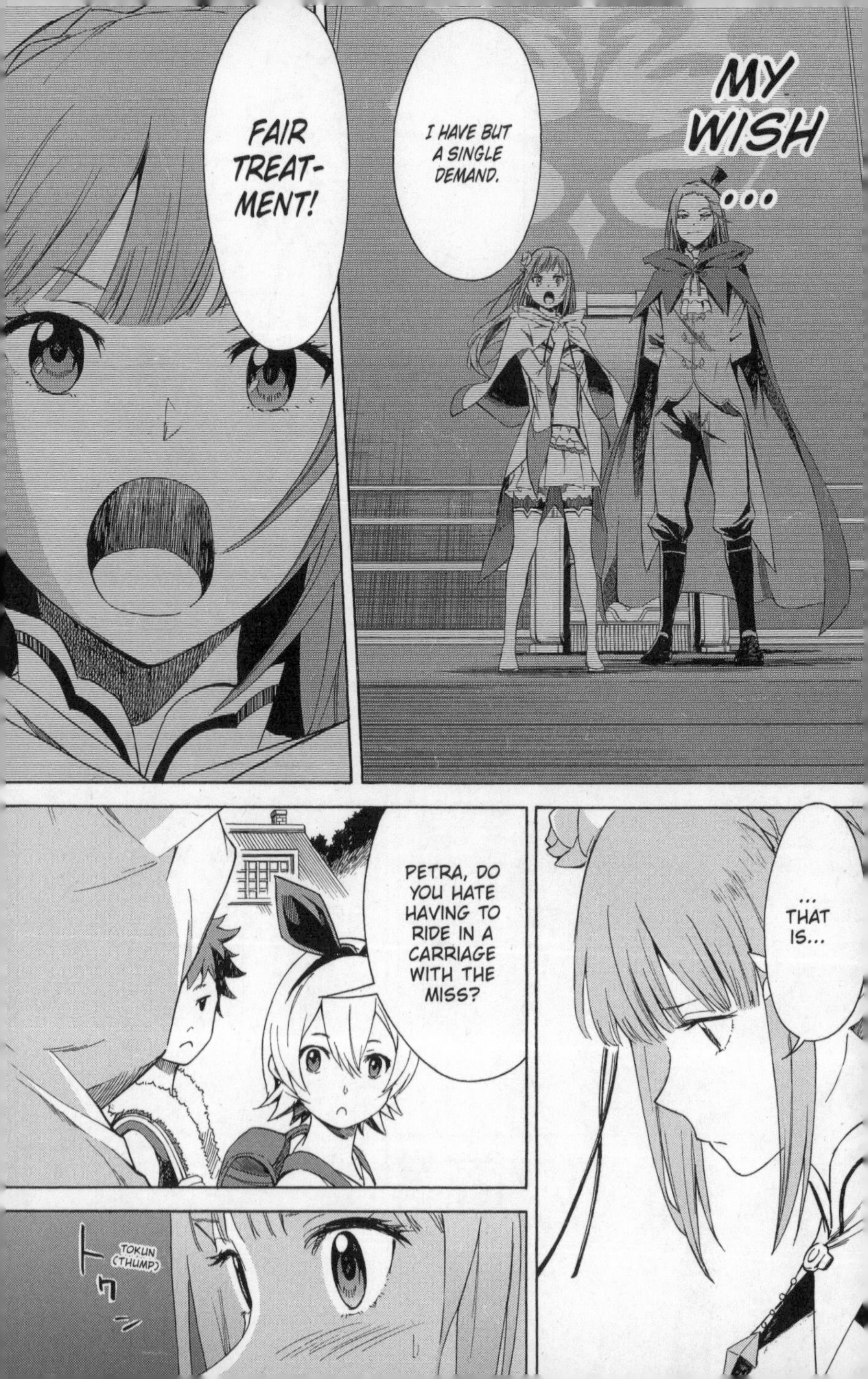
MY WISH...
I HAVE BUT A SINGLE DEMAND.
FAIR TREAT-MENT!
... THAT IS...
PETRA, DO YOU HATE HAVING TO RIDE IN A CARRIAGE WITH THE MISS?
TOKUN (THUMP)

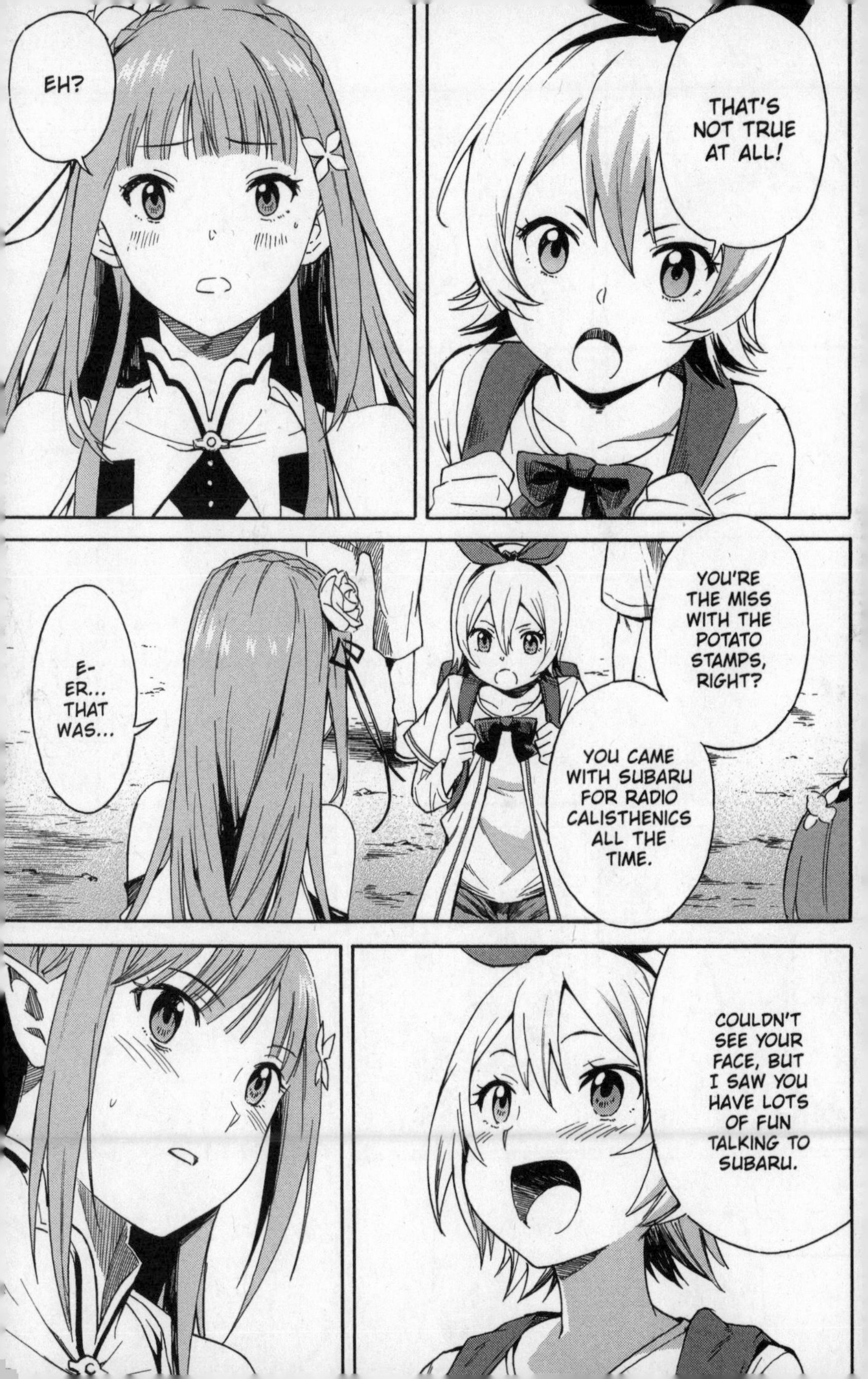
THAT'S NOT TRUE AT ALL!
EH?
YOU'RE THE MISS WITH THE POTATO STAMPS, RIGHT?
YOU CAME WITH SUBARU FOR RADIO CALISTHENICS ALL THE TIME.
E- ER... THAT WAS...
COULDN'T SEE YOUR FACE, BUT I SAW YOU HAVE LOTS OF FUN TALKING TO SUBARU.

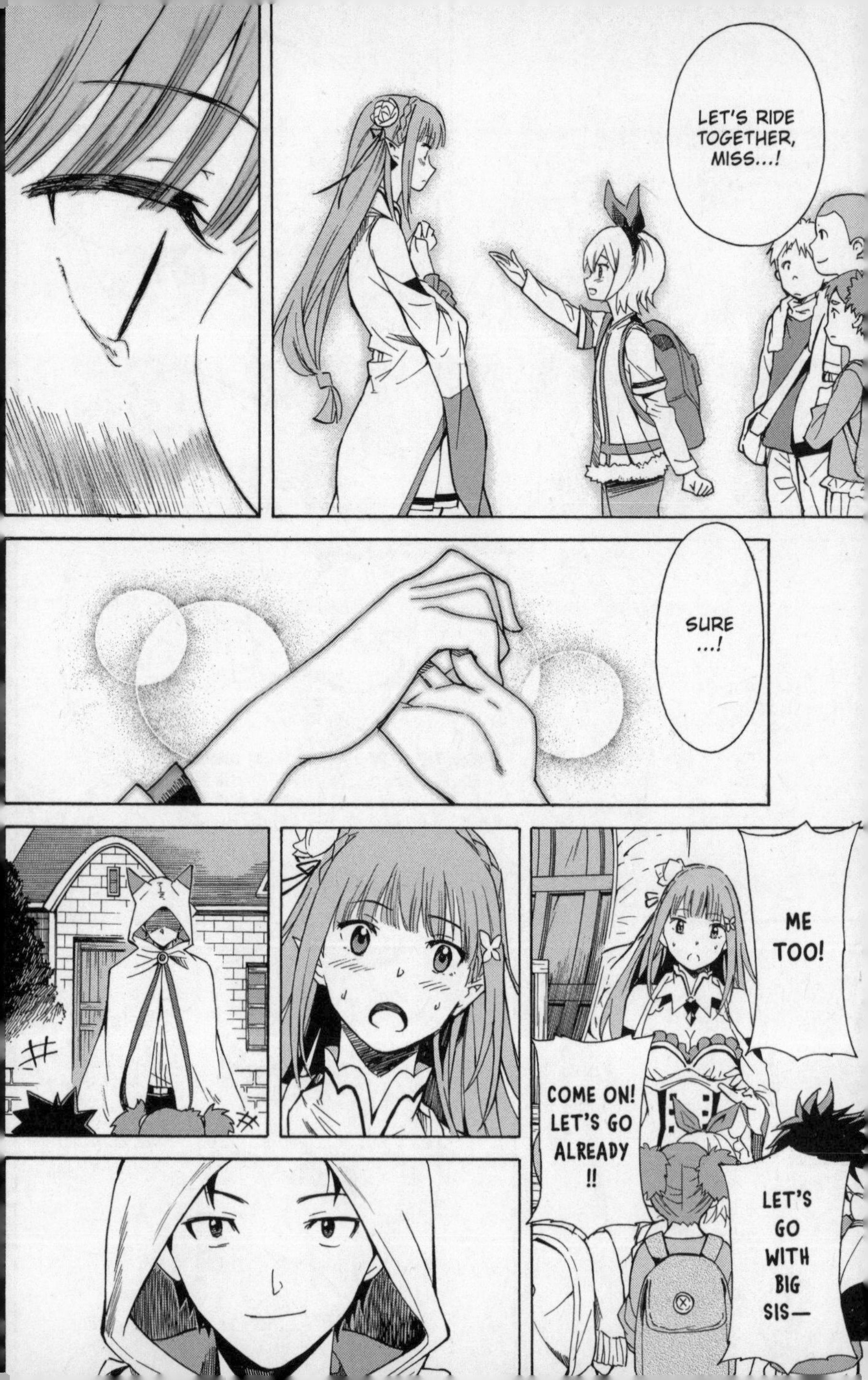
LET'S RIDE TOGETHER, MISS...!
SURE ...!
ME TOO!
COME ON! LET'S GO ALREADY !!
LET'S GO WITH BIG SIS—

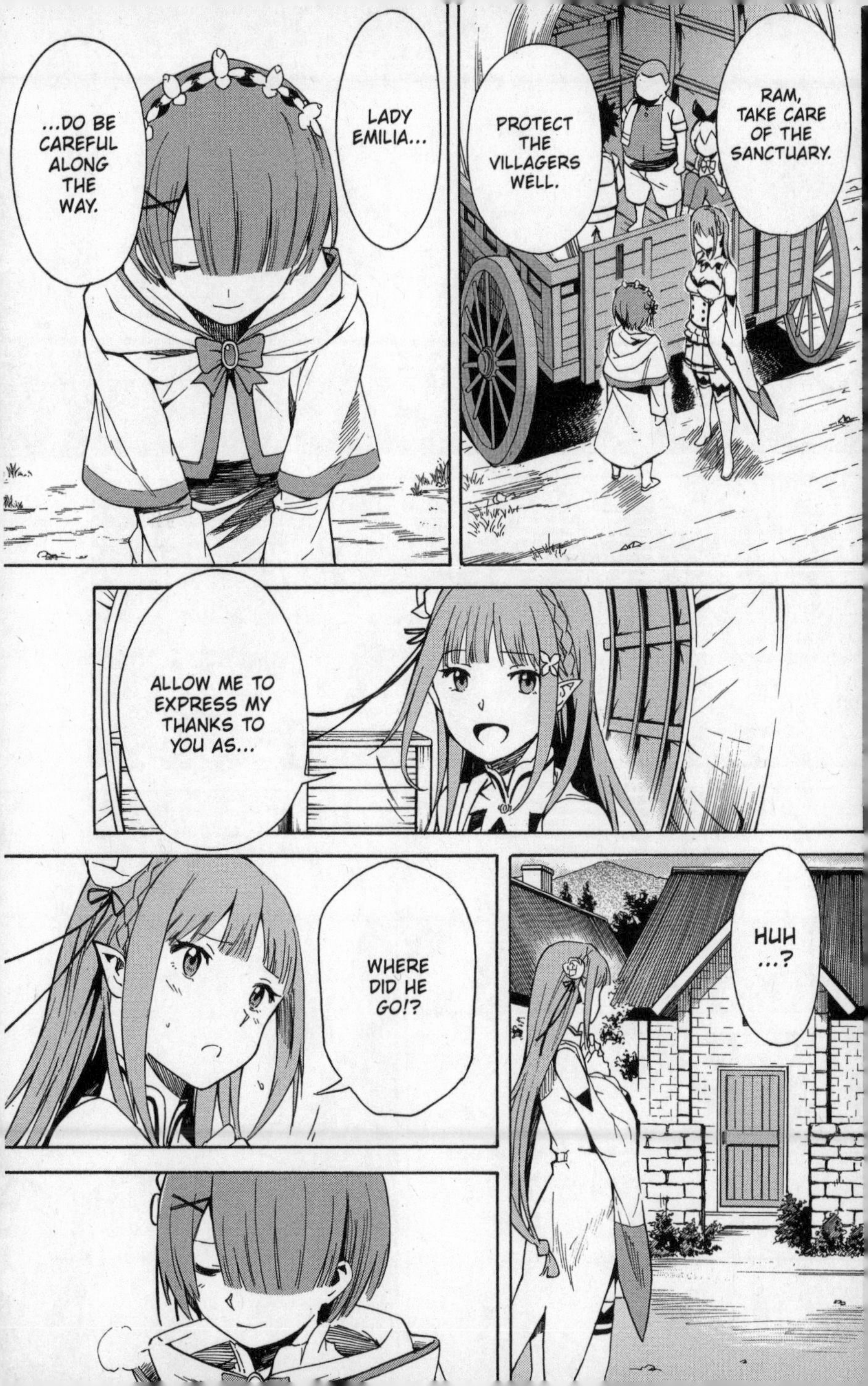
RAM, TAKE CARE OF THE SANCTUARY.
PROTECT THE VILLAGERS WELL.
LADY EMILIA...
...DO BE CAREFUL ALONG THE WAY.
ALLOW ME TO EXPRESS MY THANKS TO YOU AS...
HUH ...?
WHERE DID HE GO!?

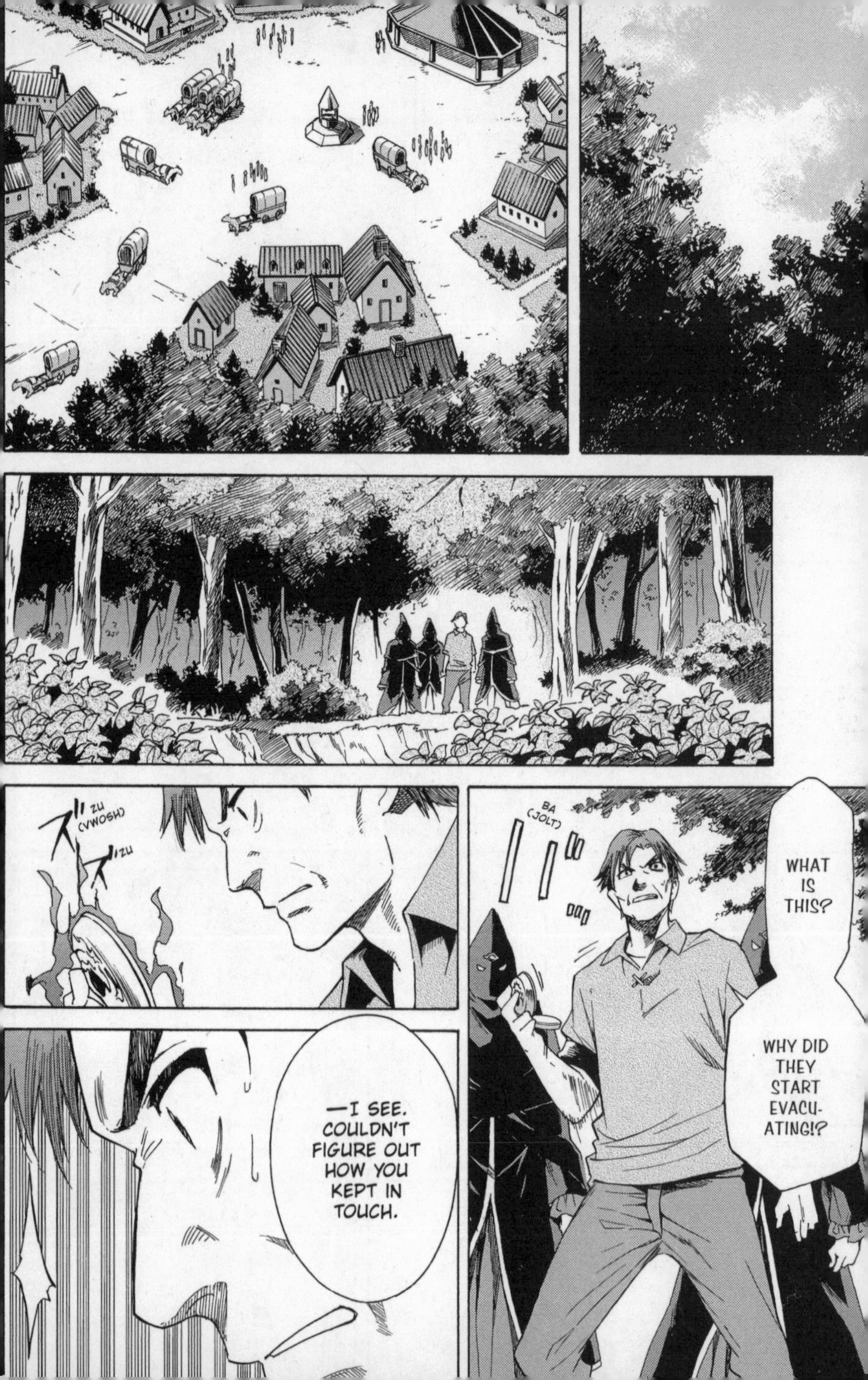
BA (JOLT)
WHAT IS THIS?
WHY DID THEY START EVACU-ATING!?
ZU (VWOSH)
ZU
—I SEE. COULDN'T FIGURE OUT HOW YOU KEPT IN TOUCH.

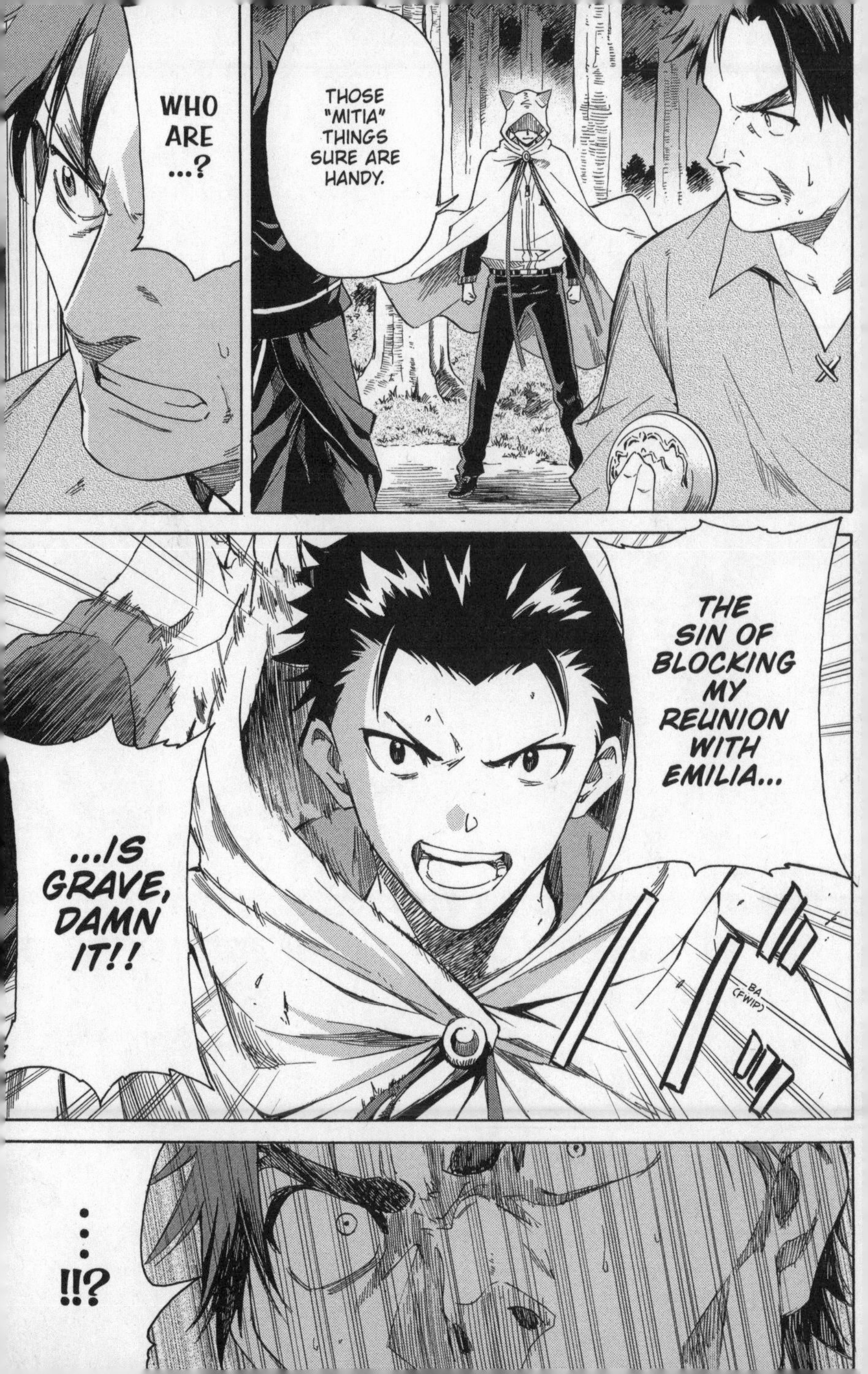
THOSE "MITIA" THINGS SURE ARE HANDY.
WHO ARE ...?
THE SIN OF BLOCKING MY REUNION WITH EMILIA...
...IS GRAVE, DAMN IT!!
BA (FWIP)
...!!?

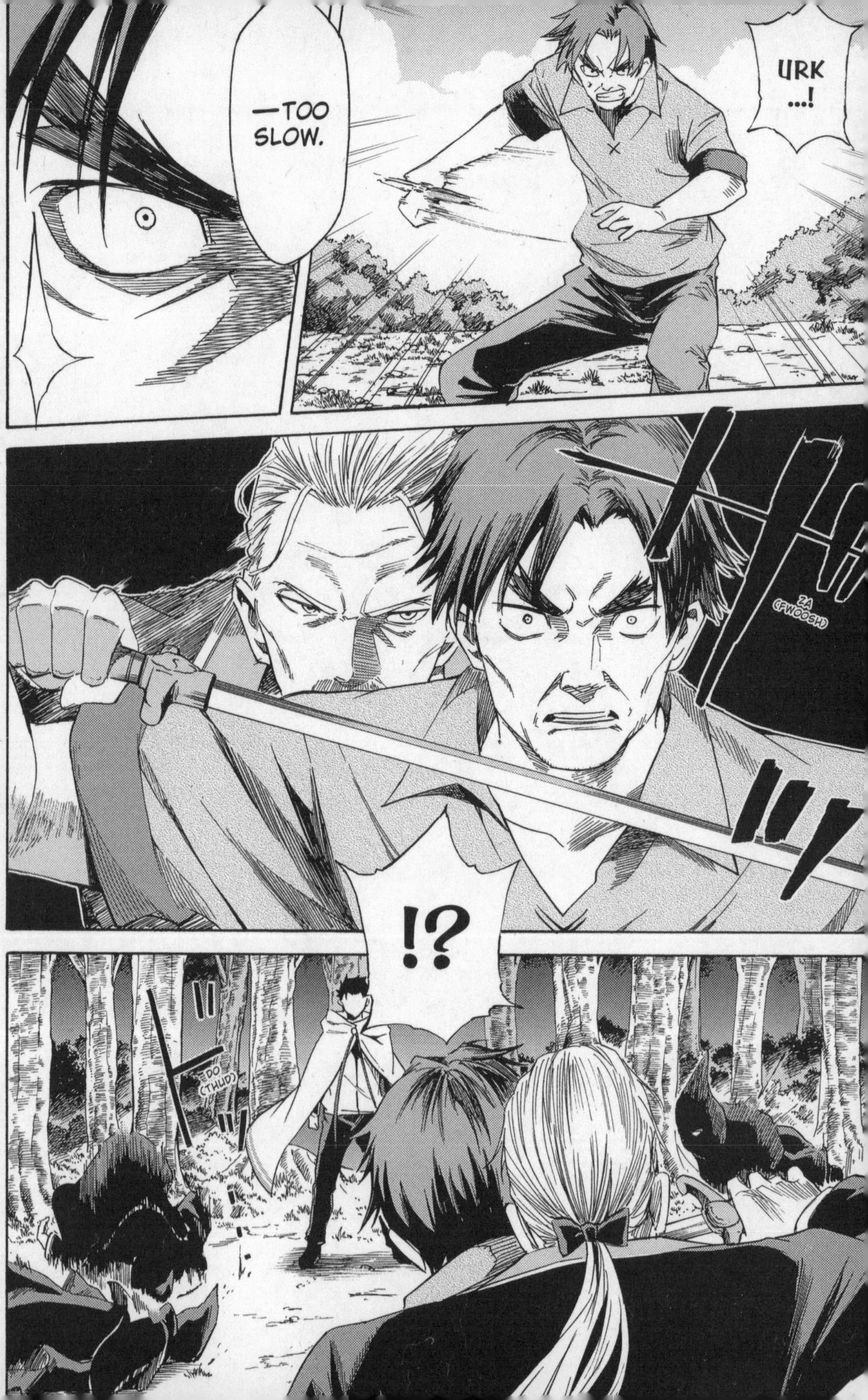
URK ...!
—TOO SLOW.
ZA (FWOOSH)
!?
DO (THUD)

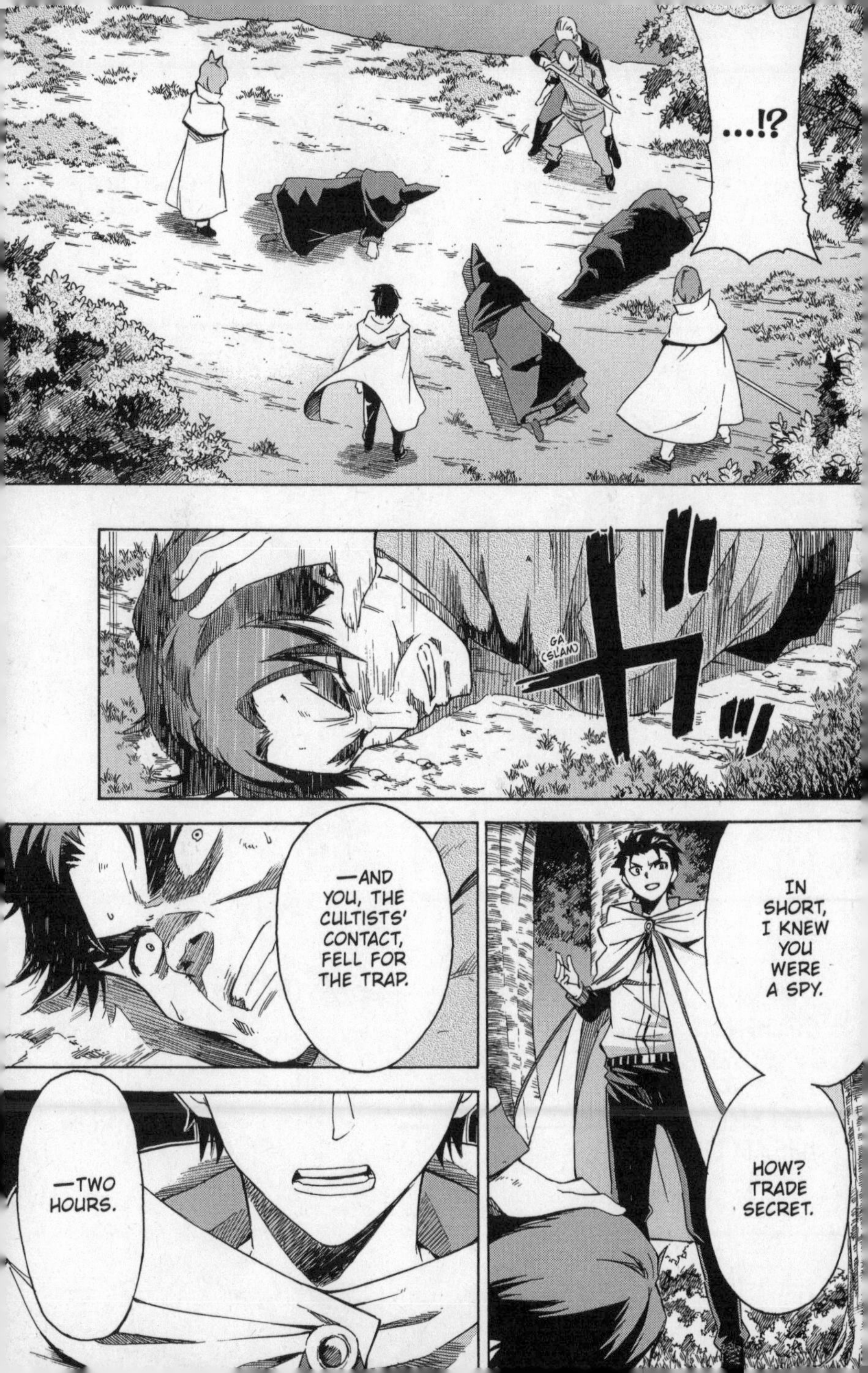
...!?
GA (SLAM)
IN SHORT, I KNEW YOU WERE A SPY.
HOW? TRADE SECRET.
—AND YOU, THE CULTISTS' CONTACT, FELL FOR THE TRAP.
—TWO HOURS.

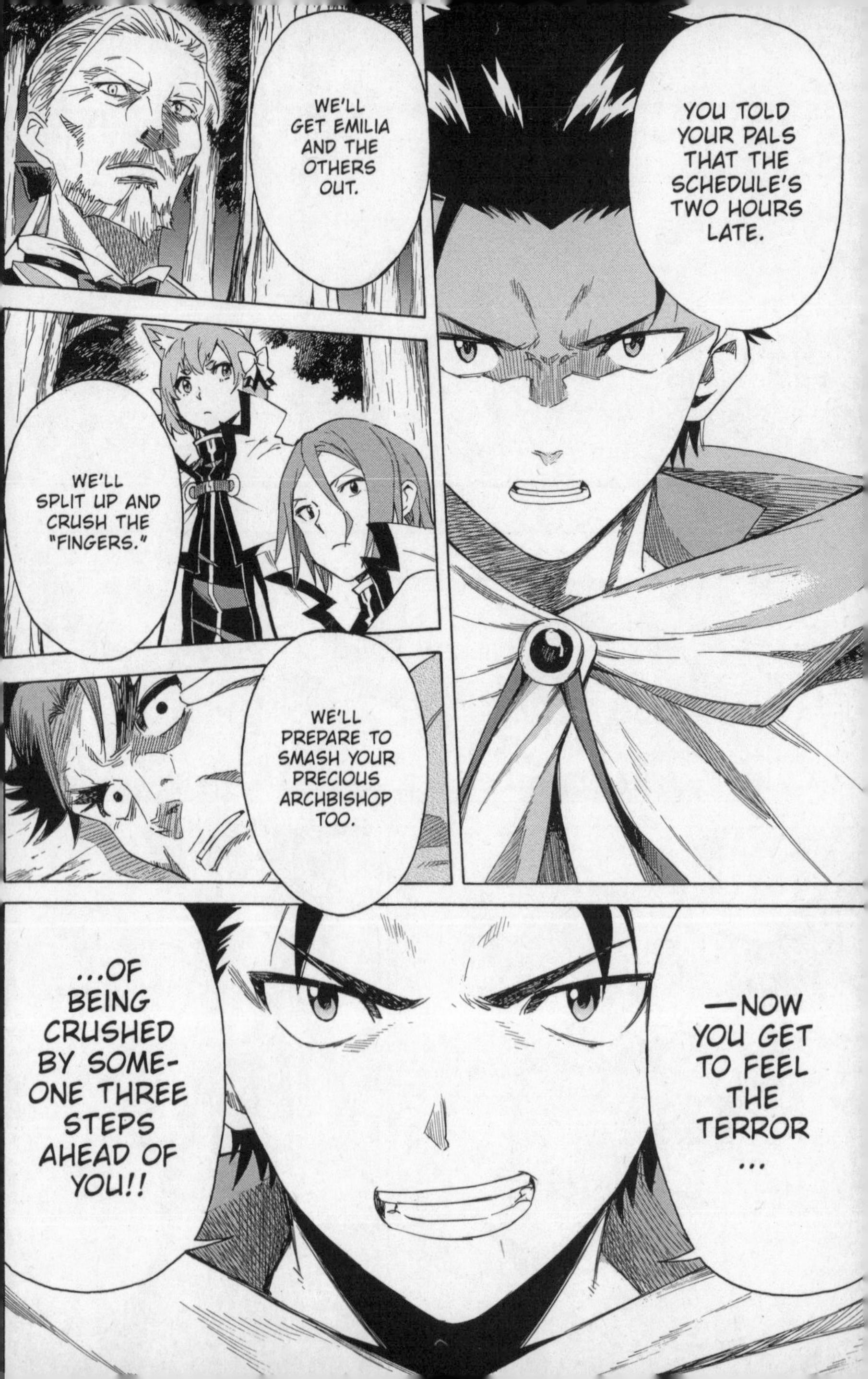
YOU TOLD YOUR PALS THAT THE SCHEDULE'S TWO HOURS LATE.
WE'LL GET EMILIA AND THE OTHERS OUT.
WE'LL SPLIT UP AND CRUSH THE "FINGERS."
WE'LL PREPARE TO SMASH YOUR PRECIOUS ARCHBISHOP TOO.
—NOW YOU GET TO FEEL THE TERROR...
...OF BEING CRUSHED BY SOME-ONE THREE STEPS AHEAD OF YOU!!

Re:ZERO -Starting Life in Another World-

The only ability Subaru Natsuki gets when he's summoned to another world is time travel via his own death. But to save her, he'll die as many times as it takes.

Truth of Zero

The only ability Subaru Natsuki gets when he's
summoned to another world is time travel via his own
death. But to save her, he'll die as many times as it takes.

Re:ZERO -Starting
Life in Another World-

Episode 42
The Madman and the Supporting Actor

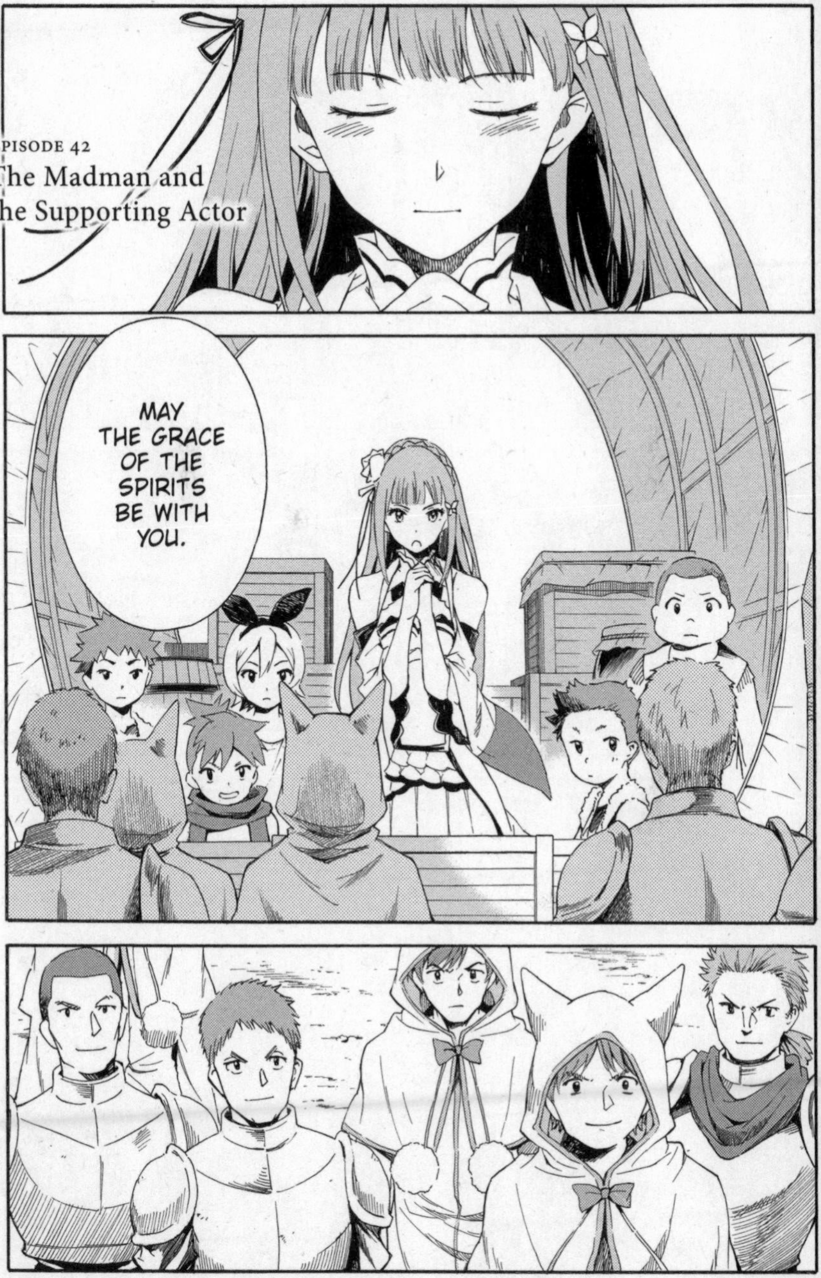
MAY THE GRACE OF THE SPIRITS BE WITH YOU.

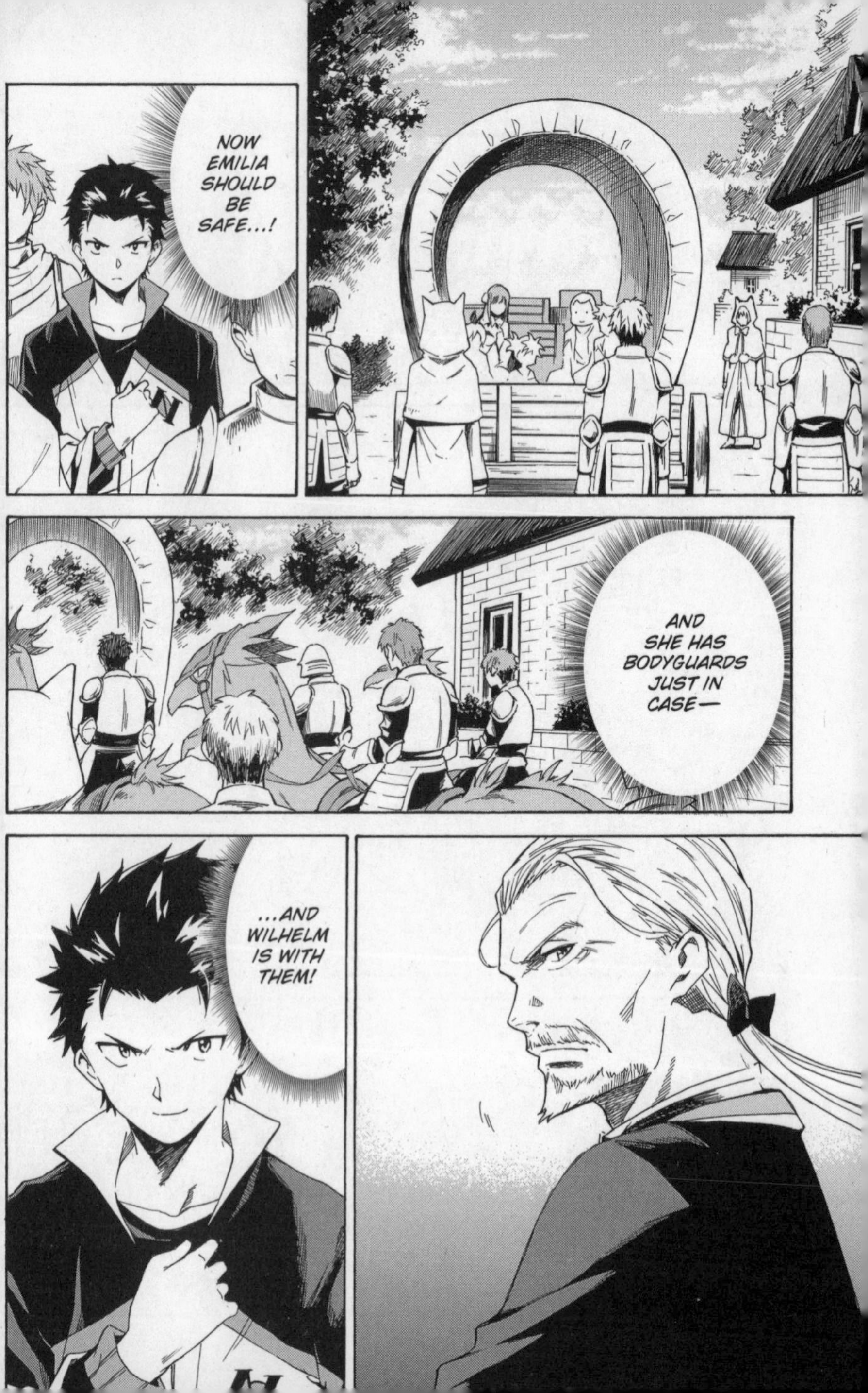
NOW EMILIA SHOULD BE SAFE...!
AND SHE HAS BODYGUARDS JUST IN CASE—
...AND WILHELM IS WITH THEM!

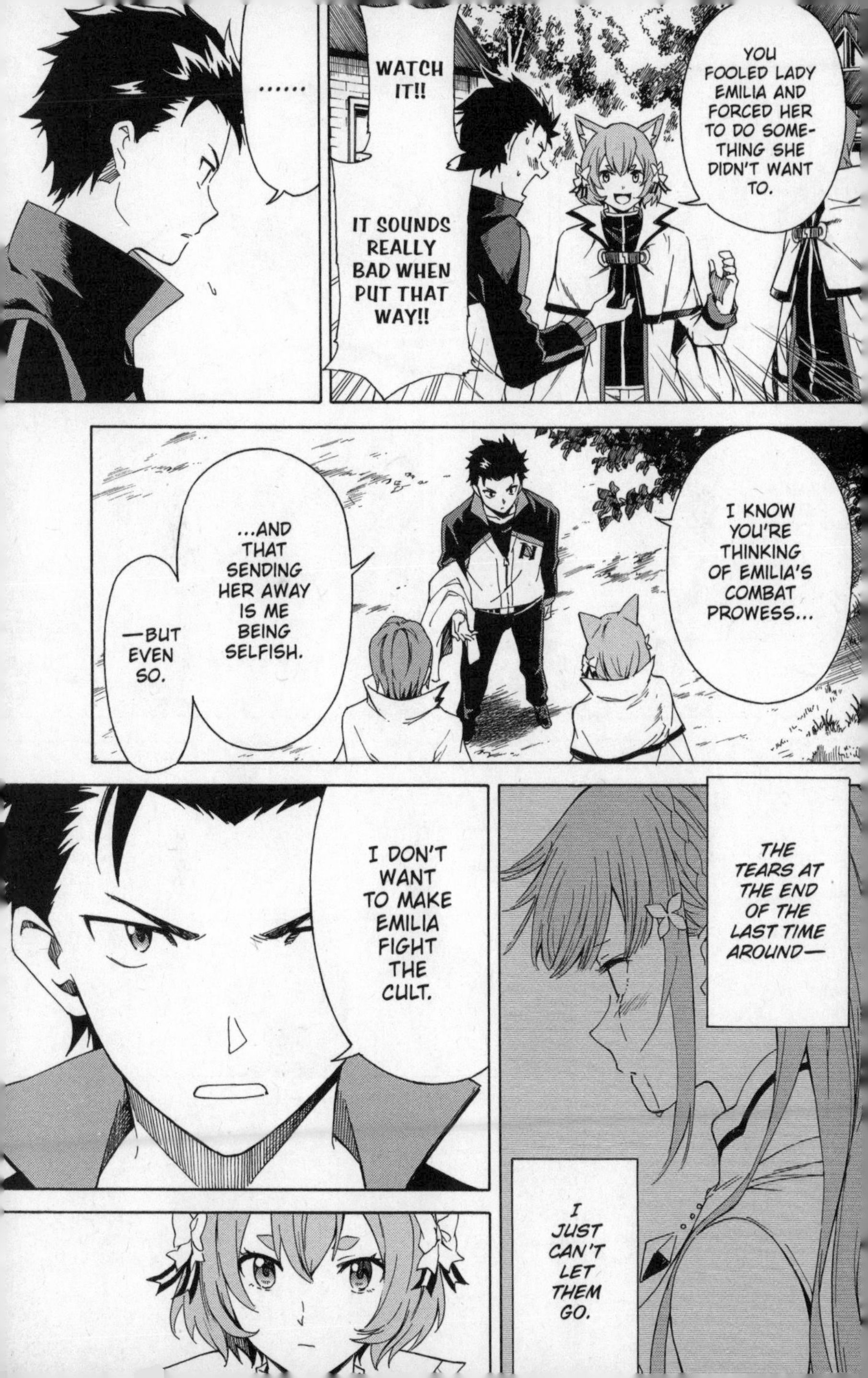
YOU FOOLED LADY EMILIA AND FORCED HER TO DO SOME-THING SHE DIDN'T WANT TO.
WATCH IT!!
IT SOUNDS REALLY BAD WHEN PUT THAT WAY!!
......
I KNOW YOU'RE THINKING OF EMILIA'S COMBAT PROWESS...
...AND THAT SENDING HER AWAY IS ME BEING SELFISH.
—BUT EVEN SO.
THE TEARS AT THE END OF THE LAST TIME AROUND—
I JUST CAN'T LET THEM GO.
I DON'T WANT TO MAKE EMILIA FIGHT THE CULT.

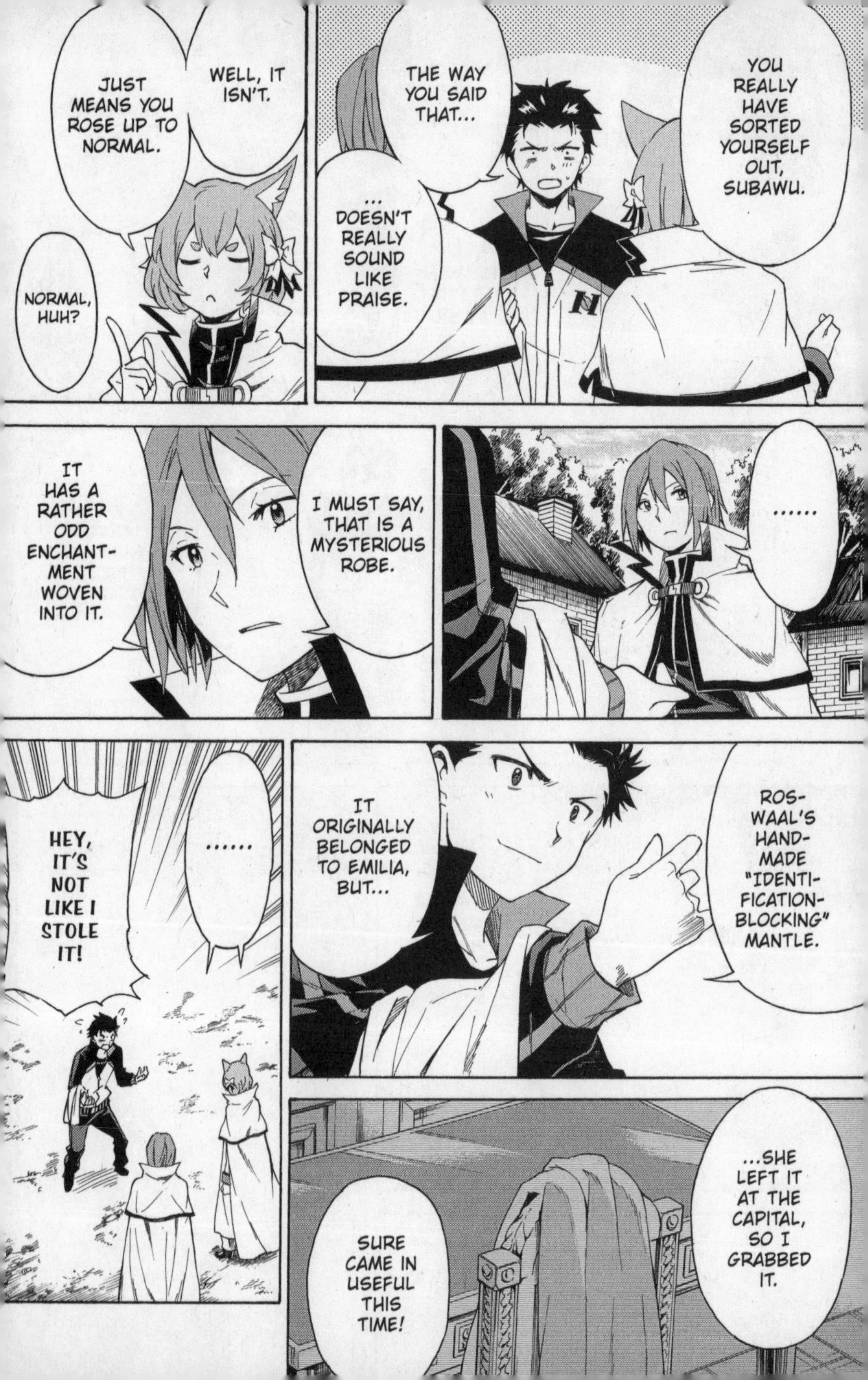
YOU REALLY HAVE SORTED YOURSELF OUT, SUBAWU.
THE WAY YOU SAID THAT...
...DOESN'T REALLY SOUND LIKE PRAISE.
WELL, IT ISN'T.
JUST MEANS YOU ROSE UP TO NORMAL.
NORMAL, HUH?
......
I MUST SAY, THAT IS A MYSTERIOUS ROBE.
IT HAS A RATHER ODD ENCHANTMENT WOVEN INTO IT.
ROSWAAL'S HANDMADE "IDENTIFICATION-BLOCKING" MANTLE.
IT ORIGINALLY BELONGED TO EMILIA, BUT...
...SHE LEFT IT AT THE CAPITAL, SO I GRABBED IT.
SURE CAME IN USEFUL THIS TIME!
......
HEY, IT'S NOT LIKE I STOLE IT!

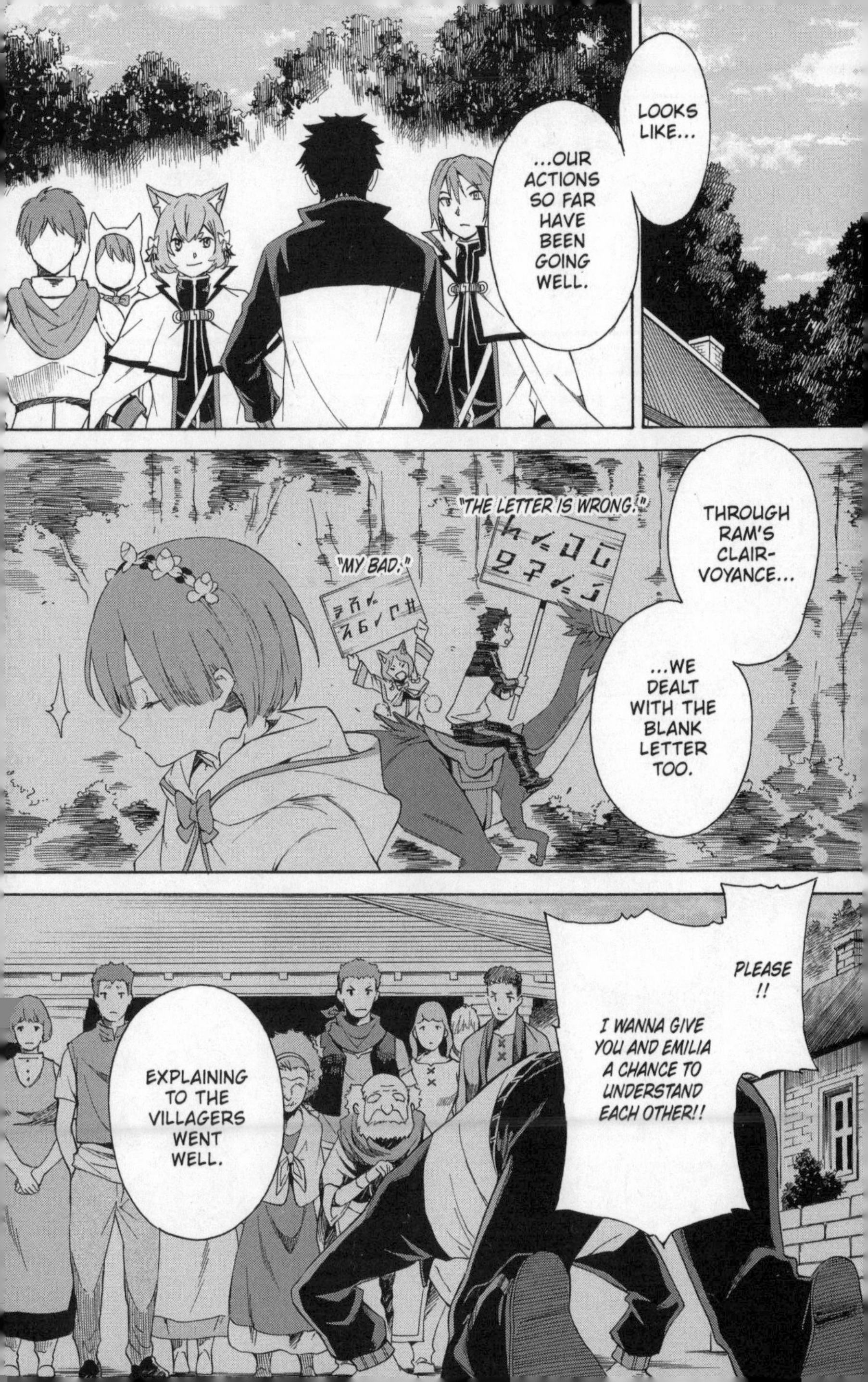
LOOKS LIKE...
...OUR ACTIONS SO FAR HAVE BEEN GOING WELL.
THROUGH RAM'S CLAIR-VOYANCE...
...WE DEALT WITH THE BLANK LETTER TOO.
"THE LETTER IS WRONG."
"MY BAD."
PLEASE !!
I WANNA GIVE YOU AND EMILIA A CHANCE TO UNDERSTAND EACH OTHER!!
EXPLAINING TO THE VILLAGERS WENT WELL.

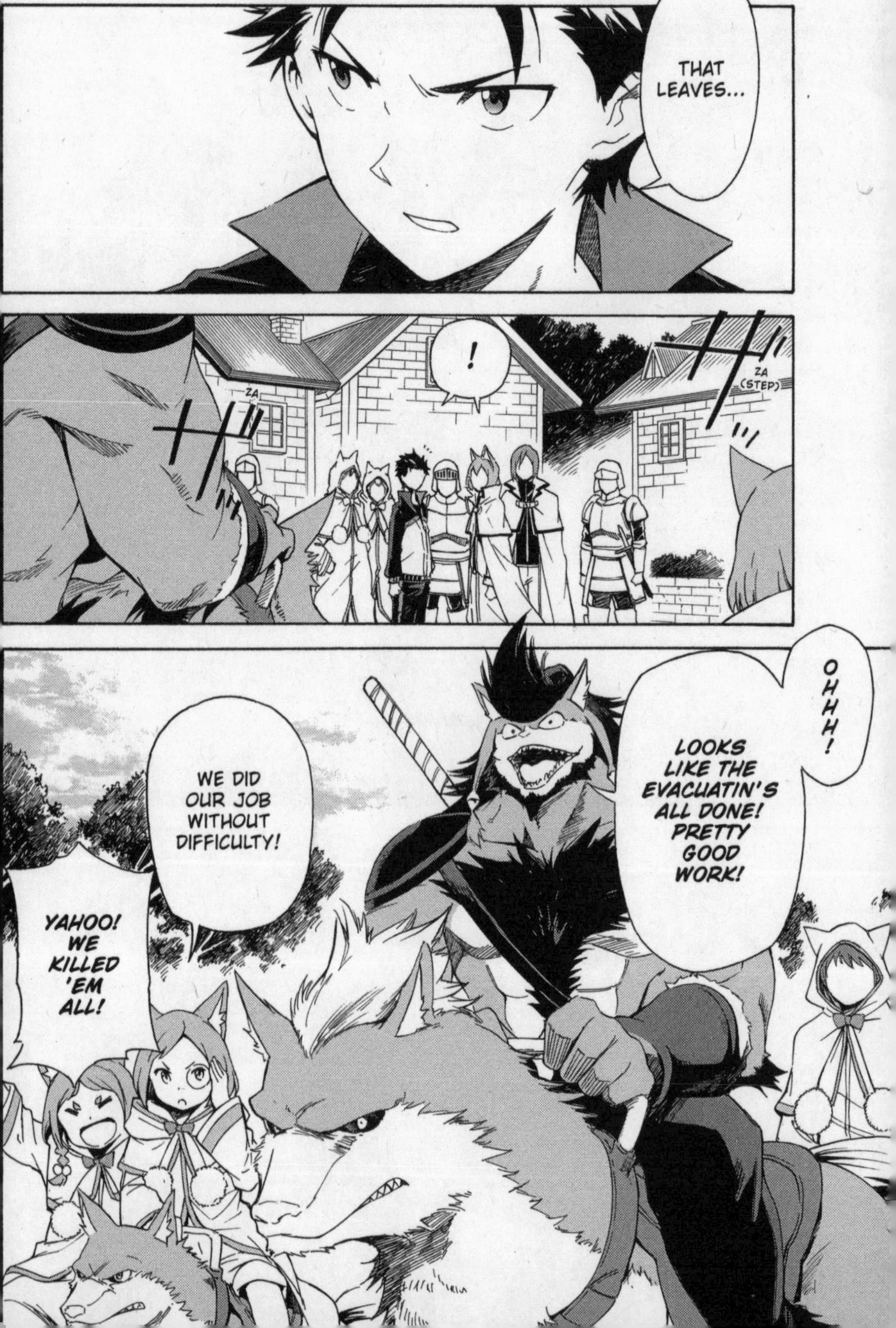
THAT LEAVES...
ZA (STEP)
!
ZA
OHHH!
LOOKS LIKE THE EVACUATIN'S ALL DONE! PRETTY GOOD WORK!
WE DID OUR JOB WITHOUT DIFFICULTY!
YAHOO! WE KILLED 'EM ALL!

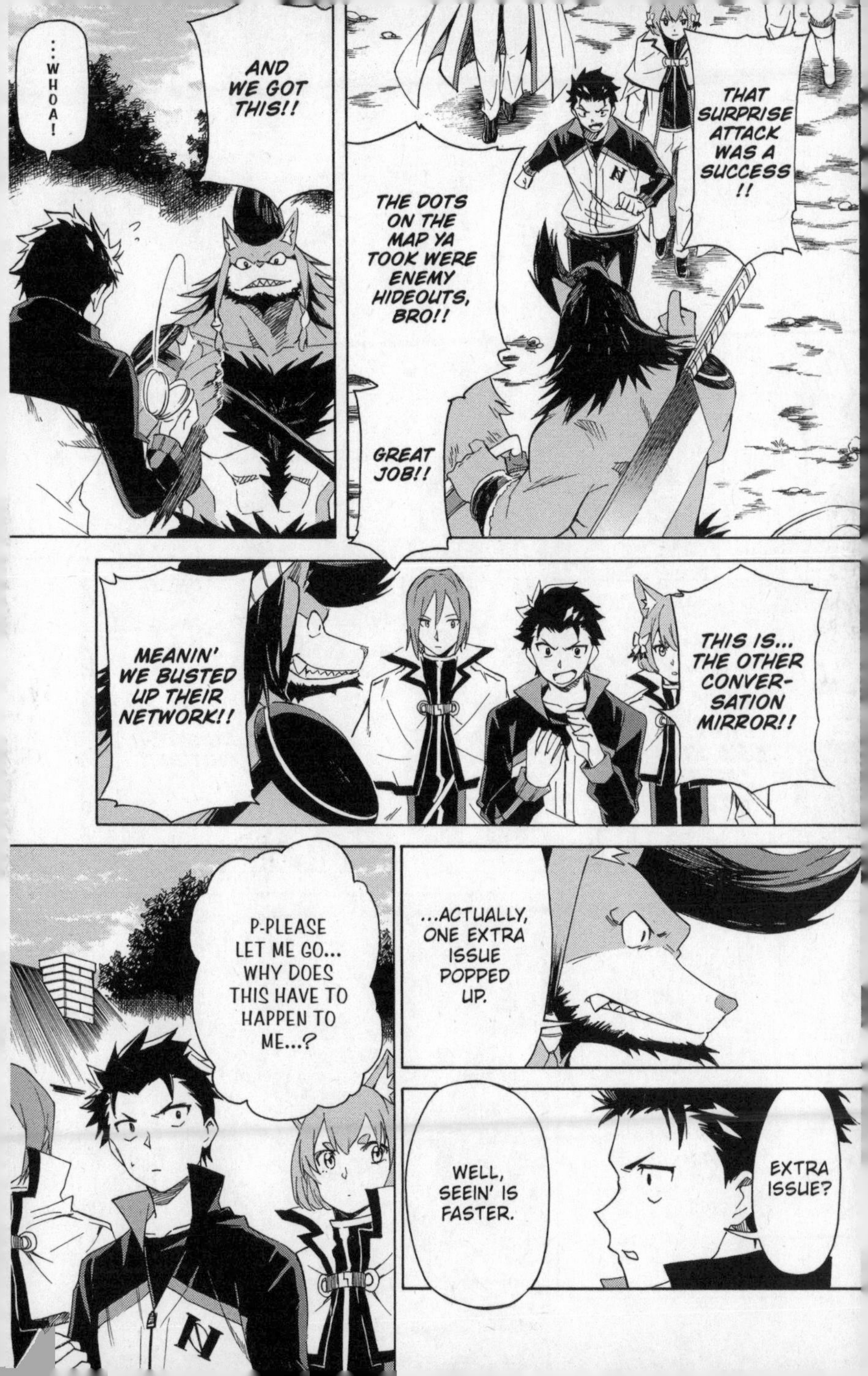
THAT SURPRISE ATTACK WAS A SUCCESS!!
THE DOTS ON THE MAP YA TOOK WERE ENEMY HIDEOUTS, BRO!!
GREAT JOB!!
AND WE GOT THIS!!
...WHOA!
THIS IS... THE OTHER CONVERSATION MIRROR!!
MEANIN' WE BUSTED UP THEIR NETWORK!!
...ACTUALLY, ONE EXTRA ISSUE POPPED UP.
EXTRA ISSUE?
WELL, SEEIN' IS FASTER.
P-PLEASE LET ME GO... WHY DOES THIS HAVE TO HAPPEN TO ME...?

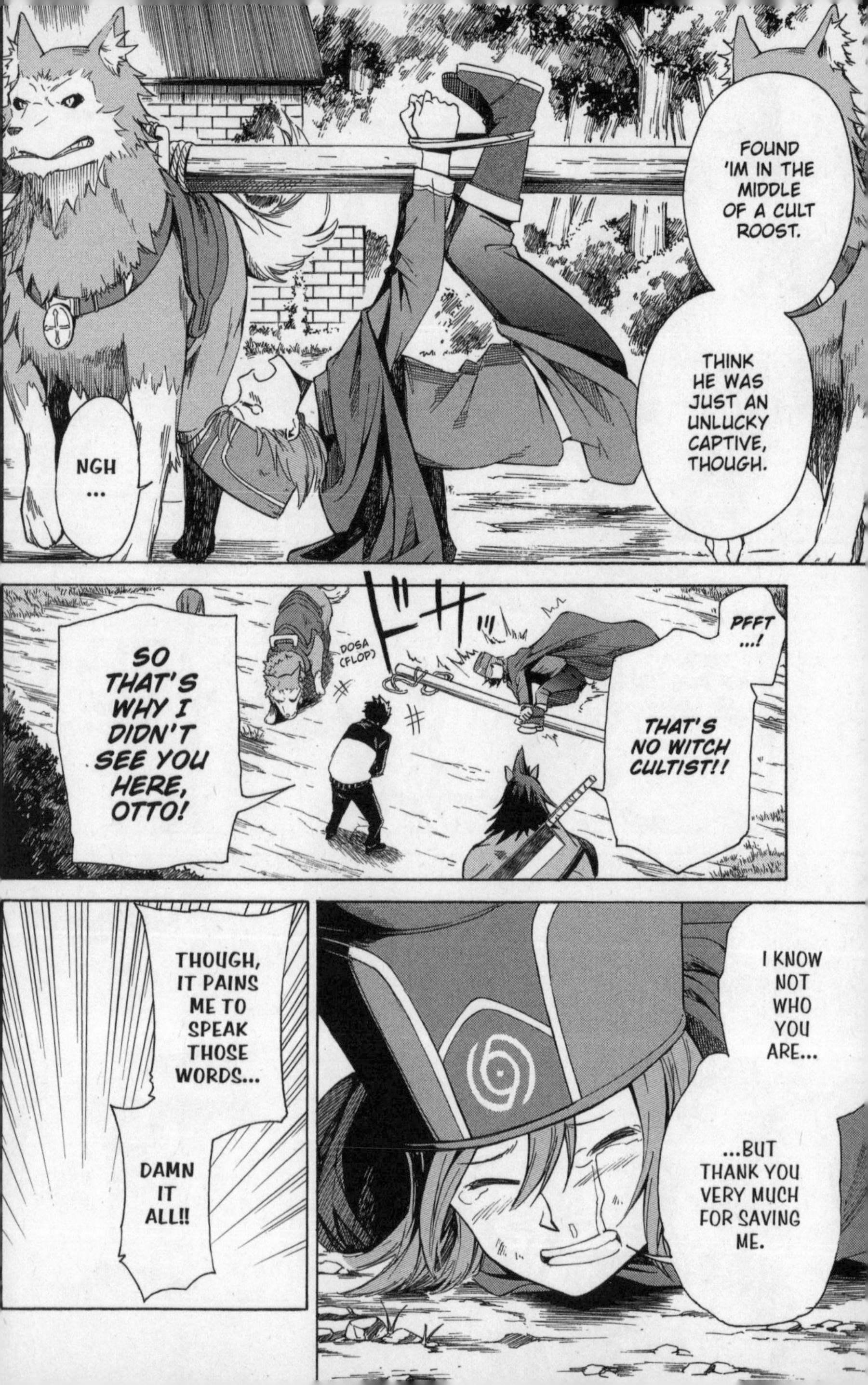
FOUND 'IM IN THE MIDDLE OF A CULT ROOST.
THINK HE WAS JUST AN UNLUCKY CAPTIVE, THOUGH.
NGH ...
PFFT ...!
ドサ
DOSA (FLOP)
THAT'S NO WITCH CULTIST!!
SO THAT'S WHY I DIDN'T SEE YOU HERE, OTTO!
I KNOW NOT WHO YOU ARE...
...BUT THANK YOU VERY MUCH FOR SAVING ME.
THOUGH, IT PAINS ME TO SPEAK THOSE WORDS...
DAMN IT ALL!!

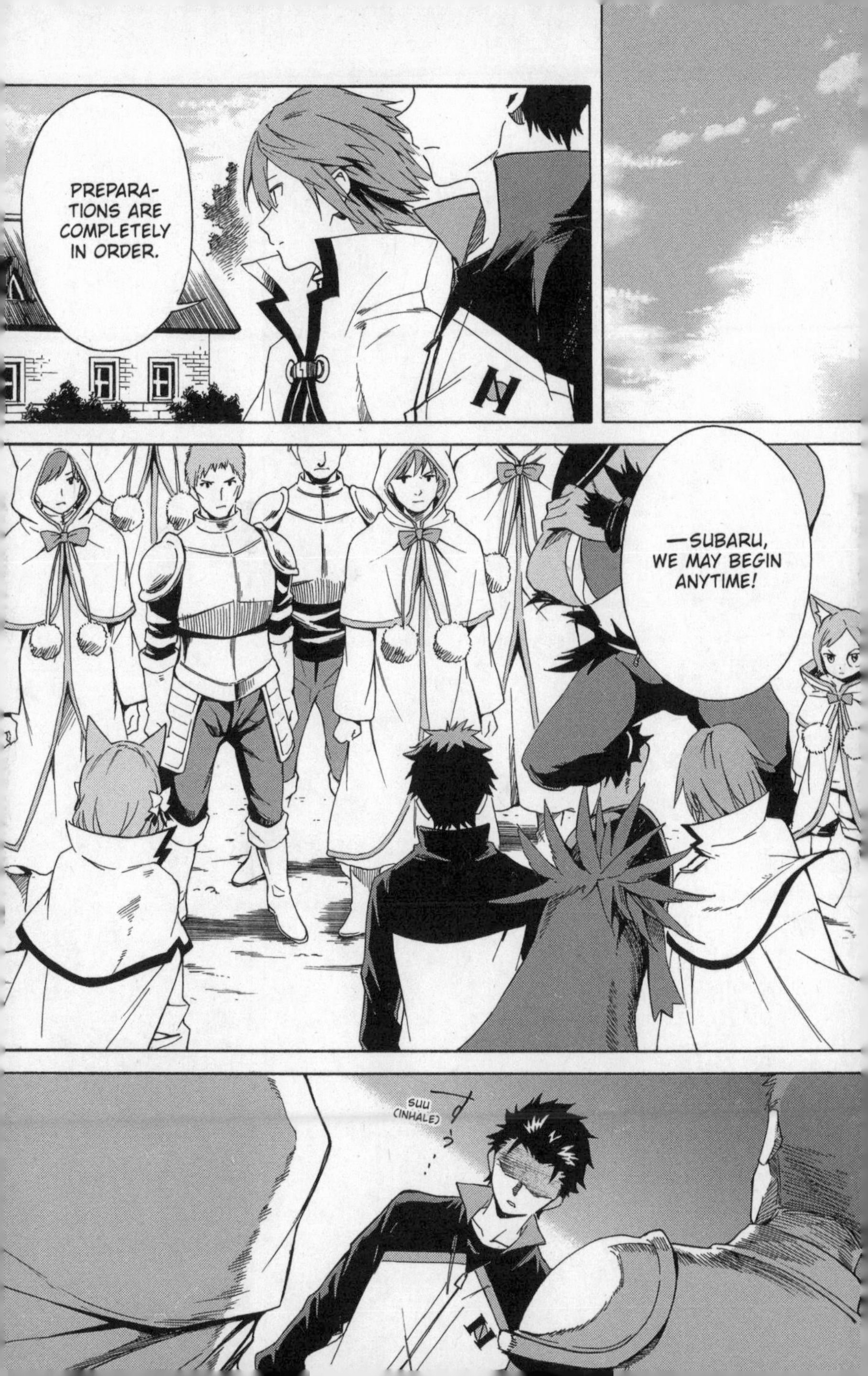
PREPARA-TIONS ARE COMPLETELY IN ORDER.
—SUBARU, WE MAY BEGIN ANYTIME!
SUU (INHALE)

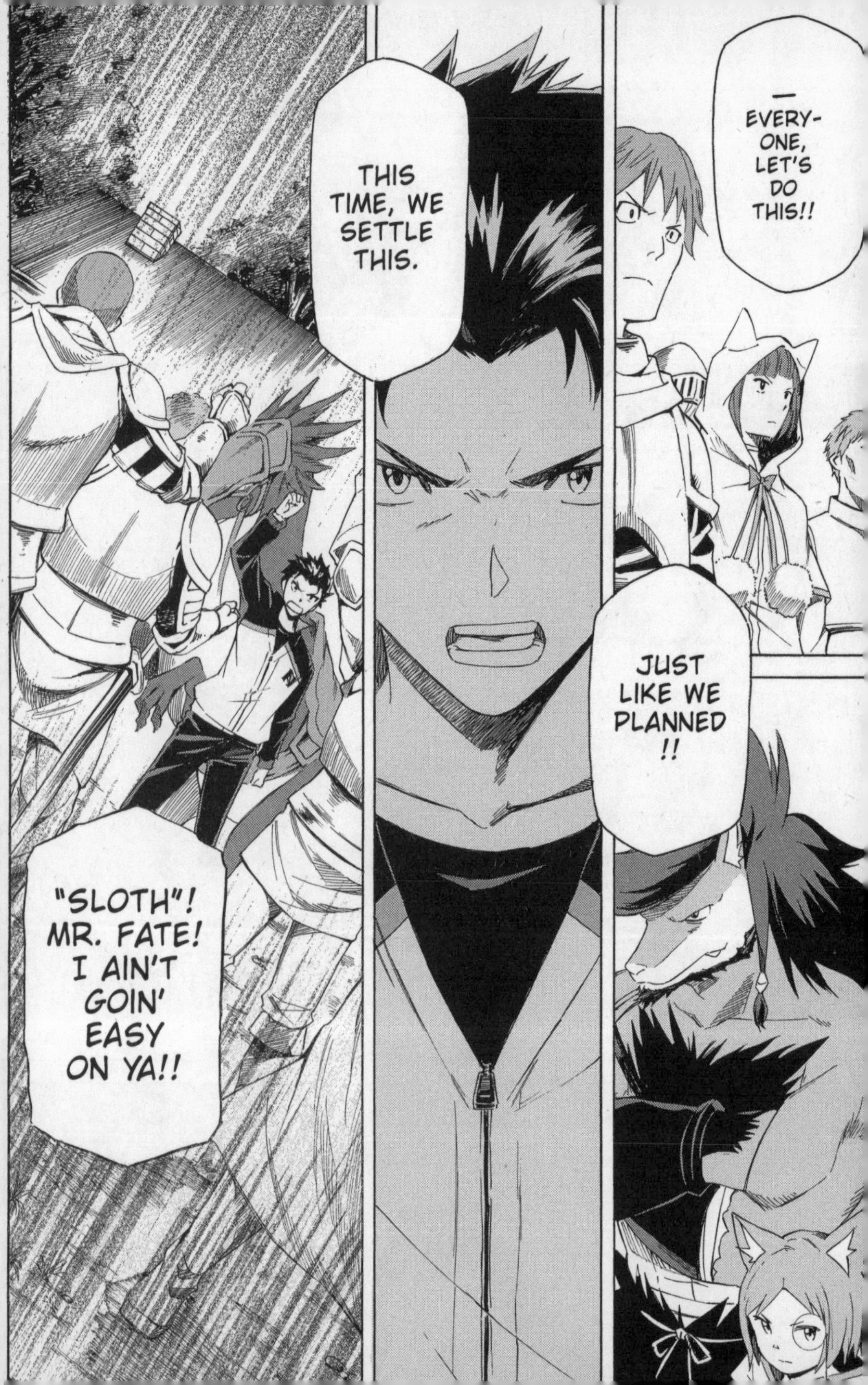
—EVERY-ONE, LET'S DO THIS!!
JUST LIKE WE PLANNED!!
THIS TIME, WE SETTLE THIS.
"SLOTH"! MR. FATE! I AIN'T GOIN' EASY ON YA!!

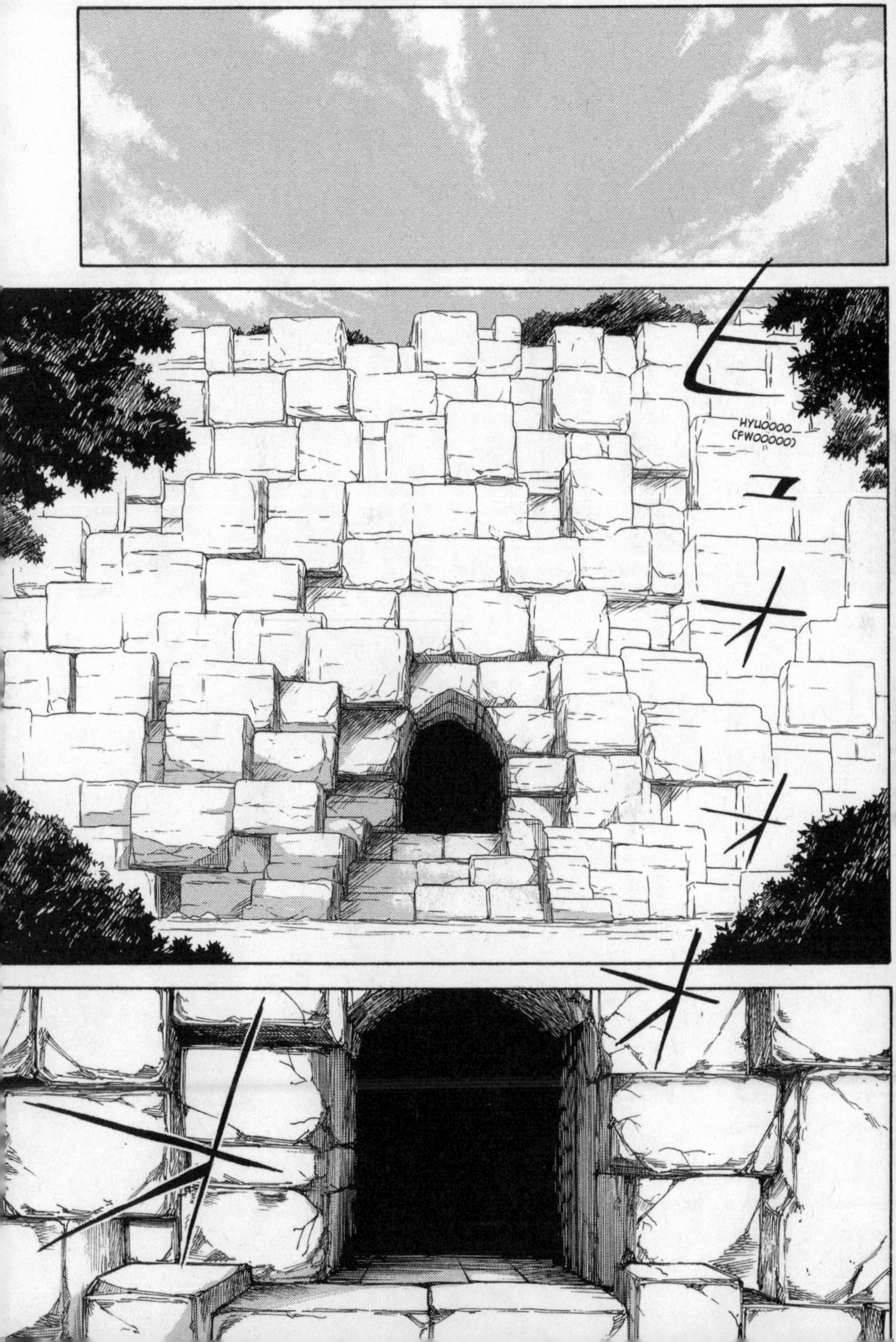
HYUOOOO
(FWOOOOO)

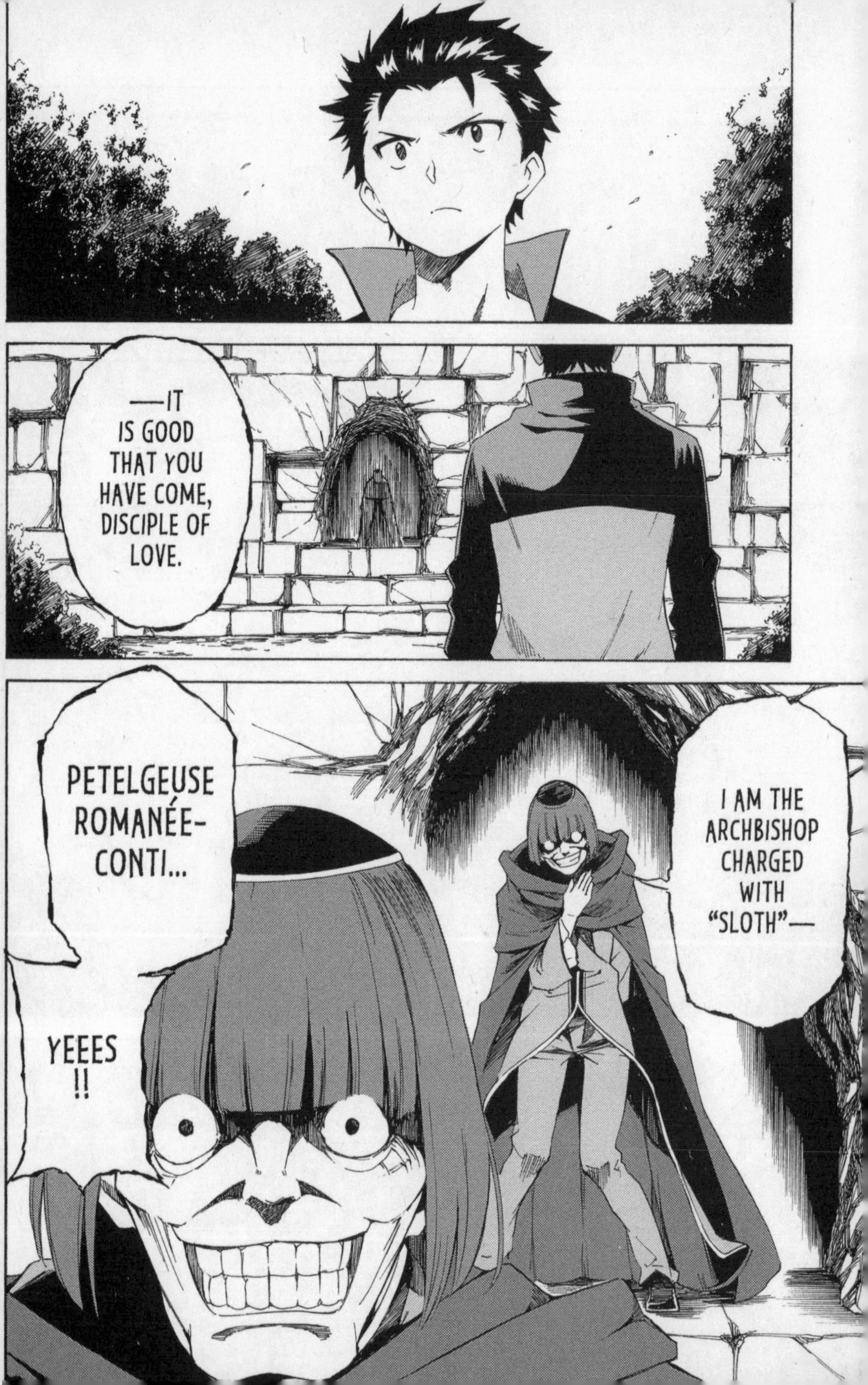
—IT IS GOOD THAT YOU HAVE COME, DISCIPLE OF LOVE.
I AM THE ARCHBISHOP CHARGED WITH "SLOTH"—
PETELGEUSE ROMANÉE-CONTI...
YEEES !!

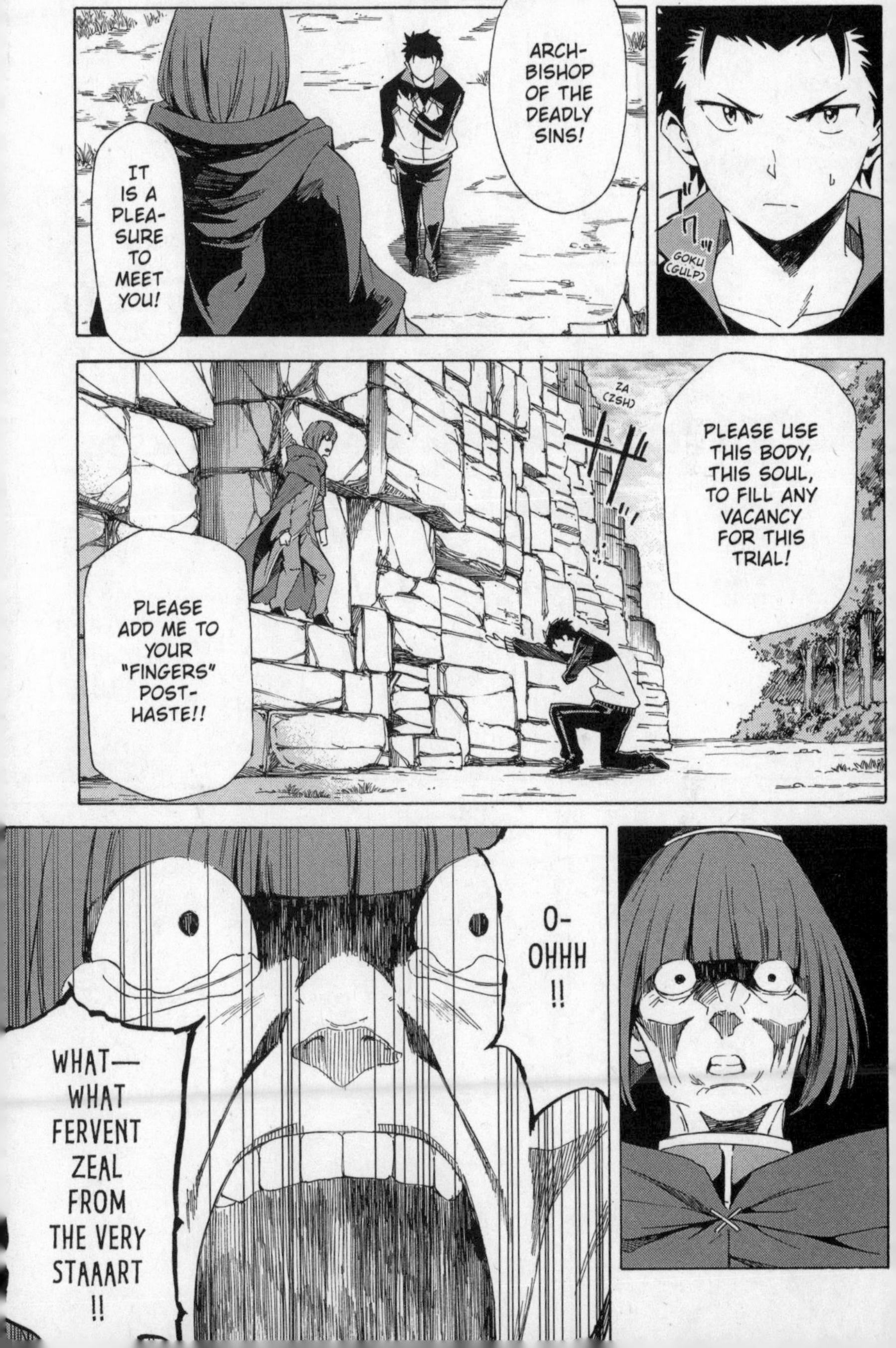
GOKU (GULP)
ARCH-BISHOP OF THE DEADLY SINS!
IT IS A PLEASURE TO MEET YOU!
PLEASE USE THIS BODY, THIS SOUL, TO FILL ANY VACANCY FOR THIS TRIAL!
ZA (ZSH)
PLEASE ADD ME TO YOUR "FINGERS" POST-HASTE!!
O-OHHH!!
WHAT— WHAT FERVENT ZEAL FROM THE VERY STAAART!!

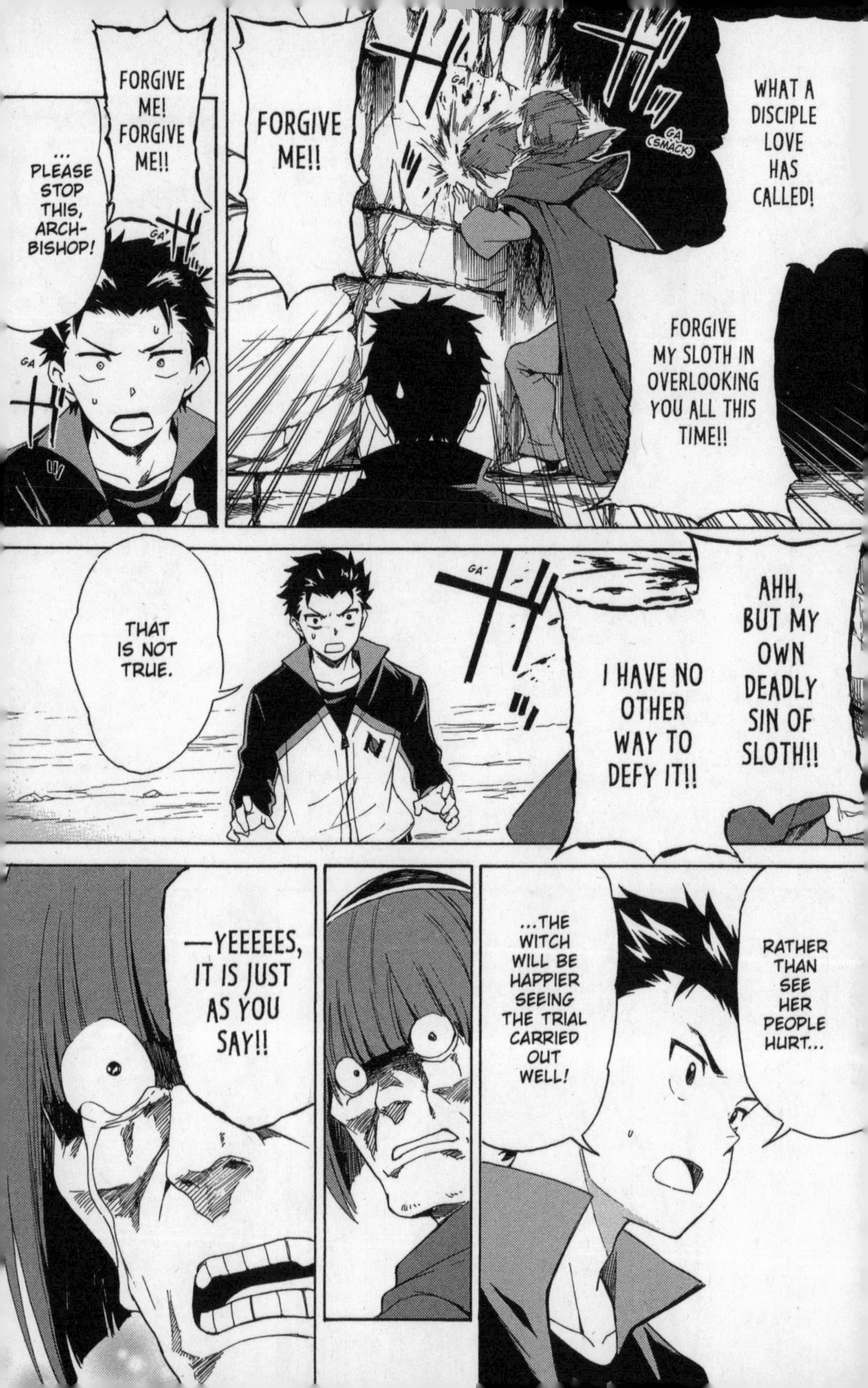
WHAT A DISCIPLE LOVE HAS CALLED!
GA
GA (SMACK)
FORGIVE MY SLOTH IN OVERLOOKING YOU ALL THIS TIME!!
FORGIVE ME!!
FORGIVE ME! FORGIVE ME!!
GA
... PLEASE STOP THIS, ARCH-BISHOP!
GA
AHH, BUT MY OWN DEADLY SIN OF SLOTH!!
I HAVE NO OTHER WAY TO DEFY IT!!
GA
THAT IS NOT TRUE.
RATHER THAN SEE HER PEOPLE HURT...
...THE WITCH WILL BE HAPPIER SEEING THE TRIAL CARRIED OUT WELL!
—YEEEEES, IT IS JUST AS YOU SAY!!

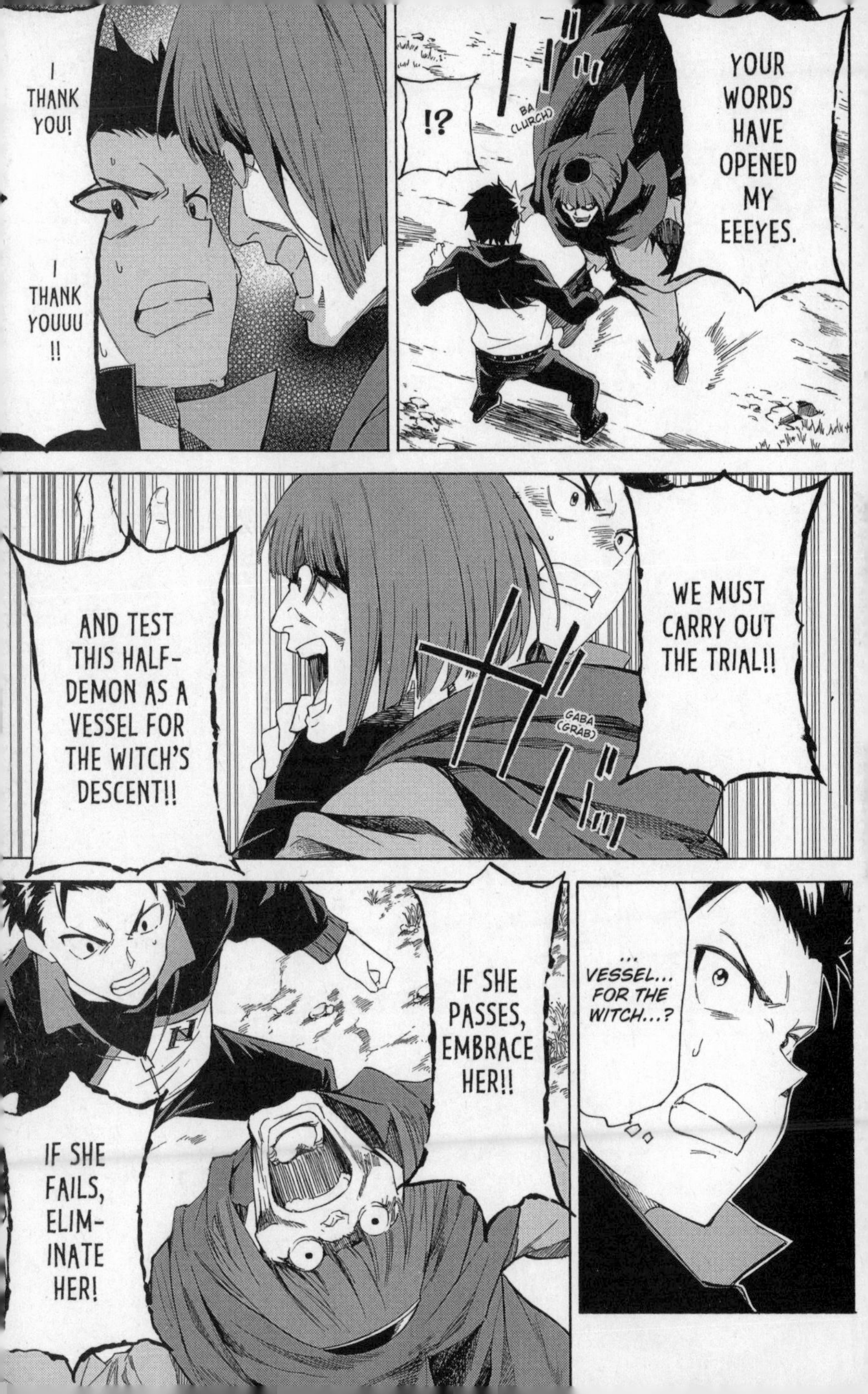
YOUR WORDS HAVE OPENED MY EEEYES.
BA (LURCH)
!?
I THANK YOU!
I THANK YOUUU!!
WE MUST CARRY OUT THE TRIAL!!
GABA (GRAB)
AND TEST THIS HALF-DEMON AS A VESSEL FOR THE WITCH'S DESCENT!!
...VESSEL... FOR THE WITCH...?
IF SHE PASSES, EMBRACE HER!!
IF SHE FAILS, ELIMINATE HER!

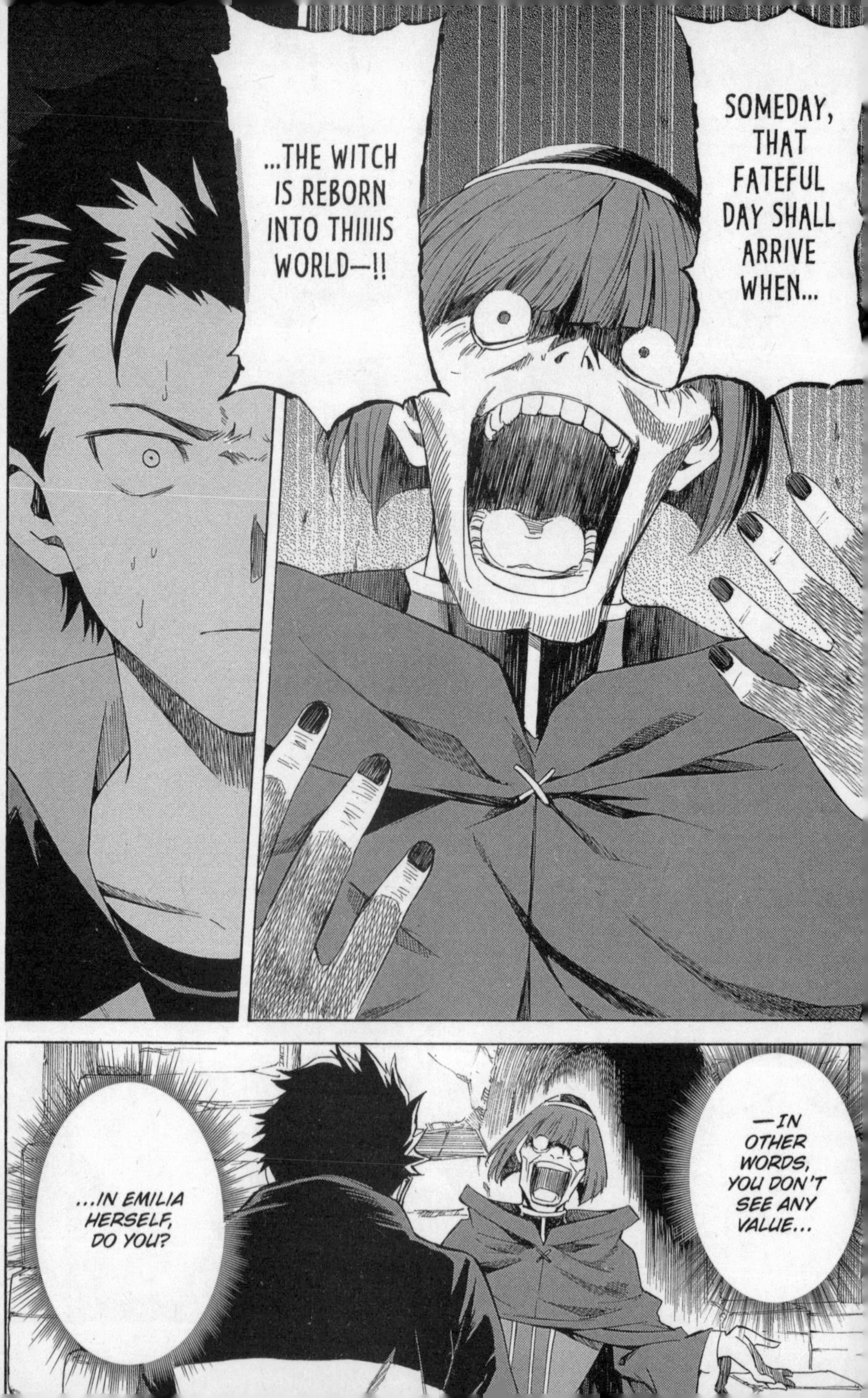
SOMEDAY, THAT FATEFUL DAY SHALL ARRIVE WHEN...
...THE WITCH IS REBORN INTO THIIIIS WORLD—!!
—IN OTHER WORDS, YOU DON'T SEE ANY VALUE...
...IN EMILIA HERSELF, DO YOU?

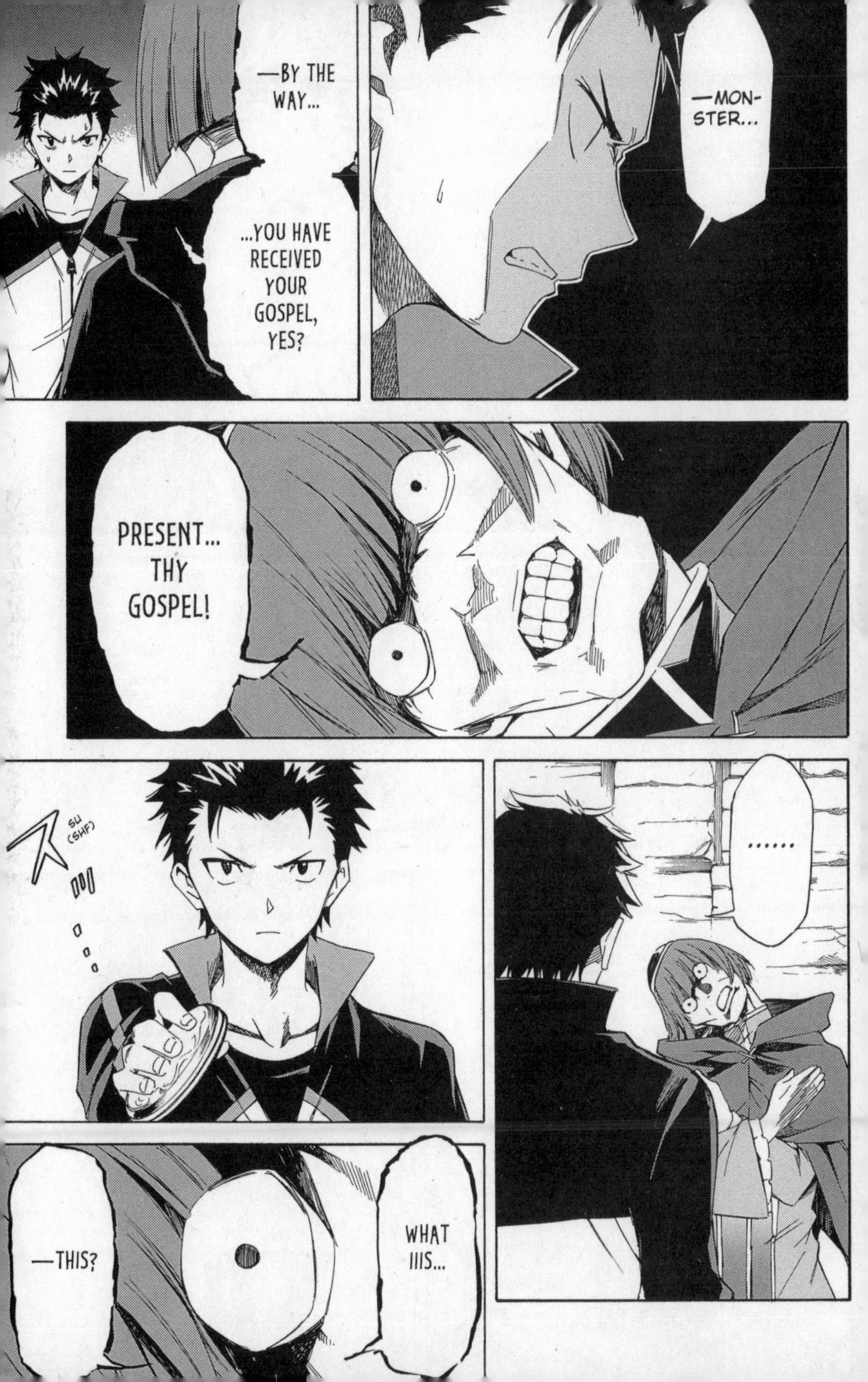
—MON-STER...
—BY THE WAY...
...YOU HAVE RECEIVED YOUR GOSPEL, YES?
PRESENT... THY GOSPEL!
......
SU (SHF)
WHAT IIIS...
—THIS?

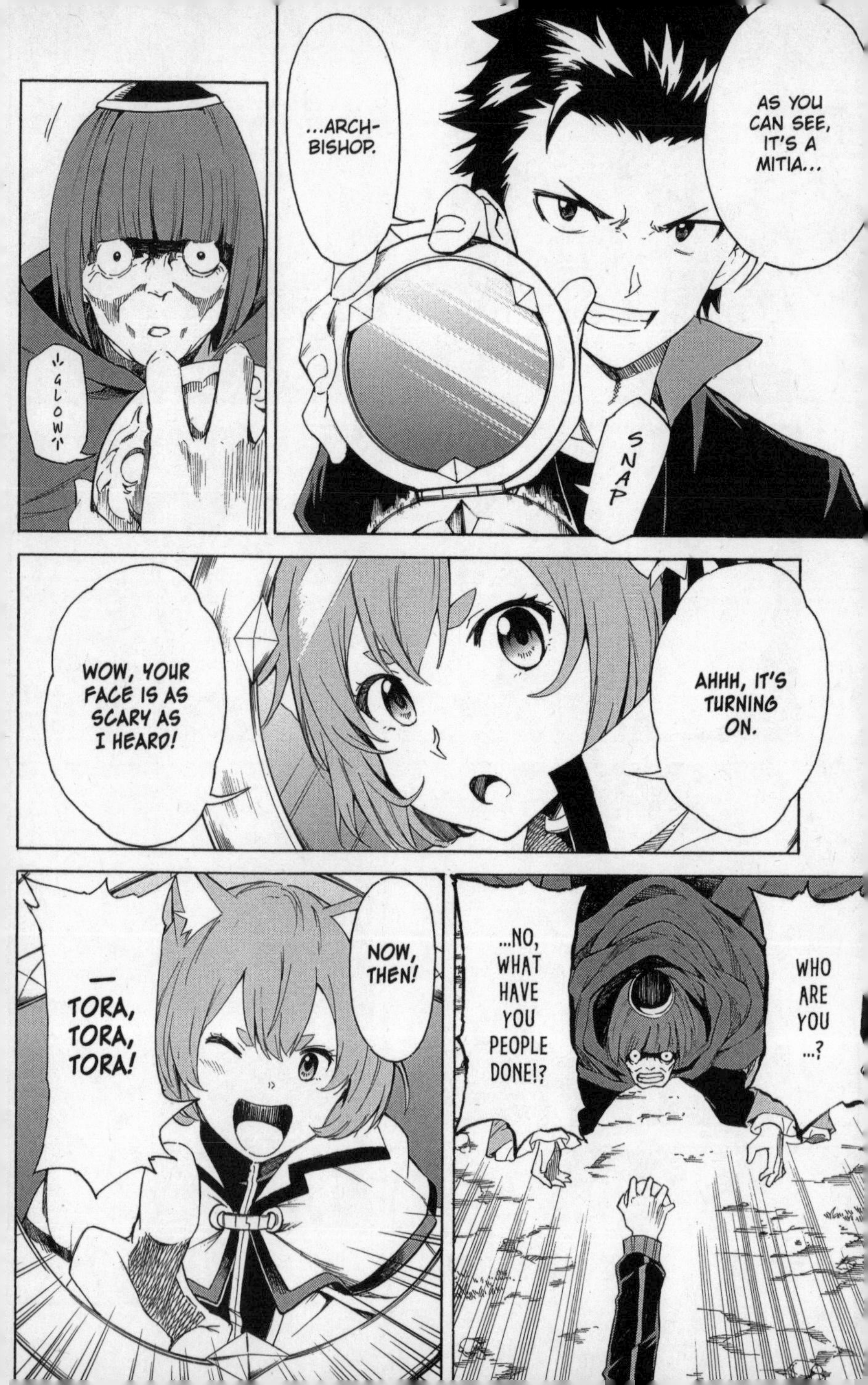
AS YOU CAN SEE, IT'S A MITIA...
...ARCH-BISHOP.
SNAP
GLOW
AHHH, IT'S TURNING ON.
WOW, YOUR FACE IS AS SCARY AS I HEARD!
WHO ARE YOU ...?
...NO, WHAT HAVE YOU PEOPLE DONE!?
NOW, THEN!
—TORA, TORA, TORA!

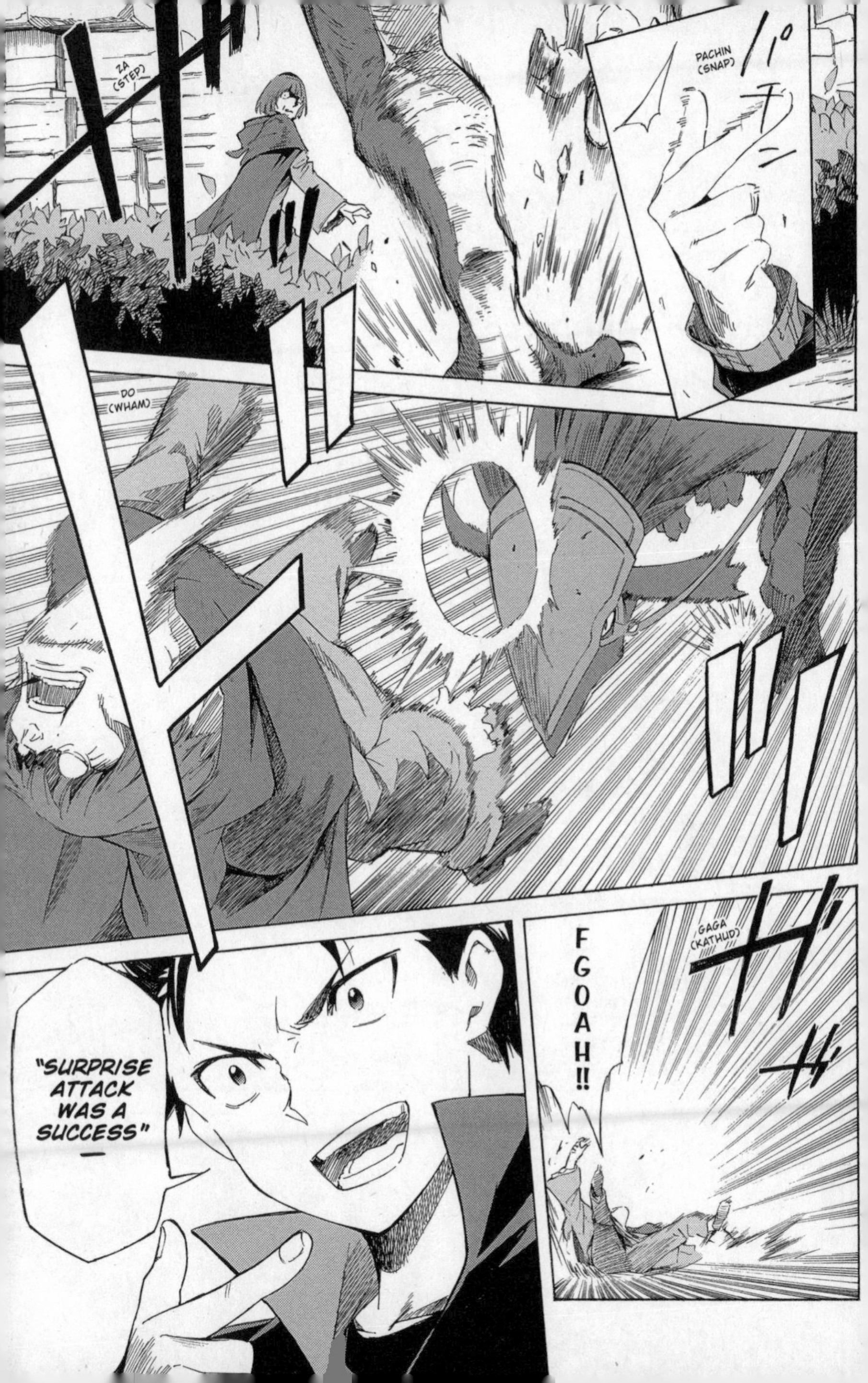
PACHIN (SNAP)
ZA (STEP)
DO (WHAM)
GAGA (KATHUD)
FGOAH!!
"SURPRISE ATTACK WAS A SUCCESS" —

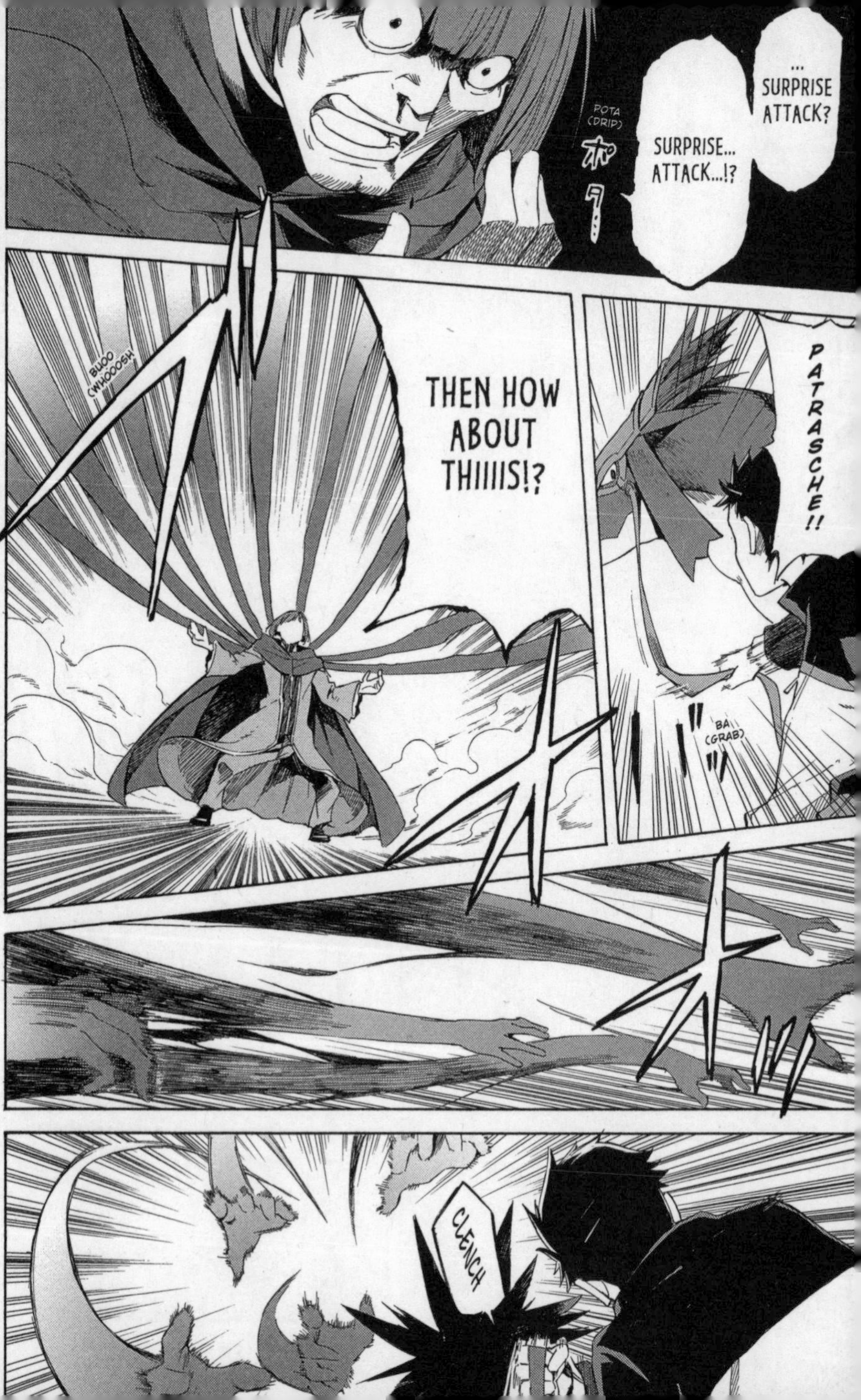
... SURPRISE ATTACK?
SURPRISE... ATTACK...!?
POTA (DRIP)
PATRASCHE!!
BA (GRAB)
THEN HOW ABOUT THIIIIS!?
BUOO (WHOOOSH)
CLENCH

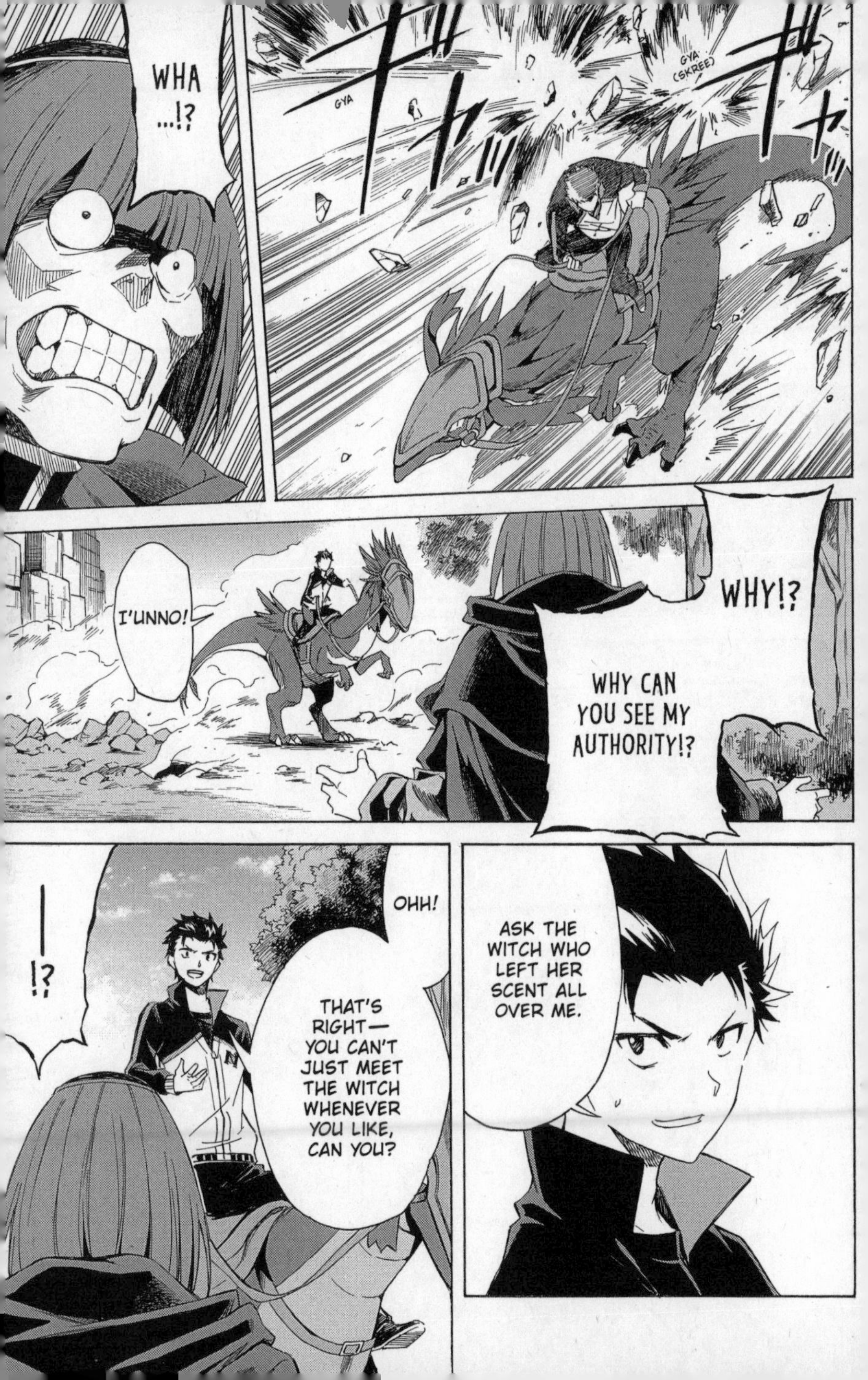
GYA (SKREE)
GYA
WHA ...!?
WHY!?
WHY CAN YOU SEE MY AUTHORITY!?
I'UNNO!
ASK THE WITCH WHO LEFT HER SCENT ALL OVER ME.
OHH!
THAT'S RIGHT— YOU CAN'T JUST MEET THE WITCH WHENEVER YOU LIKE, CAN YOU?
—!?

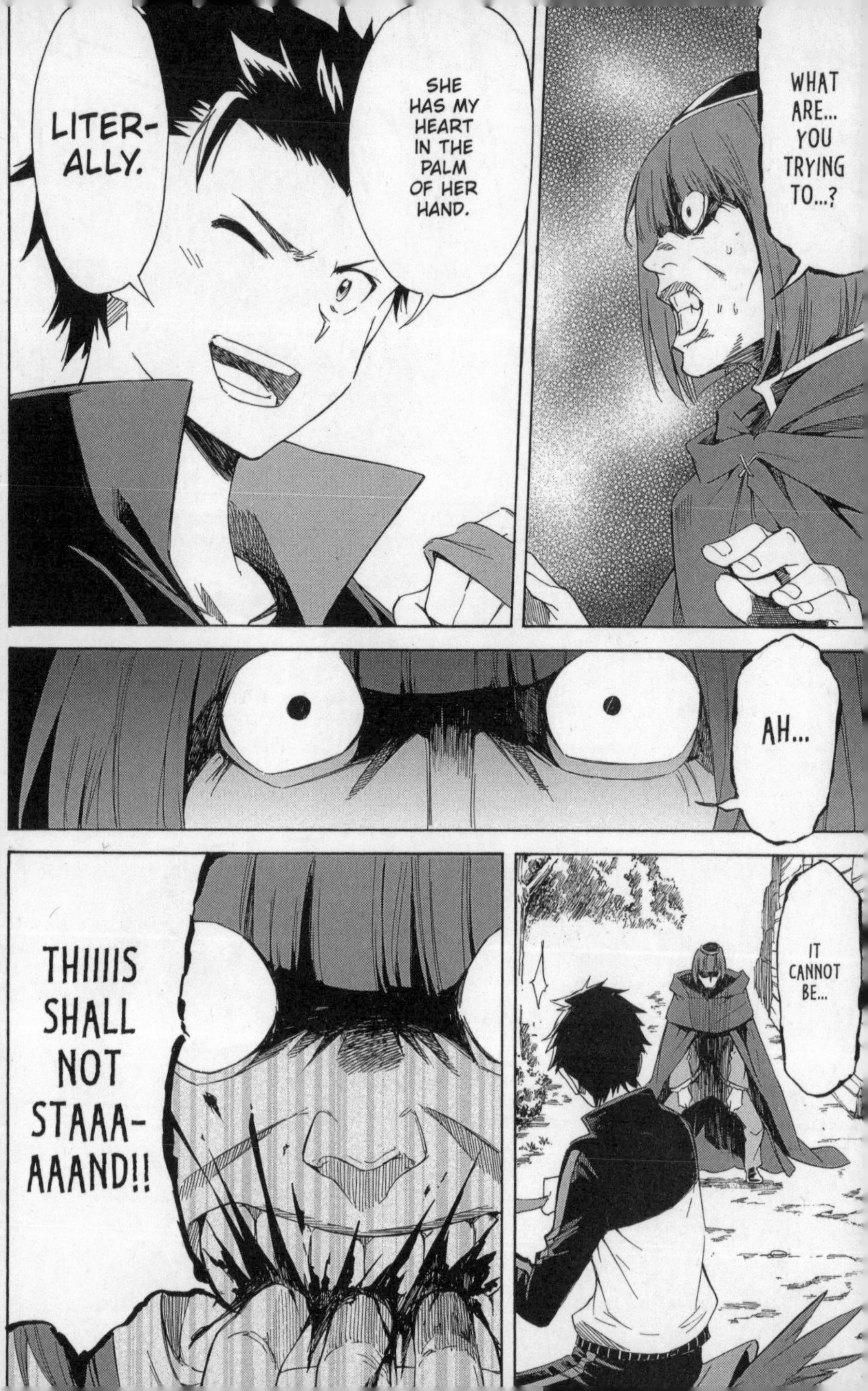
WHAT ARE... YOU TRYING TO...?
SHE HAS MY HEART IN THE PALM OF HER HAND.
LITER-ALLY.
AH...
IT CANNOT BE...
THIIIIS SHALL NOT STAAA-AAAND!!

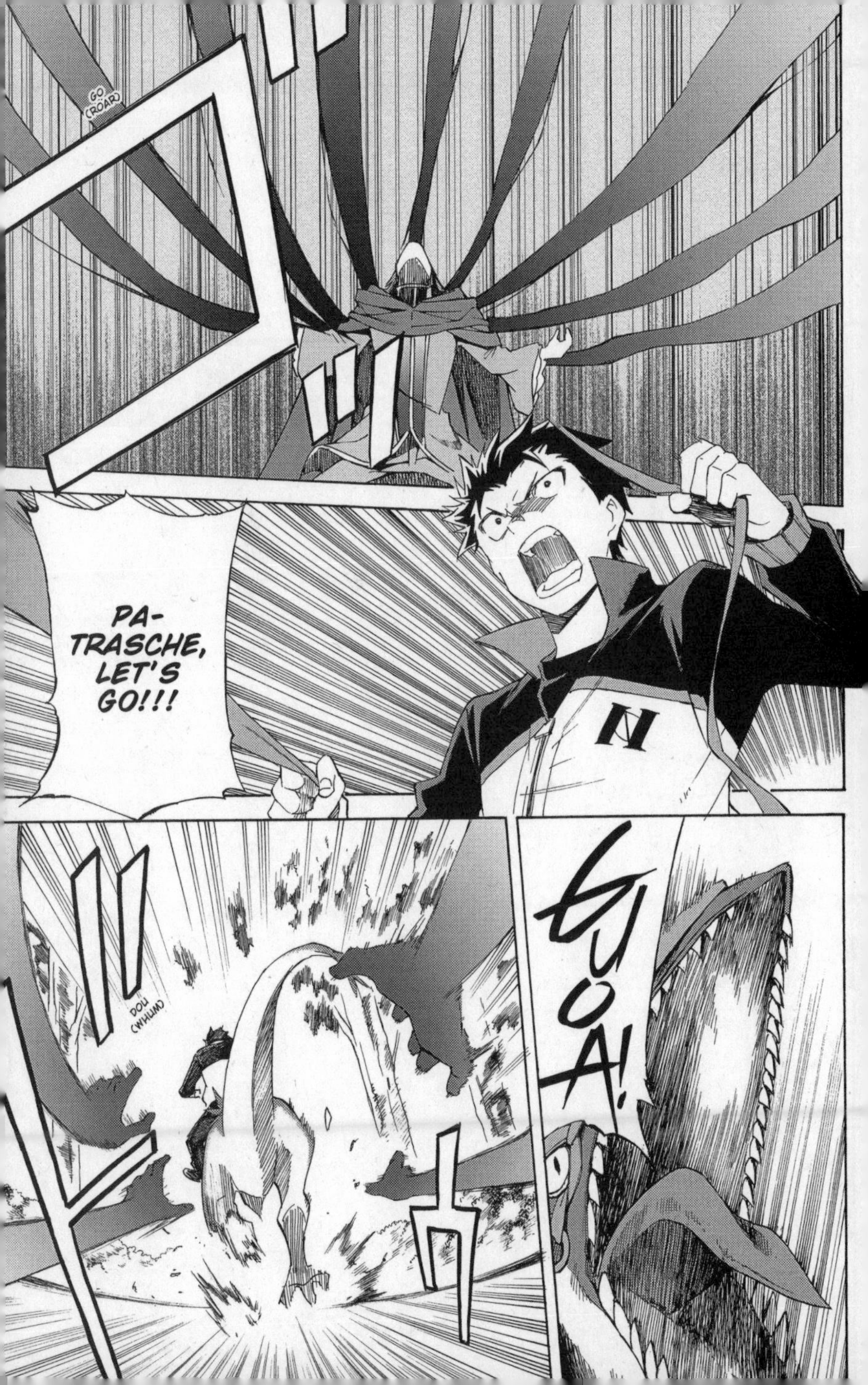
GO (ROAR)
PA-TRASCHE, LET'S GO!!!
DOU (WHUM)
GUOA!

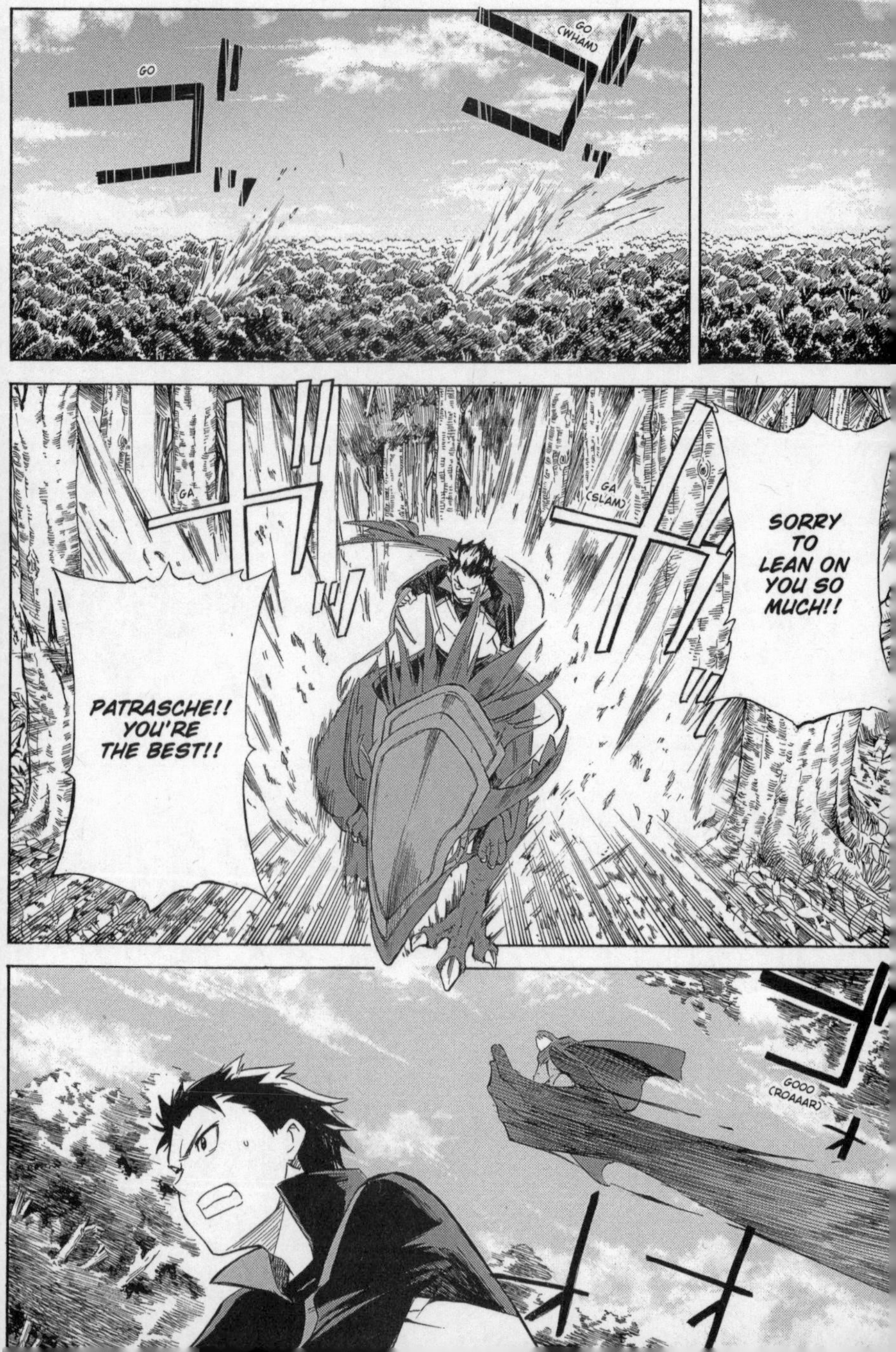
GO (WHAM)
GO
SORRY TO LEAN ON YOU SO MUCH!!
GA (SLAM)
GA
PATRASCHE!! YOU'RE THE BEST!!
GOOO (ROAAAR)

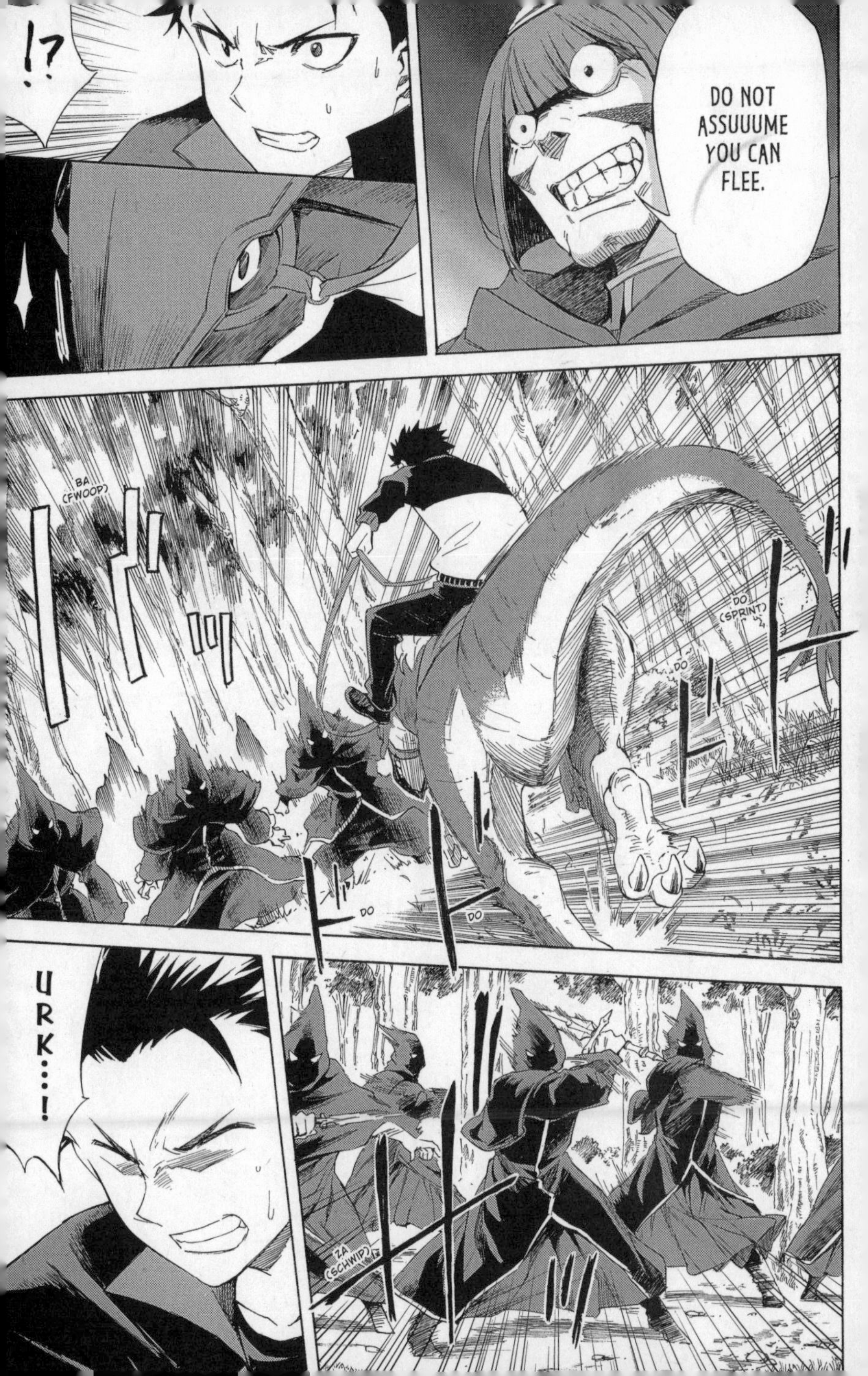
DO NOT ASSUUUME YOU CAN FLEE.
!?
DO (SPRINT)
DO
BA (FWOOP)
DO
DO
ZA (SCHWIP)
URK...!

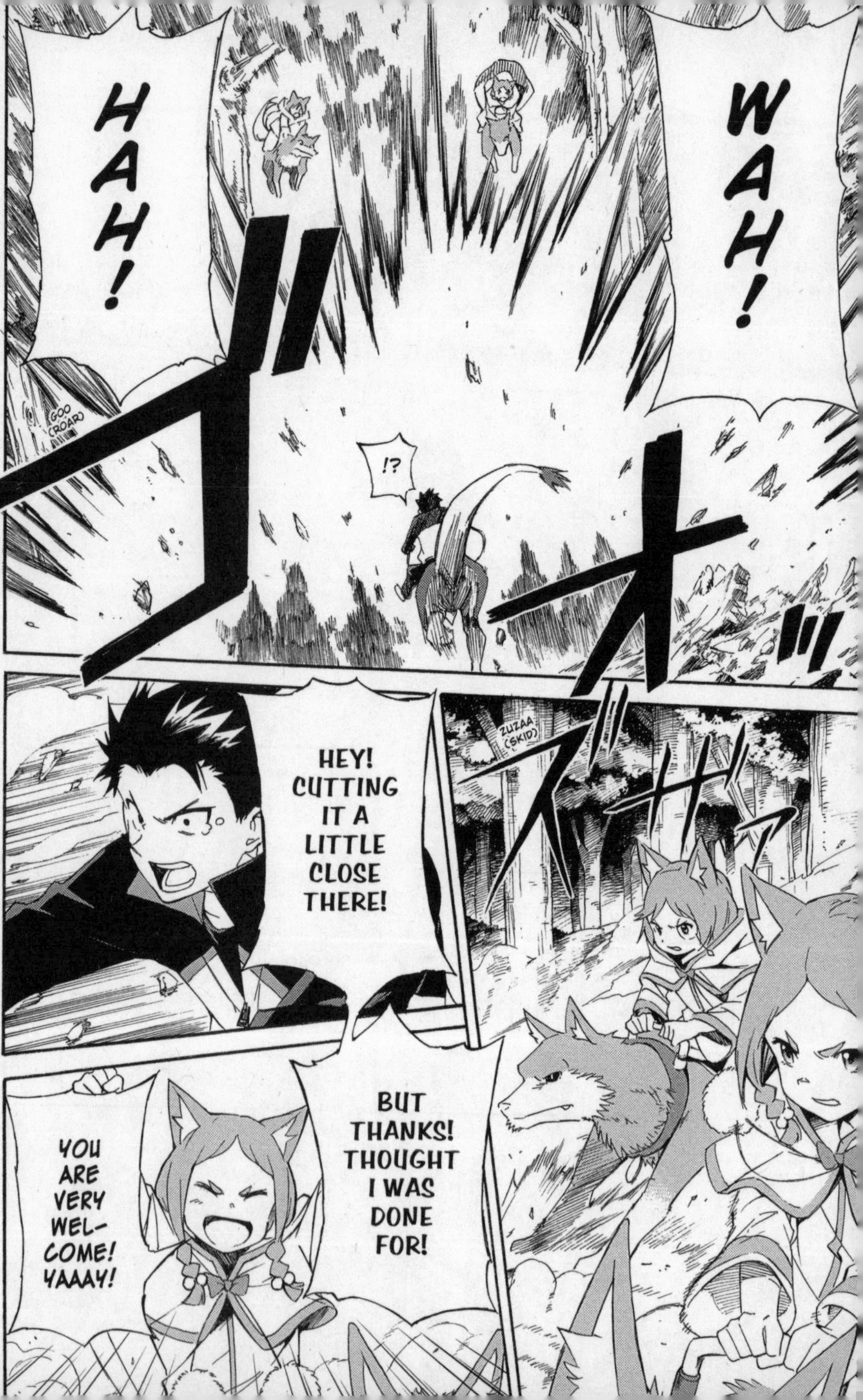
WAH!
HAH!
!?
GOO (ROAR)
ZUZAA (SKID)
HEY! CUTTING IT A LITTLE CLOSE THERE!
BUT THANKS! THOUGHT I WAS DONE FOR!
YOU ARE VERY WEL-COME! YAAAY!

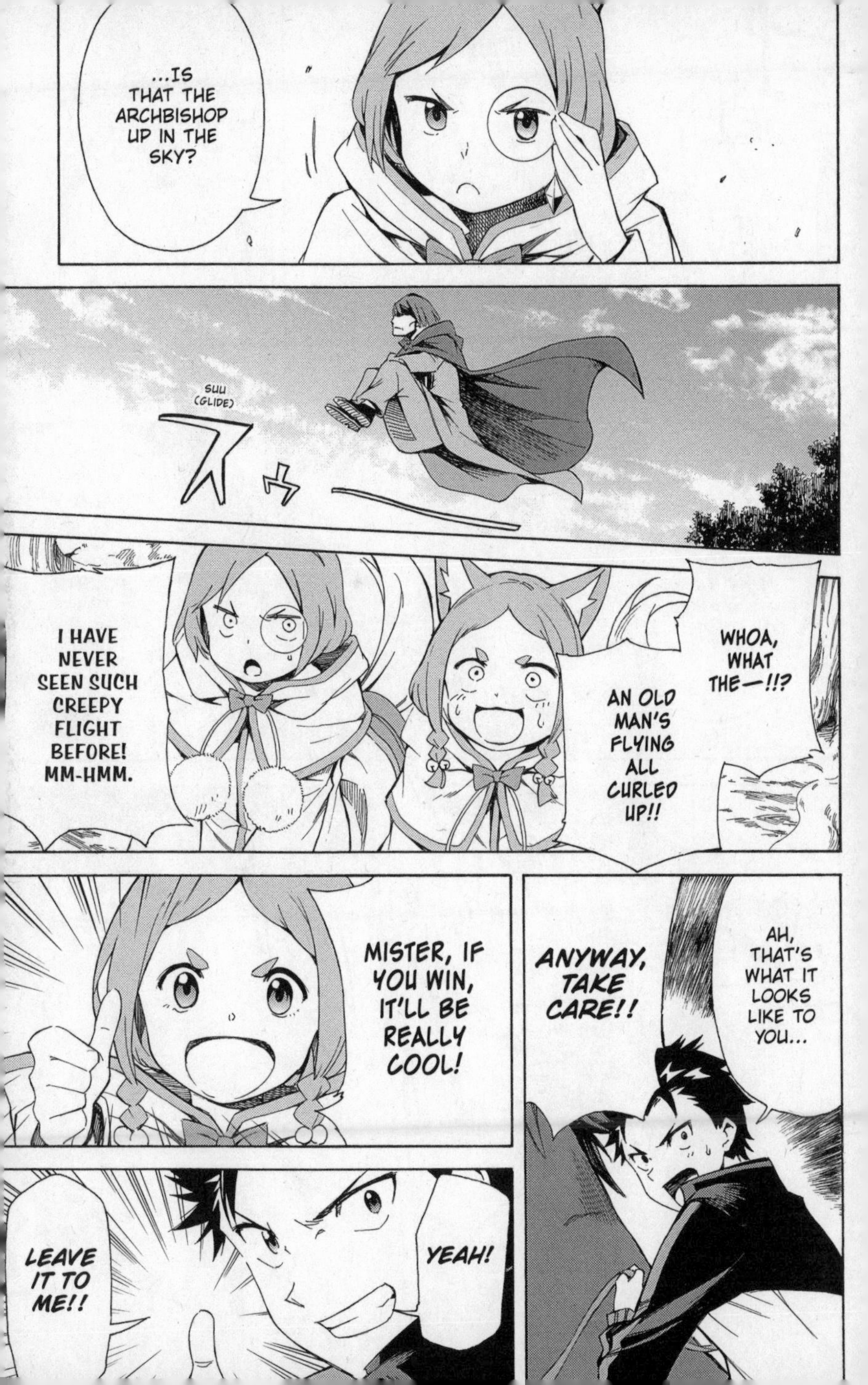
...IS THAT THE ARCHBISHOP UP IN THE SKY?
SUU (GLIDE)
WHOA, WHAT THE—!!?
AN OLD MAN'S FLYING ALL CURLED UP!!
I HAVE NEVER SEEN SUCH CREEPY FLIGHT BEFORE! MM-HMM.
AH, THAT'S WHAT IT LOOKS LIKE TO YOU...
ANYWAY, TAKE CARE!!
MISTER, IF YOU WIN, IT'LL BE REALLY COOL!
YEAH!
LEAVE IT TO ME!!

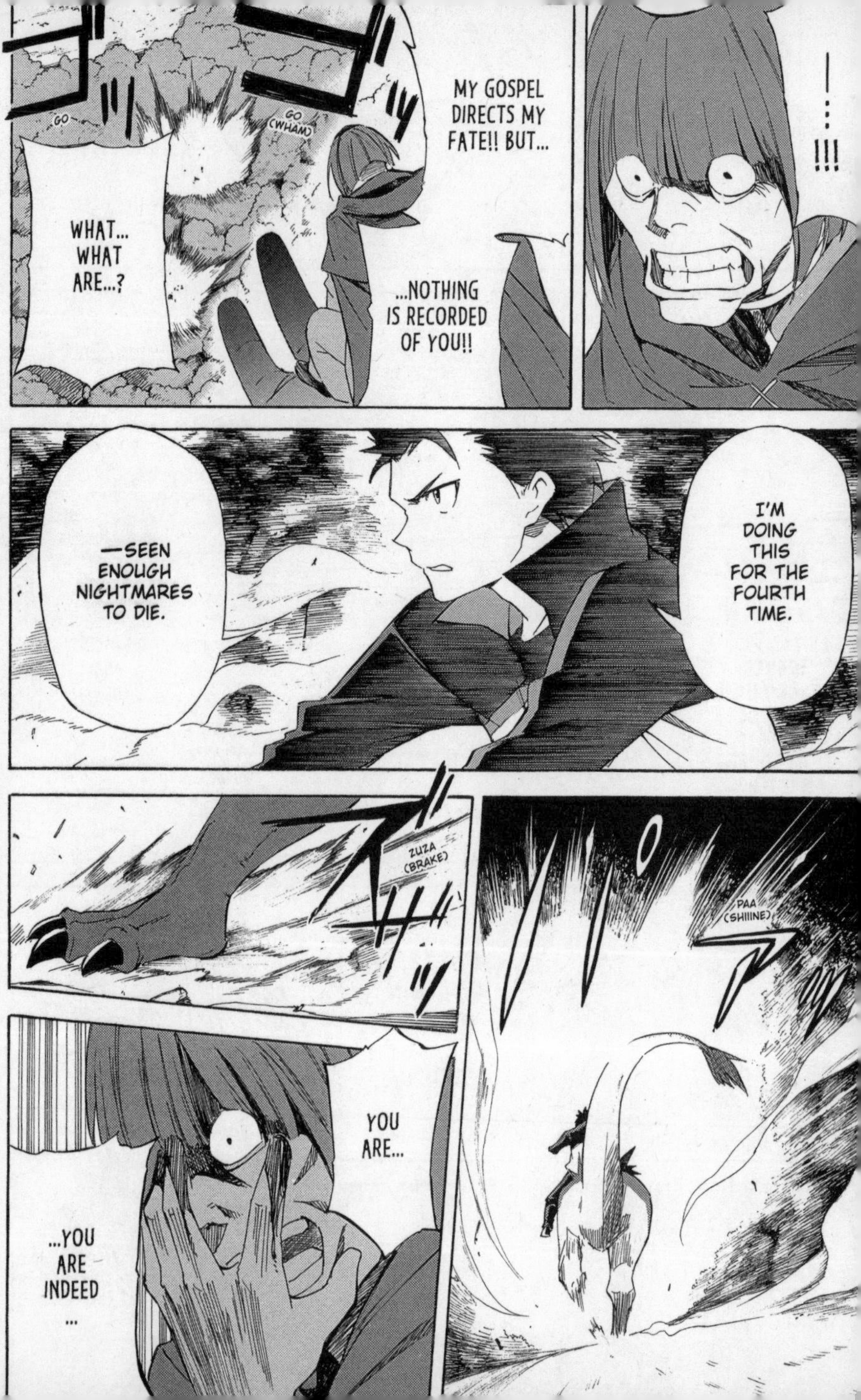
—...!!!
MY GOSPEL DIRECTS MY FATE!! BUT...
GO (WHAM)
...NOTHING IS RECORDED OF YOU!!
GO
WHAT... WHAT ARE...?
I'M DOING THIS FOR THE FOURTH TIME.
—SEEN ENOUGH NIGHTMARES TO DIE.
PAA (SHIIINE)
ZUZA (BRAKE)
YOU ARE...
...YOU ARE INDEED ...

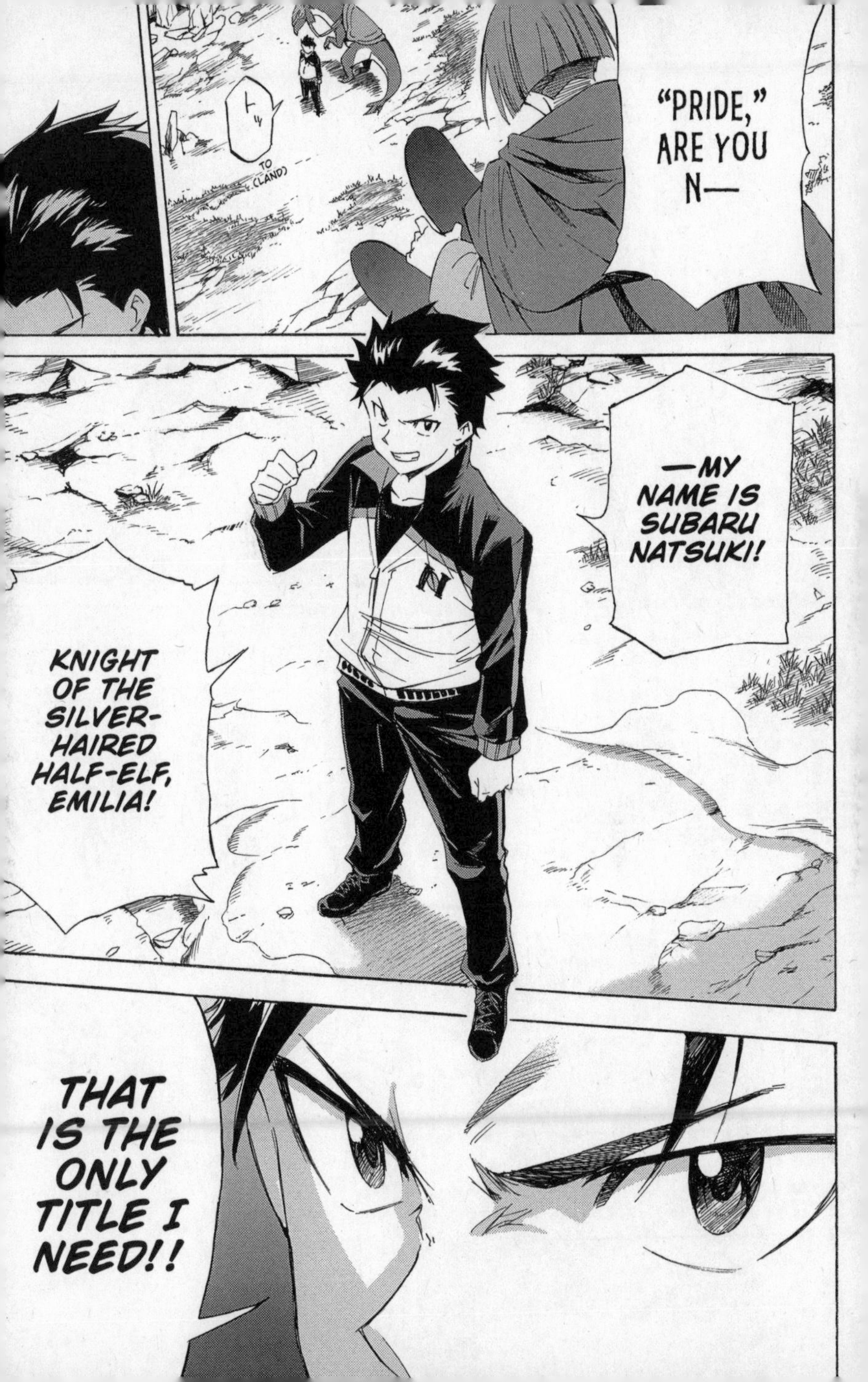
"PRIDE," ARE YOU N—
トッ
TO (LAND)
—MY NAME IS SUBARU NATSUKI!
KNIGHT OF THE SILVER-HAIRED HALF-ELF, EMILIA!
THAT IS THE ONLY TITLE I NEED!!

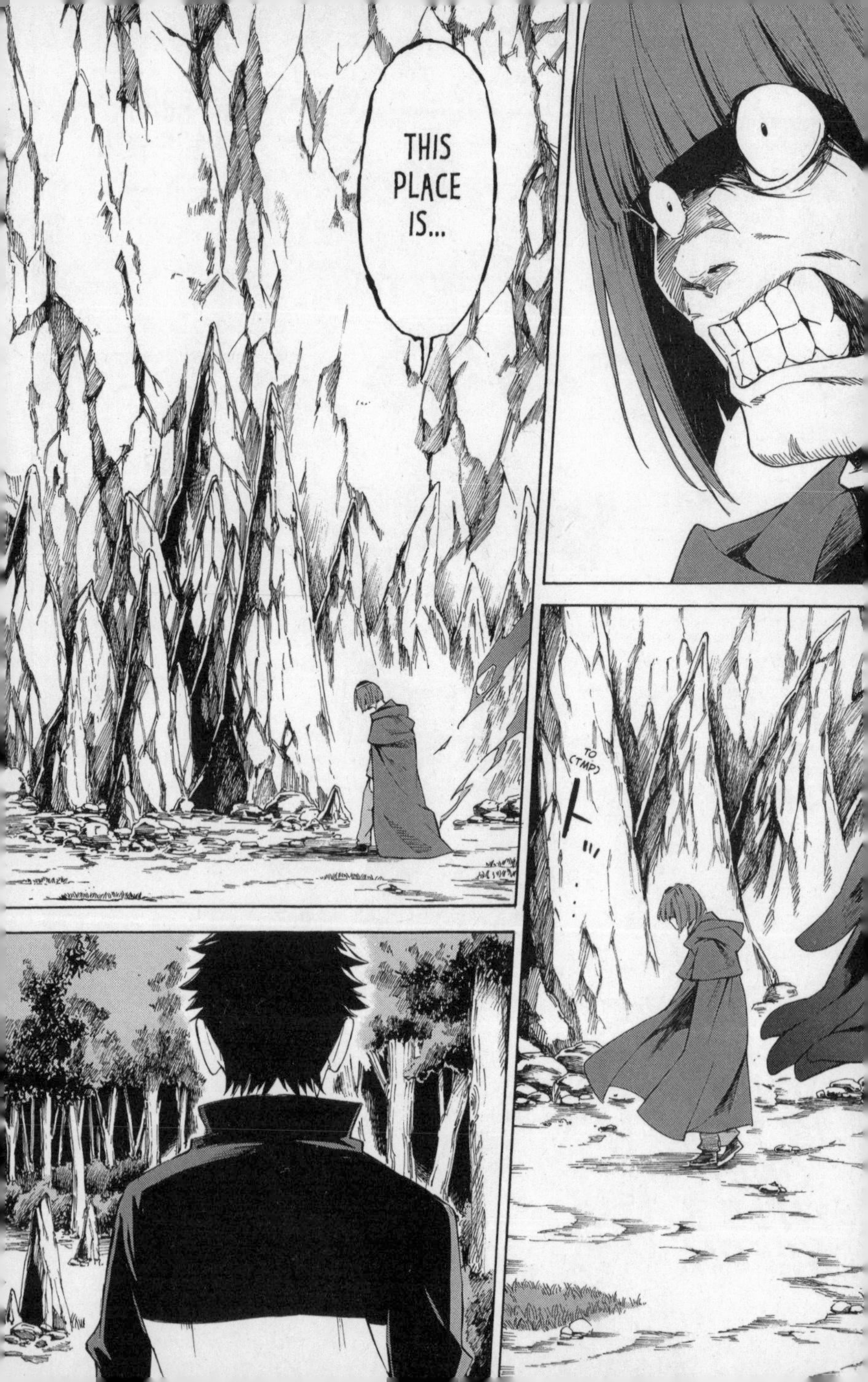
THIS PLACE IS...
TO (TMP)

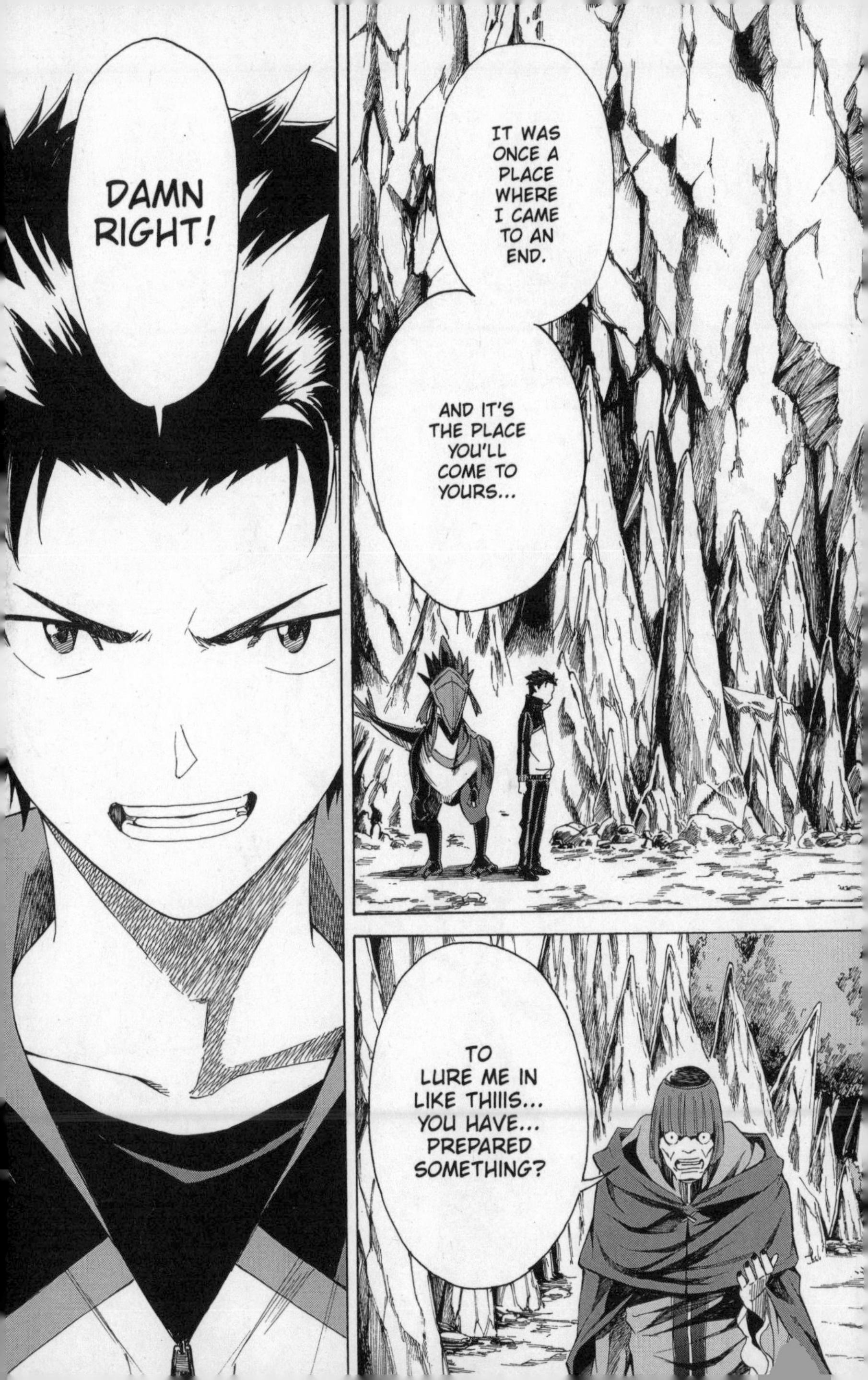
IT WAS ONCE A PLACE WHERE I CAME TO AN END.
AND IT'S THE PLACE YOU'LL COME TO YOURS...
TO LURE ME IN LIKE THIIIS... YOU HAVE... PREPARED SOMETHING?
DAMN RIGHT!

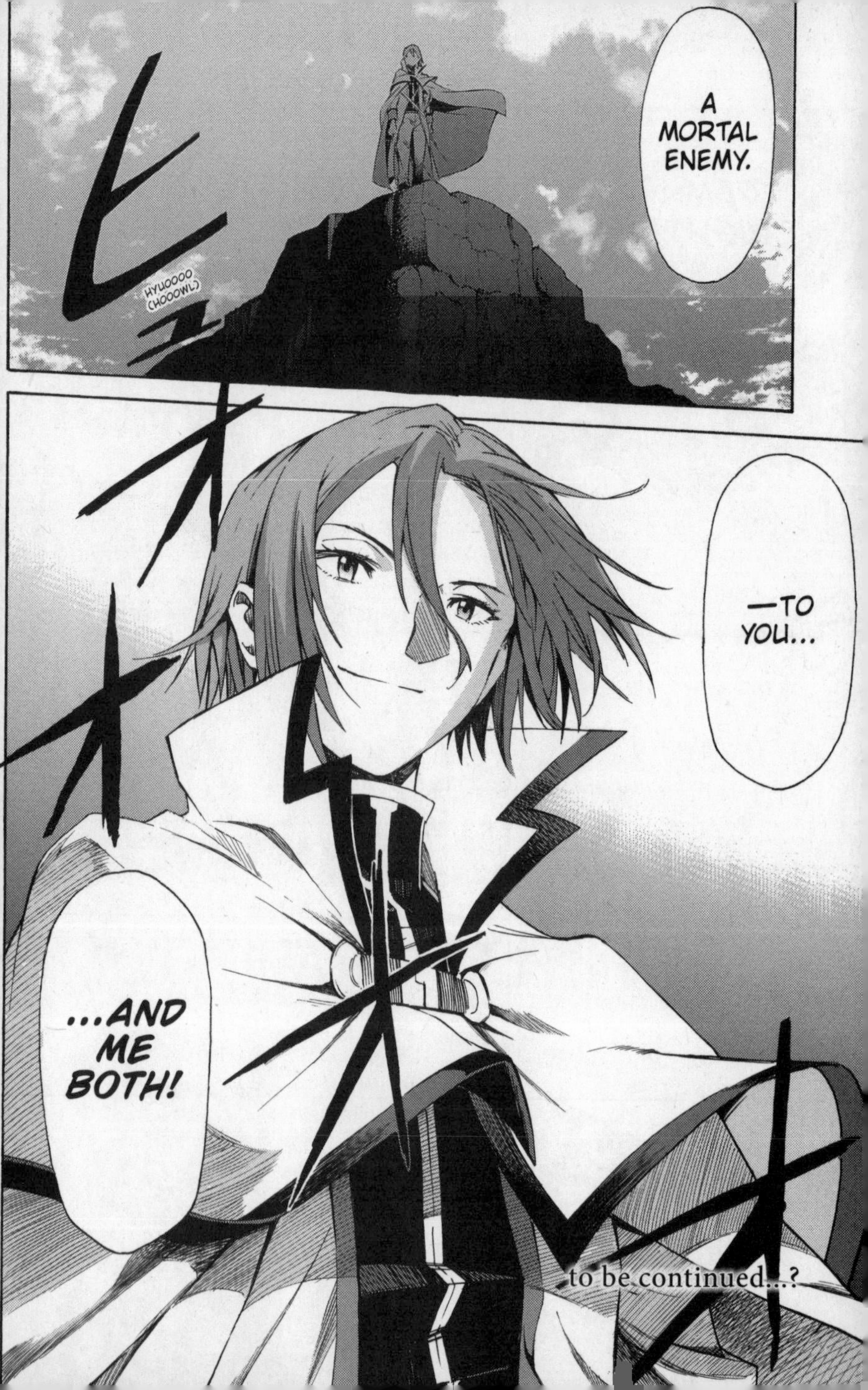
A MORTAL ENEMY.
HYUOOOO (HOOOWL)
—TO YOU...
...AND ME BOTH!
to be continued...?

Truth of Zero

The only ability Subaru Natsuki gets when he's
summoned to another world is time travel via his own
death. But to save her, he'll die as many times as it takes.

Re:ZERO -Starting
Life in Another World-

The only ability
Subaru Natsuki gets when
he's summoned to another
world is time travel via his
own death. But to save her,
he'll die as many times
as it takes.

Re:ZERO -Starting Life in Another World-
Truth of Zero

Illustration by Shinichirou Otsuka (Character Designer)

Re:ZERO -Starting Life in Another World-

Supporting Comments from the Author of the Original Work, Tappei Nagatsuki

Daichi Matsuse-sensei! Congratulations on Volume 9 of this *Re:ZERO* comic going on sale!

Emilia! On the cover! Cute! E·M·T!!

Sorry, I lost myself for a moment. Anyway, the cover does greatly stand out, but the latter half of Chapter 3, Emilia letting loose included, becomes the story of the battle with Petelgeuse!

Unlike the representation in the text of the novels, the way the manga was drawn has one Petelgeuse falling only for another to take his place. That Archbishop of the Deadly Sins is quite overworked!

However, on the heels of the melee during the Battle of the White Whale, the detailed portions of the illustrations, such as showing Subaru's emotions upon his Return by Death and on Julius and Ferris as they watched him die, show just how incredibly hard Matsuse-sensei has been working. I give the fruits proportionate to those labors a big seal of approval!

With the end of this volume, Chapter 3 truly heads toward its own conclusion, and the end to Subaru's long suffering during his "Return to the Capital" comes into sight.

Matsuse-sensei, please give us your last spurt as you head toward the ending to come!

To all of you readers, make sure you follow *Re:ZERO -Starting Life in Another World-*, Chapter 3 to the very, very end! Best regards!

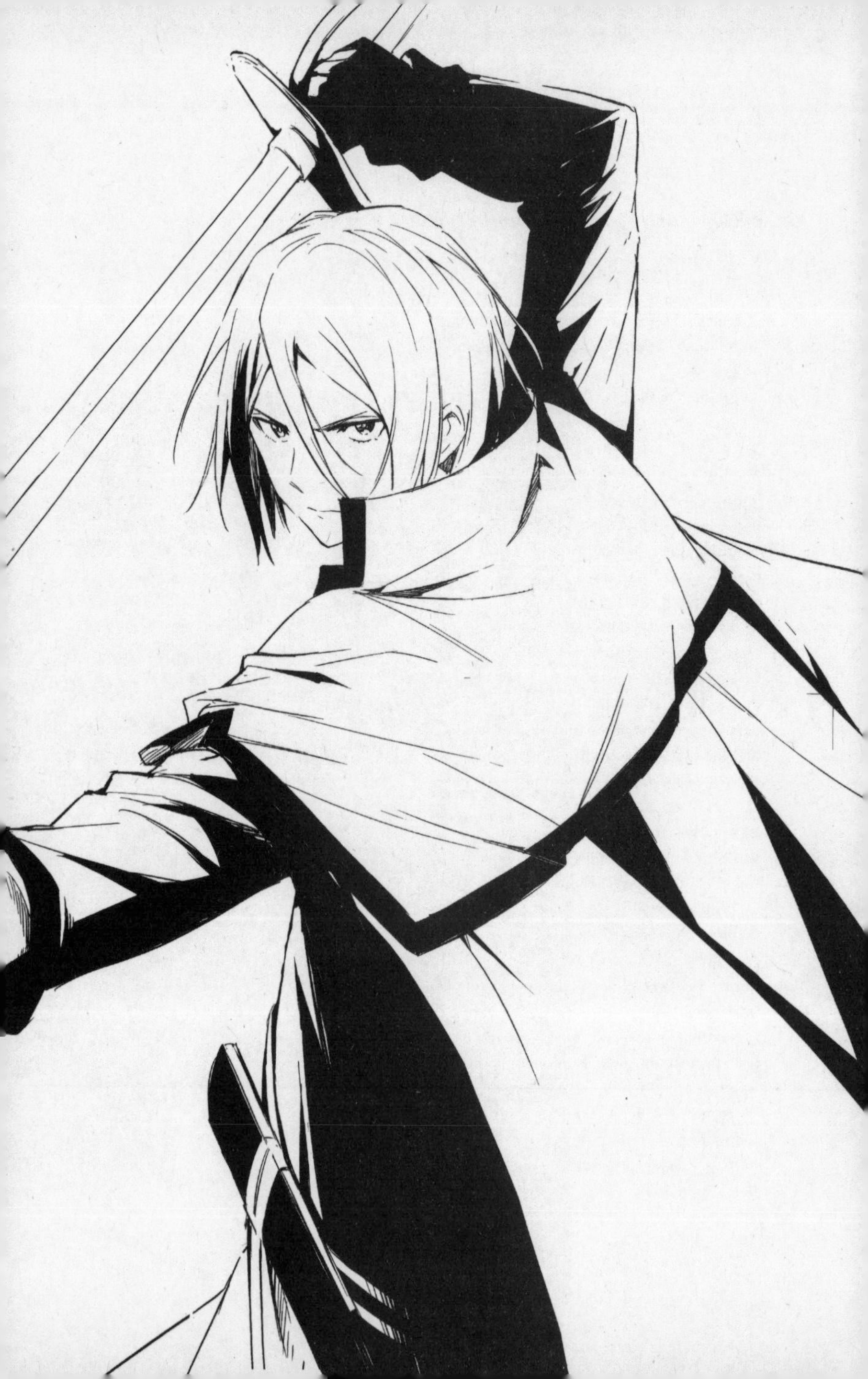

AFTERWORD

THANK YOU AS ALWAYS.
FINALLY...FINALLY, I'VE MADE IT THIS FAR!
I VERY MUCH LOOK FORWARD TO YOUR
STICKING WITH ME TO THE LAST!

—DAICHI MATSUSE

Re:ZERO -Starting Life in Another World-
Chapter 3: Truth of Zero

Artist Comments

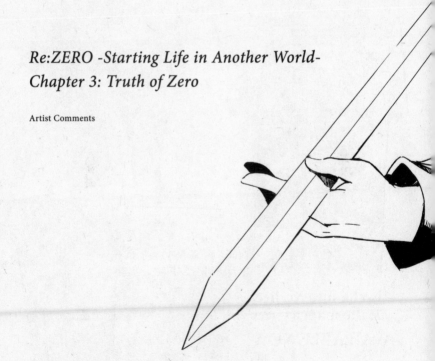

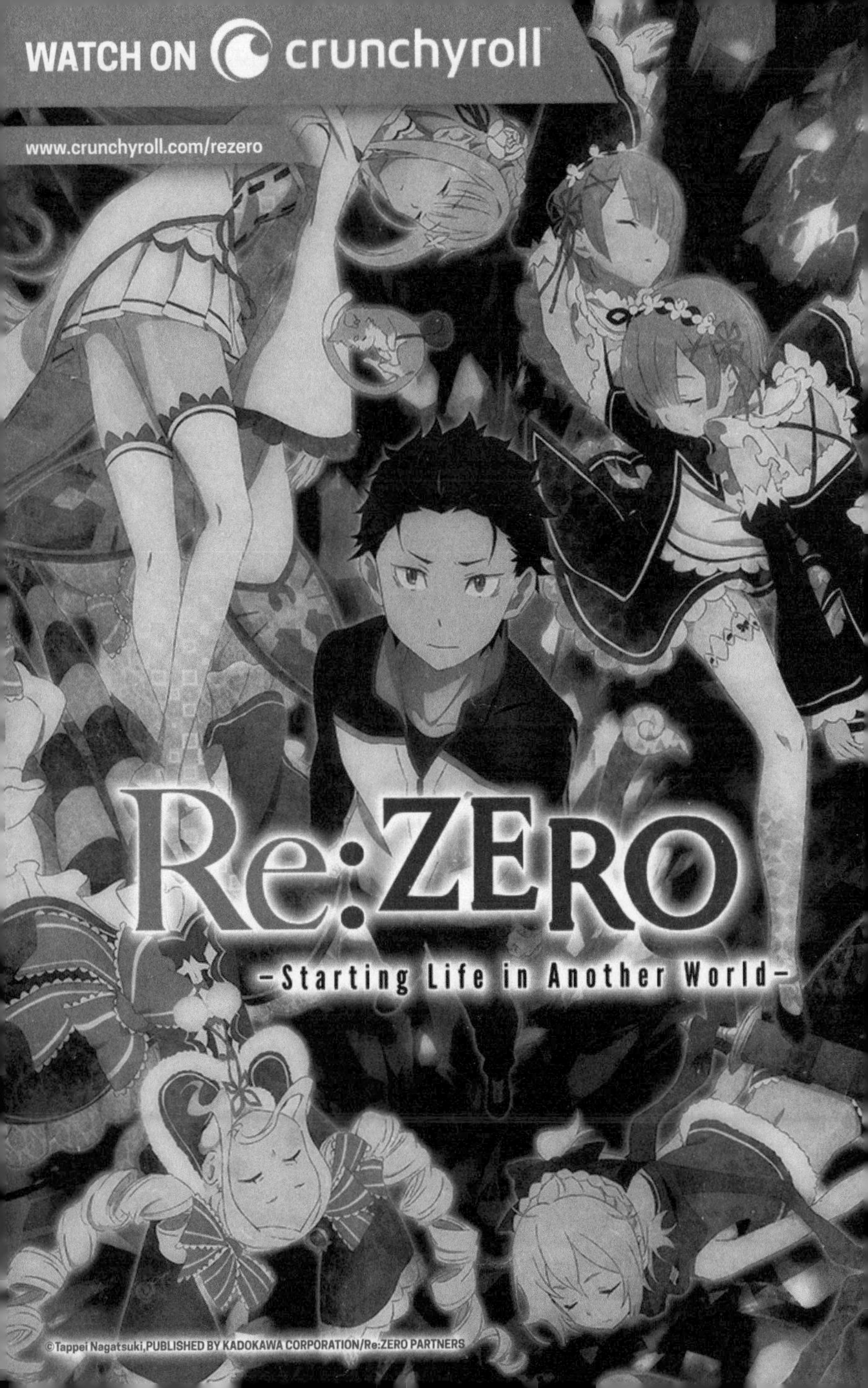
WATCH ON crunchyroll
www.crunchyroll.com/rezero
Re:ZERO
-Starting Life in Another World-
©Tappei Nagatsuki,PUBLISHED BY KADOKAWA CORPORATION/Re:ZERO PARTNERS

Death doesn't stop a video game-loving shut-in from going on adventures and fighting monsters!

IN STORES NOW

LIGHT NOVEL

MANGA

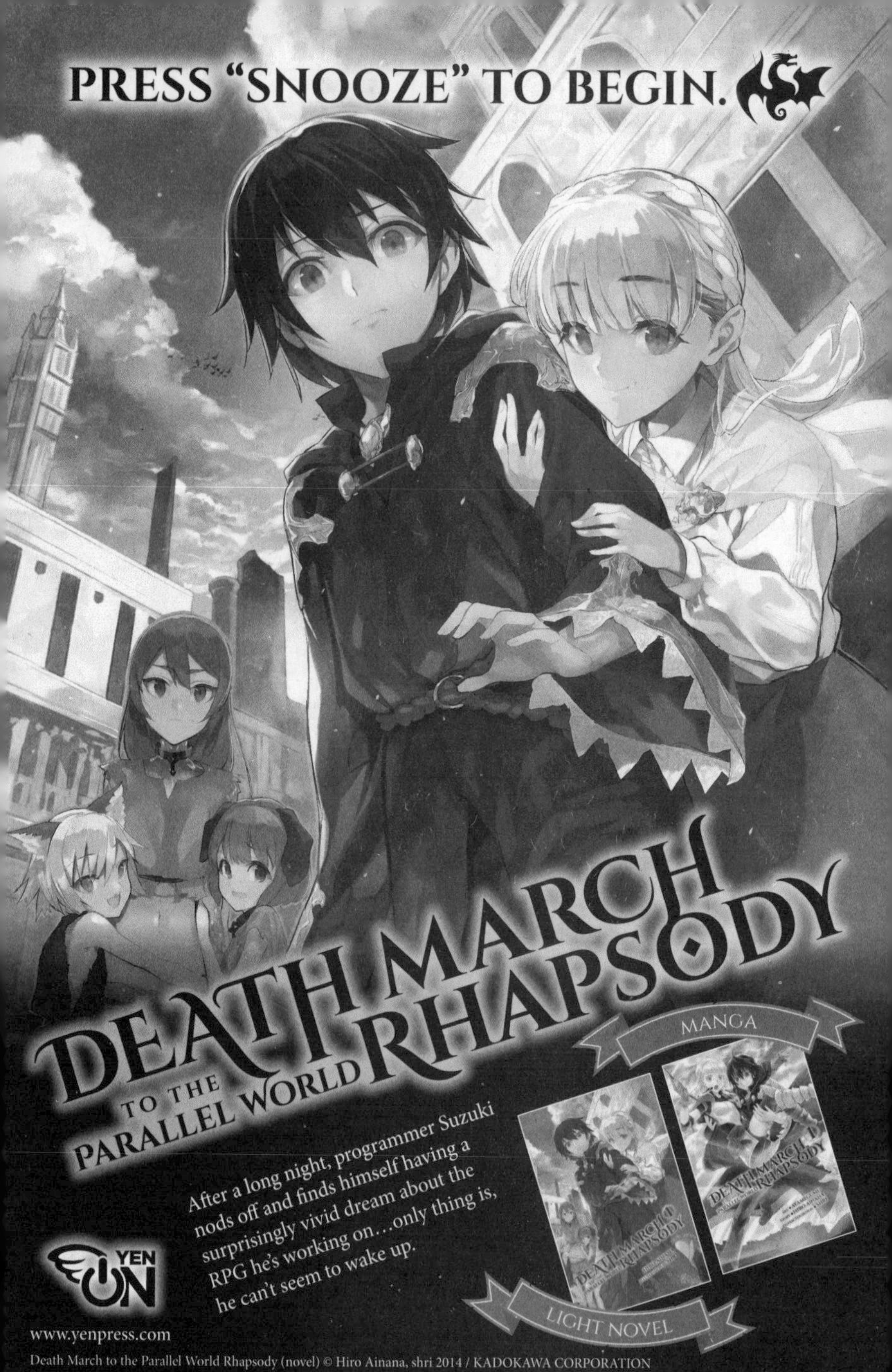
PRESS "SNOOZE" TO BEGIN.
DEATH MARCH TO THE PARALLEL WORLD RHAPSODY
MANGA
After a long night, programmer Suzuki nods off and finds himself having a surprisingly vivid dream about the RPG he's working on…only thing is, he can't seem to wake up.
YEN ON
LIGHT NOVEL

BUNGO
STRAY DOGS

Volumes 1–12
available now

BUNGO
STRAY DOGS 01

Story by KAFKA ASAGIRI Art by SANGO HARUKAWA

**If you've already seen
the anime, it's time to
read the manga!**

Having been kicked out of the
orphanage, Atsushi Nakajima rescues
a strange man from a suicide attempt—
Osamu Dazai. Turns out that Dazai is
part of a detective agency staffed by
individuals whose supernatural powers
take on a literary bent!

Yen
Press

RE:ZERO -STARTING LIFE IN ANOTHER WORLD- ⑨
Chapter 3: Truth of Zero

Art: **Daichi Matsuse**
Original Story: **Tappei Nagatsuki**
Character Design: **Shinichirou Otsuka**

Translation: Jeremiah Bourque
Lettering: Rochelle Gancio

RE:ZERO KARA HAJIMERU ISEKAI SEIKATSU DAISANSHO
Truth of Zero Vol. 9
© Daichi Matsuse 2018
© Tappei Nagatsuki 2018
First published in Japan in 2018 by KADOKAWA CORPORATION, Tokyo. English translation rights arranged with KADOKAWA CORPORATION, Tokyo through TUTTLE-MORI AGENCY, Inc.

English translation © 2019 by Yen Press, LLC

Yen Press
150 West 30th Street, 19th Floor
New York, NY 10001

Visit us at yenpress.com
facebook.com/yenpress
twitter.com/yenpress
yenpress.tumblr.com
instagram.com/yenpress

First Yen Press Edition: December 2019

Yen Press is an imprint of Yen Press, LLC.
The Yen Press name and logo are trademarks of Yen Press, LLC.

The publisher is not responsible for websites (or their content) that are not owned by the publisher.

Library of Congress Control Number: 2016936537

ISBNs: 978-1-9753-5878-5 (paperback)
978-1-9753-8676-4 (ebook)

10 9 8 7 6 5 4 3 2 1

BVG

Printed in the United States of America